Longshore Drift

Karen Gillece was born in Dublin in 1974. She studied Law at University College Dublin and worked for several years in the telecommunications industry before turning to writing full-time. She was shortliested for the Hennessy New Irish Writing Award in 2001 and her short stories have been widely published in literary journals and magazines. Her first novel, *Seven Nights in Zaragoza* was published to widespread acclaim. *Longshore Drift* is her second novel.

KAREN GILLECE

Longshore Drift

HODDER
HEADLINE
IRELAND

First published in 2006 by Hodder Headline Ireland

A CIP catalogue record for this title is available from the British
Library.

ISBN 0 340 84124 9

Typeset in Sabon MT by Hodder Headline Ireland
Printed and bound in Great Britain by Clays Ltd, St Ives plc

Hodder Headline Ireland's policy is to use papers that are
natural, renewable and recyclable products and made from wood
grown in sustainable forests. The logging and manufacturing processes
are expected to conform to the environmental
regulations of the country of origin.

Hodder Headline Ireland
8 Castlecourt Centre, Castleknock, Dublin 15, Ireland

A division of Hodder Headline
338 Euston Road, London NW1 3BH

www.hhireland.ie

For Hannah and Paul O'Grady

PART I

1

At times, I thought I saw him. His face would appear to me on street corners, where he dawdled, scuffing his sandals on the kerb, his small thumbs twisting under the elastic of his shorts as he swung his narrow frame from side to side. Through open car doors I saw him scrambling into backseats – little hands reaching up to the upholstery and clambering in. These cars were always modern, comfortable cars, designed for families, for mums doing the school run – a crazy notion in itself as the only vehicles we had ever travelled in were a series of rundown, battered vans with rainbows or flowers or the sun and moon painted on the side of them in a band of bright colours. Psychedelic death traps. I saw him running on the street, his dark hair lifting with each upward movement, a schoolbag jogging on his back, even though he had never gone to school, had never owned a satchel of books. But there were no rules when it came to these kinds of delusions and I'd grown accustomed to the absurdity of them. At times, there was another hand reaching for his, helping him up, pulling him forward, taking him from me all over again.

I'd been having these delusions for some time, although I couldn't remember exactly when they'd

begun. Perhaps they were there from the very beginning. And I knew they weren't helped by the generous
doses of marijuana I was prescribing myself. Maybe I
thought that by coming home to Ireland, I would
somehow manage to shake them off, like a dusting of
raindrops shaken loose from an umbrella. But that day
on the train from Dublin, as my head grew heavy with
sleep, breath clouding the window I was leaning
against, in my dreams I could hear the gentle breaking
of waves on the shore and I saw him there on the beach
– his tousled hair, the dimpled flesh of his upper arms,
the way he stood, all proud and fierce, his tummy
jutting forward along with his chin. His eyes were
trained on the ocean, its steady waves lapping the shore.
I had been having this dream for a long time, so in a way
I was prepared for it, having rehearsed my role of
watching and imagining – following his slow, determined movements, his bare feet struggling over the soft
sand, thinking how the shell fragments must prickle his
tender soles. In those dreams I never spoke to the boy,
never touched him. His hands were still at his sides as he
walked steadily towards the shore, drawn by the pull of
the ocean. And watching him, I remembered his early
faltering steps, the way he held his hands high on either
side of his chest, his little arms bent at the elbows as he
waddled along, poised for a fall. I felt that same snatch
in my chest as I had felt then – the pinch of anticipation
before a fall.

Maybe it was because I had been through this dream
before, or perhaps it was the sudden jerking halt of the

train, but I managed to wake myself up right before the water could dash his shin, and so spared myself that sucker-punch to the heart. Through the blurry confusion that tags on to the end of sleep, a voice announced the station and I realised that I had arrived. And sure enough, outside on the platform, they were already waiting for me – one with an anxious, watchful smile wavering on her face, the younger one sullen and solemn eyed. I felt stretched and thin and a little queasy as I gathered my belongings, and soon I was on the platform with Sorcha there before me.

'Lara,' she said.

There was a look in her eyes. There was everything in that look – my whole life and what she thought of it, the recklessness of my travels, the carelessness of my relationships, my wayward existence, and how it was no surprise to her that one day I would return like this. But there was sympathy there too, and as she gathered me up into her embrace, I surprised myself with tears that appeared in my throat and quickly swallowed them away, down into the pit of my stomach. When she let go of me and took a step backward, I could see her eyes bright and searching. Despite my firm intentions, I felt the nudge of an old irritation as she pinned me with that sad, mournful gaze.

'Come along,' she said gently. 'The car's just outside.'

The car turned out to be a big old Merc in a shade of olive green with cream leather upholstery – a real gem of a vehicle in a beaten-up, retro kind of way. It didn't suit Sorcha at all. Gripping the steering wheel, she seemed dwarfed by the size of the machine around her. Perched on the edge of her seat with her spine ramrod straight, her eyes trained on the road, she seemed uncomfortably adrift in a sea of leather as she punctured the air with questions. The trees cast dappled shadows across the windshield as we sped out into the countryside, and her voice filled the vast space between us, bright with an eager optimism, but underpinned by a quaver of nerves, hopping about like rain on a roof.

'How was your trip? Not too exhausting?' she asked brightly.

'It was okay. You know what it's like – all those changeovers. Hanging around airport lounges.'

In the backseat, Avril said nothing, swamped in her own adolescent funk. The lilt of Sorcha's voice was playing havoc with my nerves, unsettled as they were from the long flight, not to mention the five or so vodkas that had seen me through the long shunting journey from Brazil.

'Did you sleep on the plane?'

'Not really. I slept a little on the train though.'

'Well, that's something. It will take you some time to get yourself together anyway,' she pointed out with a soft vehemence.

Sheep were scattered high up on the hills and my gaze passed over them, taking in the colours of the Kerry landscape – the purple haze of trees on the horizon, the lush greenness of the grass, even at the end of summer. I thought of the landscapes left behind me – the dusty, parched plains splintered with craggy rocks, the cacti like prickly fingers pointing up to a soaring sky. I felt lucid now that I was off the train, suddenly awake, more alert than I had felt in months. Perhaps it was being back here again, or maybe it was escaping South America and the search for him, but my eyes seemed wider, like they were absorbing more, sights and sounds and smells making imprints on my senses – the screeching of gulls, the salty, smoky smell of burning turf, towns painted in a rainbow of colours. A sudden excitement gripped me and I started to talk, a torrent of words filling the car.

'You wouldn't believe the security at the airports, Sorcha. And New York wasn't the worst of it. In Rio, they made me take my luggage – and you've seen how much I have – and empty every last bit of it. Everywhere else they just put it through a machine, X-ray it or whatever. But in Rio, they go through everything by hand. And I mean everything. Toiletries, underwear, the works. Some guy with latex gloves picking over everything I own. You wouldn't want to be shy about anything you'd stowed away. I'm telling you…'

I continued on in this vein, this determined effort at cheerfulness, until I heard my own voice, the thin screech of nerves in it, and caught sight of Sorcha's flickering glance, the quick movement of consternation behind her eyes. This excitement was new to me, brought about by the proximity to home, I suppose, and the growing sense that I was moving towards a different kind of life, a break from the cycle of dark days and nights. I was giddy with possibility. But I knew there was a need to temper this excitement, to keep a handle on my wayward emotions.

'Just wait until you see the town, Lara. I'm sure you won't recognise it.'

Sorcha was gripping the steering wheel, her wedding band glinting in the sunlight, and I noticed how her hands had aged – the roughness of them, skin stretched tightly over the ridges of bones. She was sneaking glances at me too, trying to take me in, this cousin of hers that she had not seen for more than fifteen years. An expression of mild disappointment seemed to hover over her face, and it wasn't hard to see that she had expected more from me by way of demonstrative grief. I could tell from the fix of her features when she had stood waiting for me on the platform that she had been prepared for the arrival of a woman still grief-stricken, still distraught, a weeping wreck of a person. And yes, I had certainly been in that state for a time, but had since learned that to remain in such a condition sapped your energy and leeched your soul. Eventually you got to the place where you were confronted with a choice – to succumb to the interminable sorrow, or to pick yourself up, put your brave face on and try to change things. Granted, my brave face still had a tendency to slip from time to time, but it had been two years since I'd lost him, and I'd picked up a few tricks along the way.

Sorcha wasn't my favourite person in the world, and perhaps I was being unfair to her that afternoon, on account of the history between us. But some wounds fester, and I guess it still bothered me the way she had used her uterus to sabotage our plans, mine and his, all those years ago. Peeping across at this cousin, my closest living relative, I looked for the changes that had sprung up in her, in the way that women do. She was two years older than me, so she was thirty-six now. There was a thickening about her body, inevitable after children, but a surprise even so. Her eyes were still the clearest blue, large with long lashes that were coated in glutinous black mascara, giving her a somewhat startled expression. I wondered if the mascara was for my benefit. Her blonde curls had become tight and wiry over the years, as if the tension in her body seemed to have infused to the ends of her hair, so that I had to resist the urge to lean across and tug at them to loosen them up. But it was Sorcha's face beneath her hair that had changed the most, those delicate, doll-like features. It was a face that appeared tight and tired beneath her determined good humour. I was surprised by sudden feelings of warmth for her rolling over me, the passage of time softening all those hard memories. A new resolve was fastening inside me to let bygones be bygones. I could almost detect the whipping sound of my new leaf being turned over.

'It's good to see you,' I announced suddenly.

'It's good to see you too, Lara,' she said after a surprised moment. 'We were worried about you. After all that's happened. It's good that you've come home.'

Home. That word resonated in the silence that grew

around us as we passed through Killorglan and Glenbeigh. The road twisted and dipped into a valley before rising to reveal a wide expanse of sea. Light shimmered on the water, a great body of it sweeping in from the Atlantic, nestling between the peninsulas, brightly blue in the afternoon sun. I had forgotten how beautiful it was, and I felt a sudden emotion as I stared out the window, chewing the side of my fingernail, the sun warming the side of my face. The warmth of possibility began to seep into me again, like I might be turning a corner, like the worst of it was behind me now.

'Does it feel changed to you?' Sorcha asked.

'I don't know. The hills seem smaller.'

'Compared to the Andes, I'm sure they are!' Her laughter spread out and filled the car, warm and musical.

'I suppose.'

'I hope you have pictures. We're all dying to see photos of your travels, aren't we, Avril?' Her daughter remained silent in the backseat, scowling out the window. 'No doubt you've got hundreds!' Sorcha persisted.

'Sure.'

I wasn't about to explain to her that I had tipped all my photos over the top of the Sugar Loaf in Rio, watching the wind taking them and carrying them over the wide, sweeping bay, before they scattered like confetti – so dramatic an act, it drew an audience. Fifteen years discarded, thrown to the winds with one outward fling, an impulse I would later recognise as dramatic and indulgent. I remembered turning away before any could come to rest and settle, not wanting to know where they landed, scared in case I would change my mind and make an awkward scramble to reclaim them. Instead I had walked away, back to the cable car, feeling a numbness coming over me.

'Well, the house is all set up for you, isn't it, Avril?'

I watched her in the side-view mirror, this angry, pouting creature, her eyes made equally dark by the black liner around them as by the mood she was in. Avril. The little seed that was planted and growing before I left. That secret, shameful seed. Back then she was just a pinch of worry behind Sorcha's smile. All so long ago. That thin-lipped, drawn look of her father's was apparent in her small elfin face, the same richly dark, swarthy colouring. It occurred to me that it was a relief he hadn't come with them to collect me, that Sorcha and Avril had come alone. I wasn't sure how I might have reacted to him, his eyes, his soft voice. Avril was fifteen years old, a startling physical reminder of just how long I had been gone. I found it hard to keep my eyes off her.

'Do they still call it the Yankee House?' I asked her, craning my head around and favouring her with an encouraging smile. She fixed me with a hard little stare.

'Yes,' she replied tersely, evidently pissed off that I had forced this syllable from her lips, her tough little face sending out vibes of hostility. She was clearly not going to be won over easily and I had no real desire to befriend her anyway, so I turned back and waited for a glimpse of it. The Yankee House, a clapboard grey-blue cottage with a wraparound porch. Not like the traditional white farmhouses with their small windows and sloping roofs, or the new bungalows that had sprung up with their picture windows and exaggerated eaves, but a traditional east-coast American summer house with a screen door and clay pots with withered geraniums on the veranda, an ageing clematis crawling up the trellis.

I had seen it in my mind's eye often over the years, hauling the memory of it out as a comfort when I needed to, and as the car pulled into the grassy drive, something seemed to snag in my chest, memory impacting on me. Just for a moment, I almost expected to see my mother emerging onto the porch, hand raised to shield her eyes from the sun. Behind the house the waves moved in a long lazy tide, spreading out on the wet sand, the sound of the sea rolling in the distance.

While Sorcha fiddled with the lock, explaining over her shoulder that there was a knack to it, I felt a strange anticipation visiting me, something like excitement, a bright pleat of optimism at being home again. But after the door burst open and the three of us poured into the house with my luggage, something of my excitement seemed to flatten. I stood still in my mother's living room while an awareness crept over me of how little had changed. The place was exactly the same as when I had left it – the same furniture, the framed photographs of ancestors hanging neatly on the walls, doors opening out from the sitting room onto the kitchen, the bedrooms, the bathroom. But it felt smaller somehow. In that moment, I believed I could see the house through new eyes, as Avril must see it, through her young, disapproving gaze. Age was clotting up in corners, fingers from the past picking at paint from the woodwork, slow cracks, chalky flakes and the echoes of other people's voices lodged in the walls. The furniture seemed dark and austere, misshapen by years of use, the grooves of other people's bodies shaping it.

Unaware of my deflation, Sorcha, in a display of combined strength and speed, hurried into the bedroom with the bags, returning a moment later and rewarding me with the full wattage of her optimistic smile.

'I've put your things in there,' she said brightly. 'The bed is made up for you too.'

'Thank you,' I said, not sure how I felt about sleeping in my mother's bed, even though it was almost two years since she'd died there. 'You've been very good.'

'Nonsense.'

Looking about me, I was struck by Sorcha's mark everywhere my gaze fell. It was there in the swept floors and polished furniture, in the swagged curtains and the crisply cornered sheets. Passing through the rooms like a shadow, I could see that she had been in here in the time that had passed, tidying this place, wiping down these surfaces and mopping this floor. Her presence was there in the cloth neatly folded over the spout of the tap. She was everywhere, and I was nowhere.

A sudden tiredness came over me, and I heard the

voice in my head. *Hold it together, Lara. One thing at a time.* And I remembered again why I was here, why I had come back to this place, and the thought calmed me.

'Why don't I put the kettle on,' Sorcha suggested, 'make us all a nice cup of tea.'

I heard her in the kitchen, the busy hum of her industry. Reaching into my handbag, I found my cigarettes, my hand brushing against the Ziploc bag containing a packet of Rizzlas and an ounce of grass I had bought in a pub near Heuston Station. For emergencies only, I reminded myself. There was still the lingering sense of hope within me, a belief that I could get by without it. And besides, I didn't think Sorcha would be all that comfortable with me lighting up in front of her.

Flipping the lid of my box of cigarettes, I drew one out, and feeling Avril's gaze on me, I paused.

'Would you like one?' I asked, offering her the box.

Her eyes flickered to the open kitchen door, the buzz of activity emanating from that corner of the house, and she shook her head quickly. Taking a seat opposite, she watched me carefully with round, brown eyes, and I noticed how her eyes were also flecked with amber, like his. The light in those eyes had changed. There was a new respect there. Lighting up, my lungs filled, and I reached across for the scallop shell ashtray on the table. Avril would have taken the cigarette had her mother not been there. I offered a smile, but felt a residual regret at tempting her.

Sorcha emerged with a rattling tray.

'Here we are,' she said breathily, depositing it on the coffee table and lightly slapping at Avril's legs to encourage her to move up on the couch. 'This will sort you out.'

I watched the thin stream of tea splashing into the cups, the curl of her little finger as she poured the milk. There was an elegance about her that made me feel large and ungraceful, all bitten nails and messy hair.

'Oh, and these are yours,' Sorcha added, gesturing to a small clutch of correspondence tucked in behind the teapot. 'Just some post that arrived recently for you, delivered to our house. You might want to tell the post office that you can receive mail again.'

Accepting a cup, I made an effort to sit up straight, trying to match her poise. I pushed hair back behind my ears and smoothed out my skirt, tugging it down over my knees. There was an imbalance between us that I was acutely aware of – her all neat and starched, me tired and bedraggled. But more than that, there was a debt that was owed. I could feel it in the neatly kept house, an unspoken reminder of everything that went before, particularly her care of my mother, Lillian.

'These cups,' Sorcha said, regarding them with a sort of reverence, 'these were Lillian's favourites.'

The cups were small, dainty, with a curved handle too small for anything but a child's finger, and a fat pink tea rose imprinted on the china surface, trailing leaves and a thorny stem. I looked up from mine, and noticed Sorcha's mouth begin to twitch, a sudden quivering of her chin, before she recovered quickly.

'It was very peaceful,' she said softly, a hush coming

over the room. 'In the end, she went very quietly.' For a moment I was uncertain how to respond, my mind lingering over the meaning in that statement – 'in the end' – the implied episodes of pain that went before the quiet death.

'I'm sorry I wasn't here,' I said truthfully. 'I wish I could have been with her.'

'She didn't want to drag you home, that's what Lillian used to say to us. "Don't be troubling Lara," she'd say. She hated the thought of bringing you back here, when you were still looking, still searching...'

She let the sentence go and for a moment the three of us sat there saying nothing. Avril stared into her cup. I could sense her discomfort.

In the silence, something changed in the air between us, a new tension. Sorcha was mustering up to something – I could tell by the ripple of muscle in her jaw. She fixed me with an uncertain, faltering look so that I knew immediately what she was going to say.

'Lara, I was so sorry to hear about your son.'

The words seemed to hang there, ponderous and sincere, no sound around them except the pulsing beat of the sea. Avril looked up, her eyes hot on my face.

'Such an awful thing...as a mother, I can imagine what you must have gone through, how frantic you must have been.'

Those words seemed to threaten all the strength and clarity I had held inside me until then. The sense of possibility I had clung to seemed to evaporate. So, too, did my resolve to leave the Ziploc bag alone, and I can't pretend that I wasn't already imagining the moment when I could smell the scorched air around the ragged end of a lit joint.

'I'm so very sorry,' Sorcha whispered.

Sorry was what they always said. People didn't know what other words to offer after a life had been touched by tragedy. Especially the tragedy of a stolen child. But sorry was just too small a word to bring near me. And what had they to be sorry for? It wasn't their hands that snatched him. It wasn't their eyes that were averted, enthralled by another, while he disappeared into the crowd. For two years, I had been listening to people telling me they were sorry.

'It must have been awful for you,' she said again, before adding tentatively in her own sly way, 'and for your husband.'

'He's not my husband,' I responded quickly, and a little tersely. All right, I admit it – defensively. 'We were never married.'

'No, of course. I knew that,' she said with apology, shaking her head at her own mistake. 'What's his name again?'

'Alejo,' I answered, softer now, my voice a caress.

'Alejo,' she repeated, nodding with recognition. 'Your mother used to talk about him, how your letters used to be full of him. I think she liked him. Liked the sound of him. "He'll be good for her," she said to me once. Such a shame she never got to meet him. Or your little boy. Ignatius, wasn't it?' she asked, enunciating the name cautiously. 'That was his name?'

'Ignacio,' I corrected, before adding a little meanly, 'Ignacio *is* his name. He didn't die, you know.' My voice broke then, and I had to bite down on the sudden tears clambering up my throat. I held my body very still, concentrating on the tray between us, the pile of letters nudging out behind the teapot.

'It's quite an unusual name,' Sorcha said after a while, her tone quiet and forgiving. She didn't mean to cause offence. She was trying to reach out to me. I remembered how close we had once been. 'You don't really hear those old religious names any more.'

It was Alejo's idea. He had wanted to name the boy after his father. 'Why not?' I had said at the time. 'It's better than naming him after mine.'

'We never called him that,' I said, steadying my voice. 'Nacio. That's what we call him.'

'Nacio,' Sorcha repeated, testing the syllables.

At times like these, I could feel something twist inside me, the grief that had wriggled into me. It was curled up somewhere inside, behind my ribs, beneath my heart. In these moments, I felt it uncurling. It stretched like a waking cat and all my insides heaved around it.

Neither of us said anything for a moment, and then I gave my head a brusque shake.

'Sorry,' I said, forcing a smile, making a tremendous effort to lift my spirits. 'It's just hard to talk about him still.'

'Of course.'

'And it's been a long day. Weird to be back here.'

I attempted a brief laugh to lighten the tension, and Sorcha smiled graciously.

'You must be exhausted. We'll leave you to get some rest.'

She got to her feet, straightening out her skirt with one smooth flick of her hands and I watched her heels clicking on the floorboards as she moved to join Avril at the door, the hem of her skirt dashing the air behind her. Despite her sympathy and her genuine care, I knew I didn't want her here with her neat haircut, her clean and respectful life, bestowing pity, silently judging. She seemed so capable, so responsible, and I just knew that she would never have allowed anything like that to happen to one of her children, and just thinking that made me feel guilty and ashamed all over again. The door closed behind them, and then I heard nothing at all.

In the silence that followed their parting, I felt the eyes of all those ancestors staring out at me from their frames, the coolness of their gaze, the accusatorial looks. They were everywhere, sitting in judgement on the mantelpiece, coldly regarding me from their places on old walls. So I leaned forward and felt for the bag and set about rolling myself a rescue remedy. The house felt old around me. It creaked and moaned with my movements and the flurry of winds coming in off the Atlantic, battering its sides and roof. Doors banged softly and rooms whispered in corners, the swish of memory rubbing up against the walls.

I lit the joint and lay back against the cushions and for

ten glorious minutes I slipped into oblivion. And for those ten minutes, I didn't worry about the house around me, I didn't contemplate the wisdom of my decision to come back to my childhood home, I didn't think about the man in the house at the other end of the beach with the amber flames in his eyes and all the history that lay between us, and most of all I didn't consider the vast expanse of ocean that lay outside the window separating me from my son. I passed ten blissful minutes without a thought in my head. Light fell through the window behind me, casting a sheen on the coffee table littered with half-empty cups, a cloudy film forming over the cold tea. The clutch of letters was still there, and from that distance I could see a postcard, full of colour and familiarity. My heart kicked outwards in my chest as I picked it out of the pile and turned it over. The card was blank – no signature, nothing except my name and address and the postmark. But I didn't need a signature to know that it was from him. Back on the road again, following the same route we had taken together so many times before.

The postcard was of Cusco, a small Peruvian town in the heart of the Andes. The navel of the world, they called it. My eyes travelled over the grid of squares depicting street scenes – the brightly painted wooden doors; a Mestiza woman decked out in bowler hat and wide, bright skirts, her long black hair lying in two plaits down her back; the squat cathedral lit up at night; the hulking mass of the snow-capped Andes – so majestic and benign. I fingered the card and willed myself back there, back to the place we first met all those years ago...

I had been sitting cross-legged on the corner of the Plaza de Armas, in the shade of the Balcon de Cusco. There was a box of handmade jewellery, all leather straps and brightly coloured beads, lying open in front of me. I was attracting casual interest at best, selling bits and bobs to a few Swedish girls. My head was still muzzy and I was feeling occasional bouts of nausea, my body still not accustomed to the thin air and the high altitude. From my vantage point at the side of the plaza, I could take in the buildings, majestic and colonial; they seemed so solid after the series of shantytowns I had passed through since Lima. The sun was shining down on the city that day, light catching in the spurting water of the fountain, making the cobbles of the road seem cleanly bright. And towering beyond the city, the Andes seemed so colossal, so close, that they felt to me like a protective arm wrapping itself around Cusco.

I had arrived there the previous day, having finally shaken off Stan, the man I had hooked up with in Caracas, an ex-US Marine with a string of started careers behind him. He had done two years as an apprentice glass-blower in Texas, had almost qualified as a light aircraft pilot, had tried to get in on the internet business as it was taking off but had been given bad advice and chosen the wrong investment. He was what my mother would have called a no-hoper. When I met him in Venezuela, he had a sack full of ganja and an instamatic camera. He had shared his stash with me and I had indulged his hobby for photography. I didn't mind posing once I was stoned, convincing myself that it was the same as going topless on a beach.

But after a while, I grew listless and bored. The sessions in front of the camera began tearing strips off my soul, and something about the weight of his brooding silences raised fears in me about Stan, so that when I arrived in Cusco, having done a midnight runner all the way from Lima, my skin felt too tired and filthy for me to carry on.

It wasn't until much later that Alejo told me he had been watching me all that day, sitting across the road, with his stall set out in front of the fountain in the middle of the plaza. But I was too exhausted to notice anyone, overcome by the pungent smells of cooking and exhaust fumes and startled by the noise and bustle of the place – the angry honking of horns, the loud cries from the street vendors, the thunderous footfall of the hordes that descended on Cusco before venturing further into the Sacred Valley and the Inca Trail. I was nervous, too, fearful of looking up and finding that Stan had followed me, having discovered the two hundred dollars in the bottom of his rucksack was missing. He never showed. It wasn't until the sun began to drop down behind the mountains that Alejo left his stall and sauntered over, and when I looked up, it was into his small, dark eyes and that broad smile boasting strong, square teeth so bright and chalky white that his mouth seemed disproportionately big for his face. He stood with his hands in his pockets, his long black hair tucked behind his ears, the shadow of a fringe peeking out from beneath his baseball cap, slowly chewing coca leaves.

'Where are you from?' he had asked with a quick flick of his head, and I read the words on his T-shirt – 'Fit in or fuck off' – emblazoned across his narrow chest.

'Ireland,' I answered.

'Ah, Ireland.' His smile seemed to broaden, humour lighting up his face as his eyes passed over my little jewellery stall.

'You Irish – so talented, so creative,' he nodded. 'Artists and writers and musicians.'

I wondered momentarily if he was being facetious, mocking the pitiful display of beaded tat laid out in front of me. It wasn't even mine. I had stolen it from underneath the bunk of a Columbian girl in a hostel in Miraflores, desperate for anything I could hock. I couldn't bear another reversed charges phone call to my mother in Ireland, begging her to send more money. And now I sat there smiling up at him in the dying light of the day, gratefully acknowledging his compliment. If he wanted to think of me as creative, he could be my guest, although the only talent I seemed to have was a gift for picking up bad men and getting myself into trouble.

'Welcome to Cusco, Irish,' he had said with a grin and I watched him as he returned to his stall of leather goods, his belts and bags and bracelets, all made by himself.

My heart was catapulting in my chest and I thought that this meant love, when it could in fact have just been the altitude. Then again, I had always been prone to love at first sight, and there was something in the manner of his walking, the relaxed set of his shoulders, the casual drag of his feet, hands plunged nonchalantly in his pockets, that made him seem to me like someone so complete, so content, so at peace with the world that it was like nothing bad could ever touch him. I wanted some of what he had – his confidence, his easiness, his serenity. But more than that, what I really wanted, from the very beginning, was to rest my tired, worn-out body up against his.

I stared at the card, squinting to read the date on the postmark, turning it over in my head, quietly calculating. My heart was pounding in my chest at the thought of him going back there, back to the place we first met. Holding the card in my hand, feasting my eyes on the images captured there, even after all that time, I felt the nagging pull of him all over again.

2

For a moment, the car rocked slightly with the impact of the slamming door. In the silence that followed, Christy and Sorcha watched their daughter as she walked up the steep curve of tarmac to the house. Halfway up the driveway, she adjusted the bag slung over her shoulder and flicked back that flap of brown hair that seemed to swing persistently over her face. In the silence, Christy marvelled at her ability to use her body to convey utter boredom.

'Well, at least that's one of them we've managed to off-load,' he said with a short laugh, putting the car in reverse. And then, remembering his son in the backseat, he glanced at the rear-view mirror. 'No offence, Jimbo.'

The boy didn't look up, lost in his GameBoy.

'How are we for time?' Sorcha asked, flipping down the sun visor and assessing her form in the mirror there.

'Fashionably late,' he announced. He felt cheerful this evening, surprisingly upbeat, his body alert to surges of adrenalin, pulsing through his veins.

Pulling away from the kerb, he leaned on the horn and looked for Avril up the drive. She didn't respond, disappearing into the house without a backward glance.

Driving, he was aware of Sorcha persistently touching a curl coming down over her forehead, as if this continuous massaging would ensure that the curl stayed back off her face.

'I told Stella we'd be there for eight,' she murmured distractedly.

'I think she'll forgive us fifteen minutes,' he said softly, keeping his voice level.

They were going to Stella and Guy Naseby's for drinks and a light supper. How typical of Stella, he thought wryly, this pert little invitation, outlining exactly what they should expect. He could almost hear her voice announcing it on the telephone in rich, fruity tones. Usually, Christy balked at these invitations. He found Stella overbearing – 'a troll' he had called her on more than one occasion, but not to her face. Guy was more tolerable than his fat, loud wife, but Christy was naturally suspicious of these artsy, folksy types. Beneath their cheesecloth and sandals he detected a whiff of capitalism. Guy and Stella had arrived four years ago from England. 'Blow-ins,' he called them, although arguably he had blown in himself, albeit from a lesser distance. They owned a craft shop in what used to be a small church. The Old Oratory it was called, all white-washed interiors with exposed beams and stained glass windows, knitwear and pottery and an umbrella stand of shillelaghs, Enya playing on a loop. 'Fucking shillelaghs,' Christy had hissed at Sorcha the first time they had visited, curiosity getting the better of him. But Sorcha had held a different view. 'It takes a foreigner to show us how it should be done,' she had pronounced to his total amazement.

It was a fact that surprised him, his wife's dogged persistence with this friendship. For three years, ever since Stella started up her book club and reeled Sorcha in, they had been going through this pantomime of mutual exchanges – dinner parties, card evenings, fondue nights, and once – an unholy memory – a tarot card reading. But as he drove, Christy felt relieved to be spending an evening in their company. He welcomed the distraction that it provided. He didn't think he could bear a long night at home alone with Sorcha. Not this night.

Lara was back. Incredible, impossible for him to believe, after all these years. He wasn't sure how to feel about it. For a week, ever since the phone call announcing her imminent arrival, he had pitched between apprehension, doubt and a leaping excitement. At times he was almost giddy with it. All this feeling, this sudden emotion – he felt dangerous with it, distrustful of his own reactions. It was at his suggestion that Sorcha collected Lara from the station. 'She'll be happier to see you,' he had said. And all day he had avoided the beach, that stretch of sand between his house and hers, fearful of seeing her, needing to be prepared, unsure of how to approach her and her grief, while inside he was exploding with curiosity. At intervals throughout the day, he had found his mind wandering back to the house at the end of the beach, trying to imagine what she was doing, how she was settling in, what she looked like after all this time. All these questions, leapfrogging each other inside him, but he was wary of asking them out loud, of seeming too eager, too needful of information. At first, he had listened to Sorcha speak of her cousin and the changes that had gripped her, trying to adopt a coolly indifferent manner, trying to appear casually engaged, while inside he fizzed with anticipation. He felt a certain distance in his wife, a guarded restraint, so that it seemed to him as if they were dancing around each other in verbal pirouettes, neither one of them willing to touch upon the questions of the past.

Sorcha flipped back the visor, her hair finally succumbing to her will. She gave out a happy little sigh, an indication that she was looking forward to the evening after the day she'd had.

'You don't think we should have asked her to come with us, do you?' she asked, jolting him from his thoughts.

'Who?'

'Lara. I feel bad somehow, leaving her on her own like that, her first night back.'

'She probably wants to be alone. She must be tired. Give her a chance to settle in.'

'Poor Lara,' she said, and he felt that sudden beat of excitement in his chest again.

'She looks terrible,' Sorcha told him, and he found himself straining to detect something else beneath her sympathetic tone. Some trace of satisfaction. But there was none, and he felt guilty all over again for thinking of her so meanly.

'She's aged,' she added.

'Haven't we all.'

'True. But it shocked me how much older she seemed. I don't know – part of me expected to find her exactly as she was. Vibrant. Youthful.'

'Well, the sun will do that to you,' he offered reasonably.

'No. No, it's not that. She just looked so…'

'So what?' He sat there, waiting, eyes on the road, poised for the word, suddenly impatient to know, to suck up every detail.

'Broken,' she said at last.

The word chilled him. It sent shock waves through him, causing unexpected emotion to rise up inside him. At that moment the car pulled into the driveway and he saw Stella emerging onto the veranda in a mustard tent of a dress, and halting the engine and opening the door, he was grateful for the opportunity of turning away from his wife, afraid that his face would betray his thoughts.

Light supper turned out to be an opportunity for Stella and Guy to showcase their talents. They prided themselves on their self-sufficiency.

'What do you think of the goat's cheese, Christy?' Stella asked, her cheeks red and shiny in the candlelight.

'Tasty.'

'I thought you'd like it!' She chuckled loudly, her whole chest filling out. 'It has a strong, moody temperament. A bit like you!'

He thought about that for a moment, then decided to let it pass.

There was a vogue for this kind of thing, he had noticed. More and more, he found himself listening to people pronouncing on the quality of their organically produced vegetables, or of their home-pickling methods. But Guy and Stella had taken it to the extreme. They had their own goat, for Christ's sake!

Sitting on the collapsed sofa, bolstered up with a half-dozen scatter cushions, Christy, replete with food, observed the room around him amid a lazy, pleasurable fug of red wine. On the opposing sofa, Stella and Sorcha sat with their bodies turned to face each other, Stella's legs tucked up under her voluminous dress. From his position, he could see the angry red of her cheeks, the dimpling of her flesh as her face moved in busy animation. Up against that quivering mass of womanhood, Sorcha appeared slim, elfin, the way she was when he had first met her, and he experienced a flush of pride in her. He noted the effort she had made with her appearance – the mascara, the elegance of her black dress and strappy high heels compared with the bohemian garb of the troll – and felt a flickering gratitude. The women were discussing their book club. Snippets of their conversation floated across to him.

'Well I just thought it was outstanding – the humour of it, the way she captured the father's voice.'

'And the mother's.'

'Yes, but let's face it, Sorcha, the mother's voice was

never going to be difficult for her to capture. I mean, she's done it before. But the father's...'

Christy had mixed feelings about their book club. It had been Stella's brainchild, of course – a monthly meeting of women (why only women, he wondered?) in the Old Oratory, chaired by Stella, with Sorcha acting as secretary. He had read some of the minutes of these meetings typed up on his computer, and was struck by the personalities of those involved rising up off the page. Sorcha was earnest, timid, ambivalent to the material, yet eager to please: 'Sorcha thought it was well done, she didn't condone it or reject it, and thought it very well-written.' Whereas Stella was strident in her views, forthright, even aggressive, and assured of her own opinion: 'Stella declared Eugenides' latest work a masterpiece, far surpassing his early promising work, *The Virgin Suicides*. A brilliant rendering of the treachery of the gene pool, and how it can leave an indelible mark on the lives of future generations. A must-read.'

Swallowing the ends of his wine, his thoughts lingered over his own novel, which remained nameless, and wondered how it would be received by the book club if he ever finished it, what insightful comments would be offered if they had the opportunity to cast their eyes over it. Not that they knew anything about his novel – he had kept his writing firmly to himself after the fiasco of his poetry reading. Two years on, he was still haunted by the memory of it, made worse upon recollection – all those females, the naked bewilderment on their faces, and him in the middle of it all, overdoing it with his plummy tones, compensating for his nerves, taking himself too seriously. He cringed at the memory.

Elijah sat between Stella and Sorcha. A pale, skinny child of ten, he seemed to have borrowed heavily from his father's genetic material, skilfully avoiding any bequest from Stella. She was fingering the boy's long dark hair, twirling it around her finger as she spoke. Elijah didn't seem to notice, engrossed in the magazine in front of him – the *Good Food Guide*. Christy thought this child was doomed. What hope was there for him, being schooled at home by these two? Elijah was partly the reason that they were here – it was part of Sorcha's ongoing plan to foster a friendship between the two boys. His own son, sitting in a beanbag by his foot, had scarcely said a word all evening. Neither boy seemed interested in interacting with the other, Jim crippled by an overwhelming shyness, and Elijah with his preference for adult company. Christy looked at Sorcha, trying to catch her eye, but saw no apparent disappointment at the failure yet again of her efforts between the two boys. She was engrossed in conversation.

'Here we are,' Guy announced, emerging from the kitchen, a bottle of wine in each hand. 'Pass your glasses. Don't be shy.' One thing about Guy and Stella – they were generous drinkers, in spite of their health kicks.

The wine was deep and throaty, a rich Claret. He shouldn't have been drinking so much. There was still the drive home to consider. But all night his thoughts kept wandering, and he couldn't seem to control either his mind or his drinking.

'Did you show it to him yet?' Guy asked Stella.

'Oh God, I completely forgot!'

Guy crossed the room in front of him – 'stalked' was the word, Christy thought, to describe that long, lanky step – and fiddled among the bookshelves for a moment before locating a newspaper clipping.

'This is it. I saw this in the paper last Saturday and both Stella and I immediately thought of you.'

Christy let his eyes pass over the wilted clipping, absorbing the details of a new poetry competition run by *The Irish Times*, a prize of €10,000 for the best volume of poetry. Something in his chest began to sink, and he took a slug of his wine, thoughtfully considering.

'What do you think? Right up your street, huh?' Christy had noticed that Guy sometimes liked to talk like an American.

'Yes. Great. I'll need to get on to them for more details, of course. There might be rules excluding volumes according to dates of publication and so on—'

'Balderdash!' Stella interrupted. 'You'll be eligible. Of course you'll be eligible!'

Guy gave him a reassuring slap on the arm. He felt pummelled by their enthusiasm, their faith in him. Sitting amongst the volumes of books about organic farming, home schooling and good sex was the slender volume of his poems, white with the title and his name in red curlicue print – *Salmon Season* by C.E. Archibald. A leaping salmon on the front cover was Stella's

handiwork. It had been his own idea to use his initials –
it seemed more dignified for a poet. At least, that was
what he had thought at the time.

'You absolutely must enter,' Stella continued and he
smiled across at her generously.

'It's worth a try, I suppose.'

'They'll go wild for it, I'm telling you, Christy.
They'll go crazy! And my God, if they don't, then
there's something wrong with them! Something wrong
in the head!'

He continued smiling and nodding, hoping she'd let
it drop. Stella had a warm exuberance that could be
overwhelming. Sometimes Christy felt slightly battered
after talking to her, listening to that belting laugh, that
high, shrill voice. He was also privately amazed how she
managed to breathe under the weight of that heft of
chest. She had always been a strenuous enthusiast of his
work, something he had been grateful for at the start.
But now, he was beginning to feel the burden of her
enthusiasm heavy on his shoulders.

Two years had passed since the book was published,
'book' being a generous term for it – twenty-three
poems, printed and bound, paid for by himself. He had
optimistically ordered three hundred copies. Most of
them were still sitting in a drawer in his desk, silently
giving off a whiff of failure that seemed to permeate his
whole office. The episode seemed shrouded in shame –
his eager enthusiasm, stoked into fire by Stella's
exuberant support, allowing himself to be persuaded to
publish it, and the humiliation of seeing it fail so

publicly. He could still remember the deafening silence in the staff room at school that had greeted it. The few paltry words of congratulations muttered by some of his colleagues were of little consolation.

The evening being a fine one, Christy and Guy stepped out onto the veranda to smoke. In the softly complaining night, scents rose up from the garden below to greet them. He smelled lilac and the sweetness of honeysuckle before Guy lit up and tobacco scents took over. He was eye level with a tree, the boughs of which were creaking with bittersweet crab apples. Something of his earlier good humour, his cheerfulness, seemed to have faded away. It was the mention of the poetry competition that did it, a reminder of his failings. He wished they would all leave it in the past, let it go.

'Sorcha tells us you have a new neighbour.'

'That's right. Well, not new exactly.'

'Oh?'

'She lived here many years before. She's Sorcha's cousin. We sort of grew up together, the three of us.'

'Right. Tragic history, I believe,' Guy remarked, breathing smoke into the night air.

'Yes.' Christy felt a tightening in his throat. He was uncertain of Guy, distrustful of a man who wore his prematurely grey hair long and drawn back into a ponytail. A slow, ponderous kind of man, Christy had the impression that behind those small blue eyes, there was a lot of silent calculation going on. He wondered, too, just what exactly Sorcha had told them of Lara, of her history.

'So tell me, Christy,' Guy started, the hand holding his cigarette pausing on its journey to his mouth, his voice dropping low and conspiratorial. 'This Lara, is she a looker?'

His face suffused with heat. Behind him he could hear the belting tones of Stella's laughter.

'I don't know. I haven't seen her yet. I mean she was, but...it's been so many years,' he heard himself stammer, caught off-guard by the sudden lechery in Guy's leathered face.

'Something about a tragedy lends a certain beauty to a person, don't you think?' Guy drew deeply on his cigarette before stubbing it out on the banister and flicking the butt out into the herb garden, a gesture that surprised Christy, reinforcing his suspicion that the man was a phoney. 'Something very sexy about a sorrowing young woman. I don't know. Perhaps it's the challenge of comforting her. The possibilities that attach themselves to that situation. Know what I mean?'

Christy knew. A broken woman, he thought. A vulnerability. Neither of them said anything for a few moments, and in the silence, he sensed the older man's imagination ticking over and felt his own defensive shackles rising. The questions he hadn't put to Sorcha, the ones he'd been aching to ask, were clamouring in his head: *Did she ask about me? Did she mention me?* There was a certain desperation about them. He knew that he had been thinking about her all day.

Ridiculous, he scolded himself. *You're being ridiculous. Pathetic.* It was all so long ago now – water under the bridge. And after everything she had been through, what happened between them all those years ago must seem wholly irrelevant to her now.

The drive home was subdued. Jim slept in the backseat and Sorcha gazed out the window at the darkness. His own head was heavy with wine, and he drove slowly, cautiously, the headlights swinging out over the narrow, twisting roads. Sorcha's hand moved and came to rest on his thigh, stroking softly. This was a signal that she would want him to make love to her when they got home. He felt a sinking feeling in his chest. His mind wandered back through a series of Friday nights, hunched up on his forearms, moving over his wife's body, his face turned sideways away from hers into the pillow, and as she held onto his shoulders, he moved into her, giving his mind over to fantasy. Lately he'd been bothered by a nagging doubt that this act was something they were both enduring rather than enjoying.

Driving past the old barracks, taking the road across the bridge and up the embankment, the word she had spoken earlier came back to him – 'broken' – and he was surprised by the sudden stab of pain it caused him. It wasn't a word he had ever imagined associating with Lara. Even that last time he saw her, when she looked at him, her eyes brimming over with pain and resentment and disbelief, there was still something so defiant about her, so wilful and strong. He felt a bristling of nerves along his neck and shoulders as he remembered that look. But perhaps that's just what he wanted to see, to lessen his own guilt.

Almost sixteen years had passed, but the details of that day were still vivid in his memory – the cloying smell of baking that clung inside the house, the heat in that room, the hiss and spit of turf in the grate, all those relatives packed into that tight space, the kisses on the cheeks, his hand gripped by many, their congratulations ringing in the hollows of his ears. He hadn't wanted any of it – had strenuously objected to it. But at that point, he was starting to discover that what he wanted didn't count for much any more. There seemed to be a fluttering of skirts, all those women flapping around with cups of tea and plates of food, their voices shrill and high pitched, while the men sat around sullenly, eating sandwiches and drinking whiskey and passing low remarks. And Sorcha sitting in the middle of it all, face flushed with excitement, looking pleased and – did he imagine it – triumphant? His lungs had seemed to fill with heat, his collar constricting his throat, and suddenly he knew that he had to get out.

The sky was full of angry clouds that day, moving above a pewter sea, and escaping from the house, his tie and his hair were whipped back by the salty breezy. He felt confused, breathless even, his thoughts stumbling over each other. It was as if his life had changed gears all of a sudden and he wasn't prepared for it. He was only twenty-one, and yet his youth now seemed relegated to the past, chased by his new responsibilities. This chain of events he had set in motion seemed to be taking on a life of its own, unstoppable now, and he felt baffled by it, bewildered. In the confusion of his thoughts he momentarily forgot the rocks that flanked the path on either side and he tripped and fell awkwardly, hands and knees skidding over grit, feeling the ripping of skin as tiny stones became embedded in his fleshy palms.

'Christ!' he hissed, getting to his feet quickly and glancing back at the house.

He hoped they hadn't heard him. He wasn't sure if he could bear one of them finding him like this, demanding to know what had happened. He pictured them standing there in the doorframe – his in-laws – regarding him from a distance. Sorcha's father with a sullen, disapproving expression, or her mother with that pinched, anxious look, his own father's countenance heavy with sadness. But worst of all would be Sorcha, her neat face messed up by a frown, standing by silently, regarding him with those wide blue eyes. She wouldn't need to say anything. He could read everything in her face. And she would understand that all he had said to her – those few words he had uttered, his feeble attempt at enthusiasm – had been lies. He hadn't meant any of it.

He ran his hands down the front of his trouser legs, wiping the grit loose from his stinging palms, and hurried down to the grey sand, feeling it harden beneath his feet as he approached the shore. The tide was out and he found his pace quickening as he neared the water, anxious to put distance between him and the house. Reaching up to his collar, he fumbled with his tie, pulling it off over his head and stuffing it into his blazer pocket. As he came towards the end of the beach, where the rocks lay in long flat slabs of blue-grey stone, he found himself running, breath snagging in his chest, the first drops of rain dashing his cheeks. From a distance, he could see her, the wild flap of her hair in the wind and the unsteady spiral of smoke from her cigarette, as she leaned against the boulder, still wearing her navy school uniform – a protest in itself – and even though her back was turned to him, he could read everything in her posture. He knew from the defiant tilt of her head, the tension in her shoulders, the way she gripped the rock beneath her.

And as he approached, she turned to look at him and he saw tears streaking her face, chapped and ruddy from the wind. Those tears were a shock to him. He hadn't expected them.

'I'm not going, you know,' she told him in a voice stretched thin with warning. 'Don't even bother to invite me, because I won't go. I won't stand there and be a witness to that sham of a ceremony.'

'Lara,' he had said, taking a step towards her. She had looked away suddenly and tossed her unfinished cigarette into the rock pool. There was a certain ferocity in the gesture that caused him to pause. He knew he had to be careful with her.

'I didn't mean it,' he began falteringly, his voice sounding high and thin and hopelessly childish. 'You must understand that I didn't want any of it to—'

'Don't,' she interrupted, shaking her head with a finality that made it clear to him that he wasn't going to be allowed to explain to her, that she didn't care to hear his words, his paltry excuse. That one word seemed to draw a line under everything there had been between them. She wasn't interested in hearing about his pain, didn't care to know about the great splintering apart of all his hopes and dreams. It wouldn't change anything now.

'And if you think I'm staying around to watch you two playing happy families, you're sorely mistaken.'

Something heavy seemed to enter his chest as she said it, a great weight bearing down on any levity remaining inside him. His entire life, all the days and months and years ahead of him, suddenly crowded out all that had gone before and all that he had hoped would come. He was struck by the calamity of his carelessness.

'I'm going without you,' she said to him wilfully, turning to look at him so that he could see the defiance in her eyes, to show that she could be strong without him. 'You may have bailed on our plans, but I can do it without you.'

'I'm sure you can,' he said, with a gentle admiration.

Something changed about her then, her defiance slipping so that he saw the hurt that was there. She couldn't hide it from him. He felt the great gaping 'why?' echoing inside her, and a little flare of anger ignited inside him. Did she not see that it was going to be worse for him? Did she not understand that she was the lucky one? That she was still free? But before he could put this to her, she pushed herself away from the rock, turning to him, and with one hand whipped the strands of hair back off her face.

'I hear you're going to Italy,' she said coolly, trying to be nonchalant, even though it was too late for that now. 'For your honeymoon.'

'Yes,' he had answered, the heaviness entering his heart.

'It won't be the same, you know.' She fixed him with her eyes, as cold and grey as the sea, and held him there for a moment. 'It won't be the same at all.'

And then she had turned away from him, and he had watched her holding herself straight and proud as she marched up the beach, her pace quickening to a run as she neared her house, and all the while he wondered what she meant by that – the same for whom?

Did she know then how it would be? Had some shadow of intuition passed over her even then? How could it? How could she know that while he scampered around the ruins of Pompeii, Sorcha would sit politely and patiently in the shade, fanning herself with her hat, disguising her boredom, waiting for him to finish? How could Lara have foreseen that the whines of tiredness while queuing outside the Uffizi in the stifling cauldron of Florence would itch at his brain, an unfamiliar irritation? Lara couldn't know that he would have to remind himself of his new wife's condition, and that it was unfair of him to expect her to stand around in the sun. It was impossible, despite how well she knew them both, that she might have imagined how they would end up spending their honeymoon lounging under parasols by the pool of their hotel, barely speaking, while all of Italy's history and culture was locked away from him.

The fields were black, the land eerily still around him, tiredness swooping down over him as he drove, blurring his thoughts. There was a twist in the muscles of his back, angry knots working their way up and down his spine. Sorcha's hand on his thigh was still. He felt peculiar in a way he couldn't quite put his finger on. Something about the coolness of Lara's eyes on that last day came back to him, all the warmth and closeness fled from them. He tried to switch his mind off, tried to focus on the road ahead, the blaze of the headlights on the tarmac, the moonlit clouds moving over the black hump of mountains ahead. But her voice was in his head again. *It won't be the same at all.* Lowering the window, he heard the roar of the sea.

3

He interviewed me in his office, two cappuccinos from the vending machine cooling between us, froth hardening against the paper cups. I wasn't really prepared for this, given the fact that I had woken that morning to a dull pain circling my head, my stomach empty and cavernous and struck by bouts of nausea. It was a while since I'd had an alcohol hangover like it, and it had taken me some time to get myself together. Having peeled myself from the mattress, I had crouched in the bath under the hand-held shower for a full fifteen minutes before assembling the most sober, decent clothing from my collection, drawing my hair back into a ponytail, and with an assortment of cosmetics, creating the face of a healthy, employable person to wear over my own.

Somehow I'd made it on time, and reading the sign on the door – 'Alan Woodgate, Manager' – I had tried to envisage what type of person could own such a practical and plainly descriptive name. I figured him to be a tall, stiff kind of person who moved as though his joints were mechanical, a firm handshake kind of man. I was not wholly disappointed.

'So, you're from around here?' Mr Woodgate asked, not looking up from my application form. 'A local?'

'Yes, although I haven't lived here for a number of years.'

'So I see.'

His head appeared waxy under the light, wisps of hair sprouting around his crown. He was young, prematurely balding, tall and pale with a sharp, mobile Adam's apple that I couldn't stop staring at as he drank down his cappuccino. He sat hunched over my application form, a pen held to his lower lip, as he pored over the details of my life. Behind him, a window looked out onto the supermarket floor, but from where I was sitting, all I could see were the fluorescent lights suspended from the ceilings like beams, glaring against my eyeballs, still hurting from the excesses of the previous night. I was also a little worried at what information might be contained within those pages, having typed up my application on my mother's old Olympia typewriter while kind of stoned.

'Well, you've had quite a chequered career, if I may say so,' he began, looking up at me with a smug little grin, fingering his tie, before leaning his elbows on the desk.

'Yes, but you'll see from my form that I've worked in the service industry.'

'Launderettes, bars, markets, restaurants,' he droned nasally. 'And the last place you worked before leaving this country was the Wimpy Bar on the High Street.'

'That's right.'

'And tell me, why did you leave that job?'

I thought of the Wimpy Bar where I had worked

after school and during the summer holidays, me and three others in our candy-striped pinafores, frying chips and taking turns on the jukebox. Greasy windows, a layer of grime over the countertops, Madonna and Aha and Tina Turner on the stereo, and the smell of fat in my hair and on my skin. I loved that job. I would have been happy to stay there if Matt, the owner, with his six kids and belly coming out over his trousers, hadn't tried to press me against the counter and kiss me one evening as we were closing up. After that, I couldn't go back there any more.

'I was doing my exams. I needed the time to study.'

'But you didn't do your Leaving Cert. It says so here.' He stabbed the form with his pen. 'You never completed your schooling.'

'Well, no,' I said, flustered. 'Something happened, and I decided to travel then, thinking I could come back and do my exams at another time.'

'But you didn't.'

'No. I guess I got distracted.'

'For sixteen years?'

'That's right,' I said and attempted to smile like a confident woman who wasn't about to be sick at any moment as a consequence of the quarter bottle of Southern Comfort consumed the night before. Judging from the look of guarded disapproval that came down over his face, I guessed that my smile hadn't convinced. I wanted to ask him why I needed a Leaving Certificate to stack shelves. The fact is, I didn't, and both he and I knew that. I had a sudden crazy urge to laugh at the absurdity of the situation – me sitting there hungover, being interviewed by this ponderous prick to the strains of Ronan Keating piped through speakers onto the supermarket floor. I knew that he would give me the job, but not until we had gone through this rigmarole so that he could exert his authority over me, show me who was boss before I even clocked in. And so I sat there, biting down the grin that kept surfacing, strangely buoyant despite my hangover, but sure that the job was within my grasp. At last, a routine, some stability, was imminent for me.

He let it slide, and checked through some more details. Then, as he prepared to close the interview, shuffling papers into a neat flat bundle, his shoulders seemed to loosen as he sat back in his chair, looked up at me and asked, 'So what made you come back here? What made you leave South America?'

Suddenly, without warning, I was back in Chile again, in San Pedro, that dusty outpost in the Atacama Desert.

'Go home,' Alejo had told me, his hand resting light and firm on my chest so that I felt pinned to the bed, although he wasn't threatening. 'Go home to Ireland.'

I remembered the sting in my eyes, the dryness in my throat as I tried to sit up in the bed, but his hand had held me there. A protest rose up inside me and bitterness formed on my tongue, words that were barbed and sharp as knives. I let them slice through the air between us. His eyes had closed momentarily – those small black eyes, their light lost behind heavy lids – and when he opened them again, they seemed emptied of everything except sadness.

'No more, Lara,' he had said. 'No more.'

Outside, I could hear the engine of the van turning over and I knew that it was the others and that they were waiting for him – that they had chosen him over me – and I felt myself crumple underneath the weight of his hand, hit by a new sense of betrayal.

He got up from the bed, and behind him I could see his duffel bag lying by the door, packed and ready, and I wondered how long he had been planning this, his getaway.

'What will I do without you?' I asked. Even now, when I replayed the scene in my head, I hated myself for asking this, for being so feeble, so dependent. He ignored the question all the same.

'Take care, baby,' he whispered, looking down at me, his sweet face all pained and mournful, with that look like he hated having to do this, but I had left him no choice, I had pushed him to his limit, and if he didn't go now, he might never be able to.

What else could I do but come back here? What other choice did I have? He had left me on my own in a small town in the middle of the Atacama Desert. There was no one there I knew. I had little money left. I couldn't go back on that dusty road again without him. I hadn't the heart or the energy to start that whole weary cycle of searching again. *Go home*, he had instructed. Hadn't he realised the only real home I had ever known was with him?

But that wasn't the explanation I gave to this pale balding man, trapped in his own officialdom, hands folded over my successful application form, waiting expectantly.

'Because there was nothing to keep me there,' I told him.

'He's a prick,' Ger informed me on the first day. 'It's important you learn that now.'

We were standing together in the confectionary aisle, stacking cans of custard on the shelves. There was a certain artistry to the way Ger arranged the cans so that the labels were all front facing and perfectly aligned. We took a step backwards to admire our handiwork, swapping comments about Alan up in the office.

'He had the cheek to remark on the fit of my uniform,' Ger continued, curling his lip. 'I mean it's not as if it's dirty or shabby. "A little tight, don't you think?" the fucker says to me.'

Ger and I both wore blue shirts and navy trousers, but his uniform seemed to cling to his form more. Careful with his appearance, his thin black hair was pasted to his head with gel and coiffed into a lick at the front like Tintin. Rings occupied nearly every finger. He had spent the morning showing me the ropes, and I was grateful for his youth and casual charm, and most of all for his seeming ignorance about my situation. There were others in the staff room, girls I remembered from school, whose long, silent stares suggested they knew about me, had heard what had happened to Nacio.

The supermarket was called Crazy Prices. It felt cold to me – refrigerators buzzing and cooling the air. Everything was so neatly stacked, so well displayed, so clinical. The entire time I was in Peru, I didn't once see a supermarket – not once. The markets there were mainly outdoors, and any indoor ones were a far cry from this neon-lit disinfected affair. As we worked, I told Ger about the broken concrete slabs, the old-fashioned weighing scales, brown hands with chipped fingernails plucking fruit deftly from piles, or scooping grain or pulses from open sacks, the bloody tabletops dripping fat and blood onto the floor, clotting in drains, dogs sniffing and scavenging, and the noise, that constant clatter and drone of industry. He wrinkled his nose in distaste. He was a young man with a keen sense of the aesthetic. He was perpetually scented. Crazy Prices, with its anodyne music leaking from hidden speakers, was his natural habitat, so quiet and antiseptic compared to the markets I remembered.

Time passed quickly. The days were busy, and I was surprised to find the work rewarding. On the third day, Alan – or Mr Woodgate, as he insisted – informed me that in a few weeks, he'd put me on the tills.

'Once you've proved your reliability,' he said.

I had stood there staring at him as he said those words. But in truth, I was happier on the shelves, stacking and tidying and replenishing stock. I could get lost in my own thoughts while I worked. I found myself thinking about Alejo more and more – not imagining where he was or who he was with, but remembering the times we had spent together, replaying them in my head like an old film, as if by doing so I would keep them alive. One part of me feared that I would forget, now that I was gone from that place. I'd thought about writing these things down, and had even made a stab at it on occasion, but the result was mildly embarrassing, lurching somewhere between Mills & Boon, a travel guide and the confessions of a pothead. Better to immerse myself in memory as I arranged cans of fruit. It helped me get through the days.

Sometimes, Ger caught sight of me lost in my own daydreams.

'What are you musing over?' he would ask in a scandalised tone as though I were picking over lurid details in my mind.

When Alan came up and said that to me, about the tills and my reliability, I had been thinking of the day in Cusco, that second day when the rain came down from the Andes and I was soaked through, so wet that it felt like the rain had seeped through to my bones, drenching me.

I was remembering how, like so many other mornings that year in Peru, I had woken to the noise of other people, the groaning and yawning and clearing of phlegm, noises I had grown accustomed to. That hostel was better than some of the ones I had stayed in, where sleep was troubled by fear and you had to remain alert all night. I hadn't noticed the rain until I stepped

outside, so eager was I to go back there, to the place
where we had met. I hadn't felt enthusiasm for anyone
in such a long time that I felt weirdly sober and giddy at
once. I remembered those eyes, how they had looked at
me for an instant, then looked away again and how it
felt like something had pierced my chest. But when I
saw the weather, I felt my heart sinking, my hopes
plummeting with it, and something like desperation
crept up over me, gripping my body between its teeth
and sending me out into that appalling downpour.

The Plaza de Armas was deserted. The jets and spray
of the fountain were lost amid the relentless pelt of rain,
which made the ground slick and treacherous. People
took shelter under the cloisters of the Balcon and along
the promenade of shops. It was as if the activity of the
previous day had been a dream. The street vendors were
nowhere to be seen. Gone were the bags and belts and
jewellery laid out neatly on ethnic blankets. Only the
restaurant hawks were out, clutching open menus to
their chests, accosting tourists taking refuge from the
rain. I remembered standing on the corner of the plaza,
feeling the water from the drains sluicing around my
ankles, gripped by indecision, beginning to feel frantic,
so desperate was I to find him, fearing that he was
already slipping away from me. I traipsed from pub to
pub, ducking into Los Perros and the Crosskeys and the
African Bar. But he was in none of those places. I knew
that he was Peruvian, I could tell as much from his
features – his short stature and dark colouring – and
there was a chance that he lived in Cusco and I was

panicking over nothing. But I also knew the type of person he could be – the kind that felt the pull of the road, that got jumpy and nervous when staying in one place for too long, the kind that skipped town just to escape the weather, without a backward glance.

Finally, I sat down at the doors of the cathedral, slumped by the entrance, dejected and soaking and cold to the bone. *What am I doing?* I asked myself, feeling the despair forming in the pit of my stomach. Tourists were peeping out at the rain from inside the cathedral, but I didn't dare join them, fearing the bad luck I might draw down upon myself if I did – I'd had enough bad luck already. I don't know how long I sat there for, but it was long enough for the rain to pass over and the light in the plaza to change, sunlight peeking out behind a blanket of grey, winking in the water gathering in pools around the sunken concrete and the waterlogged grass. I watched the tourists venturing out into the sunlight and felt sleepy, my head as heavy and waterlogged as my limbs. And just as I was closing my eyes, I heard that voice above me: 'Hi, Irish.' I instantly forgot my wet clothes and damp hair, feeling my heart lift in my chest, something warm unfolding inside me.

We went to a bar behind the cathedral, stopping in a tourist shop on the way where I bought an Inca Kola T-shirt and changed into it in the shop, luxuriating in the feeling of dry cotton against my skin. In the bar, we sat in a booth at the back and drank *chicha* beer and talked. His voice was soft, mellow, a string of musical broken phrases. He had learned his English on the road, picking up bits and pieces from foreigners he met. He told me about himself and I shared some of my history. But somehow it seemed to me that the details of my past didn't have any effect on him. He didn't need to know where I had been or who I had met or what I had done. He looked me clear in the face with small glittering black eyes and I felt like he could see right through to my soul. I had never felt so exposed.

I didn't go back to the hostel that night. He was borrowing a room from a friend who had an apartment on the Via del Piso. It was quiet after the rain, the streets still empty, like the water had washed everything clean in the city, including the noise. And it was quiet in that room as I held him, drawing my feet up along the backs of his legs, pulling him to me. So quiet that I could hear everything – the beat of his heart over mine, the depth of his breathing rising up from his chest, the sound of his skin pressing against me.

The sensation came over me slowly that something important was happening. There was a decidedly new quality to everything around me. Things were sharper and brighter, the air amplified sound. I held onto him, wanting to get lost in him, to feel myself melting into him. And afterwards, we lay together in the darkness and I smoothed his ink-black hair back from his face and ran my fingers over the rounded curve of his cheek, tiny pockmarks clustering along the line of his jaw. His breathing slowed and his head grew heavy with sleep where it lay on my arm. But I didn't attempt to move it. I didn't want to move away from him. For no reason that I could name, I was overcome with a sense of destiny. I lay there listening to the hushed stillness, my heart quiet after the wild tumult that had visited it, and like the streets outside, bright and glistening, I too felt clean, as sleep came for me at last.

In celebration of one week as a gainfully employed citizen, I used my staff discount to buy paint. The selection to choose from was pitiful – anaemic shades of magnolia, peach and oatmeal. I lingered over the colour charts, chewing my lip before losing patience with myself.

'To hell with it,' I said, exasperated, grabbing two tins of butter-yellow emulsion, a paint roller and tray and a couple of paintbrushes.

I was sick of myself and the space I occupied. It would start with the house, I told myself – a clean sweep – before I moved onto myself.

The town was quiet for a Friday evening as I walked through it, carrying my DIY paraphernalia, and wondering again why this town seemed so elegant in my memory. I had left here in 1989, the same year the Berlin Wall came down, when thousands were killed in the Tiananmen Square massacre and the Ayatollah Khomeini declared a *fatwah* on Salman Rushdie. And now, Germany was an altogether different country, Ireland was sending trade delegations to China, and Salman Rushdie, no longer in hiding, was making the news on account of his young and beautiful wife, and I saw how the whole place had changed in my absence. It had a beaten look about it, appearing tatty and squat in the shade of the mountains. Video rental shops seemed to have sprung up and multiplied, along with internet cafés. Every building along the Main Street boasted double-glazed windows, white plastic frames and shiny panes replacing the flaky sash windows and wavy glass that I remembered.

My mother had told me of these changes to the town in our sporadic, infrequent phone conversations. They were always one sided, those calls. In the beginning, I was the one who clogged the line with my fevered enthusiasm, standing in dusty streets dropping coins into a machine and rabbiting on about all the things I was doing, places I was going, people I was meeting. Mostly, I was loaded before I made the call, and I think my mother knew this so that her silence reverberated with disapproval and worry. But once Alejo came on the scene, I think she sensed the change in me, and I began to feel her relax at the other end of the line, the tinkle of her laughter pouring into my ear. No doubt she was relieved that I had finally gotten my shit together. And so, when years later, after Nacio was born, that first year we were travelling with Roger and those two Danish girls and I began to feel the space between me and Alejo opening up, seeing something pass between him and Sylvie, the one with the hair the colour of corn, and feeling the first cold trickle of suspicion come slowly, I couldn't tell my mother, couldn't open her up to all that worry and confusion again.

Instead, I grew silent, and in those silences my mother's voice filtered through, filling the space between us, telling me of all the changes in the town, how the hairdressers' was being renovated, forcing her to go into Killorglan for a cut and dye, how the convent school was closing and there was talk of the boys' school becoming mixed, that the Department of Justice was relocating its offices to the town and a whole new building had been built down at the harbour to house it. I listened to these pieces of information without ever envisaging what they actually meant, focusing instead on the comfort of hearing my mother's voice, wrapping myself up in it. Towards the end, in our last conversations, after Nacio had gone, when her voice sounded weak on the line, her breathing laboured, yet still I didn't know – didn't realise – what this actually meant, so consumed was I by the sorrow that had opened up within me like a giant hole, I sometimes had to hold my hand over my mouth to keep from crying.

As I left the town behind me, I felt the afternoon heat on my back and found myself focusing on the road beneath my feet, counting out the rhythm of my walk in a slow, steady beat. The handles on the paint pots were cutting lines into my hands, but I persevered, my head filled with plans of redecoration, regeneration, a great need to make new. Up ahead were JCBs and steamrollers, men in orange jackets laying a new surface on the road, steam rising from the tarmac in a quivering haze of heat. I walked slowly, gazing at Killealan Mountain in the distance, purple against a white sky. Blackberries were growing in the tangled briar at the side of the road, September fuchsia budding in the hedgerows. The sun was high overhead, and I suddenly wanted to strip off my clothes and lie down in the sea, feeling the waves come softly, my body touched by foam.

I became aware of a car slowing down behind me and walked carefully into the side so it could pass, but it drew up next to me and through the lowered window of the passenger door I saw a man leaning towards me, squinting in a shaft of sunlight burning his face. It took a moment, memory stirring, before a picture of him emerged from the shadows – younger, without the beard. I sucked my breath in quickly. That face was a shock to me – the dark seriousness of his eyes, those arched brows snaking above them – a face I had once known so well.

'It's you,' I said, disbelief rising through my voice.

'Yes,' Christy smiled, and my heart, despite itself, gave out a short sideways kick.

'I saw you struggling there,' he said, indicating to the paint cans. 'That's a lot of gear you've got. I can give you a lift, if you like?'

'Oh, well…okay. Thank you.'

There was a rising commotion inside me, and I guess inside him too, tumbling up from the sealed cavern of our shared history. He was being casual with me, but I could feel how forced it was, I could sense the effort that was required of him. Putting my stuff on the backseat,

I was conscious of my own heartbeat, a nervous fluttering in my chest.

'Thanks,' I said, climbing into the front seat, pausing while he fumbled with a sheaf of papers, finally settling them by my feet as I sat in and pulled the seat belt across.

'Sorry,' he remarked, referring to the papers. 'Stuff for school.'

'Oh.'

There was a long awful minute of silence. He drove carefully, saying nothing, and all the time I was remembering back to how he had been – the seriousness of his youthful gaze, the nobility of his features, a tenderness that was there if you looked closely. There was something proud about his face, something regal about the bone structure, but it was his eyes that softened it, their warmth, their long lashes. The temptation ached within me to look at him, to really examine him, wanting to identify the changes that had sprung up in him. But more than that, I wanted to see if traces of what I had known of him, what had meant something to me, still remained.

'So,' we said together, almost on the same breath, and then laughed.

'You first,' he offered.

'How have you been?' I asked, nerves dancing in my throat, suddenly unsure of how I should feel about him. The old anger had long gone, dissipating over time, becoming overshadowed by other things, and yet something lingered – a residual wariness, an uncertainty –

as we glanced at each other across the distance of the car.

'I'm good,' he nodded in affirmation. 'I was going to…well, I was considering calling to see you, but I thought I'd give you a chance to settle in first.'

'Okay.'

'So have you settled in? Are you managing all right?'

'Sure.'

'Right.'

Alone with him in that small space, I was aware of my movements, my breathing, the bareness of my legs, the monosyllables bouncing between us. I wondered what he was thinking of me, the changes in me, hair and skin dried by the sun, lines on my face, the marks left by anxiety and grief. But what surprised me more than anything else was my desire to have him not think badly of me – an old desire, a willingness to please. I played with the zipper on my sweatshirt, my mind rifling for something to say.

'I've got myself a job. In Crazy Prices.'

'Oh?' His voice lurched up through the syllable.

'It's nothing special, just stacking shelves and that.'

'No, that's great. That's terrific.'

'It's not bad.'

'So, you think you'll be here a while then?'

'Maybe.'

He nodded his head in a contemplative way, digesting this information, and something of that youthful, studious look that I remembered returned to him, and in that moment I thought of how he had looked the first time we met, shyness and a certain arrogance battling it out on his face. Dark features, hands thrust nonchalantly in his pockets, a rare lurking smile, and the sudden twist that smile brought about inside me, inexplicable as it was.

'You must find it strange,' he said, pausing to clear his throat, 'being back here. After all this time.'

'Yes, I guess so. It's different somehow.'

'How so?'

'The house seems smaller, for a start. Full of clutter and dark corners. I can't stand it.'

He looked across at me, and I realised how dramatic I sounded and moved to dilute my words.

'I just need to do something new with it, make it clean and bright again.'

He nodded thoughtfully.

'It's a good house,' he offered.

'Sure. It's just not my house. It doesn't feel like it anyway.'

'Really?'

'It doesn't even feel like my mother's house, to be honest.' He looked at me again before bringing his gaze back to the road. 'To me, it's still Lillian's aunt's house. Hardly anything has changed since her time.'

I observed him with difficulty from the corner of my eye. His beard was dark like his hair, but speckled with the first flecks of grey. I didn't remember him having that beard. It made him look older, more distinguished. His hair was cut short and I imagined if it were longer it would still fold away in curls like it used to. It was starting to thin at the corners of his forehead and I could tell that he was pulling it forward to try to combat this sign of ageing – a small, visible trace of vanity.

'Avril tells me it's still called the Yankee House,' I informed him, and watched as the corners of his mouth reached up into the briefest of smiles.

'Well. I haven't heard it called that in a long time.'

His lips were long and straight, his beard neatly trimmed, but something of the younger softness about his face still lingered. It was there in his eyes, brown irises reflecting light through their darkness. I wondered what it would be like to kiss that straight line of a mouth again, to feel the downy softness of his jaw against my face. I ran my hand through my hair quickly, a savage movement to swipe away the image in my head.

'I was going to see if I could get Dad's old Datsun working. The walk from the town is a bit of a killer,' I said. 'It's still in the shed up at the back of the house, although God knows what state it's in.'

'I had forgotten there was a car,' he remarked pensively. 'Lillian never drove it.'

I didn't tell him that my mother hated that car – the garish red paint, the caramel upholstery. It was all my father – flash and showy. She had never understood why he left it behind him. *I leave you the car*, he had scribbled in his note, like it was some great gift to her. Did he not realise that she hated it, that she would never drive it?

'It's probably fit for the scrap heap now,' I said softly.

'I can take a look at it for you, if you like?' he offered in a quiet, measured tone, and yet there was an eagerness about the way he said it too.

His offer to help with the car surprised me. He didn't seem to be the type of man who was used to tinkering with engines. His fingernails were too clean, his clothes too tidy. He had a studious look about him, a gentleness. The quietness of his demeanour suggested someone who was more comfortable losing himself in a book than under the bonnet of a car. It occurred to me how little I knew him any more. All that I had was a collection of memories. The years that had passed made strangers out of us. Perhaps it was better that way.

'Sure,' I said. 'If it's no trouble?'

'No trouble.'

The road wound in a long, slow ribbon between the hills down to the sea. There was water in the distance, a brilliant aquamarine blue under the hazy sunshine. It felt strange to be sitting on the passenger's side of a car again – the wife's side – with a man driving, that I felt a sort of flutter of nerves going through me. There was tension between us, a silence loaded with unspoken questions. But what was the point in those questions now? Everything that I'd ever wanted to ask him seemed lost to me; all those burning questions had cooled over the years. A silence settled over us, but it wasn't hostile. I felt myself relaxing into it.

And then something happened. The radio had been playing in the background, a low drone of voices, and now in the silence, they became clearer, audible. It was a local radio station, and the broadcaster was reading out the death notices. It was one of those things that I had forgotten about this corner of the world, this quaint and morbid practice. We sat there together, awkwardness filling the air between us, listening to the details of all those dead people being listed out before he leaned across quickly and changed the station.

'Sorry about that,' he muttered, his hands settling back on the steering wheel.

The Who filled the car, strumming through 'The Seeker', and we sat there motionless, listening to those lyrics:

I asked Bobby Dylan,
I asked The Beatles,
I asked Timothy Leary,
But he couldn't help me either...

I looked at his face, saw the redness of his cheeks above his beard, and realised that he was embarrassed by the mention of death around me. His cheeks were burning up, his eyes darting about, and I could feel his mortification. Suddenly it seemed so utterly ridiculous that a great swell of laughter rose up inside me. I tried to hold it in but it burst forth in a gasp, like a loud hiccup, and his head swung around to look at me. There was confusion in his face, and I felt another giggle bubbling up. And then it just seemed to erupt inside me, this hilarity, impossible to contain, cascading out in peals of laughter. In amazement, he stared at me as tears ran over my cheeks. I couldn't control myself. And then, he too was laughing. The two of us in the front seat of the car, struggling to draw breath. And from the most unlikely source, the most ridiculous circumstances, I felt an enormous weight had been lifted from me. I sensed the release of it embracing me, the tenderness that lay beneath this shared hilarity.

When the laughter subsided and our giggles faded away, I was left feeling light and airy, like a window had been opened inside me, a fresh breeze passing briskly through it. And just like that, I knew things were going to be okay between us, that all the anger and hurt and the years that had passed would come to mean nothing. Perhaps he sensed it too, for his smile lingered after his laughter stopped. It wasn't long after that before he turned the car into the grassy drive and came to a stop.

'Well,' I said, unclipping my seat belt and darting a brief smile at him. 'Thank you for the lift.'

'No problem, Lara,' he replied gently, looking me in the eye for the first time throughout our journey.

I got out and hauled my paint cans from the backseat onto the drive, slamming the door shut, before looking in through the open window again.

'So?'

'So,' he said. 'Maybe I'll drop by some time in the next week, take a look at that car for you.'

'Sure. That'd be great.'

There was the briefest of silences before he moved to turn the key in the ignition, and as he did so a thought came to me out of the blue and I blurted it out without thinking.

'Christy? Is that short for Christopher?'

It was something I had never known, and never thought to ask before. A look of surprise tinged with confusion flickered over his face and he paused in his actions.

'Christian,' he answered softly, before adding in a different tone, 'but nobody calls me that any more.'

I don't know why I asked him that, but there was something so sad in his final admission after the joy of our shared laughter that it made me say in parting, 'Thanks for the lift, Christian.'

He waited for me to pick up my shopping and make my way to the house. I could feel him looking at me as I walked, sensing his eyes taking me in completely. It was only when I was safely inside the door that I heard the engine starting up and the car drawing away from the house.

4

After dinner, he took refuge in his study – a small room with a window looking out onto the sea – to work on his book. He opened up the Word document to chapter seven and allowed his eyes to pass over the last paragraph he had written. It had started off a year ago as a tale of jealousy and greed and the corruption of wealth – a tug-of-war between two brothers over a stretch of land, with a subplot involving a woman they were both in love with. But after getting through the first thirty thousand words, Christy had come to fear that the setting was too parochial, a nostalgic sentiment attaching to the theme, rather than the contemporary feel he had hoped for. And so he had gone back, rewriting it so that one of the brothers was involved in an internet paedophile ring, a radical move that he had a sneaking suspicion wasn't wholly convincing. Staring at the last sentences he had written, the words misted into clouds and his gaze drifted from the monitor, his eyes spanning out around the room.

A week had passed since that day in the car, and closing his eyes, he saw again her bare legs, the flicker of humour around her mouth, the dark sadness in her eyes. And her voice, the way she said his name…

Stop it, he told himself, shaking his head awake.

This study was his haven, somewhere to escape to when the voices of his family grew shrill and grating. Somewhere quiet for him to work on his book. Posters of places he planned to visit were tacked to the walls alongside his maps, some of them dating from his father's time. The atlas was his father's too, and he fondly remembered the hours spent together poring over the pink and green terrains. Christy had attempted to draw his own son into the mysteries of these far-flung destinations, but while Jim seemed content to sit and listen, there was a dullness in his eyes that spoke of boredom, disinterest. The lack of enthusiasm his children had for his pursuits, his passions, saddened Christy. They showed the same disdain for poetry, for literature. While physically they bore a strong resemblance to him, particularly Avril, their personalities seemed distant, alien to him. How could Sorcha's genes have stacked up so overwhelmingly against his? Or had it more to do with her role as a parent, the influence she had brought to bear upon them, how much more successful she had been than him at exerting her identity?

Peering at the monitor again, he tapped out a few more words, a description of the girl at the centre of the love triangle – dark hair, cut-off jeans, flip-flops, a wildness in her eyes.

His hands stopped typing. Carried away for a moment, he breathed heavily, then calmed himself. But the text in front of him seemed dull and lifeless, and he hadn't the concentration to inject some vigour into it. So instead he opened the internet and began browsing.

Since that day in the car, he'd felt a new sensation creeping through him, like something in his blood, something he couldn't readily identify. The change felt enormous. It seemed extraordinary to Christy that no one looked differently at him. And yet, he was aware of a distance growing between him and his family, sneaking in so stealthily that he had hardly noticed it. But today, over dinner, he had come to realise just how distant he had become from them. Sorcha and Avril were at the end of another long, weary row, both withdrawing to the extremes of their personalities – his daughter retreating into herself, hiding behind that curtain of hair, thick waves of fury rolling over her; his wife forcing an ebullience, a strenuous cheeriness in her efforts to gloss over things. Her voice seemed overly loud to him, and Christy found himself imagining her vocal cords, swollen and purple and glistening. Jim quietly ate his dinner, humming to himself, and Christy watched the boy's eyes drawing over the surface of the table in a lazy, somnambulant stare, and wondered not for the first time what exactly was occupying his son's thoughts. This vacant, dreamy look felt to Christy like a defence of some kind, a wall sitting solidly between them, so that his son, in many ways, was more like a stranger to him than the rest of them.

Dinner was interrupted by Avril's mobile, insistently beeping and vibrating.

'Put that away,' he had instructed as her thumb

flickered over the keyboard, texting furiously. She had fixed him with an accusing stare before dropping the phone a little fiercely onto the table.

This continuous texting incensed him – the constant movement of her thumb and the replies bleeping through, the sniggers and knowing grins they elicited. He wondered who she was communicating with, and thought back to the little girls she used to play with and how he used to enjoy them scampering through the house, the squeals and laughter that accompanied their games. But sometime over the past year or two, these innocent little girls had turned into young madams with insolent stares and a sneering disrespect. He felt awkward in their company, like he was being silently assessed. When he left a room they erupted with laughter and he felt the blood rushing to his cheeks. Avril seemed to spend hours on the phone, locked in urgent whispered conversations. It baffled him how much they had to talk about, these girls. It amazed him, too, the way his daughter's tone could fluctuate according to who she was addressing. 'Dad!' she snapped at him, short and hard, like a stab wound in the air, compared to the way her voice lifted as she spoke to her friends, the high singing arc of signing off, 'By-ye!' before swinging low into another trough of moodiness. How he missed her laughter, the simple joy of it.

'Smile, for God's sake!' he wanted to say to her, laughing to take the hardness out of it.

But she was past the stage where he could give her orders, even when couched in levity. She would see it as an act of aggression, an attempt to suppress her independence, and he already knew the response she would snap back at him: 'What is there to smile about?'

At dinner, as the air had hovered black and heavy between them, he had looked across at his daughter, seen the frown gathering in her brow, and thought to himself: *Once I loved this girl.*

Christy leaned back in his chair, his mind idling over these negative thoughts as he ran a search on Google – 'missing children Brazil'. He was startled by the number of sites that came up. Flicking through, he selected one of them, and as the page opened slowly, faces began to stare out at him, almost all of them teenage boys. His eyes passed over them, before he modified his search to boys who'd gone missing two years ago. A series of thumbprints was thrown up onto the screen – alarming how many – the curser flicking over each one, scouring for details, patiently searching. It didn't take long to find what he was looking for. Ignacio Moreno de Salvatore, distinguishable by his age, the only four-year-old among a sea of adolescence. The photo wasn't very clear – a holiday snap – and peering at it closely, he looked for traces of Lara in the small, dark face. Perhaps there was something of her about the slant of his mouth, in the mischievous gleam in his eyes. Christy felt his chest sucking in, the air in his lungs collapsing, and wished he hadn't done this. He felt like a voyeur casually looking in on this unimaginable pain.

The door opened behind him and he wrenched his concentration back, leaning forward quickly and clicking on the Word document minimised at the bottom of the screen as Sorcha closed the door behind her.

'Hi,' she said, drifting past him, and he caught the tiny fissure of weariness in her voice. 'I'm not disturbing you, am I?'

'Course not.'

She walked to the window and settled against the sill, arms folded under her chest as she stared past to the sea beyond. There was a quietness about her sometimes, a self-containment, that he found calming. Sorcha was possessed of a natural grace, which somehow seemed to take on a hue of poignancy, even beauty, in moments of sadness or weariness. She wanted something from him – he could tell by the purposeful walk to the window, the quiet pose she had adopted – and felt himself waiting for her to begin. His guess was that she wanted to talk about Avril. Most of their talks these days seemed to be about their teenage daughter, both of them bewildered and confused by the changes erupting in her.

'God, she's exhausting,' Sorcha breathed, and he felt a triumphant flush of pleasure at being right. 'Everything seems to be a constant battle with her these days.'

'It's just a phase,' he offered reasonably. 'She'll grow out of it.'

'And in the meantime, what do we do? Sit back and let her hormones take over? God, she could kill someone when she gets like that.'

'Well, we can take heart that she's unlikely to kill anyone outside the family,' he smiled up at her. 'You or I being the most likely victim.'

'Seriously, Christy. This can't go on much longer.' She shook her head, curls twitching, a look of affectionate regret passing over her. 'She told me this morning that I look like a hick. I don't, do I?'

There was such naked hurt in her face that he felt a swell of protectiveness towards her.

'No, of course not.'

It still touched him, his wife's incredulity at their children, the power they wielded over her. He could clearly recall coming home from work one day when Avril was still a toddler and finding the two of them, his wife and child, red-faced and tear-streaked, one crying indignant tears of outrage, the other grieving and distraught over what she had done. It was the first time Sorcha had ever struck her daughter in anger. He had held her against his chest that day, rocking her gently, listening to her murmuring words of contrition. Something within him wanted to feel that closeness with her again, a longing for a time when simply holding her against his chest was enough to make things seem brighter.

'Still,' she said, firmly this time. 'One of us needs to speak to her.'

'Do you want me to?'

'Would you? I'm blue in the face trying. She'll listen to you.'

'I seriously doubt that.'

'Please?'

He looked up at her, unconvinced that his words would have any effect on Avril – what had happened at dinner was proof positive of his inability to communicate

with her. It was that mask of hair over her face that finally
did it. It irritated him no end. He wished she would clip it
back, get a hair band or something. At dinner, he had sat
there watching her pushing food into her mouth, her fork
disappearing in behind that wall of hair.

'For God's sake, Avril,' he had snapped, feeling his
fingers tightening around his knife and fork. 'Do
something about that hair, would you?'

Her response had been typical, fixing him with that
empty gaze before rising from her seat, the chair scraping
back angrily over the tiles, and flouncing out of the room.

'She better come back and finish that dinner,' he had
said to Sorcha in an almost threatening tone.

'Just leave her,' was his wife's weary response as they
listened to a door slamming upstairs, chased by loud
thumping music, and he felt his appetite dwindling.

'Please?' Sorcha asked him now, and he felt moved to
appease her.

'All right, love, I'll give it a go.'

Something seemed to loosen about her body as he
agreed, a relaxing of her shoulders, relieved of their
burden. She smiled at him, her arms falling away from
her chest, and pushed herself away from the windowsill.
Stopping behind his chair, she leaned down to kiss the
crown of his head, and he reached up to his shoulder and
touched her hand that was lying there.

'Thank you.'

'Don't thank me until I've spoken to her.'

Her face resting against his head, he felt her glancing
at the computer screen in front of him.

'How's the book coming along?'

'Okay.'

'Any more news from that agent yet?'

He stiffened slightly at the mention of it, stirring in his chair.

'No, I wouldn't have, not yet. I have to send her the rest of the book first, remember? Then she'll get back to me.'

'You haven't done that yet?'

'No, Sorcha, I'm still working on it.'

His voice scratched with a sudden annoyance and he let go of her hand. He couldn't help himself – the mention of the agent made him irritable. He wished he hadn't told her about it now, regretting the version of events he had explained to her, and the way he had allowed her to casually embroider the facts, making her think that the novel was more or less completed, when in truth it was barely started.

'Did you find out anything more about that poetry competition?'

'For God's sake, Sorcha, what is this?' He sighed. He couldn't help himself.

'I was just asking.'

The air between them seemed punctured by the sudden flare-up of his temper. As if sensing his unease, his deflation at the mention of the poetry, she took a step away from him.

'Well, I'll leave you to it.' But before leaving, she added, 'You'll find Avril on the beach. I think she's calling to see Lara.'

'Oh?'

'Yes – a little bit of hero worship's going on there, I think. And to be honest, I'm not sure it's such a good idea. For either of them.'

'Why do you say that?'

'Come on, Christy. Lara's hardly the best influence for an impressionable teenage girl, now is she? And besides, she has her own issues to sort out. I don't think she's going to want Avril hanging out of her the whole time, do you?'

'I suppose not.'

'Have you seen her yet?'

'Briefly. I gave her a lift from town the other day.'

'You never said.'

'Didn't I? It must have just slipped my mind,' he said, trying to sound casual, trying to simulate a calmness that he did not feel.

'How did she seem to you?'

'Oh, you know – tired, sad, a bit distracted.'

He could feel the colour spreading to his face, and turned back to the computer so that she wouldn't see it. For a moment, a silence seemed to drift in between them, and then he heard her turning the door handle.

'Sorcha?'

'Hmm?' she said, wheeling around to face him again.

'You didn't say anything to Stella, did you? About the novel? About what that agent said?'

She looked at him for what seemed a long moment, then raised her eyebrows, her face a mask of perfect innocence.

'No. No, of course not.' And then, changing the subject, she nodded in the direction of the window, the sky darkening behind it. 'There she is.'

For an instant, he was unsure of who she meant and swung around in his chair to face the sea. But looking back at her again, she seemed to read the question in his face, and something about her stiffened to it.

'Avril, I mean,' she explained before quietly letting herself out.

He watched her as she walked, unaware that she was being observed, her hips swinging. It was a new walk she had developed, a kind of indolent sashay, embodying every last ounce of boredom she could muster. And those black shoes with their big slabs of heels, at least three inches in height. He hated those shoes, had protested vigorously when she had arrived home with them, demanding that they be returned. They were too old for her, he had argued, she was still developing, for God's sake. They would ruin her posture. But he had lost that battle too.

It seemed to him that almost everything that he had once known and loved about his little girl – his first-born – was slowly being eroded by these changes inside her. On the beach that summer, he had been shocked by the metamorphosis of her body, this voluptuousness that had crept over her, transforming her. He hadn't been prepared for the speed at which her adolescence was taking hold, her body in the grip of those pernicious hormones. Her moods swung violently. He was nervous of approaching her, mentally preparing for her sulks and strops and sudden rages before entering the house. He still loved her, but lately he was having to remind himself of that more and more.

He caught up with her by the long flat rocks, calling out her name, his pace quickening as she turned and waited for him. As he approached, he saw the suspicion in her features, the flat, hard eyes watchful of him in the darkness.

'What?' she asked sullenly as he reached her, catching his breath.

'Can we talk for a minute?'

'I suppose,' she shrugged.

'Listen, love,' he began, releasing the breath inside him, trying to adopt a reasonable approach. 'I'm sorry about snapping at you earlier. What I said about your hair—'

'There's nothing wrong with my hair.'

'I know, I know. It's just it hides your pretty face sometimes.'

She didn't look overly convinced by this and he looked beyond her at the foam licking up against the beach, and suggested that they walk on together. For a moment, neither of them spoke as they walked, and he thought about how he might approach the issue of her behaviour, the rows with her mother and the insolence that he couldn't tolerate for much longer. But there was something so companionable about the silence, almost magical, that he didn't want to break the spell of it. They used to be such good friends, Avril and he. From the moment she was born, he had been seized with a powerful longing to protect her, coupled with a sort of awe at everything she did. When she was two years old, she was fascinated with butterflies. 'Flutterbies', she called them, and he couldn't bring himself to correct her. He'd felt an ache of sadness the day she discovered their true pronunciation. And now, in the gathering darkness, he wanted again to be her friend.

'So you're calling to see Lara?'

'Uh-huh.'

'You seem to be spending a good bit of time with her these days.'

'Yeah. She's cool.'

'I suppose she is.'

'She's not like other adults, you know? Not always asking shouldn't I be at home, or won't my parents be wondering where I am, or any of that shite. She lets me do what I like.'

He bit down on the urge to scold her for swearing, and wondered what exactly Lara allowed his daughter to do that she couldn't do at home.

'So what do you two get up to then?' he asked casually.

'I'm helping her with the house. She's doing it over.'

'Doing it over?'

'You know, taking down all those ancient pictures, painting the walls, that kind of thing.'

'Right.'

He tried to remember the house as it was when Lillian was alive. There were long rolls of flypaper swinging from the ceiling, with flies like blackcurrants stuck on them. Those sticky spirals with their black corpses used to make him feel sick. So, too, did the smell in there, particularly towards the end, when Lillian was really bad, and the ugly smell of disinfectant fought against an uglier odour. But the flypapers would be gone now, and he imagined that the smell had been whisked aside in the stiff breeze passing through open doors and windows.

'I made this tape for Lara,' she told him in a shy kind of way.

'What's on it?'

'The Cure, Interpol, The Bravery, Franz Ferdinand, The Killers.' She listed them off and he could tell from the tone of her voice that she was proud of these bands, of her appreciation of them.

'The Bravery?' he asked. 'Who are they?'

'Oh, they're this really cool band,' she enthused, all her hostility dropping away. He watched as her hair fluttered around her face, her guards having fallen, leaving that breathless optimism that she'd had as a child, and he felt the blood pumping through his heart, clutched by an old, familiar love for her. 'You should see the video for their song – there's this long row of dominos in a big kind of factory and all these bits of machinery going off when the dominos reach them. It's so cool.'

'It sounds cool.'

He found that he was warmed by the easy humour that returned between them. He welcomed it after all the hard, edgy silences loaded with unspoken threats. During one argument a few weeks ago, she had called him a loser. The word had shocked him, stunning him into silence. After she said it, the word seemed to hang in the air between them, pulsing with violence. How did she know to use that word, the one name that drove straight to the heart of his insecurities, this damning word that could injure him more than any other? It was of no consolation to him that she used the word to describe others. For Avril, the whole world seemed to be populated with losers, deadbeats, morons, muppets and assholes.

The changes in his daughter were troubling to him – her withdrawal from him, this new vocabulary she employed, the negativity of it, and her newfound ability to wound him with the easiest of kicks. But for that short while walking on the beach as night closed in over them and he stared up at a scattering of stars above their heads, he was able to forget that look she sometimes gave him, that expression of something close to hate, hate and shame merged into a sneer. That look left him cold.

In the distance, at the end of the strand, above the rocks where the water crashed and splintered, a light shone out through the gloom. It was strange to see the dim, grainy glow from those windows after two years of darkness. They reached the steep run of steps that snaked up over the sandbank and the tall grass, up to the rickety porch, and he saw a shadow passing by the window, a slender silhouette, and something quickened in his chest. Lara.

For an instant, he was thrown into confusion, unsure of what he should do. He hadn't spoken to his daughter, as he promised Sorcha he would, and yet he felt that he had achieved something with her nonetheless.

'Well, I'll let you get on.'

'Okay.'

They stood for a moment, regarding each other in the darkness, the water spilling onto the sand in whispery waves.

'Oh, and Avril?'

'Yeah?'

'Ease up on your mother, all right?'

She thought about that for a moment.

'Bye Dad,' she said, and the furrow of tenderness in her voice gave him reason to hope.

He watched her climbing those steps, the optimism in the light beat of her feet over those wooden boards. Up above, he heard the door opening, his face caught in the sudden light spilling out onto the steps. Their voices were raised in greeting, and he waited for them to turn to him, but instead they left him behind, entering the house, swallowed up by the closing door.

For a moment he waited, watching the window, half-expecting to see her emerging from the shadows, calling him back, inviting him in. He stood there for two, maybe three minutes before turning away, angry with himself for entertaining such a foolish notion. He pulled his jacket around him and walked back along the strand, alone in the dark, the sea advancing beside him.

5

Sorcha sat at the back of the Old Oratory, in the place Stella called the coffee dock, waiting patiently. All around her were sounds of human voices blending with the music from the speakers, a slow, lilting air, while her two hands wrapped around a mug of coffee and she watched the steam from it wafting upwards. There was something pleasurable about sitting alone, hands warming around the earthenware mug. It felt luxurious, to have nothing else to do, only sit there and wait.

A year before, Sorcha had been to see her local GP – a tallish, decent-looking man who had been her doctor since she was a child – and confided in him about her grief. She had gone to see him, finally, at Christy's insistence. Her husband, made anxious by her persistent bouts of crying, and her own alarm at the fog of apathy that had come to settle stubbornly over her thoughts, drove her to seek professional help. It was a few months after Lillian's death and she still felt tender and threadbare, fearful of being pumped full of anti-depressants or sent to see a psychiatrist, so that when the doctor took her hands in his, looked at her intently with searching eyes and said, 'Sorcha. You must learn to be kinder to yourself,' she had felt crushed by a new wave of emotion within her, his eyes suddenly too soft, his voice too compassionate.

Coffee and cake at the coffee dock was one of her little treats to herself, a ritual she savoured. Part of her mental medication, she liked to think. Looking up, she saw Stella at the counter, serving a customer and mouthing across 'two minutes'. But Sorcha was happy to wait, idling over her own thoughts. These moments of solitude were to be treasured, plucked from the constant clamour of daily life. It was a relief that the summer had drawn to an end, she admitted to herself. Now that the children and Christy were back at school, she could have the house to herself again. This summer in particular had been more strained than others. Avril's new aggression, these sudden flare-ups in temper, had taken their toll on all of them. Christy's response had been typical – withdrawing into his study, or taking to the beach for one of his solitary walks. It surprised her still, this need for solitude he possessed. Their son seemed to have inherited something of that quality. It was another one of her worries – Jim's tendency to withdraw, this quietness of his, and what it meant. Her son's glaring absence of friends had become apparent to her over the summer months. It broke her heart to see him constantly hanging around the house, lounging in front of the TV with eyes glazed over, or holed up in his room with a GameBoy and comics. It was something she had confided to Stella in previous chats over coffee. And as she saw Stella approaching, having finally disentangled herself from her serving duties, Sorcha wondered if she should bring it up again, particularly in light of the failure the other night to bring Jim and Elijah together.

'At last,' Stella breathed, collapsing onto the narrow bench with a short, puffy sigh. Her face beamed with health and goodwill and she leaned across and clutched Sorcha at the wrists. Stella was a tactile person, a fact that Sorcha still found mildly disarming after several years of friendship. 'How are you, my love?'

'Fine. Free at last.'

'Ah yes. School's in session!' She paused to stir sugar into her coffee, tapping her spoon brightly three times against the rim. 'Guy's at home today, schooling Elijah.'

There was something quaint about their determination to home school their son, Sorcha thought. She couldn't imagine either Christy or herself having the patience to sit all day with either one of their children. An hour with Jim ploughing through his homework at the kitchen table was about as far she could stretch to.

'No Lara?' Stella asked, and Sorcha felt herself flushing, remembering her breezy remark that she would invite her cousin to join them for coffee.

'No. I'm afraid she had to work.'

'Oh, that's a pity. Still, I'm sure I'll meet her sometime soon.'

Sorcha smiled and drank from her mug and listened as Stella launched into her plans for their next book club meeting, but while she sat there silently, she thought of Lara, of the awkwardness that seemed to persist between them, and how it had threatened to split open into animosity yesterday when she had called to see her.

Lara had seemed a little stunned at first when she came to the door, blinking in the light as if woken from sleep, while Sorcha stood on the veranda smiling strenuously, her voice sounding shrill to herself as she asked brightly if it was a bad time.

'No, no. Do come in,' Lara had said, holding the door open.

Sorcha had followed her inside and then stopped abruptly, her eyes taking in the walls, brighter, cleaner than she had remembered. And then it struck her – all the pictures were gone. Those framed photographs in black and white, in sepia, in faded colours, those pictures that Lillian had loved, all of them gone.

'The pictures!' she exclaimed before she could stop herself. 'What happened to them?'

The accusation was there in her voice, she couldn't help it, and she heard Lara's response, cautious and controlled.

'They were giving me the creeps,' she said quietly, 'so I got rid of them.'

Sorcha gasped despite herself. 'But Lillian…'

'Lillian hated them.'

'No she didn't!'

Lara had looked at her then, and Sorcha knew she had gone too far – her tone, the sharp little break it made in conversation. The tension between them was there already, confrontation in unspoken things as if an argument could suddenly break open right in front of them. Sorcha didn't like arguments. They left her feeling bruised and helpless. In the end, she broke away from Lara's gaze and forced a smile around at the walls.

'Well, it looks nice and bright,' she had said feebly.

For the next twenty minutes, she had sat there making conversation over tea, listening to her own hollow voice echoing in the newly painted room, watching Lara smoking one cigarette after another.

She told none of this to Stella.

'So how are the kids settling back in?' her friend asked her now.

'Oh, you know. Avril is still getting into moods. The good thing is she's out of the house until four each day, so I have a few hours' respite.'

'And Jim?'

'Jim. Well, he seems the same, really. It's hard to say – he doesn't talk about school. I find it difficult to know what's going on in his head.'

Picking him up the day before, she had sat in the car, watching a stream of boys emerging from the gates, all of them sun kissed and healthy after the summer, before her own pale child had emerged, head down, staring at the ground, alone as usual, and she felt her worry about him deepen.

'Have you spoken to his teachers?' asked Stella.

'Not since the end of last term. They suggested we might think about keeping him back a year before sending him to secondary school.'

Stella sucked in her lips, nodding sagely. Sorcha already knew her friend's strident views on the subject.

She had listened to her boisterous opinions on the educa-
tional system, had sat through Stella's stern warnings
about bullying, and the vulnerability of boys in particular.
She had silently accepted books and magazine clippings
on the rising rate of suicide among teenage boys, and all
the while her fears had churned away inside her. There
was a time when she had shown these pieces of journal-
ism to Christy, but not any more, not since the Betjeman
poem. Stella, thinking she was helping, believing it was
necessary to go at Christy from a different angle, one
particular to him, had presented Sorcha with a poem
written by John Betjeman about his experience of being
bullied as a child – 'Original Sin on the Sussex Coast', it
was called – and she, like a fool, had given it to Christy.
His reaction had been explosive.

'What does she mean by this?' he had raged, waving
the poem aloft, incandescent with anger. 'It's bloody
typical of Stella and her second-hand wisdom!
Borrowing someone else's words to try and strike fear
into us. What does she expect us to do, take Jim out of
school? Send him down to their little hedge school so
that they can fill him full of their hippy mumbo-jumbo
and turn him into a geek like Elijah?' Of course, Sorcha
hadn't told Stella about his reaction. She would never
tell of Christy's misgivings, let alone reveal that he
believed Elijah to be overly precocious, and too thin and
bug eyed for his liking. On one occasion, she had been
shocked by his remarks that Elijah was like a character
from a science fiction novel, not really human at all.
Sorcha had noticed that her husband's remarks about

Stella, Guy and Elijah had turned nasty over the last couple of years, and suspected that the reason for this had more to do with the poetry book than anything else.

'And what does Christy make of holding him back?' Stella asked, rescuing Sorcha from the destructive spiral of her thoughts.

'He doesn't think it's a good idea, that it would only be a waste of time. He seems to think it's just a phase Jim's going through.' As the words came out of her mouth, it occurred to her that this was Christy's answer to everything concerning their children. She felt a sudden flare of impatience with him.

'Speaking of Christy,' Stella began, her eyes taking on a conspiratorial gleam. 'I rang up *The Irish Times* about that poetry competition, and it turns out he is eligible!' She leaned back, triumphantly, nodding her head as if to say 'So there!'

'Oh. Right.'

'Isn't that marvellous?'

'Of course. That's terrific!' Sorcha heard her voice and the weakness that was there, and she remembered the little sigh Christy had released when she had mentioned it to him in his study. He wasn't a man given to sighing, and that short, exasperated release of air had worried her. They had never discussed it, the great disappointment of his poetry. They preferred to leave it sitting somewhere at the edges of their marriage, gathering dust. They ignored the whole painful episode surrounding the deafening silence that had greeted its publication, the way it was ignored by all the newspapers and magazines – one review, one only, a tepid little paragraph in *The Kerryman*, barely a murmur. And then there was the embarrassment of spending all that money on copies that never sold, not to mention her own private humiliation that night in the Old Oratory as she listened to her husband reading his work aloud, wordy, verbose and arrogantly overdone. Looking around her, she had seen the blank stares of the others gathered there, and felt a sharp stab of pain registering for her husband, his pompous delivery, how ridiculous he appeared, as all at once she realised just how awful the poems were. There was guilt there, too, that she had allowed him to go through with it; that she hadn't attempted to protect him from the stings of criticism or the coldness of being ignored. She felt herself blush again at the memory.

'So be sure and tell him he's to enter that book!' Stella instructed her, tapping the table with her stubby index finger for emphasis.

'I will.'

'And if he doesn't enter it, then I'll send it into them myself!'

Sorcha knew that this wasn't an idle threat. She was aware of a sense of ownership on Stella's behalf. It was apparent from the moment Stella first read the poems and began her campaign of vigorous encouragement. These feelings of ownership were strengthened when Christy asked her to design the cover, a request Stella declared herself honoured to receive. Stella fancied herself as something of a patron of the arts, between her craft shop supporting local artists and then her willingness to hold readings and workshops after hours in the Old Oratory. It was all done out of goodwill, Sorcha knew, however misplaced it might be. Perhaps that was why she told Stella about the agent in London, something she had been experiencing little stabs of regret over since making the revelation.

'Stella,' she began tentatively. 'What I told you the other night, you know, about the agent?'

'Oh my God!' Stella put down her coffee, seized her wrist again. 'Has he heard something more?'

'No, no! It's not that. It's just…would you mind not mentioning it to anyone? I mean you can say it to Guy, of course, only you might ask him to keep it to himself.'

'Sure. Why? Is something wrong?'

'No, nothing's wrong,' Sorcha laughed, a nervous twitter. 'It's just, I didn't realise, but I wasn't supposed to say it to anyone.'

'Is Christy a little sensitive about it?' Stella asked smilingly. 'Don't worry, honey. I understand completely. These artistic souls, eh?'

'Right,' Sorcha agreed, wondering whether she should mention to Stella not to say anything of it to Christy either. Perhaps it was the cheerful ebullience with which her companion finished her coffee before leaning across to pat her hand or her own guilt fluttering inside her, but in the end she decided against it and said nothing.

Stella embraced her as they said goodbye at the door, and as she drove home, Sorcha considered again why exactly she had told her friend about the agent. She had been a little drunk at the time. That familiar flare of anxiety had ignited inside her as Stella bleated on about the poetry competition that night, and perhaps she had said it to draw her attention away from the poetry when Christy clearly felt uncomfortable about it. Or had it more to do with her own eager hope that something would come out of it? She remembered the excitement in his voice, guarded as it was, when he told her that the agent from London who he had met briefly at a writing festival had read the three chapters he had sent her and shown a definite interest. 'Definite interest' had been his exact words. Or was her reason for telling Stella about the agent based on an altogether different motive?

Driving out of town, her eyes passing over the blaze of montbresia that flanked the tarmac, the clouds scudding over the mountains ahead, it occurred to Sorcha that something had changed in their friendship. She had known for some time now that she had been making attempts to repair her relationship with Stella after the damage done to it in Clonakilty. She had come to think of it as the 'Clonakilty incident'. Such a silly thing, and yet it lay heavily on her conscience, even though she was convinced that she wasn't the one to blame.

Neither of them had discussed it in the weeks that had passed – the things that were said, the hurtful words, the embarrassing admissions. But Sorcha remembered them clearly. Stella had suggested that the two of them head off to Clonakilty for a night. There was an artist there that Stella was interested in meeting with a view to commissioning some work for the Old Oratory. They could meet him, take a look at his pottery and spend the rest of the time being pampered at the spa in the Inchydoney Hotel. As she drove, Sorcha remembered, with a degree of shame, her craven gratitude at the invitation, so delighted was she to be asked. Sorcha believed that some people had a gift for friendship – one that she didn't possess. When she looked back at her life, she saw a slew of unsuccessful friendships spoiled in some way, or else allowed to fizzle out. She worried that her son was the same. Perhaps that was why she had been thrusting him upon Elijah, in the same way her own parents had thrust her upon Lara. But Stella had the gift of friendship in abundance. She gathered people easily to herself, with a sort of magnetism that drew them in, a charm that was enveloping. Christy had declaimed it as bullying, and Sorcha was aware of the fact that there were other people they knew who found Stella repellent. But on that bright July afternoon, as they set off in Guy's Land Rover, she had felt happy to be enveloped in that charm, how willing she was to be gathered in.

Throughout the journey down to west Cork, they had talked and talked. Sorcha opened up about the worries she had over Jim, his reticence, his inability to mix with kids his own age. She talked of Avril and how her sudden moods were starting to be a worry. And Stella spoke at length about their money worries, hers and Guy's, the slump in tourism that summer and the knock-on effect it was having on their trade. She let

Sorcha in on secrets of Guy's previous marriage, and how his first wife was bleeding him dry for alimony and how frustrating it was for Stella, being forced to stand on the sidelines and say nothing.

When they reached their hotel and freshened up, they decided to crack open a bottle of wine in the bar before going to the artist's house to view his work. Sorcha couldn't be sure whether it was the effects of drinking before they had eaten or the general buoyancy of their shared good humour, but they found themselves becoming drunk quite quickly. The conversation between them seemed to shift to more intimate, personal matters. Stella told her that she wanted another baby, but Guy was adamant that they couldn't afford another child. She was heartbroken about it, and angry with Guy for being so stubborn with her while yielding so easily to his first wife's demands. Sorcha in turn admitted to the circumstances surrounding her own marriage. She told Stella how she had unexpectedly fallen pregnant with Avril before she and Christy were married, or even engaged, the shame she had felt, and the fear.

'Why do they call it that – "fallen pregnant"?' Stella had asked.

'I don't know. It's silly, really.'

'Like – oops! I've stumbled into pregnancy!'

'Help, I've tripped over my fertilised egg!'

They had giggled about it helplessly, warmed by the conviviality of their surroundings, the loosening effect of the wine.

Stella confided – well, no, in hindsight, she boasted – about her sex life with Guy. His sensitivity as a lover, his creativity, his willingness to postpone his own pleasure until she had reached orgasm.

'He's quite the gentleman then,' Sorcha had quipped, feeling suddenly shy, lost in this conversation, and wary of any onus falling on her to shed light on her own sex life in this spirit of sharing. She couldn't help but feel out of her depth, overtaken by a natural prudishness. But her remark floated past Stella, who was just getting into her stride.

'Once,' she remarked, giggling, revealing teeth stained with wine, 'before we moved to Ireland, there was another couple we were friends with. Like-minded people, shall we say. After some wine one evening – well, rather a lot of wine, actually – we kind of, you know, experimented.'

Sorcha's eyes had widened with surprise. She couldn't help it. What surprised her more was her own overwhelming sense of disgust as Stella shed light on her night of passion, the flitting from one bedroom to the next.

'Didn't you find it, well, awkward,' Sorcha stuttered, 'the next time you saw them? Weren't you mortified?'

'Nonsense! We all had a good laugh about it.' She finished with a knowing grin that made Sorcha wonder if there wasn't a second encounter or maybe even a third.

Stella had made arrangements for them to go to the artist's house – Neil Swift was his name – for supper, which he enterprisingly served on his own hand-thrown crockery. Sorcha was unclear as to how well Stella and Neil were acquainted – it was difficult to guess owing to her friend's growing drunkenness. She seemed to take command of the conversation, whisking them along in the stiff breeze of her frenzied anecdotes, her rapturous confessions, her flirtatious joking. Across the table, Sorcha silently observed their host. He had a small, compact face, with clear eyes and hair that was grey and soft looking that seemed to waft up over his head. She couldn't take her eyes off that hair. Beneath it, his skin was nut brown, weather beaten, making his blue eyes bluer. He caught her looking, and she looked away, feeling a rush of blood to her face. He laughed warmly at Stella's jokes and seemed unruffled by her liberal pouring of wine, her slurred words and increasingly vocal drunkenness. His navy sweater had a couple of holes in it, revealing white cotton beneath.

There was something slightly neglected about him that made Sorcha feel friendly towards him, protective even, absurd as that seemed at the time. Sorcha was a woman who clung to the outmoded notion that men were creatures who needed to be looked after. And looking around this man's cramped little cottage, she saw signs of neglect everywhere – in the threads of cobwebs that clung to the high corners of the ceilings, in the yellowing net curtains over the windows, the faded and collapsed-looking sofa that Stella sprawled across after dinner. In fact, the only things in the whole place that didn't appear chipped or worn or grimy were the plates and cups and bowls that he had fashioned himself, in shades of blue and grey and green, the colours rising and falling through the clay in undulating patterns like the sea.

But sometime late into the night, what had been a light-hearted drunkenness up to that point seemed to take a turn. Stella's gentle ribbing became risky, more dangerous. Sorcha felt Neil's gaze and brought her eyes up to meet it. He held her there for a long moment, and she tried to read the message being imparted. Something ugly seemed to have entered Stella's demeanour, and when she tried to get up off the seat, to Sorcha's dismay it was clear that her friend was so drunk she would be unable to walk.

'Looks like you'll be spending the night,' Neil had said. She had listened for a hint of resentment in his voice but found none.

'I'm so sorry,' she professed, feeling mortified for her friend, and worried, too. She was unsure how she felt to be staying in this man's house. He was virtually a stranger.

Together, they half-carried, half-dragged Stella into Neil's bedroom and Sorcha felt her embarrassment rise at their unexpected arrival in this most private of rooms, with its messy bed, ruffled bed linen, piles of books against the walls and clothes strewn over an armchair in the corner.

Once Stella was safely deposited on the bed, he stood beside her for a moment, both of them looking down on the half-conscious form. Sorcha was aware of his breathing, his proximity to her. And then, respectfully, he withdrew from the room, leaving Sorcha to remove Stella's shoes and get her friend comfortable. Stella was still somewhat conscious, and as Sorcha moved away from her towards the door, she heard a muffled voice from the bed.

'Who's that?'

'It's me, Sorcha.'

In the spill of light from the open door, she saw the wide face among the pillows, the small dark eyes regarding her over porcine cheeks.

'Sorcha,' she said, and something about the slow, speculative way she said it acted as a warning. Sorcha steadied herself for what would come next. 'You know, that name doesn't suit you,' Stella stated, a whisper of menace in her tone. 'You should be called Enid or Mavis. Or Iris. Something like that.'

These words came out clearly, not slurred, but punched with meanness. Old ladies' names. Sorcha understood perfectly what was meant by them.

And when she emerged into the brightly lit hallway, closing the door behind her, she felt stunned, her legs weak beneath her, and an overwhelming desire to cry rose up inside her.

'Is everything okay?' Neil asked gently, coming forward into the light.

'I...I...' She groped about for words, and then, to her absolute horror, she gave way to a giant sob.

For a moment, neither one of them moved, and in the silence, her sob seemed a large, ungainly thing.

'I'm sorry,' she said through her tears, and her voice emerged all wobbly and hysterical, which alarmed her even more.

'Here,' he said, taking her gently by the elbow, leading her over to the table, and it occurred to her that he was manoeuvring her the way you would an old or infirm person, as if her limbs were fragile, bones at risk of breaking. She felt immensely grateful that he had chosen the table sprawled with the detritus of their meal to sit her down at, rather than the awkward intimacy of the couch.

Sitting back in her hard chair, she daubed at her eyes with her used napkin, and he sat opposite at a distance, waiting for her to get herself under control.

'I don't know what came over me,' she declared with an attempt at a laugh, and he smiled and nodded, and she thought to herself, What a nice man he is, what a kind face.

'At risk of sending you completely over the edge,' he said, and raised the wine bottle and replenished both their glasses.

She lifted hers to her lips, wondering at the wisdom of it, and when she looked at him again he was staring into her eyes. Intently.

She thought of Stella sleeping in the next room, of Christy lying at home in their bed, stretched out in sleep, of her children fastened into their own dream-filled worlds. The night was stretching out in front of her, here, alone, with this strange, quiet-spoken man and his kind eyes. Silence grew around them, and it seemed to her to be elaborate, composed and possibly dangerous. There was nowhere for her to sleep, but at that moment she didn't want to sleep, didn't want to be alone with her thoughts, and at that table, surrounded by the ruins of their meal, she lifted her head, looked at him, and began to talk.

Betrayals began easily, innocently. Always in films or in novels, the betrayer seemed to profess that they didn't know how it happened, they were oblivious to the beginning of it, as if you could just slip into an infidelity, stumble over it. Fall pregnant, she remembered. Fall unfaithful. But Sorcha hadn't been unfaithful. Nothing had happened for her to reproach herself with. Talking until the dawn broke and light shone in the windows wasn't a betrayal in the strictest sense of the word. And yet, she had felt the need to conceal it. When Stella, hung-over and chastened, asked her on the drive home what she had done all night, Sorcha had replied that she had slept on the couch. She wasn't sure why she had lied – she hadn't planned on it – but in the split second before she answered, it occurred to her that it might be safer that way.

Later, back in her home, when she told Christy about the trip, she didn't tell him two things. One was the nasty episode with Stella that still sat uncomfortably with her. The other was the all-night conversation with Neil. She didn't tell him because she wasn't sure yet how she felt about either incident. It had been the strangest night. But she felt guilty for not sharing these things with him, and maybe it was because of that guilt that she told him about Stella and Guy and their wife-swapping antics back in England.

His eyes had widened, his mouth falling open, and there was the sudden explosive burst of his laughter, and then she was laughing too, so that it didn't feel so bad what she had hidden from him.

'Lord!' he had cried, wiping the tears from his eyes. 'That's hysterical! Stella and Guy, they crack me up.'

'I know. Mad, isn't it?'

'Do you reckon they're still into that?'

'God, I hope not.'

'Still,' Christy smiled, his laughter under control, and then said, almost to himself, 'It's just a shame that Stella's such an ugly troll!'

Afterwards, when she was on her own, she thought about what he meant by that comment, and as her mind travelled along that path, further questions snuck up on her. If Stella were attractive, would he have been interested in pursuing that option? Had infidelity ever crossed his mind? No. She was sure he was faithful to her. But she felt a small pang of hurt nonetheless, and realised that the pain didn't come from her husband's potential betrayal, given the opportunity, but rather at the realisation that he hadn't raised any objection to her being with Guy. He hadn't even thought to mention it. She wondered had it even entered his head, and couldn't escape the thought that maybe it just didn't matter to him.

This hurt stayed with her, clinging to her for some time afterwards. She couldn't seem to shake it off. It clustered in around the wound of Stella's words, her implication that Sorcha was prudish, old-fashioned, unadventurous. An old woman. Perhaps it was the combination of these two hurts, or the inertia that she had been experiencing for some time, but later that night, alone in the kitchen, she had taken out her mobile phone, fished for the scrap of paper in her handbag, his number inscribed on it along with his initials – a looping artistic hand, a hopeful flourish of the pen – and started keying in a text. 'You said that any time I needed to talk you'd be there,' it began.

6

He waited a week before he called to see her. He considered a week to be a respectable interval. Any less might alert her to his eagerness, although he feared this was already given away by his voice when he made the offer, the pubescent quaver in it. But any more than a week might have signified disdain, and he didn't want her to think he was disapproving or that he didn't want to see her. And besides, school was back in session, the blinding monotony of routine cranking up again, and he welcomed the distraction that a few hours' tinkering with her car would provide.

That afternoon when he had given her a lift, there was something about her, vulnerability swathed in defiance, and some part of her weakness had struck a chord in him. He had thought about it since then, whenever he found himself alone, his mind wandering back to that day. He kept seeing that dark need in her eyes, the sudden warmth in her voice when she called him Christian. The way his name, his old name, sounded when it came from her mouth.

Of course, he hadn't admitted any of this to Sorcha. He had seen the question in the raise of her eyebrow at the announcement of his intentions to help Lara get the car started.

'But you don't know anything about cars,' she had stated bluntly and he had had to remind himself not to rise to it.

'I know something,' he had replied, his voice testy despite his best efforts.

I need to get my head together, he told himself as he walked across the beach, feeling the wind stirring and blowing in from the Atlantic. These natural rhythms relaxed him, helped to quell the alarm that had visited him lately – alarm at his own behaviour, the way he seemed to slide so easily into negativity. Lately, it was as if his life was tilting sideways. He felt like he had lost his balance, unsure of his footing, of his place in the world.

The beach was empty, deserted after an incident over twenty years ago when a dead baby had washed up onto the shore. It was the way the tides whipped around the peninsula, drawing into the strand, gathering all the debris from the coast – the lost shoes and broken boats, the towels and clothes and dolls and tyres, objects discarded by their owners or stolen by the sea, even the broken body of a newborn girl – they were all deposited on the sands and shingle of this beach. Flotsam churned over the Atlantic shelf before being spat out onto the land. He remembered hearing about it – a baby, blue and swollen, picked out from underneath a coverlet of seaweed and the plastic flap of an old manure bag.

After that, the strand was deserted. People from the town stopped going there, preferring the stony cove of Cooscrom for their evening swims, or travelling the four miles to Balinaskelligs for the long curving bay of sand, the gentle rolling waves. The strand was cursed, they said, haunted. It became a lonely place, visited only by cattle that strayed beyond the fields.

He had known this beach nearly all his life. The summers he spent here as a child, staying with his grandparents up on Killealan Mountain, and then later between terms at university. But the emptiness of the beach had never struck him. Not until later, when he first moved into the house with Sorcha and they would walk along it every night. The loneliness began speaking to him; he recognised an echo inside himself. During that first year, if the night was a fine one, they would sit together in the sand dunes, looking out at the Atlantic as it washed up against the lip of the land.

'What are you thinking?' she would ask softly.

Sometimes, he told her he was thinking about his work at the school, the new curriculum, a problem with a particular pupil or a small triumph in the staff room. At other times he would wrap an arm around her shoulders and draw her to him and tell her his thoughts were of the baby leaping in her womb. But there were evenings when he looked out over the empty sea and whispered his truth to her.

'I'm thinking about all the places on the other side of this ocean.'

And then she would reach for his hand and hold it in hers, her thumb drawing back across the ridges of his knuckles. That soft stroking told of an unspoken understanding of his sorrow, that whittled loss, the relinquishing of his dreams. They didn't speak of the journeys never taken, the broken plans swept up and put away. He didn't complain of it and she didn't apologise for it. Nor did they speak of Lara. That wouldn't have been appropriate from either of them.

He walked along the strand, lingering now and again to gaze out at the empty sea, boiling as the waves gathered momentum. They hissed up onto the shore. He couldn't recall the last time his wife walked alongside him, picking their way together over the shingle and the ragged line of seaweed. The years had passed quickly and his children had grown moody and surly, and somehow he didn't seem to have the words to ask his wife to join him in his solitude. It would feel awkward somehow, like he was asking for something so much bigger. He wasn't sure how she would react.

Before reaching the house, he saw Lara sitting on the bottom step, her face locked in concentration, serious and deeply intent within herself. It caused him to pause, hesitating before disturbing her privacy. He stood there looking at her, experiencing a single moment of crushing shyness, but she had seen him and looked up, caught suddenly, a guilty smile coming over her face. It was then as he approached that he saw the joint in her hand, smelled the burning butt in the air.

'Caught in the act,' Lara said quietly, biting into her bottom lip, smiling, playful, yet still the guilt lingered. Just for a second he was swept back through the years and was stumbling upon her entwined in the arms of some nameless youth, her schoolbag flung aside in the nettles, her shirt untucked from her skirt. That same slow smile, looking up at him beneath heavy inked lids, guilt darting behind her eyes, her face as smooth as a pebble and lit up with the knowledge that he wouldn't tell, he wouldn't rat her out.

'Is that what I think it is?' he asked, his voice emerging cracked like a teenaged boy's.

'Just something to take the edges off. Care to join me?'

He looked down at the smoking joint and felt a bristle of discomfort.

'No, thank you.'

He sounded like a sanctimonious prick and he knew it, but she seemed to let it pass and took a long drag before explaining, 'It makes things easier sometimes.'

'You need a little extra help today?'

She shrugged then, meeting his gaze for a moment, her expression tender, and then looked away, almost flirtatiously. She took another, smaller puff and let it wisp around inside her for a moment before stubbing out the joint on the step and returning it to a small plastic bag in her pocket.

'Maybe not just now,' she conceded. 'Are you going for a walk?'

'Actually, I'd come to see about your car.'

She smiled up at him then, and he saw something teasing in that grin.

'Well, let's not worry about that right now,' she said, and he felt that in some small way, she was making fun of him. 'Walk with me a little way?'

'Okay.'

He waited while she got to her feet, wrapping her cardigan tightly about her, arms folded across her middle as she pushed through the soft sand, joining him as they stepped down towards the sea. For a moment, all he could think about was the joint he had caught her smoking. Where did she get it? How stoned was she? His trousers were snapping around his legs in the wind, and as they stepped across the hard marbled sand, he found himself silently recalibrating his thoughts about her, making careful readjustments to align with this new pothead impression he had of her.

'Don't worry,' she said to him suddenly.

He looked up at her with a look of confusion, not sure what she meant.

She laughed then, watching him, and shook her head.

'Look at you, the big worried expression on your face, those angry eyebrows.' He must have looked affronted, his grievance showing on his face, for she laughed again and gripped the crook of his arm. 'Honestly, you look so serious! So shocked at me!'

He wasn't sure what to make of that. Her tone was mocking, and he couldn't help feeling that she was slighting him in some way. There was a dangerous edge to her voice, and he suspected there was a chemical reason for that.

'It's just to help me relax,' she explained softly. 'Nothing for you to worry about. Here, you can take it if you like.'

He stopped and looked down at the small Ziploc bag

resting in her outstretched hand, two more neatly rolled joints nestling up against one another within it.

'Go on. I don't need them.'

He felt she was testing him, and for a moment sensed the challenge in the gesture.

'That's okay, Lara. I'm sure you can be trusted.'

She didn't laugh this time, but fixed him with a slow smile, and he felt like he had passed the test.

They turned and walked on, and something softened in the air between them, the tension dispersing on the wind.

'So I look serious, eh?' he teased.

'Absolutely. With that low brow and dark hair, those brooding looks, you look troubled, angst-ridden. Earnest.'

'Earnest?'

'Soulful, then.'

'Soulful. I like that.'

He felt his heart give out a tiny kick and knew that it was vanity, but it warmed him anyway. He smiled at her, then felt like a flirt and looked back down at his feet, sand covering the toes of his shoes. It seemed to him that they were slipping back into an old pattern. He felt the grooves of adolescence drawing them in – this easy humour, her playfulness and teasing, and his wavering, uncertain as to whether she was mocking him or flirting with him. He felt, too, the little tick of pleasure that began when she had touched his arm.

'And what about me?' she asked, darting a sideways glance at him, but beneath her smile and the teasing tenor of her voice was a nervousness. He sensed that she was fearful of what he might say and glimpsed a new vulnerability – this fear in herself, the changes that had formed in her, crouched around the sadness she carried. Beneath her playfulness there was a pleading, a desperate need for him to be kind, to be gentle with her.

'You are as you always were,' he said generously. 'Wildly charismatic.'

'Not older, then?'

'Nope.'

'Liar.' But there was humour in her voice. 'You're older.'

'Thanks a lot.'

Her laugh emerged like a punch sailing through the air, and he found himself grinning at her, hands sunk into his pockets, the wind cooling his face.

'It suits you,' she said. 'You seem to have grown into your face.'

'Grown into my face?'

'Come on!' Her elbow dug into his arm. 'Stop fishing for compliments, I've given you plenty already.'

He felt chastened somehow, grinning sheepishly. The sun was streaking the sky orange between bands of grey on the edge of the sea. They were coming towards the craggy headland, the spit of rocks falling down into the water, and he wanted suddenly to keep walking, feeling himself taken by a new, happy energy. He wanted to scramble up the rocks the way they used to, up to where the grass grew long and dry. And maybe she felt this too, maybe some sentiment of the past was wheeling around inside her, for she turned to him then, her face inscrutable.

'Is it still there, do you think?' she asked, her head tilting in that direction, and he knew immediately what she was referring to.

'I'm not sure. I haven't looked up there in a long time.'

Her eyes flickered over his face, as if quietly calculating, before she turned from him. He watched her proceeding towards the rocks, the ends of her cardigan released and flapping in the wind as she reached for a foothold.

'Come on,' she called over her shoulder.

He followed obediently, something stirring in his chest, watching her feet in flip-flops gripping the stone, her legs pushing upwards, and suddenly he was a teen-ager again, listening to her stout command, observing her leading the way, her hair untamed and billowing in the breeze. He was three years older than her, and yet that was the pattern of things between them – Lara leading, Christy following. The gap in age was swept aside by her commanding personality and his own crippling shyness. She was always the instigator of their expeditions over the headland, or across to Begnis in Sorcha's father's boat, or cycling out to Portmagee and over the bridge to Valentia Island. They slipped so easily into their roles, Lara with her busy optimism, her good-natured bossiness, a natural leader. Whereas Christy, who felt things deeply – the burden of his stammer, the wounds of cruel remarks and the loneliness of being different – seemed to relax around her boundless enthusiasm, felt swept away by her ideas and commands, and felt, too, the warm delirium of inclusion. Sorcha was there too. What he remembered of her from that time was less clear – a mass of yellow curls, a neat prettiness. But she, like him, was quiet, her presence overshadowed by the noise of Lara's busy personality. And it was always Sorcha who took up the rear, who stepped in behind him, so that his memories of her were a jumbled recollection of glancing back to make sure she was following.

He reached the top of the bank of stones and saw Lara striding through the long grass, over to the old stone where she bent low on her hunkers. Following, he looked down at the back of her head, saw the tangled hair, and stepped to one side so that he could see some of her face, the soft slope of her cheek, the angle of her brow, and admired all over again the curves and angles of her face. Her hands, long fingered and tanned, passed over the ground, dusting away the weeds and sand to reveal the flat stone in the grass, heavy and grey, the painted lettering faded but visible.

'It's still here,' she said, in a breathy whisper. 'I can't believe it.'

He stood beside her, unspeaking, unwilling to interrupt her as she read over the lines, her fingers tracing shapes across the stone.

It had been Lara's idea – a memorial to the dead baby, the child that no one came forward to claim, a grave to mark the place she was swept into by the sea. They had found the stone on the beach, long and flat and smoothed by the waves. The three of them had dragged it up here and settled it into the grass at the base of this old rock. But it was Christy who had come up with the words. It was the poet in him, perhaps. Although they weren't his words, but the words of another, so what did that make him? A plagiarist? A pretender?

And as he remembered that verse, he experienced a brief moment of regret and felt the awkwardness prickling the air. It was from 'The Stolen Child' by W.B. Yeats. It was a romantic notion he'd had in his youth, seduced by the beauty of the language, privately moved by the emotion of the piece. He'd been triumphant, too, at presenting it to the others, pleased at their reactions, their awe that he could find such a fitting piece of poetry.

Lara was reading it quietly, under her breath, but the words came up to meet him. They fluttered in the air about his head.

'Come away o human child, to the waters and the wild, with a fairy hand-in-hand, for the world's more full of weeping than you can understand.'

With that, her sorrow was alive and pumping between them. Her little boy, her loss, was present and palpable and he wanted then to reach out to her, to press down on her pain, on the coiled spring of her anger, to rock her back and forth in the cooling wind of the evening. This sudden emotion took him by surprise and he felt his body tensing to it. *Thoughts like these are dangerous*, he reminded himself.

'I'm sorry,' he said to her kneeling form, her face

partially hidden from him, eyes fixed on the stone. 'It must be painful. Those words. It must remind you.'

'I don't need a reminder.'

She stood up then and her gaze met his briefly, and he saw the clarity of her grey eyes, as grey as the fabric of sea behind her, determined and resolved and open, before she turned away from him again.

Folding her arms tight around her, she faced into the breeze, looking down over the beach from that great height, and he read the defiance in that gesture, the will not to be defeated, and something of the old Lara returned to her in that moment.

'If you could go anywhere in the world, where would you choose?' she asked, throwing the question over her shoulder. He felt the warm hum of nostalgia all around them, remembering how she had asked him this question before, so many times.

'Buenos Aires.'

'Been there.' She smiled at him then, a grin of triumph, of gratitude, of friendship. 'Do you think you'll ever get there?'

'Who knows?' He couldn't keep the trace of wistfulness from his answer.

'We were going to travel the world, remember? You and me. We had it all planned out.'

'I remember.'

'The hours we used to spend, sitting up here, talking through our lists of destinations, what route we would take, planning our voyage.'

He saw the tilt of her eyebrows, heard the lilting

slant of her voice, and sensed the challenge that was there, touching dangerously on all that had gone before, what had erupted between them.

'Well, at least one of us got to go,' he answered, somewhat disconsolately.

'True. Funny how things turn out.'

'You never wrote like you said you would.' This emerged as an accusation, when he meant it as an observation. She didn't rise to it anyway.

'No. But I was angry with you. If I had written, it would just have been to punish you, and I didn't want to write boastful, spiteful letters. There was no point in that. I had said all I had to say.'

He stood there, the wind beginning to whip around him, and heard her again, the savagery of her young voice, the hurt and disbelief gathering in the corners of it: 'How could you?' she had asked him, over and over, as if he had done it on purpose to wound her, as if it had been anything other than a foolish moment of reckless-ness. She had asked the question while he had stood there, forlornly, engulfed by his own bewildered silence.

Far below them the tide foamed in a long, thin line along the beach, like the lace hem on a petticoat. The sea seemed as still and calm as a pond, its water dull, reflecting the grey hazy clouds above. Everything seemed clear and distinct at that time of the evening. The islands in the bay appeared closer to the mainland, the rocks on the spit were glazed and smooth, and the beach arced back against the lip of the land like marble cut into the ocean.

'There were times in South America when I craved the sea,' she said thoughtfully. 'In those dusty places, those landlocked plains, I sometimes felt a longing for a body of water.'

Her face seemed to close with memory, a dullness sweeping over her features, and he could almost touch the surface of her sadness.

'Look down there,' she said, her eyes open again, her arm outstretched to the beach below. He followed her pointed finger with his eyes, down to the lone figure of a man and his dog picking their way over the ragged line of seaweed thrown up onto the strand. Occasionally the man stopped and bent down to pick up something before straightening up and continuing along his way. 'What do you suppose he's looking for?'

'I used to do that with the kids,' he said. 'When they were younger, we'd walk the beach, looking for treasure – a brightly coloured shell, or a dried-out starfish. Or sometimes I would take them up into the fields, holding their hands, pointing out the different flowers to them – the honeysuckle and the montbresia, and the rare ones, too, like the bee orchid and the Kerry lily and the kidney saxifrage.'

As he said those words, he felt a disappointment echoing up from the depths of his chest. She didn't say anything, just looked at him.

'But finding treasure on the beach was what they liked best,' he added, trying to lift his tone. 'You never knew what you were going to find. What treasure the ocean would leave behind.'

'It's funny,' she began, although she wasn't smiling. 'Since Nacio…since it happened, I keep finding bits and pieces of children's clothing strewn about the place – bibs on the beach, a lost shoe, toys, baby soothers.'

He regarded her carefully.

'And not just on this beach,' she went on, 'but on other beaches, in other places, different countries. It seems to be universal, children's carelessness with their belongings, hassled parents leaving things behind in their haste. You know, a year or so ago, I was sitting in a café by a beach in Brazil. There was a family sitting next to me, an English family on holiday. The mother was sitting at the table with her three kids, and there was this shoe on the table, a child's shoe. I remember it clearly, this solitary shoe, and all of them sitting around it, staring at it. Next thing, the father comes up from the beach and his wife asks, "Well? Did you find it?" and he shook his head. And it was like a sudden rage just took hold of her, redness exploding in her face. I remember her grabbing hold of her little boy's arm, tugging it savagely. "How many times have I told you?" she screeched at him, as fat tears rolled over his cheeks. "These things cost money. I can't just buy you new shoes every time you lose one of them!" And I watched that little boy, and something about his carelessness, the way his face seemed to crumple, his tears… something was building inside me. I don't know what came over me, but suddenly I blurted out: "It's a shoe. It's just a shoe."'

He watched her carefully, keeping his hands jammed in his pockets, hair whipped back by the wind. 'Did they hear you?' he asked and she nodded quickly, smiling up at him, trying to laugh, and he could see that she wanted to lighten things.

'Oh, they heard me all right. Looked at me with wide, staring eyes like I was a complete lunatic. They didn't say anything, just bundled their children away from the table and left. I don't blame them. I must have seemed crazy.'

She stopped then, although he felt there was something more to the story, something that she couldn't bring herself to say. And he knew from the abrupt ending, that faraway look about her, that she had been crying when she spoke to that family. For a moment they stood there together, side by side, and he could smell the salt on the wind that travelled between the six charged inches of space between them.

'What do they call it,' she asked him, picking strands of hair from her face, allowing them to be whipped back by the wind, 'the stuff the sea throws up onto the land?'

He looked down at the ragged line of seaweed trailing up the beach.

'It's called longshore drift.'

'Oh,' she said softly. 'I always wondered about that.'

After a moment, they turned and walked back the way they had come, but slower this time, not the purposeful strides that had carried them up here full of curiosity and excitement.

'We used to look for things on the beach together, don't you remember?' she asked.

'I remember.'

It was, after all, how they had met.

'Do you ever think about it?'

She asked this quietly and her question sat there now, all the air closing in around it, and he couldn't help but think that she wouldn't be asking this if she weren't stoned.

'Sometimes,' he replied.

A new sensation came over him, or rather one that he hadn't felt in a long time. That sweet sickness that was always there at the beginning. That nervousness, a sudden emotion whipped alive. He already felt how important she was becoming to him.

It was there between them, the memory of that day. He could say it to her now, tell it to her like a story: I was alone on the beach, picking my way through the longshore drift when I saw you. You were over by the rock pools, barefoot with the hem of your skirt tucked up into your pants, hands plunging into the water looking for anemones, and then straightening up, you saw me too, watching you, blocking out the light. You seemed so strong, standing there, knee-deep in water, like an Amazon, your face all dark and shadowy, that dark hair blowing around it. And I could tell from your slow smile that you knew I had been watching you. That you had felt my eyes on you. I guessed you must have been thirteen or fourteen. You said hullo, quiet and kind of bashful, and I liked your voice, liked it immediately, and something about it seemed to reach down inside me, touching my very core. I knew right then that something important was happening between us.

He didn't say this to her, though. Of course he didn't. He had already said too much, and it wasn't safe to talk about these things in that way.

They climbed down over the rocks, and once they were on the hard sand again, she turned to him, her face stoical yet conflicted.

'It was because they found his shoe, you see? Nacio's shoe. Or sandal. They found it on one of the beaches close to where he went missing.'

His breath caught in his chest and he looked her hard in the face, suddenly stricken, lost for words.

'They found several items of children's clothing,' she continued, almost matter-of-factly, 'but none of them were Nacio's. Except the sandal. I remember looking through that little mound of clothes, and finding that sandal and feeling my chest convulse with pain.'

He couldn't imagine a pain like that. Once, when Avril was five or six, he had lost her. It was a fair day, and there were farmers and jobbers, the whole place heaving with people, and him in the middle of them all, frantic with worry. When he finally found her, the red coat she was wearing shining out like a beacon, he had felt so relieved that he had come close to weeping. He couldn't imagine the pain of not finding his own child, a pain so deeply engrained that you could never shake it off. To have no choice other than to bear it, to grow used to it, until the years slipped behind you and hope faded and you found yourself grieving for a child from the past.

'I don't know how you can stand it,' he said honestly, a seam of horror opening up inside him.

She smiled at him then, a smile full of bravery and sadness. It tore at his heart.

'They thought that meant he was dead,' she said solemnly.

'And you didn't?'

'No.' There was something so plaintive, so determined, in her voice that it caused him to look deeply at her.

'Then he can't be,' he said, meaning it, and held her there in his gaze. 'You would know if he were dead. You would feel it.'

Something seemed to change about her expression. He thought he could see something move behind that stoic mask, a new understanding passing between them, something deep and resonant and unnamed reaching across the space between them.

The tide was turning, and the wind seemed to whip up around them. Evening was drawing in as they reached the steps to her house and said their goodbyes. At the bottom of the steps, he paused, waiting for her to get her key in the lock before he turned and walked down the beach for home. He wondered at some point whether she might have succumbed and at that moment be immersing herself in the oblivion contained in that Ziploc bag. He wouldn't blame her if she was. He thought again of that day on the beach, that first day, when he was dazzled by the light shimmering on the water around her long bare legs rising up out of the scintillating rock pools. But a voice inside his head was telling him to step away from that memory, that touching on the past was a dangerous thing, and what happened between them all those years ago should be left alone.

7

Three years ago, I lived a different sort of life – simpler, you might say, less mercurial. I lived with Alejo and Nacio – the men in my life – and we travelled from one place to the next without ever really forming a pattern. A sort of Brownian motion existence. Random. Not exactly Jack Kerouac – certainly happier and involving a lot less drugs – and in hindsight, the happiest time I had known. After Nacio was born, things slowed down a little, and I guess we were more careful with ourselves, less buccaneering. I remember standing at the border waiting to leave Peru and cross into Bolivia, my baby a bundle in a sling, and watching all the trucks and vans and other vehicles crossing the border, their windscreens all smashed and splintered, an indication of violence kicking off further down the road, something we had seen before and would normally disregard, willing to take our chances. But that day, standing at the side of the dusty road, Alejo had turned to me, his face grave, and for the first time said solemnly, 'It's not worth the risk.'

Some things didn't change, though. Whenever we arrived in a new town or village, I would still take the first opportunity I got to seek out a book exchange.

They were everywhere in South America, in corners of cafés or haciendas or restaurants, shelves lined with books left behind by previous visitors, a kind of massive library system over the whole sprawling subcontinent, and no library card required. I would go in and swap whatever I had last read for something new. My favourite book exchange was in Fallen Angel, Cusco, with its notice painted on the wall: 'Single male seeking book-loving friends to swap literary favourites, two books exchanged for one of my library, *Must be funky*.' While the others that we travelled with were seeking out internet cafés to check their e-mails, I was looking for my next book. I read anything I could get my hands on – Wilbur Smith, J.G. Ballard, Tim Winton, Danielle Steele, Angela Carter, Hari Kunzru, J.K. Rowling. All of these literary offerings and more I picked up, read, then swapped again along the way. It was the way we did things then, not holding on to anything for too long – a temporary lifestyle, continuously recycling.

Since returning home, I had stopped reading. There was no book exchange in this town, only a library that required a lending ticket, and I hadn't quite mustered up the energy for filling in the forms, any kind of bureaucracy being anathema to me. There was, however, an internet café, which I had begun to frequent one afternoon a week. Three years ago, I didn't even have an e-mail account. I didn't need one. The others we travelled with – Roger and Shirley, even Ernesto – used to look at Alejo and I like we were mad. Especially me. Roger once remarked that I had to be the only

backpacker in all of South America who didn't have
e-mail. But I guess I didn't really see myself as a
backpacker. I didn't see myself as anything at all. I
knew, of course, that my life was out of joint with the
times, but at that point, I wasn't seeking a label under
which to classify myself. And I couldn't see the point of
spending hours staring at a computer screen when I
could be outside sitting in the sun with a new book
open in front of me.

My relationship with the internet began after Nacio
went missing – born of necessity, you might say. And
every week since returning home, I sat for an hour,
patiently carrying out my online searches, hopeful of
turning up some piece of information, some hint of a
clue as to his possible whereabouts. But I guess that by
this time it had come to feel like I was just going
through the motions, not really expecting to turn up
anything at all. I checked my e-mails. Sometimes there
was one from Shirley or Roger, and once one from
Sylvie, which had surprised me no end. But never
anything from Alejo. Not that I really expected to hear
from him in that way. He eschewed all forms of modern
communication, preferring to send his blank postcards
instead, his own cryptic smoke signalling. In the weeks
since returning home, I had received three in total, the
latest one arriving that morning. It was from Arequipa,
that lively town in southern Peru near the start of the
great climb up into the Andes. The postcard was of
Juanita, the little girl found buried amid the ice high up
in the glacier, her body – 500 years old and almost

perfectly preserved – brought back down and displayed in the Museum of Arequipa. I remembered going to see her with Nacio, and how frightened he had been of her. She looked so unnatural, so waxen. You could still see the blows to her head – they were right there, these dents where her skull had been bashed in. And even though they had said she would have been drugged beforehand so that she wouldn't have felt the pain, I kept thinking of her there on top of that frozen mountain, how cold it must have been, and then they did that terrible thing to her, sacrificing her to the gods.

The thought came to me then – why did Alejo choose this postcard? Why did he send me a picture of Juanita when there were so many other pictures of Arequipa he could have chosen instead? But rather than send me some benign print of the cathedral or the Monastery of Santa Catalina, he had chosen an image that he knew would evoke emotion. What purpose was there in sending me a picture of a dead child if it wasn't to cause pain?

The internet was running slowly, and I leaned my head on my hand and stared out the window while I waited. I was the only person there, the rest of the town presumably down by the marina to watch the regatta. Outside on the street there was bunting strung between the buildings, rows and rows of brightly coloured pennants flapping in the wind. As I gazed out the glass, I saw the door of the betting shop open and a familiar figure emerge. It was Christy. This surprised me, as I hadn't pegged him for a gambling man, thinking of him instead as an upstanding member of the community – father, teacher, responsible citizen. He paused for a minute to stuff something into his pocket, winnings maybe, and had a brief look from side to side. There was something furtive about the way he did this, something secretive.

Bold boy, I thought to myself, smiling as he moved away from the bookies and hurried down the road.

The computer whined through its motions and the sun shone in, finding me in the corner, and all at once I knew that I didn't want to be there.

'Fuck it,' I said, getting to my feet and logging off with one hand while reaching for my jacket with the other.

Out on the street, I could hear the distant sound of a crowd of voices, the nasal squawk of a tannoy, and rounding the corner past the church, I heard those sounds grow louder. I followed some distance behind him, watching his square shoulders, the thoughtful manner of his walk, his head bent forward as though he were staring at the pavement in front of him. I don't think he knew I was there. As I walked, I was thinking of a wet afternoon we'd spent together as kids, one summer. We saw each other nearly every day, that summer. I had these tennis rackets that belonged to my father – the old wooden types with the heavy square frames that clipped around the heads to protect them when you weren't playing – and the two of us used to mark out a court in the hard sand when the tide had gone way out and knock a ball about. Sorcha would be there too sometimes, but she wasn't much into sports, and anyway, she had started to wear high heels and didn't want to ruin them, so mostly she just sat up in the dunes and watched, occasionally acting as referee when a point was disputed. Both Christy and I were fairly competitive and some games got pretty heated.

I was thinking as I walked a distance behind him about that afternoon when it was too wet to play, and it was pelting down in one of those really impressive displays of rain. We were on the veranda of my house, Christy and I, painting this wooden bench my mother had put out there. It was green and she wanted it to be blue. I started on one side and Christy on the other, and slowly we were working our way towards each other. Even though there were three years between us, it felt like we were the same age. And yet, that was his last summer before university, and I guess some part of me was worried that he would make new friends there, older and more sophisticated, and that he would begin to see me as too young, too clumsy and immature. Maybe he thought it too, for that summer we seemed to spend every spare minute with each other, making the most of the time we had left. This wasn't long before my father left, and that afternoon as we painted, we could hear him and my mother inside the house in the middle of another long, weary argument.

At first we tried to ignore what was happening behind the screen door, both of us talking, making jokes, acting like World War III wasn't kicking off in there. But at some point before we reached the middle,

I could hear the tone of the argument alter. You get used to picking up on these things, like listening to a song and hearing the melody change, a minor key taking over. Christy grew quiet, like he was concentrating very hard on his paintwork, while I grew chatty, forcing a cheeriness, trying to compensate for his silence and the things my parents were screaming at each other. It seemed ridiculous looking back on it now, the two of us there on our knees with our paintbrushes, rain thundering down, and my parents' marriage ripping apart in front of us. Then – and this is what I remember most – he put down his paintbrush, reached out and took my hand. He didn't say anything and neither did I. We didn't even look at each other. Just stayed there like that until the screen door opened and my father came out and a few minutes later we heard the engine of his car starting up. It wasn't until the sound of the car faded in the distance that he let go of my hand and we resumed our painting as if nothing unusual had happened. That was when I was fifteen years old.

I hadn't thought about that afternoon in years, but as I followed him all the way down to the marina, I kept on remembering the firmness of his hand around mine that day, the strength and tenderness that combined to give comfort. I thought of it as I watched him slipping through the regatta crowd while I hung back, undecided. I had taken great pains over the past two years to avoid crowd situations. On the rare occasion that I had allowed myself to rub shoulders with the masses, it generally hadn't ended well. I stood at the frayed edges of the gathering, craning my neck to see where he had gone, while a squall of applause greeted the reading out of the competitors.

Feeling reckless with myself, I pushed through into the crowd, bodies jamming against me. Up ahead I saw the back of his head, rising above the others. He was a tall man who held himself erect, as if each vertebra along his spine demanded its own space. I got as close to him as I could, but still there was a distance between us, and I wasn't about to start bawling out his name or waving like a lunatic. So instead I stood there, quietly observing him. A blonde-haired woman stood next to him – not Sorcha, not anyone I knew, in fact. She was holding a baby in her arms, a blonde-haired replica of herself, with large eyes that stared unblinking around it at the people gathered there. I watched the baby, the tuft of hair that stood away from its head like static, the curious grin on its soft face. It rested against the mother and she swung slightly to soothe it. I watched them there, the mother and baby, next to Christy, and seeing the three of them unwittingly grouped together, they looked so perfect, almost radiant, like an advertisement for something solid and respectable like health insurance or vitamin supplements. They reminded me of pictures from my religion book in school, the part about family values and sex as a magical gift for procreation only. For a moment, I forgot the crowds around me, so captivated was I by this glowing vision of familial bliss.

Then there was a sudden short *crack!* as the starter pistol fired, and the crowd seemed to heave in response.

The race was up and running, and all around people were straining to catch a glimpse of the boats, but I saw only a burst of light across my eyes, felt something fill my head, a metallic taste at the back of my mouth, and a shaft of acid rising up from my stomach. After which, it all went blurry, until I felt a firm grip around my elbows, heaving me from the crowd, and in the scattered images that passed before me, I saw stones on the pavement, the toes of my shoes, sky and water and the dazzle of the sun.

When I came to, I was sitting on a bench, my head between my knees, grit on the ground beneath me. There was a hand resting lightly on my back, and I heard a voice close to my ear.

'Lara? Are you back with us?'

'Yes,' I said, bringing my head up, my arms steadying themselves on the bench beneath me. 'I think so.'

I was feeling a little wobbly, the light too bright against my eyes, and I tasted acid in my throat and wondered if I had been sick.

'You passed out,' he informed me, and I turned to look at him, saw the concern marked in his face, his eyes darting from one of mine to the other.

'Christy,' I said, by way of recognition.

'Bingo.'

We sat there for a moment while I steadied myself, looking around to get my bearings. We were on a bench by the bridge, some distance from the regatta crowd, which made me wonder how he'd got me there. I had a vision of him half-carrying me over, my feet dragging along the pavement, drooling from the side of my mouth.

It wasn't a valiant image.

'That was quite something,' he said, a slow admiration in his voice. 'I've never seen anyone swoon like that.'

'I swooned?'

'Oh yes.'

'Sounds very Hollywood.'

'Hollywood black and white,' he corrected. 'Before the talkies.'

His hand was still on my back, and as if just remembering, he withdrew it quickly and sat back against the bench, crossing his legs at the ankles.

'So, what do you think happened back there?' Something searching in his voice made me think of his face when he found me smoking dope that day on the beach, the sharp disapproval in the hard little look he gave me. He had me pegged as a pothead, and probably assumed that to be the reason behind my recent rather dramatic spell.

'I'm not stoned,' I explained, my head beginning to clear. 'I'm just not good in crowds.'

'Really? I don't remember you being claustrophobic. When did you start your swooning career?'

I thought about this for a moment. 'Oh, I can't remember.' I let that little white lie drift in the silence between us.

And then, suddenly, I changed my mind, overcome by an unexpected desire to tell him. I still remembered that day on the beach, the way he seemed to understand that Nacio couldn't be dead, because if he were, I would feel it – the conviction with which he said it, like he really meant it, his eyes hot on my face. Perhaps I was still feeling light headed, or maybe it was the clarity coming over me now after my swooning spell, or maybe it was simply because he asked, but I wanted then to tell him everything, to pour out the whole story so that he would know, so that someone else here would be aware of what had happened, and that maybe I wouldn't feel so alone all the time.

'Actually, I can remember,' I began. 'It was in Brazil, a couple of years ago, around the time I lost him.'

We had camped in a dusty field by the side of a red clay road not far from Ubatuibe. The zip of the tent was open, one flap drawn back so that I could see the long grass and the wire between the fence posts catching the light. Beyond the low apple trees, there was the flick and swish of horses' tails batting at the black flies. Other beasts stood in the fields with the horses; I had heard them during the night, the braying and low moaning and the barking of dogs. At one point after midnight, the noise had grown so loud and frenetic that I had stuck my head outside the tent to see what was causing the disturbance, but there was just the red glow of the dying campfire and a smattering of stars across the vast blackness of sky.

Nacio had been restless during the night. Lying between the two of us, he had kicked out in his sleep, his small body wriggling beneath his blanket, hair matted to his forehead with sweat. That morning as I tried to dress him, he seemed cross and irritable. Clamped between my legs, he resisted my instructions and I had to struggle to force his arms and legs into his clothes. Outside, I could hear Shirley's voice, thick and strong, and Roger's rich baritone laughter belting out gloriously into the stillness of the morning. Sounds of tin pots and cutlery impacting met me there in the tent as I pressed Nacio's feet into his worn sandals, buckling them and pulling him towards me for a quick hug. I remember the smell of him, that milky smell, his body still warm with sleep. I would give anything to have that moment back.

Alejo was outside and called out to me that he was going to the market with Sylvie, and I could see her there behind him, dressed and ready and waiting in the sun.

'Hang on,' I said quickly, 'we'll come with you.'

I looked about for my flip-flops and bag, tucking my hair back behind my ears. The tent was awash with blankets and sleeping bags, clothes strewn about, and in the confusion that lay there, I couldn't find Nacio's jumper. Outside, I could see Sylvie laughing, her long yellow hair braided and glinting in the sunlight.

'Oh never mind,' I said aloud, abandoning my search for it. In the nights that followed, that decision made in haste came back to haunt me as the cold crept in over the land and snapped at the air and I thought of my little one out there with only his light black shorts, his orange T-shirt and those scuffed sandals,

and I felt my brain pounding with remorse. Why
didn't I take the time to find his sweater? Later, I found
it stuffed away in my rucksack, a red jumper with blue
patches at the elbows. I remembered holding it up and
pressing my face into it, his smell coming back to me
with a sudden shock.

We walked together, the four of us, along that dry
clay road, Nacio skipping along next to me, his hand
gripped in mine, stopping to pick up oddly shaped
stones and placing them in his bucket. By the time we
reached the narrow streets of Ubatuibe, the weariness
of his lost sleep had caught up with him and I felt the
nagging pull of his arm as he hung back, dragging his
feet, reluctant to go any further. The path to the market
was broken, giant fissures running through concrete,
and we had to step carefully. Outside the town hall there
was a commotion. Crowds had gathered. There were
banners, and middle-aged women with sullen faces in
white T-shirts, their arms folded under their breasts,
stood around gazing about them distractedly. I held
Nacio's hand tightly as we moved past. Up ahead, I
could see Alejo and Sylvie sauntering along. Once or
twice they looked back for us and then stopped and
waited until we caught up. In the main square, soldiers
in combat trousers and khaki T-shirts were white-
washing the small stone church. They were shouting to
each other and laughing while they slapped paint onto
the walls. They seemed so cheerful, so youthful on that
beautiful morning. I remember afterwards seeing some
of those young men dashing around the marketplace

with the others, their faces stretched and drawn, paint splattered on their T-shirts, eyes searching as they called out my son's name.

We reached the market and the noise washed over me: the squawking chickens, dogs barking and the loud drone of industry rising up and bouncing off the ceiling. The whole place was crawling with activity. A thick pall of cooking was clotting in the air, and I could sense Nacio's excitement tinged with fear as he clung to me, his eyes darting all over the place, drinking in the sights and sounds and smells. It was a market like so many others I had been to in Peru, Chile, Bolivia, Brazil; they were all the same. They were held in great big skeletons of buildings, a high roof perched on a frame of long spindly columns, like the shell of a factory. And inside, the stalls would be lined up in rows, some covered over with tarpaulin or blue industrial plastic sheeting, mostly rickety tables on uneven ground. The merchandise was varied – sacks of pulses with silver scoops, the sacking turned down neatly; mounds of vegetables and fruit, weighing scales suspended overhead; meat counters where the dogs lingered, licking blood in puddles off the floor, flies swarming overhead. We passed a counter where a small, squat woman with a shrivelled, raisin-like face sat cheerfully chopping the heads and feet off chickens, her meat cleaver gleaming in the light, and I felt Nacio's grip on my hand tightening as he leaned in close to me. Tourists amused themselves trying on hats and gloves made from alpaca wool – so much to choose from, and yet those stalls were always the same: blankets and dolls and panpipes, beads and belts and wallets, ponchos and T-shirts in bright, gaudy colours.

Nacio wanted to go and look at the reptiles, a stall with various spiders and snakes caught in glass cages and displayed in front of enthralled spectators.

'Please, Mama,' he pleaded with me, flicking the hair out of his eyes, eyes so dark they were like pools of ink.

'Go,' Alejo encouraged us. 'Sylvie and I can get the shopping. We will come and find you later.'

Something in me sank as he said this, a protest welling up inside me. Sylvie smiled at me, her big teeth so white and healthy, turquoise bra straps biting into the flesh of her shoulders, and I felt in that moment unsure of everything. There was a long silence, longer than it should have been. I struggled for something to say while Alejo's face flattened a little, sharpness entering his eyes. 'Just go, Lara,' he said, a testy note in his voice that I hadn't heard before, and they began to move away from us.

I watched them for a full minute before I lost them in the crowd. They didn't glance back. So we turned, Nacio and I, to wander back to the snake stall, but I couldn't resist glancing back once more, and there they were at the very end of the aisle – he, shorter than her, with that relaxed roll of his shoulders, that laughing flick of hair; and she, with her long, slender back, that yellow plait swinging over her pink cheesecloth dress. She was throwing back her head, laughing at something he was saying, and he reached out to touch the small of her back.

The reptile counter drew a crowd, faces queuing up, peering over each other, or pressed against the glass. The air was humming with that drone of hushed excitement. I could feel Nacio grow tense next to me, his little body filling up with the delicious anticipation of horror that small boys have. The reptiles lay inert in their glass cages, drugged or bored or terrified, unmoving among the straw and sawdust. Every so often, one would stretch languidly and a ripple would pass through the crowd, fingers pointing and necks craning.

'I can't see, Mama,' Nacio complained, tugging at my arm, so we moved closer, pressing up against the other bodies gathered there. The smell was over-powering – the filth of the cages, the unwashed, sweaty smell of the men gathered there. The heat and the odours rising up from the crowd and the nagging doubts scraping around my mind all reared up and swaddled me in a blinding headache.

'Come on, Nacio,' I said sternly, a new fear nipping at me.

'Just a minute,' he pleaded, leaning forward, inching closer.

Did I know then that something terrible was about to happen? Could I feel some change in the energy around me, some new and pernicious life force drawing near? In the desperate weeks and months that followed, I tried to revisit that moment, to tunnel back through time, and all I wanted was to go back there and to act on that instinct, be more decisive, more trusting of myself, more authoritative. Why didn't I drag him away from there, draw him towards me, away from danger and those reaching hands? But time forbade going back. And so I was forced to remember that moment for what it was – a terrible weakness.

There were two American boys, not much more than teenagers, rapping on the glass of the spiders' cage. Three local women with straw hats and long black braids were standing idly to the side watching them. As for the others gathered there, their faces didn't impress themselves on my consciousness. In time, I think I created faces for them, so often did I strain to remember them, dipping deep into the murky waters of memory, trying to coax their features to the surface. In my head I created round faces, gold glinting from mouths amid teeth stained yellow, coarse unwashed black hair, toughened skin like leather, small, watchful eyes. Which among them did it? Which one of them turned his gaze away from the snakes and spiders, lured by the strange desire that was whipped alive at the sight of a small boy, his cleanly dark, shiny hair and clear, unblemished face? Was it the delicate set of my boy's features that drew him into danger – that small *retroussé* nose, those high, proud cheekbones, eyes that seemed enormous in his elfin face? Or was it the small frame of his body – narrow shoulders swathed in orange cotton, skinny legs emerging from shorts, dusty feet pressed up on tiptoes, his little calf muscles straining?

I should have been watching those faces, taking them in, always alert to danger, but instead my face was turned away, my neck craning, eyes fixed on a flash of pink skirt in the distance, that golden plait tossed about like a tail. I strained to see Alejo's hand, to see where it was placed, but my view of him was obscured and so I imagined the worst. I had known that it was coming, if it hadn't happened already. I had known from the start, that first day in Buenos Aires when Roger had brought her back to the hostel. Something about her vivacious laugh, her wide-eyed humour, her perfect diction, that refined English accent like cut glass had irritated me. But the others had warmed to her, drawn by her overwhelming sociability, and it was Roger's van after all, so there was nothing I could do except bite my tongue and hope that I was wrong about this one.

But in the weeks that followed, as we made our way up through Argentina, hanging around the border by the Iguaçu Falls, I hung back, observing, feeling the knot in my stomach tightening. And I saw everything. At camp in the evenings, I watched Roger and his burgeoning joy and rapturous laugh. I watched Sylvie and her assured displays of affection towards her new lover, but her eyes gave her away, the flickering flirtatiousness of them, eyes that seemed to send out invitations. And I knew to whom those unspoken entreaties were directed. Not to Ernesto, with his shy smiles, retreating back into himself. I knew from Alejo's silence, the brooding quietness in him, what his response would be. I remembered sitting at the campfire, Nacio's sleeping body humming in my arms, watching that whole bizarre play being performed around me, and looking across the flickering flames, I caught Shirley's eye – wise, sensible Shirley – and I read the warning in them, and without speaking, I knew that she had seen it too.

I felt a sudden fear that morning in the marketplace. I had seen something. It wasn't some crazy paranoia. I could sense there was something growing between them. Standing there, my eyes straining to see them, my heart thudding with that slow, creeping fear, I knew already that it was too late. The die had been cast. And as I stood there, feeling that new horror washing over me, I heard a sudden shriek. Turning, I found that one of the Americans, through his persistent tormenting, tapping at the cage, had succeeded in getting a scorpion to crack its whip-like tail against the glass. A cry of delight fed by horror rose up from the crowd gathered there, and it was then that I looked down and saw my hand was empty. He had slipped my grasp without my noticing.

At first I didn't panic, reasoning with myself that he couldn't have gone far. Shouldering past the others, I found myself pressed up against the glass cages, face to face with the frightened captives. But my eyes weren't fixed on them; instead they were darting around, beginning their long, arduous and in time, obsessive, hunt for my four-year-old boy. I asked the two Americans had they seen a little boy with dark hair and an orange T-shirt and they answered politely, 'No ma'am,' before turning back. In broken Portuguese, I asked the local women, but they just stared blankly, shaking their heads. The crowd around the stand was dispersing and suddenly my eyes were everywhere, rifling through the faces gathered there, feverishly searching him out. My mind was washed clean of pink skirts and yellow plaits and all the treachery that came with them. Something was taking possession of my body, raw maternal instinct. A dry tightness was starting in my throat as I felt the beginnings of a new desire, a desire so strong it slowed the breath, focused the mind absolutely.

I kept expecting to see him, kept expecting to turn around and find him emerging from underneath a table or from behind a flap of blue plastic, drawing me into some new game of hide-and-seek. But in my heart I knew my boy was too nervous, too frightened of strangers to initiate such a risky game in a crowded space. He wasn't the sort of child that wandered off, preferring to stay close to either of his parents or to one of the adults in our group that he knew and trusted. The first dark thoughts strayed into my mind and I felt a buzzing in the back of my head.

Quickly I moved down the long aisle of stalls, past the piles of fruit and the stands of toilet rolls and detergents, past the carved wooden bowls and spoons, down to the last stall where the woman with the meat cleaver was still hacking away at chicken carcasses. Seeing the glint of the blade, coldness sliced through my heart, remembering Nacio's fear as he had passed her. I knew he wouldn't have strayed past her alone. I was running now, pushing people aside. I called his name, flinging back curtains that obscured stalls, ducking under tables to see him. I stretched up on my toes, feeling the ache in my calves as I scoured the crowd for him. My heartbeat quickened, my movements became frantic. I was screaming his name at this point and people were beginning to stare at me. Faces turned towards me and I could see the cold gleam of understanding in them. Within moments, people had gathered around me and somehow, amid my trembling panic, I managed to convey a description of him, all the while wanting to push through them, needing to get past them and find my boy. He had been gone nearly a full ten minutes and I couldn't escape the gnawing feeling that something awful was happening to him.

Faces around me were alert and stretched with worry. Over and over I heard his name being called. Market traders were coming out from behind their counters, abandoning their stalls in the search for him. My tears were coming thick and fast. At one point, I bent over double, thinking I was going to be sick, dry-retching until my stomach was all twisted up inside. Something was gathering in the air around me, something dark and threatening and full of foreboding. Years later I still woke sometimes in the night to feel the shadow of it pressing up against me. I had grown accustomed to it by then. But that was the first time, when the blackness of it rolled over me, sucking the air from me, bleakness collapsing in on top of me, a horrible weight entering my body like a sort of dread. And by the time I found Alejo, the tears were coming so fast, my whole body caught up in that crazy, convulsing anxiety, that I could barely get the words out, and when I opened my mouth to tell him the truth – that our child had been stolen – all that emerged was a howl, so lonely and remote it seemed to take on a life of its own, beating black and angry in the air about our heads.

For a moment afterwards, neither Christy nor I said a word. I felt a sort of exhaustion at having told my tale, at having enunciated all those words that had been churning around inside me. But I felt strangely calm as well. He was leaning forward, his arms resting on his long thighs. For the duration of my story he had held his eyes firmly on the ground in front of him. He hadn't once looked at me. And now, as he let the air out of his lungs, releasing a long breath into the warm afternoon sunshine, he turned and fixed me with a gaze that was at once tender and filled with horror.

'I cannot imagine what it must be like,' he said slowly, each word pensive and clear, and I felt the honesty there. One part of me was dreading that he would say sorry and start apologising like everyone else, but he didn't, and the fact that he didn't gave me such hope that I was ashamed to find my chin trembling with emotion. He didn't seem to notice. 'I don't want to imagine it,' he added flatly, a little too honestly.

He was still looking at me, and I felt something prickling on my skin underneath my clothes. I wasn't used to being looked at so intently.

'It's the guilt, you see,' I found myself saying. 'I feel so desperately guilty about it all. Sometimes, I can't help but feel that if everything else ever goes away – the sadness, and the fear – even if one day I find him again and he's all right, he's not damaged in any way, I think that the guilt will still be there, like it's part of me now. I won't ever get free of it.'

He seemed to think about this for a moment, and I felt sort of shaky having admitted this to him. When I looked back at him I could see his eyes all brown and warm with those little sparks of amber, and they seemed to be filling with something – a kind of wisdom, or compassion.

'A few years ago,' he began softly, 'I let Jim fall. I was carrying him on my shoulders upstairs to bed, and we were kind of joking about. It all happened very quickly. We were in the bathroom and I sort of tripped, and he came off my shoulders and fell against the toilet.'

'Was he hurt?'

'His front teeth were chipped. God, he was hysterical. And I think I must have been too. But the sight of his teeth – and he'd had such beautiful teeth, the frills on them were perfect – and then this ugly sharp gash across them. Those lovely frills just gone.' He shook his head regretfully, and I could feel the pain there, the remorse. 'I couldn't believe it, couldn't come to terms with what had happened. And even after he'd been to the dentist and had them capped, I still couldn't forgive myself for it. The guilt was horrendous. For days, I could hardly bring myself to look at him.'

'Accidents happen.'

'Yes. And nobody blamed me for it. Sorcha never said

a word to admonish me, although she must have wanted to. She must have ached to. And in a way, I wish she had. I wished she would scream at me, demand to know how I had been so careless with him, so cavalier. It might have helped to assuage my own guilt.' He paused, chewing on his lower lip, and I felt that he was weighing something up in his mind. 'I'd had a couple of drinks after work, you see. She didn't know that. And I'm not saying I was drunk – I wasn't, but still, I can't help but wonder if I hadn't had those drinks, perhaps I would have been more cautious. Perhaps I wouldn't have had him on my shoulders in the first place, and then I might have spared him that pain and anguish. He might still have his beautiful teeth. So you see, what I'm trying to say is that there is always guilt when you're a parent. Worry that you're going to mess them up, and then remorse when you do. Guilt is part of the package.'

Neither of us said anything for a moment, then he looked back at me and said solemnly, 'You know I've never told anyone that before?' and I felt so up and down all of a sudden that I didn't know how to answer him. We were sitting next to each other and in that moment his presence seemed so warm beside me, so comforting, that I wanted to lean against him with my head resting on his shoulder and feel that warmth seep through my clothes to my skin.

The regatta crowd had drifted away and it seemed very quiet. The sun was beginning its descent, and with nothing left to say, we got to our feet.

'Can I give you a lift home?' he offered decently. 'The

car's just around the corner.'

'That's okay.'

'Are you sure? I feel bad, I never did look at the Datsun for you like I said I would.'

'Really,' I assured him, 'I'd prefer to walk. It's such a beautiful evening, and I could do with the air.'

'All right then,' he said, but before leaving, he turned to me and just then we embraced. It was unexpected and a little awkward at the start, but we seemed to hold on to each other for a long minute, and I could feel his arms tight around my waist, the side of my face resting against his roughened jaw. My arms tightened about his neck and I could tell that by holding me like this, he was trying to impart some sympathy, that he was holding not just me, but my lost child too, and the void left by his absence. There was fear in that embrace, as well as sympathy and strength and a sort of shy affection.

Drawing back from him, I felt him hold on to me a second longer before taking a step backwards.

'Well,' I said.

'Well.'

For a moment, I just stood there blinking up at him, not really sure what I wanted to say to him.

'See you, Christian,' I said eventually, turning away.

'See you,' he replied softly, the sun bright behind him.

8

Sorcha was used to asking people questions. 'Any gossip?' she asked Stella when they met for their coffee mornings. Listening to the back door banging and the kitchen inhaling the children through it, she gathered her questions in her mind, lining them up, preparing to be spoken. 'Did you have fun in class today?' she invited her son as he sat at the kitchen table, hunched over his homework. 'How was your day?' she tested her teenage daughter tentatively on her return from school. 'What's on your mind?' she gently asked her husband, quiet and thoughtful over dinner. She asked these questions partially out of habit, but also because she believed it was her role to tease information out of them, to keep communication alive. A relationship that didn't involve communication was one that grew dangerous quickly. That is what she believed.

When the children were little, they did an exercise in school called 'Our News'. Each day, alone in the kitchen, savouring her solitude, Sorcha used to think of them, their clean, bright faces, their neatly laundered uniforms, sitting in their classes and discussing the small occurrences that made up the fabric of their lives. When they would come home in the afternoons, she would look through their copybooks and read 'Our News' transcribed in their childish handwriting and feel like she was peering through a window into their worlds. They had long since grown out of the stage where they would grant access to their copybooks so readily, and so she tried to tease it out of them with her gentle probing – patient, at times devious, always loving. They answered her compliantly, sometimes giving the information in bouts of excited exuberance, other times shrugging off her questions with one-word evasive responses. She asked them nonetheless. But lately, it had grown apparent to Sorcha that when she asked her family questions, they didn't ask her back. Not one of them asked her how her day was, or whether she had any news. It chipped away at her, their selfishness. It was forgivable in her children, for that was what children were, that was what she had bargained for when she gave birth to them – to care for these selfish, irresponsible creatures, nurture them through their whimsical, egotistical beginnings. But Christy – what of him, her husband, her life partner? What of his questions? Privately she suspected arrogance on his part – were there news, it would be he who brought it into the house, as if she were incapable of going out into the world and finding her own strange and unusual things, incapable of possessing her own secret life.

Lately her questions had changed, or rather, the tone in which they were asked had altered. There was something shrill and sharp about them, a desperate edge skimming along the surface. It was becoming harder for her to cover over her worries, to mask the underlying grievances overtaking her. She worried about her daughter – she was too thin – and found herself watching Avril as she ate, silently assessing how much she consumed. 'Why are you looking at me like that?' Avril asked waspishly. 'I'm not looking at you like anything, darling,' she replied. Another day, she might have retorted, 'The cat can look at the queen.'

She worried about her son, too, but for different reasons – his silence, the way he seemed to inhabit his own inner life, closing them all off. She wondered sometimes was it merely an intense shyness. At other times, her mind filled with more sinister theories – autism, or Asperger's syndrome, or some other frightening malady. Today was no different. If anything, today was worse. It happened when she saw the GameBoy peeping out between copybooks in Jim's open schoolbag propped up on one of the kitchen chairs. His head was lowered over his homework, his straw-blonde hair falling forward, hiding his face, a pencil moving laboriously over paper, knuckles white with effort. She felt a flick of annoyance at the sight of the GameBoy and reached for it in the schoolbag, auto-matically inhaling deeply, as if needful of a deep breath for the lecture that would follow. They had told Jim countless times that he wasn't allowed to bring it to school. Sorcha feared that he would spend his lunch break hunched over this gadget instead of mixing with other boys, making friends. But as she pulled it out of the bag, her breath caught in her chest. A short spasm of shock registered in her stomach. The screen had been completely shattered, smashed in. She looked at the cracks lacing through the glass, all of them emanating from this central wound, and she imagined a heel coming down firmly, stamping on it.

'Jim,' she began, hearing the slice of panic entering her voice, 'what happened to your GameBoy?'

He looked up expectantly, saw the smashed toy in her hand, and something seemed to close about his face, like a curtain falling over his expression.

'Nothing,' he said blankly, addressing his homework.

'What do you mean, nothing? It's smashed. Someone broke it.'

'It fell out of my school bag, that's all.'

'Are you sure? It looks like someone stamped on it.'

There was a brief silence, and she sensed that he was considering this, wavering over how he should answer.

'You know, you can talk to me, love. Whatever it is, you needn't ever worry that I won't—'

'It fell, I said.'

There was a finality about the way he said this, and reluctantly she let it go.

But later, after dinner, she brought it up with Christy. Alarm was nudging at her, fear gathering in the outer reaches of her consciousness.

'It probably did fall,' he said flatly, pulling on his boots and leaning forward to tie the laces.

'It did not. Some kid clearly put his foot through it.'

'I'm sure he'd tell us if that were the case.'

'How can you be so sure?' she asked, impatient with

him now. 'You're a teacher, you know what boys are like. Some little thug has done this, and Jim is too scared or humiliated to tell us. How can you not see this?'

'You're overreacting. And anyway, it's probably a good thing that it's broken. All he ever seems to do these days is play with that damn thing.'

'So that's it?' she asked then, watching him getting to his feet. 'You're not going to do anything about it?'

'Look, I'll talk to him later. Have a proper chat with him, *mano a mano*. All right?'

With that, he clasped her shoulders, planting a perfunctory kiss above her forehead, before heading outside. She watched him from the kitchen window, his brisk descent to the beach, his long stride, head bent leaning into the wind. And still a shadow of worry hovered over her. When did he become so hard to reach? It seemed to Sorcha that it was becoming more and more difficult to fasten him down on anything.

She poured herself a generous glass of red wine and leaned back against the kitchen counter. The house seemed to sigh around her as she savoured the warmth of the wine in the back of her throat. Jim's smashed GameBoy was lying on the table, along with his copybooks and pencil case. A pile of CDs belonging to Avril had collapsed across the counter. The children's lives filled the house – their things were everywhere, crawling into each room. Sometimes it irritated Sorcha. She longed for a sense of order, for surfaces empty of clutter, clean lines and a bright whiteness bouncing off everything. The children had their own bedrooms, and

Christy had his study. But what about her? What about Sorcha's need for her own space?

In the cupboard behind the ironing board, she kept a plastic bag full of magazines. This was her consolation, her secret treat when feeling down – decorating magazines. She collected them avidly – *Ideal Home, House and Garden, Irish Homes, Image Interiors*. Last week, in the newsagents, the girl at the counter had passed comment on her interest in decorating. Was it really that obvious? She hid these magazines from her family, this private indulgence, keeping them firmly to herself. What harm was there in such a benign fantasy, she asked the empty room? What had she to feel ashamed about? Some days, when they were at school, she sat at the kitchen table, poring over the glossy photographs of white walls and soft carpeting, the plush furnishings and stately gardens. And then she might wander through the empty rooms of her own house, imagining.

She had lived here all her life, in this house. She knew every corner, every shadow, the smell of each room, the sand that caught in the corners of the windows, the way the wind whined around the eaves. Some people couldn't conceive of spending their whole life in the one place. But Sorcha loved this corner of the world. She knew that she was lucky to wake in the morning and look out upon the ever-changing sea. The beauty of this place wasn't lost upon her, as she sometimes expected it was on others. She hadn't become immune to it, but rather was constantly surprised by new facets to that beauty – the call of the kittiwakes and gulls, the flocks of oystercatchers strutting along the sand, the surprise of colour in the flowers that blossomed amid the wild grasses, the tawny hills prickling with gorse.

And yet, the house, much as she loved it, seemed lacking somehow. It didn't have the same sense of style as other houses had achieved. Shortly after her parents died, they had redecorated, stripping the house of its predecessors' style so that they could put their own stamp upon it. That's what people did – used their houses as a means of expressing their personalities. They had ripped up carpets and stripped the walls bare, thrown out the old furniture and replaced it with new. But in their haste to make their mark, Sorcha feared that they had made mistakes. There was too much pattern, for instance, and no uniformity of colour. She regretted some of the furniture they had thrown away – she had felt twinges of prostrate disappointment at spying the return of some of those old designs into new houses in her magazines. Some relics of her parents' time still remained, like the stone lions atop the pillar posts at the end of the drive. Recently, she had felt a great longing to take a mallet to them, lob them cleanly off their posts. If a house was a reflection of the owners' personalities, then what did this house say about them, she wondered? That they were hasty, regretful, uncertain of who they were, conflicted over who they wanted to be? Were they to do it over, there were many changes she would make. And Sorcha believed that it was about time for

a change, for sweeping changes. Yet she suspected her
husband wasn't so keen on the idea.

Yesterday, lost in one of her decorating daydreams,
she had found herself standing in his study, taking in the
décor he had amassed there – the maps and posters
lining the walls, the old bookcase lined with volumes of
encyclopaedias (from her parents' time) and atlases and
dictionaries, the *Writers' and Artists' Yearbook*,
several volumes of poetry, and of course, all those
National Geographics with their yellow spines
outward. And standing there, in that light-filled room,
she had felt the tranquillity of the place, the swish of
the sea outside the window, the dust motes dropping
through a beam of light, and the thought crossed her
mind: how come this room was his? The study, they
called it. And before it was Christy's, it had been her
father's. But on his death, Christy had claimed it as his
own. There had been no discussion about it, no debate
as to what to do with the space there, he had merely
gone in there one Saturday, cleared out the old desk,
sorted through the papers and books and junk, and set
about installing himself in there.

It was almost with undue haste, Sorcha thought, that
he had swooped down and seized it for himself. And
what right did he have to do so? It was her father's house,
her father's room, and yet it had never occurred to
Christy that she, Sorcha, might have some hankering
after a space of her own. Instead, he had assumed that
she could make do with the kitchen. Standing in that
study, she had been surprised by a fresh wave of anger

towards him. This room seemed the embodiment of his selfishness – she felt pushed out by it, excluded, isolated. These maps, these far-flung destinations that he dreamed of were a mark of exclusion. They always had been. First, they had been something that he had shared with Lara, quiet whisperings and musings over what routes they would take, when they should go, what they would do there; and then later it became something he nursed in private, like licking a wound. Now that Lara was back again, it was like he felt a new sense of impatience to see these places, to put his dreams in motion. And he planned to dedicate all the money from his salary that he had been siphoning off for years to his travels. There was no question that this money be put to another use. No possibility of it being utilised to redecorate the house, for instance.

Now, standing alone in the kitchen, the sea pulsing outside behind her, she couldn't get the thought of that room out of her mind. Glancing behind her, she saw the far-off figure of her husband moving steadily away, up the beach. In the next room she could hear shouts and blasts of gunfire from the TV and she felt a vague twinge of concern about the violence that seemed to fill her living room on a regular basis, her children absorbing it through dull eyes. But she also recognised it as an opportunity. Slipping out of the kitchen, past the living room door, she found herself sidling up to the closed door of the study. Pushing it open, she felt a nervous flutter in her stomach, then wondered angrily what it was she had to feel nervous of. There should be no secrets between husband and wife, she thought primly, before remembering her own secret and feeling a blush of shame.

Closing the door softly behind her, she pulled the chair out from the desk and sat down, placing her wine glass on the surface in front of her. Her husband was a tidy person, fastidious, even. Everywhere her eye settled in the room she saw neatness, order. Books were arranged on the shelves in neat stacks, graduated in size. The surface of the desk was empty apart from a penholder and a tray full of blank pages waiting to be fed into the printer. It occurred to her that of all the rooms in the house, this was the one she loved the most. Why was that? Was it because it was Christy's, his sanctuary? Had it something to do with the aspect of the room, the view from the window, the light that filled it? Or was this love derived from something darker, envy, perhaps? He had this room as compensation for being the sole breadwinner. This was something that he had never admitted, something they had never spoken about, but Sorcha knew that this was the reason. And what if she had a job – would that change the balance of things, entitle her to some space of her own? Some months ago, she had contemplated asking Stella whether there was any possibility of her working a few hours each week in the Old Oratory. She had discussed it with Christy first, and he had greeted the idea with cautious optimism.

'Well, there's no doubt that you're capable of working there,' he had said at the time, 'and you might well enjoy it.'

But he had left the sentence hanging, keeping

something back to himself, and into that space her doubts poured in. Would it test her friendship with Stella? How would it affect the dynamics of their relationship were they to spend so much time together? She voiced these fears aloud to Christy, and he had nodded solemnly, not offering an opinion either way, allowing her to talk herself out of it. And then the 'Clonakilty incident' had happened, and asking Stella for work became out of the question. Nevertheless, she was left with the notion of feeling inadequate, underused, as if being a mother and caring for her family, looking after this house, wasn't work enough in itself.

She sipped her wine, leaning back in the chair, feeling the comfort of the room wrap around her. It would be a while before Christy returned. These evening walks stretched out to an hour, sometimes more. *What does he do in here?* she wondered. All those lonely hours he spent in here – doing what? Writing poetry? Working on his novel?

At Christmas last year, Sorcha and Christy went to a party in her sister Margot's house in Limerick. Margot's husband was a lecturer at UL, and the party seemed particularly bloated with academics. She wasn't sure, looking back on it now, whether it was because of all the wine she'd had to drink, or whether it was something deeper – a nascent insecurity at being in the midst of all these intellectuals – but in conversation with a tall, thin man with a wispy moustache, Sorcha found herself blurting out that her husband was writing a book. She had said it with a kind of pride, and perhaps it sounded boastful. The man had fixed her with a patient little smile and said, 'My dear, who isn't?' She had felt the sting of those words, felt reduced by them, belittled. Looking across the room, she had sought out Christy with her eyes. She found him by the cabinet locked in conversation with Margot, and there was something about his face in that moment, a kind of eager innocence, that caused her to experience a sudden jolt of fear for him. That was the first time it occurred to her, that he was fastening all his hopes on this book, hopes that it would distinguish him in some way, bring him up from the mundane drudgery of teaching. And in a way, she was pinning her hopes on it too. It was ridiculous now in hindsight, given the fact that she had never even read any of the book, didn't even know what it was about. He was loathe to talk about it, he told her, fearing that some-how the book wouldn't be completed if he spoke of it too often.

'Some writers believe that it's bad luck to discuss a book before it's written,' he had said to her, and she had wondered at the time whether any bad luck would attach to passing oneself off as a writer before anything had been published.

But what if the book didn't work out? What if nothing came of all this writing? Sorcha didn't like to think of what that might mean. The shadow of that time when the poetry failed still lingered over them, and she wasn't sure how he would cope – how either of them would cope – with another failure. Sitting at the desk now, gripped again by this fear, it occurred to Sorcha that where she had failed to manage his expectations with the poetry, perhaps there was still room for her to protect him with the novel.

Almost without thinking, she placed her empty wine glass back on the desk in front of her and reached for the top drawer. Pulling it out, all she found was some magazines and a few notebooks with his thoughts scribbled through them – poetry mainly, not what she was looking for. The second drawer contained copy-books awaiting correction from school, but the third drawer, when she tugged at it, was locked. She knew that the book must be in there. Leaning forward, she emptied the penholder onto the desk, and among the spilled-out pens were a set of tiny keys. She felt a little flick of pleasure at being able to second-guess him so easily. She unlocked the drawer, aware of a dull feeling behind her eyes – guilt, perhaps, a degree of shame about snooping around behind her husband's back like this – but the feeling faded when she found what she was looking for. A blue folder holding a sheaf of paper. She withdrew it carefully, setting it down in front of her. Her heart was beating loudly in her chest, a thud of anticipation, as well as fear at what this might contain. Opening it, she saw that the pages had been separated into bundles, each one held together in an elastic band. The first one was the largest, and on the facing page were the words 'First Draft'. Quickly assessing them, she found that there were four bundles – four drafts – each draft smaller than the one before. Alarm nipped at her as she assessed each one, the first containing eighty pages, the second, fifty, the third forty-two, and finally the last a mere thirty pages. On this final bundle, he had printed the words, 'Submission to Shelly Cormack'. The agent. Her heart was pounding in her throat. So this was what he'd sent to her. She discarded the rest and tried to ignore the panic rising inside her that what she had understood to be an almost complete novel was nothing like that. As she flicked through the prose gathered there, reading snippets here and there, a page fell out from the sheaf onto her lap before wafting down onto the floor. Bending forward, she picked it up carefully and could see that it was a printout of an e-mail he had received. She read it carefully:

Dear Christian Archibald,
Many thanks for sending me your sample chapters, which I read over the weekend. I don't think this is something that we could take on at this point, although I did like the writing, in parts, a lot, particularly the strong opening, which immediately catches the attention.

My feeling overall, as a reader, was that when it felt as though you had 'relaxed' into your own voice, the narrative worked well and flowed smoothly. In other parts, the tone felt slightly more self-conscious, a little bit more formal, and that occasionally appeared to 'muffle' the 'real' voice that we sense underneath. I'm aware that that may well be a function of the fact that you are still finding your way 'in' to the novel (I'm not sure how advanced the work is at this point) but perhaps if you are still in the early stages I imagine that it is possible that you will later revisit these chapters and that they may alter their shape, depending on how the narrative ultimately develops.

I hope this is helpful, rather than confusing, and if the novel has not already been taken up by someone else by the time you have finished it, I would be happy to take another look then.

With best wishes,

SC

As Sorcha finished reading, the first wave of betrayal came over her. He had betrayed her by leading her to believe that his novel was almost complete, and then compounding that falsehood with news of the agent. 'Definite interest' – those were the words he had used. But how could he have gotten that from this polite but clear rejection? Her temper rose to the surface suddenly, and she swallowed it down with the remainder of the wine. These secrets he kept from her brought a new worry. Although she knew that he wasn't alone in keeping secrets – she remembered with a rush all those text messages she had sent, and the ones she had received and savoured, reading them over and over – the knowledge of his betrayal seemed huge to her, enormous. Moved by an impulse she would later recognise as petulant, indulgent and dramatic, she found her mobile phone in her pocket, and for the first time in weeks, she texted him – right there at her husband's desk. 'Are you home? Need to talk...'

9

Almost without realising it, my days fell into a pattern. A blissfully simple, happy pattern. Every day I got up and went to work; in the evenings I set about redecorating my house, and then, before the closing light of day, I walked the beach. The evenings were still mild enough, yet there was a turn in the air, the promise of autumn whispering on the wind. Sometimes I met Christy on the beach and we strolled along together. Our conversations followed a pattern too. He talked about his family and his work. He seemed preoccupied by his teenage daughter, the ravages of her adolescence. When he talked of her, bewilderment leaked into his tone, a brittle disappointment at her newfound anger. He told me that he was planning to travel, as soon as the kids were sorted out, he said. I'm not sure what he meant by that, but there was an almost innocent eagerness about the way he questioned me on South America, and somehow, I found it heartening to talk to him about it, to share my memories with him, releasing them into the wind. I had begun to look forward to these walks, the comfort I drew from his presence, and on those nights when I walked alone I felt touched by disappointment that he wasn't there. I didn't like to think about what that meant.

But on Friday, there was a deviation from the pattern of things. It started when Alan Woodgate approached me after lunch, hands behind his back, a patrician smile on his face, and informed me that I had proved my reliability and could graduate onto the tills.

'Fucking fabulous,' Ger said wryly. 'How do you feel?'

'Happy as a pig in shit,' I said.

'Right then. Let's celebrate.'

It was a Friday evening custom that the staff of Crazy Prices spilled out into the car park, travelled to the other side of the street and entered the drinking establishment formally known as Larry Malones, but commonly referred to as the Hub. I had never learned exactly why. Up until that point I had avoided this slip-stream of humanity sucked into the Hub on account of my unwillingness to get drawn into any drunken con-versations, as much as my own fear of crowds. But on this occasion, I decided to make an exception. After a slight detour around the back behind the pallets where we shared a sneaky joint – 'Oh, pure wickedness,' Ger whispered, dragging deeply – we sauntered across and into the Hub, already filling up with its Friday night regulars.

I had first discovered this place when I was fifteen and it was in its heyday as a haven for underage drinkers. Entering behind Ger, I saw that in twenty years the place hadn't changed much, and if anything had deteriorated. The bar was long and narrow with a carpeted floor that felt sticky underfoot. Odours fought against each other

in the stagnant air, spilled beer and detergent and
something like stomach acid. A group of women from
work sat together in a booth inside the door and some of
them glanced up at me as I walked the length of the bar,
then looked back down again, not really interested after
all. I perched myself on a high stool at the far end of the
counter and Ger gave our orders to a grim-faced
barman, his white shirt, black trousers and red bow tie
seeming out of place somehow. There wasn't much light
in there, barely a faint glow cast from lamps shaded in
dark colours with gold unravelling tassels. My Southern
Comfort and red arrived in a short squat glass with a
thin red straw for stirring, and as I lit my cigarette, the
barman told me I wasn't allowed to smoke. 'You're
kidding,' I said with faint disbelief, and he answered in a
weary tone, like he'd answered this question a million
times before. 'It's the law.'

'Jeez, you really have been out of it, haven't you?' Ger
remarked, testing his Bacardi and Coke before setting it
down, satisfied. 'So what do you want to do? Go over
and join the others?'

I followed his gaze over to the band of people all
sitting, chatting animatedly, tut-tutting and sucking in
their lips in disapproval, and I wondered what they were
talking about.

'I don't know,' I said hesitantly. 'What do you think?'

'Well, only go over there if you're prepared to discuss
what you plan to do with the money in your SSIA
account – that's what I'd say.'

'What's an SSIA account?'

He stared at me then, a blank expression on his face, before erupting into sudden laughter.

'It's like you've been dropped in here from another planet, do you know that?' he laughed, shaking his head. 'Lara, you crack me up.'

We stayed at the bar, drinking and talking, and without a cigarette I drank more quickly than I normally would. There was a TV above the bar showing horse racing, and the grass of the track looked luridly green. I sipped from my straw and stared up at it with dull eyes.

'So what about Alan?' Ger asked, the weed and the alcohol making him gossipy. 'Would you or wouldn't you?'

'No way.'

'He's not gay, you know. He's married. With kids.'

'Even more reason not to,' I said, a little sanctimoniously, and he cocked his eyebrow and let it slide.

'So?' he asked, his voice rising speculatively through the syllable. 'Is there anyone?'

'Nope.'

'What? How long have you been back here? You must have your eye on someone.'

Without warning, a thought strayed into my mind and I saw again those brown eyes flecked with amber, like tiny flames licking around his pupils. Once, many years ago, I had told him that. I wondered if he would walk the beach tonight alone, if he would miss our conversation. Sometimes, on our walks, we didn't talk at all. There was something comradely about the silence between us, listening to the hush of the calm, empty sea.

'There's no one,' I said quickly, banishing those thoughts from my head.

Some men in suits entered and paused briefly for some friendly banter with the women in the booth before approaching the bar. The one nearest to me looked over and nodded a hello. He was wearing a striped shirt with a blue tie and I noticed that his sleeves were pulled up and held in place by some sort of suspenders clasped about his upper arms.

'What the fuck are they?' Ger said out of the side of his mouth.

I nodded hello back curtly before turning my eyes away.

'What about him?'

'Who? Short arms?'

'Yeah. He's cute in a butch medallion-man kind of way.'

'Why don't you have him then, Ger?'

Sounds zoned in and out, battling for attention, the loud pings and bells and tinny music of the slot machines competing with the pop music seeping from speakers and the conversation rising up around me. There was something so familiar about it, in a way I couldn't put my finger on, and then as Ger launched into an elaborate bitchy account of goings-on in the men's toilets, it came to me. This bar was like the one we went to in Ubatuibe, after the sandal had been found on the beach. The same noises, the same undercurrent of seediness. I had needed a drink that day, and so had Alejo, and so we'd sat across from each other, two cold beers between us, and I'd felt so light and papery, like I was transparent or smoky or hardly there at all. Neither of us had slept throughout the eleven days that had passed since Nacio went missing, and looking across at him, his eyes were like hollows in his face, small, black eyes sunk back into their sockets. He'd looked so forlorn and bewildered that I wanted to put my arms around him, to draw him to me, to feel the comfort of his body against mine. I put my drink aside and leaned my arms across the table and took his hands in mine.

'So,' I said softly.

'So. I guess that's it.'

A shiver passed through me as he said this, a bristling of nerves like raindrops across my back and neck.

'What do you mean?'

'His sandal, Lara,' he said wearily, a struggle in his voice. 'You saw the blood on it.'

His hands felt heavy in mine, and my fingers relaxed around them, my grip loosening. 'You must have known it would come to this,' he said quietly.

'Come to what?' My voice came out crisp and hard and I let his hands drop on the table, feeling something hot and defiant rising up in me. His voice, his demeanour and the defeated slump of his shoulders were all scaring me.

He put his thumbs up to his eyes and squeezed them into the sockets. 'Don't make me say it.'

'No,' I said, shaking my head, a warning in my voice. 'It's not true. Don't even think it.'

And then he took his hands away from his face and I saw the misery in his eyes and he said those words to me, the words I didn't want to hear.

'He's dead, Lara.'

A protest rose up inside me, like a great yawning despair, a furious rage at his defeatism, his easy surrender. Suddenly, everything changed. The shared anxiety, the comfort and closeness brought about by our desperate loss while clinging to that thin thread of hope was all gone now, cast aside with the declaration of his loss of faith. In the months that followed, our pain seemed to separate, each of us locked in our own private grief – my grief for a lost boy, his for a dead one. We were no longer on the same side. We nursed our own separate heartaches, unable to confide in each other. He hid behind the veil of language, claiming not to be able to express his pain in words that I would understand. But that was a cheat in itself, for I caught him sometimes, whispering to Shirley or to Sylvie, letting his sorrow pour out to them in shuddering noiseless sobs. In the meantime, I sealed myself within a fortress of anger. I built a shield of it, red and fiery. Refusing to let go of my belief that he was still alive, I railed against anyone that dared suggest otherwise, my temper roaring and spitting.

We continued like that for months, Alejo mourning in private while I led us all on that frantic, desperate search for Nacio, pushing ahead, burying my despair and indignation at their half-heartedness. In the silence that grew between us, our wounds began to fester, spawning new resentments.

I had just ordered our fourth round when the man in the sleeve suspenders came over to me. Ger had slipped out to the gents', leaving me alone, and suddenly there was a shadow cast along the bar counter next to me.

'You all right there?'

'Fine, thanks.'

'You look a bit lonely, sitting there, drinking by yourself.'

'I'm not alone. My friend's just in the toilet.'

'I see.' He took a second, as if silently appraising whether it was worth continuing on, before his face cracked into a wide, confident grin, and I could tell he wouldn't be put off easily. 'Well, maybe I'll just sit here until he gets back?'

'Sit where you like,' I said as he eased himself onto the stool next to me. 'It's a free country.'

'That it is.'

My companion began telling me about himself. I forgot his name instantly, and his profession, zoning in and out of the conversation. He didn't appear put off by my terse, noncommittal responses to his questions. He bought us more drinks, and by that stage I had realised that Ger wasn't coming back, having abandoned me to my fate with Short Arms. I didn't protest when another drink was put in front of me, even though the voice in my head was telling me this could have consequences.

'So how come I haven't seen you around here before?'

I thought about this for a moment before answering.

'I lived abroad for some time. I only recently came home.'

'Whereabouts?'

'South America, mainly.'

'Wow. I bet that was incredible.'

I nodded, sipped my drink, and thought about maybe terminating this conversation, but Short Arms had launched into a tirade about always wanting to do the Inca Trail, to see Machu Picchu. Then he started telling me about some documentary he had seen on Channel 4 about Peru.

'There's this museum in Lima, in the catacombs of some monastery, I don't remember the name. But there were all these skulls and bones laid out, I mean thousands of them! All spanning out in this display like a sunburst or something. Have you ever been there?'

'We never went to museums,' I answered. 'Alejo didn't agree with them – they were temples to empire, he thought, full of white mock-liberal tourists.'

'Who's Alejo?'

I considered this for a moment, trying to calculate at that time what exactly he was to me.

'He's just a guy I used to travel with,' I said.

'Oh.' He watched me for a moment, then, satisfied with this answer, nodded slowly and picked up his drink. 'And he didn't like museums then?'

'Not really.' It came back to me in a rush. 'It's funny, he's a quiet, easy-going man, but one thing used to always wind him up – the rape of the land by the Spanish invaders. The blood on their hands, their greed for gold – it used to drive him crazy. I remember his face, white with rage, in the cathedral of Lima. The display of gold was so ornate and gaudy. I thought it was vulgar, but he thought it was criminal. Preserving a tomb to Pizarro – it was like venerating Hitler, according to him. So you see, museums were never a part of the agenda for us. It wasn't worth the hassle. And we didn't have the money for it either, so that was that.'

Neither of us said anything after that, both of us a little surprised by my volunteering all this information.

'Well, that's something I hadn't heard before,' he said, looking no less eager.

The light from the bar was catching the side of his face, lighting up only one half of it, making his cheekbone stand out more, and it occurred to me that he wasn't bad looking. I smiled across at him like a flirt, an echo of that old weakness rumbling inside my head. It had been a while since I'd felt the attentions of a man, and I welcomed it after the brush with sorrow that came with the familiarity of this place.

When I was fifteen, I used to try my luck at getting served in the Hub. And sure enough, as we started in on the next round of drinks, a blast of cold air heralded the arrival of a group of young girls. They were all shadowy eyes and black eyeliner, short skirts and high boots, plunging necklines and garish jewellery. The over-emphasis on their sexuality drew attention to their youth. I watched as they took their seats behind me, feeling my head spin as I turned to look, but they didn't notice me as they giggled amongst themselves. Avril was with them – taller than the rest, a slash of red lipstick signalling a brazen confidence. They gave their orders to the lounge boy, who was too intimidated by their clamouring sexuality to dispute their ages, and giggled loudly as he walked away.

I didn't think Avril saw me. Perhaps she did and pretended not to. But it wasn't until later, when my companion had drawn his stool right in next to mine and had turned the conversation down a more intimate avenue, that Avril came over. She walked to the bar with a confident strut, teetering on high heels, and almost shrieked my name.

'What are you doing here?' she demanded before dropping her voice to a breathy conspiratorial whisper. 'You won't tell Mam or Dad I was in here, will you?'

The man I was with seemed momentarily put out at Avril's lingering presence before masking his annoyance and offering to buy us both a drink. Her eyes lit up at the prospect. She had a Southern Comfort and red like me, and looked pleased with herself as she sipped it, but made no attempt to move away from us.

'How's the decorating going, Lara?'

'Okay, I guess.'

'You should see her house,' Avril explained to him. 'It's like an American beach house or something. We've been renovating it, haven't we Lar?'

I ignored this and took a gulp from my glass. I was drinking too quickly, but was past the point of caring. I yearned for a cigarette but didn't trust myself to walk the eight or nine yards to the front door. The room seemed full of hard surfaces. Everything was spinning around me.

'Did Lara tell you she's just back from South America?'

'Yeah, she mentioned it.' He answered Avril's questions but his eyes were all on me, and that's where they stayed as I heard her listing the countries I had lived in, all so remote and distant from me now, and as I gazed at the glassware assembled in rows behind the bar, I felt a loneliness washing over me, an emptiness like the slate-grey sea. I had an urge to get out of there, but then I thought of the long walk home, my limbs weighed down by alcohol and the shadowy rooms of my house at the end of it, and I took another sip of my drink and wondered just what it was I thought I was doing back here.

Voices buzzed around me, lights and colours blurring. Avril moved away to rejoin her friends and I couldn't be sure if she was peeved at me for my silence, my senses too dulled to pick up on her perceived grievance. The man next to me moved in close. There was a wedding band on his finger that stared back at me, full of accusation, as I felt his shoulder pressing against mine.

'I'm here for the night,' he told me. 'I have a room upstairs.'

He glanced at me, his eyes dark and a little shiny, and my cheeks grew hot and I looked away. He had a cheeky, optimistic charm about him. It had been so long since I had been with a man, so long since I had felt the comfort of another's flesh, that the temptation ticked over inside me as I tried to locate in the blur of my thoughts just exactly what I wanted from him. I finished my drink and could feel him still looking, so I stared back at him and saw the dark wanting in his face, and suddenly I was so sad that I seemed to be crying inside my head and the feline grief in my chest was stretching and clawing all over the place, and what I wanted more than anything was to feel someone putting their arms around me, folding me into them, and right then I didn't care who that was.

With that old dark feeling taking hold of me, I moved across and found his mouth with mine. We sat on our stools, leaning into each other, open-mouthed and hungry. I didn't care what the sour-faced barman thought, or Avril and her friends sniggering behind me, or my work crowd in the booth, their eyes out on stalks. I allowed my body to be overtaken by desire, a new sensation after all this pain.

It wasn't until I drew away that I saw Christy standing at the door, his face pale, his eyes bright and shiny. He'd obviously been searching for Avril and had finally found her at the Hub. He took a moment to register shock and disappointment as he stared at me draped all over this married man, this stranger.

Understanding came quickly. He dragged Avril out

of her seat, his voice just a pitch below screaming. I tried to say something to him, feeling guilty about my own performance and somehow culpable for Avril too, for not doing anything to stop her, but I was too drunk to be coherent. My tongue felt thick in my mouth.

'I can see you don't require a lift home,' he said to me, and the words were spat out, full of hiss and venom, his eyes all cool and flinty. In that moment I felt so small and worthless beneath his cold disapproval that it was all I could do not to cry.

As they left, the air seemed to collapse around me, closing in on me, dark and oppressive. The man moved towards me, but I waved him away. He mumbled something then, called me a name. 'Prick-tease,' he said. But I was beyond caring. I climbed down off the bar stool and stumbled out into the night.

10

All week the storm inside him raged. It erupted on that first night and hadn't abated since, although the house had grown quiet and hostile around him. He knew that that night would go down as a black one in his history.

After tearing Avril away from her friends, he dragged her outside to where he had parked across the street. She seemed shocked by the latent violence of his actions, and he felt like something within him might snap. Once inside the car, Avril found her voice and instead of being penitent and remorseful, instead of begging him not to be mad, she hit him with the force and shrillness of her fury. How dare he, she screeched at him, how dare he embarrass her like that? How dare he violate her privacy, her independence? He had no respect for her, she spat out, tears of rage springing in her eyes. Did he not know how much he had shamed her and himself, dragging her out like that?

His knuckles grew white and bloodless as his grip tightened around the steering wheel. Hot tears of rage came suddenly in his throat and he had to battle to swallow them away. Avril's tirade continued throughout the short journey home, and all the while he said nothing, struck dumb by this new rage galloping through him. He glanced across at her and saw how ugly her face became with the poison she seemed willing to speak. Leaving the car parked in the drive and watching her strut ahead of him in her high heels and obscenely short skirt, dressed like a slut, he felt the hot blood filling his hands and fingers, his heart pumping blood like molten lava out into his chest and flooding his limbs. As they entered the house, Avril kicked the front door behind her so that it came flying back, landing a glancing blow to his arm and shoulder, and suddenly the rage seemed to rise up inside him in a glorious jet of pure hatred so that for a second he thought he might kill her.

He slammed the door shut and the noise of it reverberated through the entire house. He rushed after her and caught hold of her arm savagely, shoving her back against the wall. He stood there, yelling in full voice, his face pushed up close to hers so that he could see something move behind that defiant mask of hers – she became hurt, perhaps frightened.

'I am your father,' he screamed at her, 'and I will not have you treat me like I'm some piece of shit you've just trod in. You will show me some respect, or by God I'll kick you out of this house so fast your head will spin. Don't think for a moment that I won't!'

Sounds came to him from upstairs, the creaking of floorboards, and Sorcha emerged, wrapping a robe about herself, her face wreathed in worry, coming down the stairs demanding to know what was going on. At the sight of her mother, Avril's face dissolved into tears, but the rage was out of him now, spurting upwards in hot jets and he couldn't stop himself.

'No daughter of mine is to parade herself around this town like a slut, like a whore. You are not to set foot outside this house again without some decent clothes on you. And you're to wipe that muck off your face as well. To look at you now makes me sick!' he spat as Sorcha advanced towards him, hissing his name with shock in her voice, as if to say he had gone too far. But there were flames in his stomach and he turned to his wife, her face pale and drawn, and instructed her to keep out of it, it was none of her business.

Maybe she sensed that her mother was on her side, but when Christy looked back at his daughter, Avril jutted out her chin defiantly, her tears all gone, and said coolly and quietly, 'Go fuck yourself.'

He slapped her then, hard across the face, then felt the tremble in his chest as he realised what he'd done. And while he knew that it was wrong, knew that it was something he would always regret doing, in that instant, as he lashed out at her, feeling the impact of his flat hand against her wet cheek, the words 'little bitch' running through his head, what he felt more than anything else was a glorious satisfaction – satisfaction at giving vent to the purest of feelings, instead of suppressing them as he should have done. He had grown tired of doing the right thing, the decent thing. His passion, his rage had finally been released, had at last broken free of the confines and rigours of decency.

And as Sorcha swooped down, shoving him aside and gathering her hysterical daughter up in her arms, cursing at him, 'God damn you, Christy! What the hell is the matter with you?' he had leaned against the wall, his hands creeping over the wallpaper behind him, a new power pulsing through his chest.

It fastened inside him, this tantalising sense of power, of possibility. It nestled up against his anger, coupling with it, spawning a new range of emotions. As he lay awake in bed that night, listening to his wife breathing through her troubled sleep, he felt that somewhere in the quietness of the house, his rage was lingering. It was out there now, finally unleashed, lurking in the shadows, ready to spring into action again.

The next morning, as he'd stood there buttoning his shirt while Sorcha tried to tackle him on what had happened the night before, her voice all shrill and shaking with disapproval, he had stopped what he was doing, turned to her slowly and raised a finger to silence her, flashing a warning glance. He saw the fear entering her eyes, the memory of his fury bouncing off the surfaces of the room, and turning away from her to resume buttoning his shirt, he had sensed her slinking away from him, unspeaking, and felt a tingle of excitement, the power inside him expanding and filling out his chest.

His daughter looked pale and wounded as she sat opposite him at breakfast, and he felt a twinge of guilt as he viewed the red shadow across her cheek. Normally, after a row, Christy felt compelled to clear the air, to resume some kind of amicable arrangement. It seemed to him that he was always the one to capitulate, to make the first move. But not this time. Suddenly now he was conscious of the new presence he brought to a room. He felt bigger, as if the rage inside him was filling out and demanding more space.

Battle lines had been drawn up in the house, with the women forming a wounded, aggrieved front, Jim remaining neutral and disinterested. They hardly spoke, the four of them – Avril not at all, and Sorcha only in short bursts of frustration. Christy's voice felt loud to him; it resonated with authority. He didn't speak to Avril, wanting to show that he could be every bit as wilful, every bit as stubborn as she could be. This time, he would not give in.

For a week this stand-off continued and he grew used to the silence. At times, he felt a hot impatience move inside him and he came close to throwing his hands up in the air and exclaiming, 'All right, you win.' Yet still, he held on.

In the night, when he couldn't sleep, he went down to the kitchen and poured himself a drink. He turned out the light and stood in the darkness staring out at the gloomy night sky, the white foam licking the shore and breaking over the spit of rocks at the end of the beach. At times, there was a light on in the clapboard house with its wraparound porch and run of wooden steps, and he thought of Lara – her eyes flat and staring, her speech slurring, that dark-haired prick wrapped around her, the indecency of it, slobbering all over him in a public place.

And he was visited again by those stabs of jealousy, coming at him from the past, when he had found her outside the barracks, that playful look of guilt on her face; or when he had to listen to some boy or another talking about her, bragging about what he had done with her. How easily she gave of herself to other people, and yet with him there was always this distance, as if she was holding him at arm's length. He remembered all this and felt the heat of his temper flashing through him, that same angry resentment and stinging hurt.

On Wednesday, it rained again, a torrent of squally showers coming in off the ocean. He felt a stab of guilt, thinking of Lara walking home in the rain. He had promised to look at her car for her. But his guilt was swept aside by the push of his resentment. Why should he look at her car, he thought angrily. What did she think he was, some kind of lackey? She had spoken to him of love, of loss and sorrow and disappointment, and he felt that something had passed between them, something old and remembered, and he felt her opening up to him, allowing him to glimpse inside her terrible pain. That and something more – the memory of that embrace, the way her body felt when clasped to his. Something vague and hopeful had washed through him, raising hairs on his flesh, making his heart thump loud and full in his chest.

And then she had done that thing, had cheapened herself. No, he thought to himself as he swirled the ice cubes melting into his drink and watched the rain beating down. She could wait a little longer.

*

In the end, a week passed before he finally called to see her. He waited until Sunday afternoon, that lazy hour of the weekend that felt like a pause or an intake of breath before the whole week started up again. The sun was bright on the ocean and the wet sand glistened as he walked across the beach. Mounting the steps to Lara's house, he heard the lonely cries of the choughs echoing out around the bay. The screen door was open, and feeling brazen, made bold by the perceived insult he had suffered, he pushed through after a brief peremptory knock and found Lara on her knees on the bare floorboards, struggling to open a tin of varnish. She looked up in surprise, and seeing him standing there, a darkness came over her face, her surprise chased away by a chilly suspicion.

'Oh, it's you,' she said, and he could hear in her voice that she was aggrieved and wondered what it was she had to feel injured about.

'Yes, well, I said I'd come and look at your car, didn't I?' he replied in a sharp, testy voice full of shards of ice.

'You certainly took your time.'

She looked away then, having delivered her blow, and continued the struggle with the varnish.

'I've got other things to do, you know. I'm not here to be at your beck and call.'

'Fine. Go and do those other things then. Don't do me any favours.'

He heard the defiance in her voice, read it in the firm

set of her shoulders, the tension in her neck, and despite his anger and the injurious mood he had wallowed in all week, he felt suddenly moved to touch her.

'Look, why don't I just take a look at it and we'll say no more about—'

'No, really,' she cut across him, eyes flashing. 'I'd hate to be beholden to you.'

'Oh, for God's sake!' His anger was bubbling up again. 'You wouldn't be beholden to me. Jesus!'

'Just go, will you?'

'That's just lovely.' He gave a hard little smile, gritting his teeth, his eyes narrowing. 'That's all the thanks I get for helping a friend out?'

'We're not friends,' she said, just loud enough for him to hear.

'No. I guess we're not. But that's your choice.'

'Just go, would you?' she whispered wearily, her whole body shrugging with exasperation.

'Why don't you go, Lara? Go back to the Hub and get tanked up and find another scumbag to ram his tongue down your throat. No doubt you fed him your sob story too, huh?'

She stared at him in horror, a slow realisation creeping over her face, mixed with a flicker of satisfaction. He was rooted to the spot, not quite believing that he had said that, horrified at being so petty and snide and cruel. She looked at him now, reading everything there was to know about his jealousy, his dark desires.

'I knew it,' she breathed, shaking her head. 'My God—'

'What do you know?' he said, voice rising, over-reacting, feeling his heart pounding up into his throat, suddenly terrified of what she might say.

'I knew it,' she repeated. 'That night in the bar, the way you looked at me. I was pissed, but I remember that look. And that's what you've been doing all week – avoiding me, sulking, wallowing in your own self-pity.'

'Don't be so fucking stupid.'

'I had forgotten how jealous you could be, Christy. How petty.'

'It's Christy now, is it? I'm not Christian any more.' He heard the pettiness of his tone and realised that he had proved her point in that one sentence, and hated himself for it.

'When did you get to be so self-righteous?'

'I'd ask you when did you get to be such a slut, but I already know the answer.' These words emerged quickly, heedlessly, and he felt his regret instantly.

She looked away as he said this, choosing to ignore him. She appeared so smug sitting there, trying to lever the lid off the tin with a knife, and he suddenly felt small and insignificant and exasperated, all his anger deflated and worthless when up against her sneering disrespect.

'Here, let me do that,' he said, reaching for the can of varnish, but she held it away from him, insisting on doing it herself. He watched her struggle for another few seconds and felt the impatience building inside him. 'Just give it here and let me do it,' he said, the irritation creeping into his voice, and suddenly he made a swipe for it, but she held on and he found himself leaning over her, battling for the tin. 'Give it here,' he gasped, reaching down and grappling with her for it, so that he was kneeling on the floor next to her, scrabbling over the tin, and he felt things change between them – a new intensity, a new ferocity – so that it was no longer about the varnish, but a struggle with a stronger desire. The tin fell from her hands, hands like claws. He grabbed her wrists as she tried to scratch at him, holding her back. There on the floor beneath him, she struggled like a wildcat, her grey eyes on fire, and all the while he held her away from him until he felt like he could bear it no more and he released her wrists and her hands flew up and grabbed his head, and he was drawing down on her suddenly and their mouths met, and he felt the savagery of the kiss, her teeth sinking into his lips.

He had never felt such a huge emotion. It was like a live, thumping, physical thing. Her arms were reaching up for him, drawing him down, and in his bones he knew this was wrong, in the quickening of his heartbeat and the thickening of his breath, he knew this was wrong. Everything happened quickly. He was lying between her knees, pausing above her when she untucked his shirt and he felt her fingers creeping around his waist, touching the hairs at his belly, fingering the elastic of his shorts and he felt like his body was splitting open, his thoughts crowded out by the sensations ripping through him. He found her mouth again, and this time it was softer, less savage, and her lips parted beneath his.

Sunlight found them through the open window as they stretched out on the bare floor. He felt exposed somehow, here in the daylight, as she guided his shirt over his head, peeling it from his body. His mouth moved over her jaw. He kissed her neck and pushed away her straps, tugging at her vest, pulling it down. With his mouth he moved over the plump warmth of her breast, and finding her nipple hard and erect, his tongue swarmed around it and she moaned and rose beneath him. Something was pulling inside him, drawing him on like the tide, and he felt for her legs, lifting her skirt, his hands underneath her, thumbs hooking elastic, inching cotton down over her knees, past her ankles. He felt her knees open to him again. Hands roamed over his stomach, quick fingers working his belt, tugging at his shorts, and he leapt free of them, the warmth of her fingers and palm suddenly wrapped around him. There were explosions in his head, sparks fizzing up and down his spine, ricocheting off the inside of his skull. He looked at the length of her, her eyes half-closed with a look he couldn't read, lost in herself. He took her hand away and, cradling into her hips, pushed gently and found her. She seemed to tense before her legs moved around him, gathering him in, and he felt something take hold of him, his throat thick and plugged with emotion. Moving inside her, he stared down at her. She seemed to make no sound, her back arching, her hips working below him. His arms strained, holding him up, and he swooped down and kissed her and in that moment everything was perfect and whole.

Waves were crashing in his head, a symphony of

sound flooding his body. He poured himself into her. Coming to a rise, she shuddered around him and he felt himself bursting apart, and in that instant, something broke open inside him, a bright new space, a chink of light, relief flooding through it, drowning his rage.

PART II

11

Sorcha pegged the washing onto the line and squinted in the sun, inhaling the freshness of the clean clothes and the salt on the wind coming up off the beach, and felt the first breath of autumn in the air. The sheets billowed and snapped in the wind as if they had a life of their own, and reaching the end of the line, her eyes cast out beyond the clean line of clothes, pure white against the green of her garden, to the sea beyond, the black hump of Begnis Island rising up out of the water. At the end of the bay, Lara's house lay quiet – no smoke from the chimney, no open windows, no presence on the veranda. Sorcha looked on it for a moment, felt a deeper silence reverberating from it, and she thought of the awkwardness that existed between her and Lara, a prickliness that she couldn't seem to shake. But then she bent down, plucked a pillowcase from her basket and put the thought out of her mind.

All morning she'd had this lazy, lethargic feeling, a kind of floating, like nothing about the day was real or grounded. It started when she awoke in the early hours before dawn and found that she was lying alone, sheets and blankets kicked back on the other side of the bed. Sounds from downstairs travelled up to her – taps spilling water into the sink, the low hum of a kettle boiling, feet pacing over the kitchen floor, and then silence. What did he think about sitting alone in the dark, hunched over the table, his fingers wrapped around a mug of tea? For the third time that week she had found herself lying in bed listening to her husband's nocturnal movements, turning things over in her head, fighting the urge to go down to him. Some instinct within her told her that joining him would have consequences, and in the dark hour before dawn, her worries whispered to her, clamouring and building in pure voice.

Bending to pick up the basket, she straightened up and saw Christy at the kitchen window drinking a glass of water, his free hand raised in greeting. She waved back and smiled, feeling a sudden lurch in her chest as she walked towards the house. He seemed cheerful this morning, overly affectionate, and the thought kept crisscrossing her mind that this was owing to the fact that she was going away for the night.

She had told him a week ago, on Sunday evening when he came back from his walk. He seemed flushed and a little edgy, but she was edgy herself, nerves jumping inside her. And yet it amazed her still, the calmness with which she had told the lie.

'I've decided to go up to Margot's for a night,' she had said carefully, keeping her voice even and firm. But beneath her calm exterior ran a torrent of nerves.

'Oh?' he had looked up at her, genuinely surprised. 'What brought this on?'

'No reason. I'd just like to get away for a little while, that's all. On my own.'

'When were you thinking of going?'

'Friday,' she said.

He seemed to consider this, hands on his hips, and for a moment she thought he might ask her if it had anything to do with the tension in the house since the night of the row. But he didn't. Instead, he had looked back at her and smiled warmly.

'Sure. Well. Absolutely. It will do you good to get away for a bit. Have some time to yourself without us lot making demands on you.'

And there was real warmth in the way he said it that made her wretched little heart lurch with happiness before being chased away by the misery of her deceit.

Coming in through the back door, she found Christy pouring her a cup of tea.

'Here you go,' he said, handing it to her and taking the wash basket out of her hands. 'Sit yourself down there.'

She allowed herself to be manoeuvred into the chair and looked down at the toast he had buttered for her.

'I didn't know if you wanted marmalade or honey,' he explained.

'What's all this?' she asked, instantly regretting the words, the sad truth contained within them that it was a rarity for him to spoil her like this.

'It's breakfast, Sorcha,' he said with amusement and

she noted how smart he looked today in a crisp pink shirt and matching tie that she had bought him last Christmas. She had worried about the colour at the time, anxious that he would balk at wearing such a feminine hue. But he looked handsome in it, his hair gelled back off his forehead. He looked *sexy*. That was it.

'What time is your meeting?'

'Ten-thirty,' he said, glancing at his watch.

'And what will you do while I'm away?'

She watched him as he gathered up his things, putting papers into his briefcase, and shrugging his shoulders into his jacket.

'I'm taking the fifth-years to see a film later, and this evening, I guess I'll just work on my book.' He said this cheerfully, and she thought again about the meagre chapters squirreled away in his desk, with that letter from the agent.

'There's spaghetti sauce in the fridge,' she began, 'you just have to heat it up, and there's loads of pasta and—'

'Relax,' he said then, leaning over her and planting a kiss in her hair. 'Don't worry about a thing. The kids and I will be fine.'

'Well, if there's anything—'

'Sorcha. Go, enjoy yourself. Really, I can take care of everything here.'

'All right,' she said, feeling miserable at the tenderness of his voice.

'Give my love to Margot,' he told her from the door.

'I will. Oh, and don't forget to take in the washing...'

He smiled at her from the door, and then he was gone.

For a moment, she sat and thought about what he had said. Or rather, the way in which he had said it. There was a new cheerfulness about him. In the last week, something had changed. A lightness had crept over him, a levity of spirit. She was uncertain about it, suspicious of where it came from, or what it grew out of. As the silence of the house stretched out around her, new doubts reached her, rubbing their questioning hides against her, and she sat there considering her mug of cooling tea and the toast growing dry and hard on the plate, and tried to remember the last time he had made her breakfast before going to work. Was this a conciliatory offer, some kind of apology for the last few weeks? It seemed to come from out of the blue and she couldn't help but wonder what it meant, this gesture, this peace offering.

She got up and threw the tea down the drain, the toast in the bin. Her appetite had dwindled in the last week, guilt and excitement mingling in her stomach. As she set about putting her house in order, thoughts of Christy preyed on her mind. There was a new quality to his reticence, something that she couldn't quite put her finger on. Sorcha couldn't help feeling that behind his quiet exterior, he was full of words, of unspoken things. First there was the book that he refused to talk about, his unfinished work, and then there was that night – that terrible night – that still lay heavily on her memory, the image of him, black and threatening and full of rage, standing over their daughter, his fists clenched, his arms raised and drawn, that tension in his body from the taut stretch of his neck down to the firm stance of his feet, and her sudden fear, shocking and new, that he was going to punch his own daughter square in the face. She had never seen that in him before. That night he brought something new into the house with him, and suddenly she was afraid of him.

But that was two weeks ago, and things had calmed down since then. The terrible stand-off between her husband and daughter had drifted into an uneasy truce, but anything was better than the anger of that night. And while Avril still lurked behind her injured stance, something seemed to have melted in Christy. Perhaps he'd had a change of heart, Sorcha thought optimistically, or a twinge of remorse, but twice in the last week, she had happened upon him alone, staring into the middle distance, his mouth resting into a gentle little smile.

Before leaving the house, she rang Margot. She listened to her sister's voice ringing out bright and muscular and forced herself to express a cheerfulness that she didn't really feel. Her older sister had always possessed the uncanny knack of being able to pick up on Sorcha's worries and frustrations, and today she wasn't sure if she could withstand Margot's persistent ferreting, cajoling and subtle bullying tactics. She was frightened of what she might admit to. Today, she felt her life would be no match for the bright, shiny surface of Margot's domestic bliss. Yet she had to ring her, she couldn't risk her sister phoning later that evening in her absence and the confusion that would stir up as a result. The phone call was brief, a cursory exchange of information without ever really saying anything.

Afterwards she left a note, instructing her family to bring in the sheets when they were dry, pointing out the food that was in the fridge. Signing off with a flourish, she scored three sharp little Xs at the end of the page. She stood there for a moment and she contemplated these kisses, one for each of them, before scooping her car keys from the kitchen window and reaching for her bag.

'I don't suppose she'll commission any work from me now.'

These were the words Neil offered into the silence that fell between them in the wake of Stella's drunken rant. A certain wryness entered his tone as he said it, and she had looked up at him, seen his arms folded neatly on the table in front of him, his nut-brown face under that cloud of grey hair twitching with an uncertain amusement. For a moment, she was lost, forgetting their reason, hers and Stella's, for being there in the first place.

'Perhaps not.' For some reason she felt apologetic, almost responsible, but this was whisked away by the casual shrug of his shoulders before he sipped his wine.

'Not to worry.'

In that moment he seemed to be so relaxed, a person who didn't get ruffled, so content and at ease in his own

environment that she couldn't help attaching a certain
envy to her idea of him.

Since that night, she had thought of him often – more
often than she should, she suspected. As she drove, she
heard his words again, tried to fix on an image of him in
her mind. That was the difficult part. With passing time,
his image had become distorted. She was no longer sure
how tall he was. She remembered his hair, and his eyes,
as blue as a swimming pool, and the glint of irony in
them. She remembered, too, his arms folded on the table
in front of him, long, thin forearms, almost as brown as
his face, dark hairs feathering out over them. But trying
to fit all these physical parts into one clear individual
seemed just beyond her grasp. She was beginning to fear
that she wouldn't recognise him. Or worse, that she
would be disappointed by what she found.

Three times along the way, she considered stopping and
turning around. One time she actually pulled over onto
the hard shoulder and caught her breath, thinking to
herself: *What on earth am I doing?* Sitting there,
breathing heavily, she knew that the reasons why she
should turn around and go home were manifold and
profound, whereas the reasons for continuing on were
more blurry and indeterminate, less intellectualised and
more of a deep need within herself, a longing that
propelled her onwards.

Starting the engine again, she drew out onto the road
and headed south, glancing briefly in the rear-view

mirror and seeing the face of a woman who was tired of being good and upright and decent, weary from giving of herself to those people who inhabited her life. A doormat, that's what she felt like. Well, now she wanted to rebel, to break away from all that was safe and dull and imprisoning. She refused to go quietly into middle age. She was only thirty-six. Thirty-six! Stella's words still lingered in her head – those old lady names she had thrown at her. For weeks now, she had nurtured her secret life – the clandestine text messages, the furtive phone calls and lately the slow, languorous conversations in the day when the house was her own, and she could sit at the kitchen table with the phone pressed to the side of her head, his words pouring down the line into the whorl of her ear. They talked about all sorts of things: his business, her children, her fears that Jim was being bullied, his mother dying last year and how he had felt shaken with grief by it, Lara returning home, her childhood, his failed love affairs, the distance that was growing in her marriage, Stella and Guy, Christy's writing. She told him about the feelings of resentment towards Christy's study that she was lately assailed by. How she longed for a room of her own.

'The worst part is, I know he's not getting anywhere with his book. I know it,' she had muttered forlornly.

Then telling him about the chapters she had found, the pitiful note from the agent, she wondered briefly was this infidelity in itself, declaring her lack of faith in her own husband? 'I wish he would just let it go. Admit that he's not getting anywhere with it, and move on.'

'Maybe it makes him happy,' Neil had suggested, 'just working on it. Just dwelling within the possibility that it might become something.'

'Perhaps.'

Sorcha wasn't altogether sure what would make him happy. In many respects his happiness felt removed from her, a vague, shadowy, intangible thing that she couldn't approach.

They picked through and tossed about all of these things between them in hours over the phone. She thought to herself: *I could say anything to this man.*

Not since her friendship with Lillian had she felt she could be so open and honest with another person. She missed her friend, and felt the void deeply after her death. It had been a surprise to those around her, how profoundly she was affected by the loss. For weeks after the funeral, the tears kept coming; they wouldn't seem to dry up. It was exhaustion, she had told herself. Caring for Lillian during the final stages of her illness had been an all-consuming, emotionally wrenching ordeal. All she needed was rest. And still the tears came. 'Aren't you relieved it's all over?' Christy had asked her, his face quizzical, when she had tried to talk to him about it, tried to explain to him the loneliness she felt inside. 'No!' she had shrieked with exasperation, suddenly furious with him for not understanding, for being so callous. Did he not know? Could he not see? All those years spent living up the beach from Lillian. Those long days stretched out behind her. After Sorcha's parents died and Lara had left on her travels, and Jim and Avril were at school, it was just Sorcha and Lillian – that brisk walk up the strand, coffee on the porch underneath the clematis, or in the wintertime, curled up on Lillian's sofa, a dainty cup and saucer balanced on her knee, listening to the gentle softness of Lillian's voice. All those mornings that they sat together, looking out at the vast expanse of ocean, and the things they talked about – love, babies, sex, betrayals, disappointments, hopes. Sorcha had harboured the small hope that Lara's return might mean a return to her of something, some part of the closeness she'd felt with Lillian. Sorcha missed her friend. But Lara was too damaged, too wrapped up in her own grief, for any closeness to exist between them.

She had explained all of this to Neil and he listened closely. There was something strong and undemonstrative about him, a warmth in the silence on his end of the line, so that she felt he was absorbing every detail she uttered, and felt, too, that when he spoke it was with a measured deliberateness, as if he had thought through each word.

But they hadn't discussed what would occur between them when they met.

'Why don't you come and visit me,' he had suggested, 'and we can talk properly.'

She wasn't sure which one of them suggested that she stay over, but the implication was there by virtue of the distance she had to travel. *Something ought to be said*, she thought, *some parameters set in place*. 'My husband is the only man I have ever slept with,' she said to herself. Perhaps she should tell him this from the outset, so that he knew, so that his expectations were managed. But another part of her felt that these things were better not discussed, that somehow the magic would evaporate under the weight of those words. Better to let it play out as it will, she decided, to let it happen. A surge of excitement took her as her mind idled over the possibilities, and her foot pressed on the accelerator as she hastened south.

12

Christy sat into the stiff leather chair and peered across the vast desk to the tight, fastidious form of Arthur Douglas, the headmaster and his boss, who had summoned Christy to his office for what he termed 'a little chat'. This was to be a dressing down of sorts, and not something that Christy found wholly unexpected, and on that bright Friday morning, he wasn't too sure he cared. The kids had nicknamed the headmaster Seymour after a character in *The Simpsons*, and the name had stuck. So while Arthur began the meeting with an interrogation of his lungs, a deep guttural hacking and coughing, Christy had sat there masking his revulsion, thinking to himself, *Well that's just charming, Seymour.* All that was required was that he appear plausibly alert for the duration of the meeting, so he sat there, nodding his head gravely, his mind shifting to the curve of Lara's neck, the declivity of her chest, while half-listening to Arthur holding forth in fruity tones on the need for unity in disciplinary matters, the fall-off of interest in the more traditional subjects and the disappointing results of the previous year in some areas of study.

He daydreamed in fragments and found himself

staring past Arthur out through the glass partition to the office beyond where Alice Blake, the school secretary, sat tapping away at her keyboard. She was sitting in a parallelogram of light cast onto her from the window, and Christy found his eyes drawn to her arms, mottled and corpulent like corned beef emerging from her sleeveless blouse. *That blouse is a mistake*, he thought. On occasion, during the tedium of various staff meetings, he had found himself thinking about Alice Blake in a sexual way, but only as a fleeting fantasy, a passing whim during these endless droning hours. Looking at her that morning, Arthur boring on, Christy's cheeks grew hot at the memory of it. For now he had much richer fantasies to occupy his imagination. Fantasies that he intended to make a reality later that evening.

After what seemed an eternity, Arthur got to the point.

'The first half of the term is almost over, Christy, but there's still time. Let's see it for what it is. An opportunity.'

'Right.'

'Are you ready to grasp this opportunity? Ready to make the most of it?'

'Sure. Absolutely,' he replied dutifully, trying to hide his bemusement.

'Good, good. Let's hope this year brings some decent results then, eh?'

'Of course.'

'Because we can't afford to have another year like last one.'

'No,' Christy agreed, feeling a shift in the tone of their conversation, the underlying pull of seriousness entering the space between them. In the creaking silence that followed, he felt Arthur building up to something.

'I really couldn't overlook another year like the last,' he said quietly, intently, fixing Christy with the fullness of his porcine gaze. 'Do you see what I'm saying?'

Christy shifted uncomfortably in his seat, felt the sweat creeping down his spine, and cleared his throat.

'I think I understand you, Arthur.'

Fuck you, Seymour. Fuck you.

'Good. Good. A change in attitude is what's called for, Christy. We all go through periods of disinterest, of boredom, especially in this job. Don't think I'm not sympathetic to this. But we can't continue to overlook the results, now can we? Whatever it is that's bothering you, it's about time you snapped out of it,' he said, before nodding dismissively, reaching for the sheaf of papers in front of him and shuffling them brusquely, an indication that the meeting had reached an end.

In the long corridor following their little exchange, Christy considered the words that had been spoken, and wondered if there had been a threat implicit in the warning given. Was there something searching and insistent in that hard little glance Arthur gave him? Did he hear weariness in the headmaster's voice, the weight of disappointment and the anticipation of failures still to come?

The words and their tone stayed with him, bouncing off the inside of his skull, as he made his way down the corridor in the direction of his next class. Sure, the

Leaving Cert results in Geography, History and English
hadn't been great, he reasoned with himself, but they
were no worse than the last few years. Certainly no
worse than the grades in some of the other subjects. He
felt the heat of a new anger crawling up his neck and
flooding his face. Why him? Why had he been singled
out for this dressing down when there were so many
others on the staff far worse than him? Hell, there was
a whole assortment of alcoholics and pedagogues and
narcoleptics for Arthur to pick from. But after fifteen
years of service to the school, that was how he was to be
treated? With snide comments and faithlessness and a
weary despondency? Christy understood the tone it was
swathed in, that underlying current of mistrust. The
twitch in Arthur's moustache and the sneaky, sideways
glance that had accompanied the remarks said
everything there was to say.

But as the day passed, the sting of those remarks eased
away, withdrawing into the recesses of his memory. In
fact, the anger and irritation that ensued seemed to
trickle away quicker than they probably should have.
The truth was, Christy admitted to himself, he really
didn't care too much one way or the other. The passion
he had once possessed for the job – and there had been
a time when he was a committed and dedicated teacher
– had ebbed away long ago. Was it during the fourth or
fifth year that it began to dawn on him, the dullness of
everything, the routine monotony? Was it before or
after Jim was born that he began to feel the nagging
doubts, the awful, cloying regret?

*

It had been arranged two weeks ago that he accompany his fifth-year history class to the cinema that afternoon. The film was *Downfall*, a German movie about Hitler's last days in the bunker. Not a cheery prospect, and part of him balked at the idea of the boys groaning their way through the subtitles. He briefly considered feigning illness to get out of it, wanting to make the most of the opportunity while Sorcha was away. But it was on the curriculum, and he felt it might be no bad thing to sit in the dark for a couple of hours, losing his mind to the fantasies that had been lurking there since the affair began a week ago.

When they arrived at the cinema, there was a mad dash from the cars they had travelled in across to the small, depressed-looking movie theatre, and Christy had to endure several heart-stopping moments watching his students dashing out in front of moving vehicles. The foyer was empty, apart from a few stragglers, so that the boisterous presence of the boys seemed to overwhelm the place. Christy queued for the tickets, an envelope of money in his pocket, while his class busied themselves at the vending machines. Stepping away from the booth, ticket stubs in hand, he caught sight of Mike Atwood, another teacher and a colleague from the early days before Mike had defected to the girls' school. He was sitting on the steps waiting for the theatre to open, and there was a dejected look about him that made Christy forget for a moment that they had never really gotten along. Instead he found himself crossing the foyer in long purposeful strides, smiling as if in recognition of an old friend, something he was not.

'Mike!' he announced, offering his hand and feeling the weak, clammy grip before withdrawing it quickly. 'It's been forever since we've seen you. How've you been?'

'Oh, not so bad, I suppose,' was the response of a man making a strenuous effort to pitch his voice somewhere towards cheerful optimism, but falling well short of the mark, sliding back down into the trough of his anxiety.

'Are you going to see this movie then?'

'Yes. I thought I might as well. I see most of the movies they put on here.'

His eyes seemed bulbous and shot through with blood vessels as they cast about him warily at the boys scattered around the foyer.

There wasn't much to say between them, and it wasn't long before Christy found himself asking the inevitable question.

'And tell me,' he began, 'any luck on the job front?'

It was common knowledge that Mike had been fired after an ill-conceived, and by all accounts, disappointing love affair with a student. The news had surprised Christy at the time, having always thought of Mike as sexually ambivalent. But apparently, he had become obsessed with the shadowy delights that lay beneath the gym slip of one Angela Lennox. It was three months before Mike discovered the vast plains of vacuity that occupied her pretty head and called time on the affair. But the damage had been done. Angela had taken her empty head and her gym slip treasures and gone crying all the way to the school board. What happened after that was brief and stunningly painful for Mike, followed by a long period of dispirited unemployment and reckless self-loathing. Sitting on the steps, shaking his head grimly, Christy couldn't help but feel a wave of regret for this desolate soul sitting bunched in his anorak. There was something so lost about him that before he knew it, Christy was suggesting that they should go for a drink some time, the two of them. Catch up on old times. Mike seemed to brighten a little at the prospect.

Later, as he sat in the darkened auditorium, watching the flickering sequence of images on the screen, Christy wondered what it was that had compelled him to proffer such an invitation. No doubt it was an impulse born out of pity, but secretly he suspected that it had more to do with those new stirrings of benevolence inside him. It was certainly that, but also the common ground between them – they both knew what it was like to succumb to those dark forbidden desires that can haunt a man's days and nights.

The shuffling, agitated movements of the boys died down as they became sucked into the world of Hitler and Eva Braun and the dark chaotic days deep in that Berlin bunker, and in the darkness, Christy wondered whether Mike too had felt those first shocking feelings

of excitement tinged with fear at the start of his
romance with Angela Lennox. Did he find at times,
while engaged in routine, pedestrian things like teaching a class, or doing the dishes, or putting petrol in the
car, that the realisation of what he had done, of what he
had become engaged in, hit him forcefully, so strong
and surprising like a sudden shock, like a punch in the
belly, that he felt winded by it? Even at that moment, in
the quiet solitude of the cinema, Christy felt himself
reddening, remembering Lara's leg slung over his hip,
her arms light and slender entwined about his neck and
the long steady strokes as she dragged her foot up and
down the back of his legs, her eyes lost to him as he
looked at her face, her gaze inverted, that glorious
darkness, a pool of mystery. He had felt his heart
stirring in his chest as if each ventricle were pumping
out something new, something raw and powerful. 'All
my life, I have wanted this,' he told her. 'All my life.'

A week had passed since that glorious first
afternoon, and in that week he had experienced such
tumultuous feelings, such sensory delights. He thought
of their chaste evening walks, the thrill caused by the
sudden brush of her hand against his, the pounding in
his heart as he clambered up over the rocks after her, up
to where the grass grew long above the lip of the land,
where they were able to sink into the sand, and he could
feel the press of her lips against his all over again. And
then that stolen opportunity, a diamond glittering in his
memory, of a secret entanglement in the back seat of his
car parked in the deserted grounds of the abandoned

and dilapidated Reen Roe Hotel. The risks they had taken took his breath away. But the memory of those stolen kisses, those deep bodily explorations, were stored up in his mind and savoured during the time when he was away from her.

On screen Eva Braun was dancing on a table in a backless dress. She was all flashing sequins, red lipstick and tight blonde curls. But she held his attention for only a fleeting moment before his imagination wheeled away again, bringing him back into the arms of his lover. He loved the way her head bent to the side when she looked at him in those private moments, deep and intent, yet always with that humour in her eyes. He loved how her hair fell across her face and how she reached up to swipe it back – the curve of her slender arm, those long fingers. He loved the sprinkle of freckles on the bridge of her nose, the slight overlap between her two front teeth – those tiny imperfections, how they made her so much more real, more perfect to him. His mind spent hours idling over the contours of her body – her narrow hips, the crevice of her back, the languid roll of her shoulders as she lifted and stretched – or reliving the taste of her smooth lips, her salty skin. Last night he had kissed her eyes, had felt the delicate flutter of lashes beneath his lips. These things, these details, consumed him. They fed the longing inside him that lasted from the moment he left her until they were together again.

At lunchtimes, he battled with the temptation to call to Crazy Prices just to catch a glimpse of her, the flash

of her smile. And after school he sat in his study,
fidgeting or pacing the floor, or trying to tap out a few
solitary words on his dismal novel, the end of it
receding ever further away from him, all the time
whiling away the hours until dinner. He wolfed down
his food, anxious to be away, out into the evening
sunlight. It troubled him that a change in the weather
was imminent, fearing what it would mean for them,
praying that the Indian summer would last a little
longer. At least, tonight, he didn't need to worry about
it. Sorcha was away, and the possibilities that opened up
to them filled him with a new excitement. He stirred in
his seat, a flush of adrenalin passing through him, and
breathed quickly, feeling the desire climbing his spine
again.

Through the blur of his thoughts, he was aware of
movement on the screen in front of him, terse voices in
German slamming against his eardrums, his eyes too
distracted to pass over the subtitles, and something else
– a smell invading his nostrils, thick and piney, stirring
something up from the fund of memory. A miasma of
blue smoke two aisles in front of him confirmed his
suspicions, and before he had even risen from his seat to
investigate which one of his charges was smoking pot in
the cinema, he already knew who it would be.

There was an immense deal of shifting and private
grumbling as he made his way past pulled-in knees,
stepping on toes, and then strode down to where Carl
Ring was sitting, his knees folded up in front of him and
resting against the seat in front, a fat reefer clutched

between his thumb and index finger while he peered at the screen through the misty veil of marijuana smoke.

'You,' Christy said tersely, pointing at Carl with a stabbing finger, then pointing at the exit. 'Come with me.'

Carl moved his head slowly, elegantly, addressing Christy with a vaguely confused, condescending look as if to say 'And you are?'

'Come on,' Christy persevered, aware now of the heads turning around to glare at him, the tut-tuts and whispered irritations emanating from the shadows. 'Out. Now.'

Turning on his heel, he felt Carl's lumbering movements behind him, and emerging into the light of the foyer, blinking rapidly after the darkness, he turned to look at the boy, suddenly enraged to find that he was still clasping the reefer in his grubby hands with their bitten-down nails.

'Give me that,' he hissed, snatching it and hurrying to the ash can, stubbing it out viciously.

Turning back, he walked slowly, observing the boy, taking in Carl's deep-set brown eyes above high cheekbones, a long aquiline nose and the full lips of a tyrant's mouth. His hair stood at crazy angles from his head, but the face beneath was a handsome one despite the hard mask of acne that had formed like a shell over Carl's cheeks and chin, interspersed with black stubble like iron filings. The stubble gathered in a heavy shadow above the mouth and Christy watched that mouth as it drew back into a sneer.

'And you can wipe that smirk off your face too.'

Carl smiled serenely, looked away, and then looked back again, his face more serious this time, a patient expression coming down over it.

'You know you could be expelled for what just happened back there.'

'Why? It's not like we're in school.'

'That's not the point. Smoking marijuana is illegal.'

'Not in Holland.'

'We're not in Holland, Carl, or hadn't you noticed.'

'Sorry sir, but I thought we were in fuckin' Germany.'

'Don't you swear in front of me.'

Carl rolled his eyes and whispered 'whatever' under his breath. Christy felt the anger in him beginning to rise, sweat beading on his forehead near the line of his hair. The boy was the same height as him, so that they were standing eye to eye, and he held Carl's stare, saw the flicker of rage mirrored in those pointed eyes, and willed himself not to lose his temper. This boy was a troublemaker. Christy knew of other teachers who frequently refused to have him in their class, who shouted and screamed and ranted at him, who sent a litany of letters home to his mother. Christy had had his fair share of run-ins with Carl, perhaps more than most. But Christy didn't do any of those things. He couldn't see the point, recognised the futility of it. Yet still he felt the boy continued to test him, trying to push him over the edge.

'Look, Carl,' he began, adopting a reasonable tone, trying to be fair with the boy, trying to level with him. 'You just can't go around smoking pot in public places.

Or anywhere, for that matter. You could get into serious trouble. And I don't mean with the school, I mean the police. Is that what you want? A conviction for drug use before you even do your Leaving Cert?'

Carl shrugged. He didn't look overly concerned by this, so Christy took a different tack.

'You do know that if you smoke too much of that stuff it could lead to impotence.'

'Not so far, it hasn't,' he countered, sharp as a tack, that sneer nudging its way back over his face, and all at once, Christy had a vision of the boy recounting this conversation for the lads on the way home, embroidering it of course to make Christy appear more stupid, more gawkish and imbecilic, while redeeming Carl as the quick-thinker, snapping out one-liners to floor the gombeen teacher.

'Well, whatever.' He decided it was best to let the innuendo slide. 'But I'm giving you fair warning, Carl. You continue along this path and there'll be nothing but trouble. And if I get wind of this happening again—'

'Yeah, yeah,' Carl cut him off. 'Can I go back inside now sir? I'm missing most of the movie. You know it's my education that you're jeopardising here.'

The insolence jumped up at Christy, socking him in the mouth. But there were other things on his mind. And maybe it was the thought of a Friday evening, alone with Lara, or maybe it was the sudden image of her leg slung over his hip, but he nodded his head at the boy in defeat.

'All right,' he said. 'Off you go.'

And left it at that.

Later, as they left the cinema, he glimpsed the hunched shoulders of Mike Atwood leaving from the side exit, and he thought again of their conversation and felt a sudden stab of guilt. Guilt for what he had taken on with this affair, the betrayal he had instigated. But then he stopped in his tracks, his breath snagging in his chest, caught up in the vivid memory of her legs wrapped around him, locking him to her. His mind drifted easily as he followed his charges out into the sun, his eyes gazing inwardly to the softness of her limbs, her skin darkened from years of exposure to the sun, the tangle of hair and all the pleasure he found there. These images drew an ache within him, the pain of longing, every impulse in his body impelling him to go to her.

13

It seemed to me that everywhere there were people kissing, embracing. They were all around me – in work, on the street, in the pub at lunchtime. *Does this go on all the time?* I asked myself, *this pressing of flesh against flesh, these open displays of affection?* Or had I not noticed that they had always been there, so lost was I in the daze of my own thoughts?

At work, music was piped through the speakers, and lately I had noticed love songs spilling out into the vast space. I imagined there was some psychology behind this, that love songs nurture an atmosphere of generosity and well-being, which no doubt promotes spending. Nonetheless, it amazed me how shoppers could go about their business, loading up their trolleys, without once pausing to listen to those words sighing through the sound system. When I took my break and slipped outside for a cigarette, around where the empty pallets were piled high against the wall, I stumbled across a couple kissing. They broke away from each other, red-faced and smiling. 'Sorry,' I mumbled, embarrassed, before stepping away.

At lunchtime, Ger and I walked briskly down to the Anchor, falling in line behind a small group of men in shirts and ties emerging from an office in front of us, their talk punctuated with easy laughter. They smiled across at the young women sitting outside the Red Rose Café, and in those glances exchanged, I saw a sexual recognition, a flirtation. As we ate lunch, I was transfixed by a couple at the next table, the girl stroking the hairs on her boyfriend's forearms in small, cat-like movements that seemed to me unbearably sensual.

It seemed to be an epidemic. These lingering touches, the intimacy of limbs, all rubbed up against me, swamping my imagination, reminding me of what had passed between us.

'So what's new with you?' Ger asked, a bemused look on his face. 'I mean, you're like a different person. You look different. Don't get me wrong – you look great. Are you on something? Some kind of health kick or something? You look kind of glowing. It's like there's a spring in your step. And I'm not the only one who's noticed. Just yesterday, Pamela from the bakery was saying the exact same thing. She reckons there must be a man in your life. But I said that's impossible, 'cos if there was, you'd tell me. Right?'

The first time had been fast, almost frantic, like both of us were worried that the other would change their mind halfway through. I felt the twisted tension in him, and my own urgency bubbling and simmering, wanting that intimacy so badly, clasping him to me, and as he gave a high strangled cry, something fluttered within me, a glorious relief. The second time was slower, more languorous. We moved to the bedroom and fell against one another beneath the sheets. We made love slowly, savouring each lingering kiss, each sensory delight. We didn't speak, the only sounds caused by the friction of our bodies, the moans and cries, and the movement of the bed beneath us.

We made love until we grew hungry, ravenous, and he got up and left the room and some moments later I heard the hiss and crackle of eggs spitting in oil on the frying pan. When he came back, he was carrying a tray with two plates piled high with buttered bread, runny eggs and bacon, the rind all brown and crispy, and two mugs of coffee. I saw that he had put back on his T-shirt and shorts and I pulled the sheet up to my armpits, resting my plate in the dip the sheet made between my knees.

'Cheers,' he said, raising his mug, and I clinked it with mine, and we sat there together, a comradely spirit weaving between us as we ate our food. The eggs were salty, a film of grease left coating the palate of my mouth, and I realised that I hadn't eaten much in days.

'This is great,' I said, tucking in hungrily, and he turned to me, giving me that curious little smile, and said, 'Yes, it's wonderful,' and I could see he didn't mean the food.

There was a bottle of wine in the kitchen and I thought briefly about getting it and bringing it into the bedroom, cracking it open between us, but part of me felt a little shy at getting out from beneath the sheets and being naked in front of him, and another part of me felt that I really didn't need a drink right now. I was still floating along on what had just passed between us. It occurred to me also that it might not be a good idea for him to drink with me – Sorcha might grow suspicious at alcohol on his breath. The smell of sex hung in the bedroom air between us, and I wondered whether he would shower before he left. I thought, too, about how he would explain his long absence. My mind became cluttered with all these new deceits, shooting guilt through what we had just done.

He picked the plate from my lap, stacked it with his and put them on the floor. Then he leaned across and wrapped his arm around my shoulder, drawing me to him, and I leaned into his chest, felt the warmth of him through his cotton T-shirt, his arms tight about me, and my guilt evaporated. There was a stillness in me that I hadn't felt in so long. He held me there for several minutes and I began to feel sleepy listening to the thrum of his heartbeat.

'I have to go,' he said softly, his voice deep and echoing through the wall of his chest. I didn't want him to leave and held on to him more tightly, feeling his sigh as he fixed his lips to my scalp through the tangle of hair.

'Lara,' he murmured.

'Don't go.'

'I don't want to, but it's getting late.'

'Just a little longer,' I pleaded, feeling the ache of separation opening up in my chest.

He squeezed me tight, with all the strength he could muster so that it hurt just a little, before releasing me wordlessly. He stood over the bed looking down at me, a little wistful look about his eyes and mouth. And there was something else there, a longing. In the short time since that first afternoon together, I hadn't been able to stop thinking about him, that dark need in his eyes.

A change was happening inside me, I could feel it. Waking in the morning, I felt it taking hold of my limbs, that sweet, heady sensation, that busy commotion. It propelled me into a series of actions, it carried me through the hours and minutes and days between our meetings. The time I spent away from him was accompanied by the sweet taste of memory of the times we had been together, those few stolen hours here and there, the long quiet walks, the sweet intimacies between us in his darkened car, and one glorious afternoon in the heat and comfort of my bed. But the taste was tainted by a large dose of guilt. Although we didn't speak of his wife and family, it still troubled me – don't think that it didn't. But I had become expert at managing my thoughts, at tucking them away in the dark recesses of my mind. There was a happiness about him that I found strangely endearing, an almost painful innocence to the openness of his feelings. The way he looked at me sometimes with such unabashed joy made me worry that he might be falling in love. He didn't use that word, but it whispered on my skin with the touch and trail of his fingers. I felt it in the tenderness of his kiss, the softness of all the other words he spoke. But mostly, it was there in his eyes, that shadow of intensity, that gleam of happiness that I knew only I could bring. His whole body betrayed his deepest emotions – he couldn't help it.

I was distrustful of my own feelings, aware that I had always been prone to falling abruptly in and out of love. My inconstant heart was not discerning. But the change in me, this new happiness, this ready and eager benevolence, flooded my whole being, warming the coldest parts of me, so that I was disposed to look on the bright side of things, to be positive. There was something about him that I found comforting, that I had always found comforting. The pain was still there. I couldn't get free of it, but I didn't feel it every minute. Perhaps it was just an illusion, a trick of the mind, this temporary banishment. But even if it was a trick, I was glad of the reprieve, the relief it provided.

I was disposed to think better of people, to look brightly at the world. That was what love did to you, wasn't it? Favoured your outlook, so that you see the positive in place of the negative? Perhaps that's the reason why I wasn't upset by the postcard that landed on my doormat that morning. Under different circumstances, it might have sent me over the edge. But I was too buoyed up by recent events to allow myself to be floored by it.

When I had found it on the doormat that morning, I had felt the tightness in my chest, the shortness of breath and that hot tide rinsing over me, the same feelings evoked by its two predecessors. This one was from Chile, the Atacama Desert, the place where Alejo left me. I had stood in my nightdress, feeling the heaviness in my legs as I remembered that dusty place, the sick feeling in my stomach as he sat on the bed looking down at me with those sad, mournful eyes, saying, 'No more, Lara. No more.' The postcard was of the Valley of the Moon and my eyes feasted on the blueness of the sky pitched against the grey-gold of the sand and rock, rising up and spreading out into that lunar landscape. It could be another planet, so different was it to the lush greenness to which I had been transplanted. The postmark was from San Pedro, the last place we stayed in together, that frontier town on the borders with Bolivia and Argentina, a pocket of pain in my memory.

But today I chose to remember it in a different way. Disposed to look positively at the world, I chose to remember San Pedro as it was the first time we went there together, that rosy time in the first burst of love, when we were blissful in our poverty.

We arrived there tired and dry mouthed after the long journey over several days, passing from vehicle to vehicle. Starting in Arequipa, we had hitched a lift down to the border between Peru and Chile before being deposited in Arica, where I had stopped at a supermarket and given thanks for a toilet that flushed and running water that I splashed over my face, stripping down to my bra, water lapping my underarms and back and stomach. We reached San Pedro during the night and found space to pitch our tent at a campsite outside the town. It was dark when we got there, and noisy with barking dogs and braying beasts. It wasn't until morning that I saw San Pedro in all its coolness and quirkiness, its narrow streets lined with short, squat clay-coloured buildings, its pretty square with whitewashed church blazing in the sun, Spanish and colonial looking, but simple with its low roof and short steeple, its humble hanging bell.

Alejo found a place in the corner of the square and set out his stall. It was such a relaxed little town that no one bothered him, no one was troubled by our presence there. I left him to it, wandering off alone, looking for a book exchange and sauntering through the market aisles, poking my nose into the various haciendas, the shops where you could rent mountain bikes or sand-boards, the pottery and jewellery emporiums with their brightly coloured beads, fishing for ideas, for new designs, looking to spy something I could make myself.

Back at the campsite that evening, I got chatting to some English guys who were driving their minibus out to the Valley of the Moon to watch the sun setting. Begging a lift, Alejo and I sat in the back between their boards and thermarests as the van rolled and lurched over the humps in the desert. Outside, I watched the sky change colour, becoming a deeper, darker blue, indigo. Rocks rose up out of the sand like pillars, rugged and jagged in shape, and the sand itself seemed to climb upwards into great hills so that it felt like we were driving into a giant sand dune. I looked across at Alejo and saw his face transformed into a watchful awe, and then he saw me and the corners of his mouth rose into a grin and he winked at me so that I felt warm despite the cold growing steadily in the air.

The minibus stopped and we all got out and stood there looking around us. We seemed to be standing in the middle of a vast plain, grey and dusty, surrounded on all sides by steep sand hills.

'This way,' Alejo said to me, taking hold of my hand and leading me towards a sloping hill where the sand was pocked with footprints.

The climb was tough, particularly towards the end where the sand was soft and our feet sank deep into it and the muscles in my thighs began to ache. And then we were at the summit. Sand poured down from our feet into deep valleys far below, giant fissures in the desert, like the land had been wrenched apart, plates banging and repelling each other in an earthquake. There were people gathering along the peak, moving in a line towards a high point in the distance where the sun was dipping down. But Alejo and I peeled away from the others. We found a different peak and picked our way across the rock and sand until we found a ledge to sit on. We sat there together and watched the sun slipping down, casting the whole place in a glow of orangey-red. Peeking past my feet, I felt my heart jump up into my throat at the sheer drop down into the crack in the earth.

'Do you think it looks like the moon?' he asked me.

'Yes,' I said and he began nodding his head slowly in that way that I was just becoming used to.

After three weeks together, we were starting to become familiar with each other's traits and mannerisms – the way he liked to touch, to use his senses, to fill his chest with air and puff it out like he was sucking life itself from the atmosphere around him. His sudden laugh, so light and airy and ripped through with joy. The way he grew quiet and solemn when he was being thoughtful or serious. He seemed that way now, a faraway look in his eyes, his thoughts far beyond me, and I wanted suddenly to lighten the moment, to hear him laugh.

Looking out at the lunar landscape around us, I began to sing: 'Fly me to the moon, and let me sing among the stars.'

He looked at me with that wrinkling of his nose like I was crazy. He didn't know the song and shook his head at me, and still I kept singing.

'Let me see what spring is like on Jupiter and Mars.'

'You're crazy.'

'In other words, please be true. In other words…'

'I love you.'

He didn't sing these words, but said them – slowly and clearly.

'You do know the song,' I said, feeling my heart beating loud and slow in my chest, the colour leaping up into my face.

'No.'

'Then…'

'No song. Just that.'

Just that.

That was the first time he said it. There were other times after, and I can remember most of them. He didn't say it often. We weren't the types to go around telling each other how much we loved each other all the time, as if needing to reassure each other as to how we felt. But I remember that time the best, because it was the first. And because it was so unexpected, the way it seemed to come from nowhere, its arrival perfect and beautiful as the sun grew red and huge over the Atacama before dropping away into night.

I was lying on the bench to the side of the porch, smoking a long, lazy joint and thinking of that setting sun over the desert, when I saw him coming. His stride seemed purposeful; his upper body bent forward as if leaning into the wind, but there was no wind that evening. Instead the air was strangely still, like a held breath, as if waiting for something. Gulls cried out before swooping low over the sea and I felt my heartbeat quickening as he trudged across the beach through the shingle. I closed my eyes, feigning sleep. I didn't yet know how it would be between us. It was so long since I'd been in this position that I felt self-conscious, unsure of myself, a certain weakness expressing itself through this pretended doze. That evening with Alejo in the Valley of the Moon, I was so sure of my own feelings. But now, everything inside me seemed opaque and indeterminate. And Christy was an altogether different kind of man. It was so long since I had felt any kind of warmth inside that my heart felt sort of hollow and I didn't trust my own desire to fill it.

His step as he came up the stairs was slow and certain and there was a pause when he got to the top, before his footfall came towards me, and my heart stilled itself, my whole body poised for his touch.

'Lara,' he said softly, his voice hovering close to my head, and I felt his fingers touching my forearm, just for an instant, leaving a warmth on my skin that reached somewhere deep within me, and I could tell before I opened my eyes that there was desire in his face.

'Hey,' I said sleepily, opening my eyes and stretching languidly.

Behind him, the sky was filled with bands of red and purple, the sinking sun lost behind the clouds, and his face seemed open, taken with a new optimism. I felt him touch me again, his hand grasping my ankle, his fingers hot against my skin, and his eyes were hard and bright, filling with something dark and needful, and I felt an almost electrical current in my legs, sparks charging up through my body.

He sat down next to me, and for a moment we were both silent.

'I haven't been able to stop thinking about you,' he said at last in that low honey voice of his.

Something leapt within my chest, a wild hope, and I felt so grateful for it that I had to hold myself back from springing into his arms. Instead, I uncurled my legs slowly and reached for his hand, feeling his fingers instinctively lacing through mine.

'I've been thinking about you too,' I said.

Shyness crept over me, and I felt a slow blush spreading up my neck. He held my gaze and I recognised the same wild hope, the same crazily happy expectation in his eyes.

He leaned in and kissed me for a long time, his hand cupped around my face, fingers combed into my hair, and it didn't take long for the desire in me to be whipped alive, my limbs reaching for him, looking to tangle themselves about his.

'Sorcha is away for the night,' he whispered into the crook of my neck, and despite the lurch I got at the mention of her name, there was that sneaking knowledge of opportunity shouting down the persistent question in my head: *What about his wife?*

'Come inside,' I said, getting to my feet and leading him in.

Almost as soon as the door had closed behind us, he was kissing me again. I couldn't see his face in the shadows, all I could hear was the gentle hush of the ocean and the slow, steady beat of possibility.

14

He took her to a small pub called An Sugán. From the moment he drew back the door, she felt a wave of conviviality washing over her, drawing her in. They stood at the entrance and looked around.

'What do you think?' Neil asked.

Sorcha observed the crowded room, taking in the low ceiling, the deep green walls with their racing prints and a heavily framed painting of Daniel O'Connell, and the fire burning brightly in the grate.

'It's perfect.'

They found a table next to the fire and sat down facing each other. The flames crackled and spat in the grate beside them and for a moment, the first since they had met earlier that afternoon, they were at a loss for words.

'I hope you're hungry,' he began after the waiter brought the menus.

'Starving.'

'The seafood here is first rate.'

'Yummy.'

Yummy? Why had she said a ridiculous thing like that? What was the matter with her, using childish words? It wasn't as if she was with her children. Here she was at dinner with a strange man, the whole night studded with possibilities, and all she had to say for herself was—

'John Dory for me, I think,' Neil said, folding his menu decisively. 'How about you?'

Her eyes scanned the list, her mind frantically turning over the possibilities. Why did she feel so nervous?

'Em...oh, yes. The black sole. It looks—'

'Yummy?'

Looking up suddenly, she caught his eye, blue and winking with merriment, as a smile slowly spread across his face, broad and toothy, and she began to laugh. She couldn't help herself. It was nerves on her part, and maybe on his too, but she felt the relief of it, like letting all the air out of her lungs, her insides relaxing.

They gave their orders and he asked for a bottle of Chardonnay, checking if that was okay with her, and she smiled and nodded, watching him hand the menu back. He was wearing a light blue shirt with navy box stripes and little cuff links with no tie. The shirt looked crisp and well ironed, the blue bringing out the colour of his eyes, and it crossed her mind that he must have ironed it himself. She had a vision of him standing over an ironing board in that humble cottage, earnestly working through those creases, and the thought of this touched her.

The waiter poured the wine, and suddenly bold, she raised her glass to his.

'To us,' she said and he followed suit, clinking her glass and repeating, 'To us.'

At the party in her sister's house the previous winter, Margot had taken her to one side and pointed out to her – discreetly, of course – the various people in the room engaged in adulterous relationships. 'The woman over there with the purple jumper and the glasses? Her and the tall, handsome one with the Kevin Costner look. And did you see the woman Jeff was talking to, the one with the blonde hair? For years she's been sleeping with Edward, who I just introduced you to. *Years.* Everyone knows about it.' At the time, she had felt a level of disquiet over these revelations. She had never thought of herself as particularly prudish, but these infidelities seemed to bother her. It stayed with her for days, Margot's words rolling around inside her head like marbles. It was some time later before it finally dawned on her what had irritated her so much. It was Margot's tone as she pointed out these sexual pairings. It had seemed boastful, as if she were proud to have all these adulterous people counted among her friends, as if it lent an air of glamour to the occasion. Sorcha had felt baffled and quietly disheartened by this attitude.

She wondered to herself what Margot would make of her own little sister telling a lie to her family, a lie that involved Margot herself, in order to spend the evening in the company of a man who was not her husband, next to this crackling fire, eating fat crispy chips with fish so tender it broke free of itself and crumbled with the slightest press of the tines of her fork. For a second her mind wandered beyond the meal and what might happen afterwards before she pulled back, steadying herself, not ready to consider that just yet.

'So I finally rang Stella,' he told her, fingering the stem of his wine glass. 'She's decided not to go for it.'

'No.' She put down her knife and fork, feeling a twinge of sadness for him. 'Neil. I'm sorry.'

'It's no big deal. Hardly a surprise when I hadn't heard from her in all this time.'

'Still. Did she give you a reason?'

He smiled then, and above the flickering glow of the candlelight, she saw his face, those gentle eyes, the seriousness of that straight mouth, such a dignified face, and she thought she could imagine him as a boy, all solemn eyed and watchful.

'She said they were too similar to the stuff she sourced in Dingle. That mine isn't original enough to warrant a separate purchase.'

'What?'

'It's no big deal,' he said again.

'But that's ridiculous,' she gasped, feeling the bloom of anger inside her. 'I've seen the stuff from Dingle and it's hardly similar at all, and certainly nowhere near as good.'

'It doesn't matter.'

'This has nothing to do with the quality of your work. This is Stella being embarrassed about the state she was in that night and being too childish and bloody minded to get over it.'

'Sorcha.'

She looked up then. It was the gentleness about the way he said her name that made her do it, and looking at his face, she realised how worked up she had become, how shrill her voice had grown. She must sound crazy. This man in his blue shirt with his kind eyes must think her insane. But he didn't appear to. He smiled at her in a way that was easy and companionable before refilling her glass.

'Sorry,' she murmured.

'Don't be. I'm flattered that you're offended on my behalf.'

She watched his hands as he replaced the bottle in the bucket beside the table, noticed the size and breadth of his fingers. There was strength in those hands, power in the grip. A raised vein on the back of his hand ran straight up under the cuff of his sleeve and she found her imagination running after it, tracing it like a cord over his forearm, up, up to his shoulders, narrow for a man, certainly not as broad as Christy's. Instantly she shook the thought from her head. She would not go there, would not start making comparisons, would not think of Christy at all. So far neither one of them had mentioned him. And yet, he had been weaving in and out of her thoughts from the moment he had kissed her goodbye that morning. She kept thinking of the warmth in his voice, the sudden kindness of his breakfast gesture, and thoughts of him at home in his study, earnestly tapping away at his novel, brought an ache to her chest. Neil hadn't asked her what she had told him in so far as where she was, or where she would be spending the night. A memory came to her of his bedroom, Stella passed out on that messy bed, and she felt the blood gathering in her cheeks at the thought of going back there again.

A silence fell between them. It seemed to arrive without warning, and lingered while the waiter cleared away their plates. Sorcha fingered her wine glass, drank again from it. She watched a bead of water trailing down the glass from where her thumb had been. She followed its progress with her eyes all the way down the stem.

The silence refused to lift. It seemed to magnify the gap between them and she became aware of the placement of her hands, and of the hands themselves, nails that were short and unpainted. She felt mildly ashamed of them. The insecurity took hold of her and she felt suddenly large and ungainly. It had taken her hours of thought and prevarication before she had finally chosen her red silk crossover blouse that tied in an elegant looping bow at the back, along with a slender black skirt with a daring slit, as her outfit for the evening. She thought it would make her feel elegant, regal, sexy. But now in the blistering ill-ease of the persistent silence, she felt prickly beads of sweat forming on her back beneath her bra strap, followed by a nip of panic that the sweat might seep into the silk, forming little ragged circles. Just what was she doing here anyway, having dinner with a man she hardly knew? She had a sudden premonition of the awkwardness of paying the bill, splitting it between them, Neil insisting that he pay in a display of chivalry.

Perhaps he was feeling the same way, thinking the same thing. She looked across at him, watched him studying the beam above the bar. He was looking at it intently, his arms folded over his chest, his head held to one side. He had a small, neat face, and she felt in that moment that there was something quite delicate about his features, and wondered suddenly what type of man he must be, inviting a married woman to dinner and by implication (owing to the distance she had to travel) to stay the night?

Their initial meeting, the thing that had connected them – Stella Naseby's verbose, rude, embarrassing drunkenness – now seemed flimsy and weak, wholly removed from what they were now. And all those long, lingering conversations on the phone seemed to have evaporated, losing their magic now that they were here together face to face. At that moment, they were just two people, nursing their own quiet grievances. They seemed to her a pathetic pair.

After a minute, the waiter brought over their desserts, a welcome interruption, and looking down at the creamy tiramisu in front of her, she regretted choosing it, feeling sick at the sight of all that cream, those heaped-up layers of soggy sponge. Across the table, her companion was going at a slice of cheesecake with his fork, pausing briefly to look across at her.

'Would you like to try some?' he asked.

'No thanks. I don't eat cheese.'

Why on earth did she say that? For a start, it wasn't true. Why could she not just have said no thanks and left it at that? How pathetic she was. And now the silence had opened up again between them, and she thought of passing the whole night under the dark morose blanket of it, and a shiver went through her. She was acutely aware of the weight of this occasion, this sad little dinner and all it had come to mean to her in the week of planning it and thinking on it. The candle-light, the wine – she felt the burden of expectation pressing down on them, the questions that remained unspoken over what would happen next.

The waiter approached.

'Everything okay?'

'Great,' they answered, beaming up at him.

How dull he must think she is. Glancing across at his head bent over the last of his dessert, it occurred to her that he must be regretting this whole thing, must be dreading bringing her back to his place and having to endure the whole painful process of getting this over with. She thought again of Christy, how he had kissed her goodbye, the fleeting joy of his backward glance as he went out the door. She thought, too, of her children, their faults and frailties – Jim's reticence, Avril's moodiness – but despite everything, she loved them still. The distance between them seemed to magnify that love, and the thought that they were unaware of this secret betrayal she had orchestrated brought a sudden pang of longing for them, so great it was physical.

'Would you like some coffee?' he asked.

'I'm all right, thanks.'

'Tea?'

'No, fine, thanks.'

The silence hovered over them, and she couldn't bring herself to look at him. And then he reached across the table and took her hand in his. The gesture surprised her, took her unaware, and looking up she saw his eyes fixed on her, patient and empathetic.

'Sorcha,' he said softly.

She felt the understanding in his voice, the shared feelings of awkwardness, insecurity tinged with longing, and the hard edges of the silence seemed to disintegrate, curling away into a mist.

'Let's get out of here,' he said solemnly.

To her great relief the silence didn't return. When they got back to his cottage and settled onto the sofa – shoes kicked off, her feet raised up beneath her – they sipped from glasses of Bailey's and talked. It was like tapping into their long luminous telephone conversations, the awkwardness of dinner evaporating in the renewed spirit of their friendship. They talked, it seemed, for hours, and part of her felt like she had slipped back in time to the first night they had met, the stillness of the cottage around them, this warmth at the centre of their conversation that seemed to draw the most closely guarded thoughts out of her.

'You were very quiet over dinner,' he commented. 'I was afraid you were beginning to regret coming here.'

'Regret? No.' She watched him carefully, the bare slope of his cheek running into the hollow of his eye.

'So what were you thinking about?'

She had been thinking about her husband, her children, and considered for a moment telling him something different, making something up, then decided against this. And as she told him, she watched his face, looking for a reaction, but he kept his eyes steady, his face an empty page.

'Sorcha,' he said slowly, 'have you always been faithful to him?'

She looked at him then, surprised by his question, the way it seemed to arrive so suddenly, and the emotion it stirred up within her.

'Yes,' she answered. She might have added *of course*.

She had heard people say that there is someone for everyone – a phrase that is trotted out as a comfort, she supposed, to appease those who are lonely, who feel incomplete. But of course, that wasn't true. For people did end up alone, didn't they? Some people spent their whole lives alone. And yet, Sorcha had chosen him. She had chosen Christy. It wasn't love at first sight; there was no thunderbolt, no sudden realisation. It had dawned on her slowly, that gentle side to his nature, the quiet, brooding spirit, all the passion that lay hidden beneath the surface. Three summers in a row he came to stay with his grandparents, and in the months leading up to that third summer, when she was in the last year of school and feeling anxious and impatient and fearful about what her life might become, she was touched by a new feeling, one that she couldn't readily identify. Anticipation at his arrival, excitement, perhaps, yet it was quieter than that. Maybe it was a kind of hope. And some time during that summer, she had sat with him on a wall outside The Point, drinking beer at the fading of the day. It was the first time they were alone that summer, and it seemed to her that they were both aware of it, a certain timidity entering the air between them. It was then that he had first shown her his notebook, the scribbled writing, his poems. There was a bashfulness about him that day, his face tanned, caught in the glow of the evening sun, a silent need in his eyes as she felt them on her, watching her as she read. She felt him looking – how could she not? – and it was all she could do to keep reading. 'It's not much,' he had said, and she had looked up then, 'just a few bits and pieces I've jotted down.' This look he had then – like he was a boy again, like the eagerness for her approval seemed to strip away the man he had become. And it was at that moment that she recognised the feeling for what it was. They say it can happen like that, don't they? That everything can change in an instant.

Neil was watching her carefully and she felt it must show in her face, that old love, grown tired and a little worn, but still there.

'So what are you doing here with me?' he asked softly.

He was looking at her thoughtfully, seriously, and in that instant she was unsure of everything. She thought of Stella's coldness, the spite of those names she had called her. She thought, too, of the aching sense of betrayal that had assailed her on finding that letter in Christy's study, the cold feelings of disappointment that had opened out within her. But she realised that she wasn't here for those reasons. Looking inside for an answer, she was confronted by darkness and doubt.

'I don't know,' she answered truthfully.

Everything seemed to still in that moment. Slowly, and with deliberateness, he leaned forward, placing his glass on the coffee table. He turned and looked at her for a long moment, before moving towards her, his hand going up to her cheek, fingers threading into her hair, and she watched his eyes and awaited his kiss. His mouth felt dry against hers, lips like paper, gently touching hers, soft, and yet...and yet... A protest rose up within her, so strong and unexpected, that she found herself pulling away from him. For a moment they sat there, stunned by her hasty withdrawal, the revulsion that seemed to be implied by this sudden retreat, and she felt instantly mortified.

'Oh God, I'm so sorry,' she said in a small, shocked voice, hardly able to bring herself to look at him.

But he just sat there saying nothing, and then slowly, with the same deliberateness, he retrieved his glass of Bailey's and sat back in the sofa. But despite the relaxed pose he aimed for, there was a stiffness about him now, and she felt the air prickle with awkwardness.

'Neil.'

'It's all right, Sorcha.'

'I feel so ashamed.'

'Don't be,' he said, but there was a hardness in his voice that she hadn't heard before, something accusatory.

It was clear to both of them that nothing further could happen between them. The knowledge of this wove through the air between them, enmeshed in awkward feelings of distance, of misunderstanding.

'I'm sorry,' she said again, taken with a new sense of failure, embarrassed by her own innocence, her lack of backbone. And yet, she felt relieved too. 'I thought I would be able to do this.'

'You still love him, don't you?'

His question surprised her, the tone it was asked in as much as the question itself. She sensed the reproach in it and had to check herself suddenly, felt the racing of blood through her veins, a lump in her throat.

'Yes,' she admitted in a small voice, feeling the truth of that statement. All night, he had been there in her thoughts. She carried them with her always, her family, and realised now that it was a burden she treasured. 'It's a strange thing. We were so young when we were married. Everything was new to us. I gave myself to him wholeheartedly, without doubt or regret. With hope. I don't think I could do that again, with some-one else.'

He nodded his head thoughtfully, then turned his head to her, giving her that long-eyed look again.

'Can I ask you a question?'

She nodded, apprehensive now.

'Do you think he's being faithful to you?'

She looked at him then, honing in on the doubt laced through his words. Faithful. Such an old-fashioned, solemn, far-off kind of word. Was her husband faithful to her? She believed that he was. It wasn't something she had ever questioned before, and yet she knew that marital infidelity was commonplace. All around her were instances of it. She remembered Margot's party, her sister gleefully pointing out adulterers. But Christy…

'Yes,' she said at last, arriving at her decision uncertainly, her voice quavering with a nagging doubt.

'Really?' he asked and the speed at which this word emerged from his mouth caused her to rock back from it.

'I think so,' she said, wavering. 'Why?'

He shrugged then.

'I don't know. I suppose I just thought you might have found it a little odd that he spends so much time with your cousin.'

'Lara?'

'I'm just saying—'

'It's not that much time. He's just helping her get settle in, fixing her car for her and that.'

'Right, of course,' he said, appeasing her now.

'And sometimes he bumps into her on the beach in the evenings, but there's nothing wrong with that.'

'Of course not. And I'm sure you see as much of her as he does.'

They let that sit there between them for a moment, both of them knowing that she had told him of the awkwardness between her and Lara, a friendship that had been forced and difficult in childhood and now seemed prickly and remote as adults.

'You think there's something between them.'

'Sorcha, come on. What do I know?' he said amicably, trying to make amends. 'So what if there was history between them once? That was like a million years ago now, I'm sure.'

She watched him all the time he said this. And now, as he took a final drink from his glass, she realised what he had done, what he had nudged out from her. This seed of doubt. That is what he had wanted to achieve, this harsh little cut, this subtle tear in the faith she had in her husband, punishment meted out for leading him on, the ugliness of reviling him. It surprised her now, as sometimes you are surprised by a twist in a story, a film where one of the characters turns out to have been dead all along. She hadn't detected this side of him, this small, mean, vindictive shadow.

'Why did you ask me here?' she began, feeling bold and perhaps riled by his achievement. 'You knew I was married. What kind of a man invites a married woman to spend the night?'

He stared into her face, a hard knot in his brow.

'Because I felt there was something between us. And I know you felt it too. Yes, I realised you were married, but I've been married before. I know what it looks like when you're coming to the end of it. We all move on. Some of us need a little coaxing. And that night, there was something about you that I found…' She watched him trying to locate an adjective. 'Interesting. I was curious to explore it further. But I told myself I would wait, that I'd let you make the first move. Let her contact me, I thought. And then, when you texted me, and I replied, and it continued on, I knew that you wanted more. I thought to myself, it's *your* marriage, your responsibility.'

He delivered this last sentence matter-of-factly. It left her cold. She was struck by the hard reasoning of his response, the cool machinations of his thoughts, so at odds with her own foolish notion that there was something noble about their friendship, meaningful and comforting, that might have led to something more. And almost at the same time she thought of her marriage vows, how easily she had lost faith in them, how close she had come to violating them, and in that instant she felt ready to return to that old and tired love, ready to make strident efforts to reinvigorate it.

'This couch folds out,' Neil said then, and she saw the sky black outside the window behind him. 'There's bedding in the hot press. I'll make it up for you.'

15

If he was honest with himself, Christy never intended to meet Mike Atwood for a drink, not for a second. Even as the suggestion was emerging from his mouth, accompanied by that earnest nodding, that generous smile, he knew in his heart that he wouldn't honour it. Which is why he was surprised to pick up the phone a few weeks later and hear that tentative voice at the other end of the line, that gentle stammer: 'So how about that drink then?' And why he was even more surprised to find himself sitting in the Rod 'n' Reel on a Wednesday evening, sitting across from Mike with Al Green playing on the jukebox.

The Rod 'n' Reel had been Mike's suggestion, a relic from the 1970s with sticky carpets underfoot, embossed paisley print paper lining the walls, and now in its new smoke-free environment, there was a whiff of something chemical in the air, bleach perhaps, undercut with less pleasant odours. They were sitting in a snug beside the empty dancefloor, Mike with a look of happy concentration on his face that surprised Christy, who was expecting to find him dour and dispirited. On closer inspection, Mike appeared a lot brighter than on their last encounter. He was wearing a plaid shirt open at the collar and appeared to have had a shave and a haircut. Sipping his pint, Christy quietly observed this change in him, a marked recovery from his stumble into painful love. This thought turned in on itself as Christy wondered what might lie ahead for him – pain or redemption?

A month had passed since that first Sunday afternoon, and in those days and nights he had seen the workings of his life come asunder, turned on its head. He couldn't sleep at night, and in the day he was distracted, his mind working over all the fractures in his life – the faultlines in his relationship with his wife, this new unhappiness that lay between them that they were both strenuously trying to ignore, his children's futures, what impact his own choices would have on them. His moods swung between misery and pure joy, a kind he hadn't experienced before, a kind he hadn't thought possible, growing as it had out of a deception, a betrayal. And yet, when he was with Lara, all he could feel was this warm commotion, this busy love. It gathered inside him, a living, breathing thing. She talked to him of the places she had been to and he latched onto these descriptions, adding to them his own hopes and ambitions, a future forming in his head for them – one that he hadn't discussed with her yet. And then there were days when she was quiet, when her eyes seemed to invert, staring into the depths of her melancholy. Bad days where she smoked one cigarette after another and he couldn't make her return his smile and he knew that she was thinking of her son. On those days, she became lost in herself, and all he could do was sit with her, silently offering comfort, waiting for her to come back to him again.

'So. Thanks for coming out tonight, Christy. It means a lot to me.'

'No problem. You're looking well. You seem in much better form.'

'Well, I'm celebrating.'

'Oh? What's the occasion?'

'My new beginning.' Mike smiled sheepishly, his cheeks pinking slightly, and Christy found himself sitting up, interested now. This wasn't what he had been expecting. All day, he had nursed a slight dread at the thought of an evening in the company of a morose, beaten man, envisaging a couple of lonely hours spent watching his vague attempts at cheering Mike up collapse in a pool of defeat. But the prospects for the evening now seemed quite different, and while he welcomed this new enthusiasm, part of him worried that Mike might want to extend the celebration over the course of several hours, while Christy had been planning an early exit. He had arranged to meet Lara down at the old Reen Roe Hotel at ten o'clock. Glancing at his watch, he saw that it was already eight-thirty. He looked back at Mike, adopting a quizzical air.

'New beginning?' he asked, and judging from the look of excitement coming over his face, it wasn't hard to see that Mike had been dying to tell someone his news.

'I've got a new job.'

'Mike, that's fantastic—'

'No, wait. That's not all.' He paused for dramatic effect. 'It's in Africa.'

'Africa?'

'Yes. Uganda, to be precise.'

Christy felt a small pearl of envy bubbling up in his chest, and this surprised him.

'Wow,' he said, making his voice larger than he felt. 'Doing what?'

'Teaching.' The reply came with a slight shrug, as if to say wasn't it obvious.

'And when…how did all this come about?'

Mike smiled, put down his pint and leaned forward, his arms resting on the table in such a manner that Christy knew he was in for a lengthy account, packed full of wisdom and humorous asides and a good degree of pedantry, and he thought again of Lara, sitting in her car waiting for him, and felt a murmur of impatience in his brain as he settled a smile on his face and listened to Mike launching into how he had just decided that enough was enough. He needed to change his life and change it radically, so he had contacted a friend who worked for an aid agency, and after a few phone calls, an interview in Dublin and some reorganisation of his affairs, it was all sorted.

'I leave Friday week,' he announced with a triumphant nod of his head.

'That's fantastic. I'm delighted for you,' Christy said. 'Really I am. You deserve a change. A new start. It will be the making of you.'

He listened to himself doling out these platitudes

and felt vaguely annoyed at the patronising tone in them.

'You know, Christy, that day I met you, that day in the cinema, I think that was the turning point for me. Seeing you there, with all those boys. When I went home that evening, I got to thinking how fucked up my life had become, and how different it could have been. The mistakes I've made. But meeting you reminded me of how it could have turned out, if I'd only stuck to the script. If I hadn't been so weak...' He broke off suddenly before shaking his head with a renewed determination. 'I should have married, you know? Someone like Sorcha. That evening after the cinema, I got to thinking how comforting it must be to go home to someone like that. Someone warm and reliable and supportive.'

Christy closed his eyes for a second and thought of Sorcha, and opening his eyes again, he looked across at the empty dance floor, remembering a time long ago when they had danced here together, back when everything was different. He thought of the whip of her skirt against her legs as she wheeled around, her head thrown back with laughter. And that thought unleashed a whole series of images spiralling down through him. He thought of the gentle bend of her neck when she leaned over the cradle to kiss their baby goodnight; of the pockets of her old duffel coat full of shells and sea glass at the end of a walk on the beach; of the way she tucked her head into the crook between his neck and chin; of an evening spent many years before, on a wall outside The Point, sharing a cold beer while looking out over the drift of water between there and Valentia Island, and it seemed to him that he loved Sorcha in the vague inexplicable way that he loved all of those things. But he felt, too, that his love for her was an awful lot like an old photograph, fading and curling at the corners.

Lately he felt he hadn't the strength to face her. There was no pleasure in deceiving her. As they started in on a new round of drinks and he listened to Mike speak of his plans, Christy's mind turned to last night, in bed with his wife, when he had felt her hands kneading the small of his back, read the message that was there, and then shamefully had turned over, feigning sleep. Afterwards, he had lain there, listening to her crying softly into her pillow, and he had felt so small and cowardly that it was all he could do to lie there unmoving. *Why am I doing this?* he had thought to himself. Despite the affection that persisted in their daylight exchanges – the small kisses in greeting, the encouraging smiles, the tactile gestures of conciliation and support – it had been a month since he had made love to his wife, and he knew that this silence that had fallen over their marriage bed couldn't continue unexplained for much longer. He was charged with guilt over the hurt he was causing, even unknown to her. And yet, the guilt was not enough to counteract the intoxicating draw of his new love. It had him in a stranglehold, a gloriously pleasurable embrace that he couldn't summon up the courage or the desire to break free of. It seemed to Christy that he had spent most of his life waiting for something. Throughout all the major events – his marriage, the birth of his children – there was always this little hum of impatience, of longing. He yearned for a sense of arrival. But what he had been waiting for was less clear. Until Lara.

'Mike,' he began, taken by curiosity, by a new need to know, and made bold by the three pints he had consumed. 'What made you do it?'

It was something that he had speculated upon on several occasions, and more recently he had been revisited by those old wonderings. And now, in the quiet confines of this stagnant old pub, his heart heavy with the knowledge that he was shrugging off his old love, making room for the only future he could imagine now, he felt that what Mike might tell him, what secrets he might share of his downfall, might in some way act as a guide for him through the current turmoil he was feeling.

His companion seemed to think about this for a moment, examining his pint, and sucking in his lips.

'I'd like to say that it was an act of madness, a sudden weakness, but I don't suspect you'd buy that.'

'So what was it? What made you act so recklessly? You must have known what would happen if you were found out.' He lowered his voice all the way to a whisper. 'Were you in love? Tell me, or was it just sex?'

'Love, sex…it can be hard to tell the difference when you're up close to it, you know? I think it started out from loneliness. And compassion. She showed me compassion.' He broke off suddenly, momentarily spinning away in his own thoughts before fixing his eyes on Christy again and persisting with the telling. 'I never told you this, but when I started at the girls' school, it was…God, it was just awful. I had no idea what they could be like, how vicious they could be. At that time, I was the only male teacher in the school, and foolishly, I actually thought this was kind of cool. What an idiot I was. And yeah, I was a little turned on by the thoughts of all those girls – especially the older classes, young women really – being under my tutelage. A welcome change after all those boys. The younger girls were okay, the first and second years. But the older ones, it was like anything I said, they put a sexual spin on. Some of it was just flirting, but then it seemed to get more serious. More aggressive. And it was constant, all the time, this sexual innuendo, this open leering, plaguing me with questions about my sex life, asking me was I gay. Nothing I did to discipline them, to try and get them to stop, none of it worked.' He shook his head at the memory before looking Christy clear in the face. 'I was a mess. I couldn't cope. And among all those little vixens, she was the only one to feel compassion. I remember that day so clearly, when things had gotten out of hand during one particular class and I was dangerously close to just walking out. I remember her turning around and hissing at her classmates to shut up, to leave me alone. I could have cried with gratitude for that one little spark of compassion. Of solidarity. Stupid, isn't it?'

But Christy shook his head. He understood how these things could clutch at your heart, how small gestures became magnified under those circumstances. He knew what it was like to be vulnerable, to lay oneself open to such tentative gestures of the heart.

'So what happened after that?'

'Things calmed down at school. The headmistress stepped in, laid down some threats, there were a couple of suspensions and after that classes seemed to return to a kind of normality.'

'But the girl? Angela, was it?'

'Yes, Angela. Angie.' His voice softened as he said this, and for a moment, Christy caught a glimpse of the trace of his fondness, his desire. 'I suppose I favoured her in class after that. But she wasn't very bright. She struggled with her work. And when she approached me at the end of class one day and asked me could I help her after school, we both knew what was going to happen. That was the first time I kissed her. God, how insane it was – how risky! But I didn't care. It was reckless, but thrilling. And while in the beginning it was just kissing, it soon began getting more serious. We'd meet after school, I'd take her places in my car...'

His explanation petered out, and Christy guessed he didn't want to divulge the sordid details of their affair.

'You must think I'm pathetic, Christy. A living, breathing cliché.'

'No. Really. I understand better than you think.' He paused. 'Do you regret it?'

Mike nodded slowly. 'Every day for the past two years.'

There was something chilling in the way he admitted it, something dark in his voice that made Christy feel suddenly cold. He glanced again at his watch. Lara would be leaving her house now, climbing into that rusty old Datsun, and soon she would be there, waiting for him. A sudden shaft of acid rose up from his stomach into his mouth, and he couldn't tell if it was excitement or sudden fear that was the cause. Sitting there opposite that ruined man, living proof of the damage the heart could do, he should have been resolving to end it between them, to return to his old life, be grateful for what he had. But he knew he wouldn't do anything of the sort. He was too far gone for that. Christy recognised himself to be completely and desperately in love. And it wasn't an accident that he had gotten involved so deeply. He knew that too. He'd intended to get mixed up with Lara from the moment she'd got into his car that first day, to get entangled with those long bare legs, those nervous fidgety hands of hers, with the dark mop of hair that fell recklessly around her shoulders, with the teasing good humour that masked deep wells of hurt that she tried so hard to battle against. He intended it right from the start, when he learned that she was coming home, or maybe even earlier, when he first saw her standing in a rock pool, bare-legged with long arms plunging into the water, grasping around for anemones. He knew it was inevitable from the moment she said his name.

*

During the short journey to their meeting place, he briefly considered telling her about his conversation with Mike – the revelations about the affair, the guilt, the remorse. But he decided against it, uncertain as to how it might affect Lara, careful of anything that might spoil what they had between them. Turning the car in off the main road, he sped up the long deserted avenue, overarched with ancient sycamores, the twinkling night sky peeping through occasional breaks in the canopy of branches. At the end of the avenue was a large cement-grey building, more like a prison than a hotel. It had been abandoned years before and remained a hulking, brooding tomb of concrete, its windows all boarded up. At one corner of the car park, a giant chessboard had been painted onto the concrete. When the hotel was open the chequered board was home to giant chess pieces, each one the size of a child, and he remembered bringing his own children to play here, their delight at being able to jump from square to square, his own little pawns. As he drew up into the flagstone car park, he saw the red Datsun parked alongside the chessboard, its sole occupant visible as a silhouette against the lambent dashboard in front of her.

Pulling the Merc up alongside, he waited for her to get out of her car, and what he saw then was a glorious swathe of green silk, dappled with light from the beams of his car. She shut and locked the door behind her and walked slowly across to him. He stayed where he was, didn't take his eyes off her as she got into the passenger side and turned to face him. Her hair was down around her shoulders, still wet from washing, and her eyes had been brought out with eyeliner and mascara so that they appeared bigger, wider. They regarded him cautiously, guardedly, but her dress and her high-heel shoes and her make-up filled him with hope. He felt the glorious beat of anticipation booming in his chest.

'Thought you'd forgotten me,' she said, a small pleat of accusation in her tone.

'As if I could.'

He leaned across, took her face in his hands and kissed her passionately, caught the whiff of something smoky and piney on her breath, and when he drew back, her face had softened and she leaned her head back on the rest.

'You look beautiful,' he said wildly, impulsively, and was rewarded with a slow smile that crept over her face and lit up her eyes.

'You okay, Christian? Everything all right at home?'

She assumed his lateness was as a result of some incident with Sorcha or the children, and he moved to correct her, explaining briefly where he had been and with whom.

'Good,' she said, her chest heaving with relief. 'I worry about you, you know? How awkward things must be for you at home. Having to lie all the time.'

'It's worth it,' he said, reaching for her hand and holding it in his. 'And you know, it's not so bad lately, with Sorcha.'

'Really?'

'Yeah. And with the kids. I can't explain it, but it's as if everything has suddenly become calm again.' He didn't admit to the tears in the night, didn't refer to his own inability to make love to his wife, this further insult to the health of their marriage.

For weeks now, he had been alert for changes in Sorcha's voice, poised for some hint that would indicate suspicion. But there had been nothing, only this silence in the bedroom. He knew that it was only a matter of time before the silence spilled over into the rest of their lives. And still the guilt lingered, not overwhelming, but promising to bloom into something larger, something less compromising. It was inevitable, given what he wanted to do. Given the plans he had started making for them.

'And you're sure she doesn't suspect anything?'

'Positive. She hasn't got a clue.'

He remembered saying goodbye to his wife that morning. He had been on his way out the door and she had caught hold of his hand suddenly and drew him to her, kissing him warmly and tenderly on his lips. 'Bye, you,' she had said lightly and with affection and he had felt his heart dropping like a stone down through him. It was unusual for her to be like this with him, and he felt a certain poignancy in the moment, the weight of meaning in their parting, almost as if he would never see her again.

'I can't be sure,' he began, 'but she seems to be making a concerted effort to be nice to me. To be affectionate.'

'Oh?'

'It's like she's trying to make something up to me.'

'Perhaps she's trying to start over.'

'What do you mean?'

'Things haven't been great between the two of you. So she could be trying to rectify that.'

He shook his head at the thought. And besides, the affection between them that had crept back in over the last few weeks had been partially instigated by him, affection born of guilt, a shameful cover-up. And yet there was a certain honesty to his feelings. Since this had begun, his nerves were rattled; his senses were heightened, watchful for any searching glance, listening for the suspicion in his wife's voice. It seemed amazing to him that life among his family, in his household, could carry on as normal, at the same mundane pace, while this momentous thing had happened to him. Joy rose up inside him, swelling his heart, this unbelievable explosion of happiness, and all he wanted to do was tell someone. He had come close to admitting it to Mike, but knew that it wouldn't solve anything, knew that it would only instigate a plaintive entreaty to end the affair, to return to the safe kernel of his marriage. He knew in his heart that he couldn't tell anyone. Instead he had allowed his happiness to spill over into these waves of benevolence, this goodwill towards Sorcha and the kids. He felt an overwhelming need to connect with them again, to share some of the warmth he was feeling. Over the past week he had reached out to each of them in turn, being close with Sorcha, allowing for small treats like breakfast in bed, spoiling her. And she had responded lovingly, with an almost guilty affection. With Jim, he had made an effort to sit with him at the computer, masterminding the endless games. Avril seemed determined to thwart his efforts, still smarting over the ugliness of their argument those weeks ago, steadfastly refusing to speak with him, denying him any leniency.

'You know,' he had said to her two nights before, 'I admire you for your stubbornness.'

She had looked at him with eyes loaded with suspicion, scouring his face for some hidden meaning, some sly attack. But there was none. And when he had left €20 on her bedside locker as a peace offering – completely wrong, he knew, buying his way back into her affections – she hadn't thrust it back at him, but merely looked up briefly from the book she had balanced on her knees, leaning back against a wall of pillows, before looking away again. But as he closed the door behind him, he thought he heard a mumbled 'thanks' emerging from the shadows, and with that came a surge of feeling, warm and close.

'Anyway,' he said to Lara, 'it's a good thing, this new spirit of calm in the house.' The fact that it was because of a deception and a betrayal so great that he could hardly breathe when he thought of it was beside the point.

'I found something today,' she told him, a cautious optimism taking hold of her voice, 'an article on the internet. A woman in the States who found her child several years after her baby supposedly died in a house fire. She saw her at a party and recognised her from the dimple in her face. Can you believe it?'

'Yes,' he nodded slowly, imbuing his voice with a solemn belief.

'The child had been stolen by a friend of hers who started the fire to lead everyone to believe that the child had died. All these years, she had been raising the little girl as her own.'

He watched her carefully, saw the flickering hope inside her, this never-letting-up of her belief that she would find her boy alive, and he thought of the file she kept filled with newspaper clippings and articles printed off the internet, her notebook full of scribbled leads, thoughts, anything that might prove significant, anything that could some day lead back to him.

'There, you see?' he said. 'These things do happen. You must never give up hope.'

She smiled at him then, and he felt it reaching into his chest, the spark of possibility igniting within. His heart, made dry and dusty after all those years, parched with longing, was quickly aflame.

'I love you,' he said, his words offered out into the darkness. It felt different, saying it out loud. The exhilarating fear in uttering those words, the delicious nerves in his voice, the thud of anxiety awaiting her response, the risk he was taking!

She looked at him for a long moment, his wretched heart desperate to hear those words repeated back, but her response when it came was more measured.

'Christian. You mean so much to me too. You always have.'

And he felt the hope stirring up again inside him, rekindling the flames within him. There were so many words within him that he wanted to say to her – so many thoughts and emotions that he wanted to lay at her feet like an offering, a sacrifice, words to test her, to draw her out, to wrap around her, to consume her. But before he could say anything, she leaned across and kissed him full on the mouth, and he felt her hand reaching up into his hair, clasping his head with a tenderness that sent sparks shooting up into the dome of his skull.

A thought crawled into his head, a thought of his wife and family at home in the house on the other side of the bay, all the windows lit up from inside, oblivious to the action taking place in the front seat of the family car. But his hand moved down to her breast and everything seemed to slow down, and he pushed that thought out to the furthest corner of his mind and broke away from her lips, bending to kiss the neck she offered to him. He felt her body rising to his kisses, heard the low moan like purring in her throat, and in no time at all she had moved from her seat to his and was hovering over him, her green dress up around her waist, as they became locked in that slow, deep, steady rhythm.

I can't live without you, he found himself thinking. And yet, all his life he had lived without her. Years and years had passed where he had gotten through each day and each night without her presence. Something huge had changed in him. The emptiness he had felt, that great void inside him, was suddenly occupied so fully and completely he imagined that to rip her out of his life, out of his heart, would cause such pain to him as to be almost physical. Such a wrench must involve the ripping of skin, the tearing of muscles, a searing pain, the spillage of blood. *I can't live without you.* He wasn't sure if he could bear such pain.

Afterwards, she rested her head against his shoulder, curled up on his lap, her face nuzzling his neck.

'Will you be all right?' he asked, his hands kneading the small of her back.

She nodded gently and then drew back to look at him.

'How about you? Will you be okay?'

She meant would things be okay when he went home to his wife, and he sighed deeply and kissed her gently, reading the worry etched into the crease of her brow.

'Why don't you let me worry about that, hmm?'

She seemed to bite her lip, as if trying to bite down on the questions tumbling up suddenly from deep within.

'Do you think she suspects anything?'

'Lara.'

'I don't think I could cope with—'

'Lara,' he repeated, firmer this time, more authoritative. 'It's fine.'

'She can't ever find out, Christian.'

He considered saying that she would have to find out eventually. Considered telling her that he couldn't hang on much longer. The need within him had been growing steadily, his resolve forming to leave his wife. But the hour was late, and he wasn't sure if he was ready for that conversation yet, preferring to work out all the details himself first before presenting her with a *fait accompli*.

'She won't find out,' he said soothingly, kissing her neck again, and she allowed herself to be appeased.

'I need to see you again soon,' he whispered in between kisses. 'Will you wait for me to contact you?'

'Okay,' she agreed, her voice warm and sleepy.

'It won't be long.'

'Promise?'

'I promise.'

He waited until she was safely in her car, with the headlamps on and the engine humming, watching her turning the old Datsun out of the dark cement-locked space onto the road with tufts of grass sprouting up the middle of it, slowly following, keeping a distance behind her. It was as the car swung out onto the main road that he thought he saw something, a sudden movement, something grey and shadowy in the weeded tangle behind the chessboard. His heart gave out a beat of alarm and he strained in the darkness to see, but all that was there was an old hydrangea bush strangled by climbing weeds and throttled by the wind.

16

He told me he couldn't live without me. Such a strange thing to tell a person really, when you think about it. It's like there's a warning implicit in this expression of love, a need that's almost aggressive. His arms were around me at the time, and I could feel the warmth of his breath against my neck, and I probably should have felt happy hearing those words, elated perhaps, but all I could feel was the undertow of something missing. I couldn't put my finger on what it was. Like when he talked about when we were kids, navigating the difficulties of adolescence, and his voice became tender and wistful, recounting the things we had done together, the innocence of it, and yet there was always this longing in his voice, all these 'what-ifs' stacking up unspoken. What if we had acted upon feelings that were clearly there between us? What if he hadn't caught me that day with some boy whose name and face I could no longer remember? What if he hadn't reacted the way he had? What if there were no pregnancy, no engagement, and instead there was a journey? What if? What if? But I didn't like to follow these questions too far, wary of where they might lead, the events and people and history they might erase. I was finding it hard enough to cling on to my memories as it was.

In truth, I wasn't so comfortable discussing that part of our history, partly because I found it difficult to answer that question he never asked, but that was always there between us nonetheless. How come it had remained a friendship for so long, a friendship with a strong mutual attraction, almost as if there was a promise of something more, without ever actually developing into anything? Even trying to explain it to myself was difficult. But I knew that what had existed between us, this promise or expectation, had been kept in balance because of the distance we kept from it. Almost as if we were saving ourselves for the right time. I remember having this need – this bewildering, inexplicable need – to hold off, to wait, to save it for later. And while I went with other boys, exploring that side to me, there was always the promise of him in the future. It wasn't nothing. In a way, it was everything. But I knew that it would be dangerous to try it too soon, when we were still so young, to see it fall and come apart and then lose everything, our whole friendship, at a time when I needed him more than anyone. I didn't want to see it bloom and then die, and then have to look back on it bitterly, with regret.

But there were some things about that time that I liked to remember. Like the time we knelt together on the veranda, the rain falling all around us, my hand clasped in his. Or that one time after my father left and my mother was in the middle of one of her blue phases, where she would sit motionless at the kitchen table for hours staring into nothing, suspended in a kind of horrified torpor. There was nothing I could do for her when she got like that, and I remember that afternoon when we had left her sitting there, Christy and I, and gone to my bedroom. We just left her there, staring at the TV, *The Cosby Show* playing, but she wasn't laughing at the jokes. She wasn't doing anything at all. And once in my bedroom, he turned to me, his voice soft and concerned, and asked if my mother was all right, and then, without warning, I had begun to cry. We sat together on my bed and he held me against him. He didn't try anything on, just held me there, and I remember the sweet surprise at the softness of my face against his.

He still held me in that way, imparting comfort, when I talked to him of South America, what unfolded in the days and weeks and months after Nacio disappeared.

'Tell me what happened,' he asked me as we lay in bed together.

And so I told him of the interview in the police station that day – the first of the interviews – when I sat across from a police officer whose face was worn and leathery, jowls hanging down like a dog, weary eyes that seemed to flicker when he asked for our address and we explained our situation to him, our nomadic way of life. He had been taking down notes, filling out forms, and this piece of information seemed to jar with him. I remembered watching his pen hovering above the page, a low rumble coming from his throat. I was calmer then. There was something vaguely reassuring about being in that place, with its clinical surroundings, its forms and gun holsters and fluorescent lights. I kept my voice steady, concentrating carefully on marshalling all the facts that I could remember, speaking slowly, endeavouring not to become impassioned, needing to be clear in my thoughts and in my words, somehow feeling that this would speed up his discovery. And after leaving there, having listened to words of assurance, convinced that they would do everything possible, would explore every single lead, commit every available resource to his discovery and safe return, Alejo and I found ourselves wandering back to the marketplace.

Night had fallen and the place was deserted, all the bustle and hysteria of the day a distant echo. We stood there together, looking up at the iron structure rising up in front of us, black and enormous, and high up overhead I saw the stars, thousands of them, winking and silent from their far-off constellations. Everywhere, there was a deep silence. Neither one of us spoke, both of us straining to hear something, as if our son might suddenly emerge from the shadows. We stayed there like that for maybe twenty minutes, maybe half an hour, before wordlessly turning and walking away.

'But somebody must have seen him,' Christy persisted. 'A boy can't just disappear from a crowded marketplace without anyone noticing him.'

There were many accounts of what had happened to him that day – some said they saw him with a group of children playing in the square outside the church;

another reported seeing him being hurried away by a man in a navy anorak, a baseball cap on his head; another saw him on a bus bound for São Paolo; still more thought he had been sighted down by the harbour sitting alone as if waiting for someone. It seemed that small dark-haired boys were ubiquitous, and while the police had reassured us they were following up all the leads, it soon became clear that they couldn't cope with all these conflicting stories. And so, when the sandal was found on the beach and identified as Nacio's, I couldn't help but think that there must have been a measure of quiet relief among the officers that a resolution had presented itself, tragic as that resolution was.

Everything went quiet after that. All work on the case was suspended. Case closed. Despite my refusal to accept it, my furious disbelief at the police's reaction, there was little I could do to dissuade them. When I learned some weeks later that a woman had phoned the police to say she had seen Nacio playing in the back garden of her neighbour's house on the outskirts of São Paolo, I was incandescent with rage at their callous indifference to this lead. Christy had held me against him as I told him how I had stood in that police station screaming at that officer's dog-like face that he had to do something, that I refused to accept their inaction, their incompetence, their downright bloody criminal negligence.

'Lara,' that officer had said to me, summoning up all his patience, his compassion, his firmness. 'What you must understand is that this woman who rang us, she rings the police almost every day. She sees a poster of a missing person and she calls to tell us she knows where they are. Last month, she rang the American Embassy in Rio to tell them her neighbour was hiding Ossama bin Laden. For months before that she was plaguing them with reports of new information surrounding the Kennedy assassination. She calls us all the time about plots she has uncovered to overthrow the government, about UFOs she has seen hovering over her house. This is a crazy person we are talking about. I'm very sorry, Lara, but you are unfortunate that she has heard of your son, and simply taken it into her head that she has seen him.'

I had stood there in front of that large man, felt his strong hand on my shoulder as I cried hot tears of rage, and heard his voice soft yet firm, telling me all over again that my son was gone, and that I had to accept the fact that he would not be coming back.

When I told Christy this, I could feel the steady thrum of his heart beating through the wall of his chest. He didn't say that it was unfortunate, but I could tell that was what he was thinking. And for some reason, I felt the beginnings of disappointment in him. I'm not sure how I had expected him to react, but perhaps I'd been hoping for some show of anger, of disbelief that what could have been a positive and genuine sighting had been so casually disregarded. Instead what I found was a limp acceptance, no better than all the others, and it made me wonder just how much I should tell him. I thought about the enquiries I had been making into private detectives in Brazil, contemplating telling him how I was putting the last of my mother's money into employing some stranger I had found on the internet to go do the police's work for them. Perhaps it was his failure to react in the way I'd hoped, or some other deeper unease, but in the end, I said nothing at all.

One time, I was with a married man – before Christy. One time only. It was back in San Francisco, during those last days before I quit my job at the dry cleaners and moved my stuff out of that flea-pit that served as an apartment and took the bus all the way down to Mexico. I didn't leave because of this man, but you could say that he dug the spurs in to speed my exit. Or rather, his wife did. I had met him in a bar, south of the city, the kind of place that did happy-hour cocktails from five until seven, where the waitresses wore striped red and white shirts, braces punctuated with rows of pin-badges, and short black skirts that barely covered their asses. I was sipping a margarita, killing time before my shift at the launderette, and he was sitting next to me at the counter, tucking into a French dip. His name was Pete Polanski, and he had that strong, hungry Slavic look, eyes that scorched you with intensity like an ice burn. He was in sales and carried that same tension in his shoulders that all salesmen seem to have, along with the sharp eyes and the smooth tongue. He bought me another cocktail and then another one and it wasn't a tough decision to skip my shift. We spent that night flipping on the mattress on the floor of my scummy apartment, and for the next three weeks alternated between there, the Holiday Inn and the back seat of his Isuzu Trooper. I never asked about his wife, never enquired as to whether he had kids. The band stayed around his finger the whole time, even when we were lying together stripped of everything else.

And then one day at work, standing in my pink gingham smock ironing a pile of shirts, I heard the bell above the door and looked up to see a short, busty, warm-eyed woman with a voice full of shaky nerves.

'I want you to stop,' she said clearly, and I knew at once who she was and what she meant. 'I just want you to stop.'

We stood there regarding each other until I remembered the iron just in time and lifted it from the cotton. Steam rose up from the shirt and I felt the heat in my face. Everything seemed clear and distinct under the neon light of the shop and I felt the heat move around my heart, the shame of it trembling in my stomach. I couldn't look at her, couldn't hold her gaze, and looked away, lowering my head, and in that moment I thought of my mother – her cool dignity, the strips my father and his girls tore off her soul. In that moment I felt too small and filthy to look that clear-eyed woman straight in the face.

While my situation now was not exactly *simpatico*, there was still a fairly large streak of shame running through the complex pattern of my affair with Sorcha's husband. The guilt was unavoidable, especially seeing as she frequented my place of work. I made it my business to engage in sudden urgent flurries of fruit-stacking, or hurried trips to the storeroom whenever I saw her pushing her trolley through the aisles. On the few occasions that she approached me, I was polite, smiling feverishly and casting my eyes upwards towards Alan's office, as if to indicate that I was being monitored and couldn't really stay and chat. Always, as I watched her retreating form, the sad squeak of her trolley wheels, I felt sodden with shame and equally resolved to stop this thing before it got out of hand. But my resolve had a tendency to evaporate when I was with him, and those conversations in the front seat of his car that started 'I mean it this time. We really must stop this,' seemed to terminate with the two of us enjoying the luxury of the vast leather expanse of the Merc's back seat.

So when I emerged from the bank onto the street that bright blustery October afternoon and walked straight into Sorcha, for a moment I was so completely startled it was all I could do not to stand there opening and closing my mouth, grasping around for something to say. I stopped, my stomach convulsed in panic, and suddenly all the guilt I had been suppressing came clawing out at me from the cavern of my chest.

'Lara!' she cried out and I noticed the colour running into her cheeks. 'There you are!' As if she had been searching for me everywhere.

'Here I am,' I croaked, barely able to get the words out, and the two of us stood there facing each other, her with a look of expectation on her face, and me with my mouth opening and closing, no words emerging, gripped by a sudden fear that any movement I made, any words I uttered, would give away everything I must conceal from her.

'I've hardly seen you at all these past few weeks,' she exclaimed, her eyes searching over my whole face.

'I know. I've been busy getting myself sorted out. Sorry,' I blurted out, 'I meant to call on you, it's just that—'

'It seems that my husband has seen more of you than I have.'

I watched her face carefully, looking for signs that she was fucking with me. But there was nothing there besides an eager willingness to please, and in the next breath she was asking if there was anything she could do to help me get settled in, so I guessed my secret was safe for now, at least.

We stood there nodding and smiling at each other, and I felt my nerves jumping all along my spine. I was anxious to get away from her, but feared what she might read into any sudden gestures.

'Well, you're looking wonderful. So much better than you did when you arrived, if you don't mind me saying.'

I didn't mind and said so.

'And you're settling in now,' she exclaimed, 'finding your feet.'

'Getting there, Sorcha,' I said, shifting my weight

from one foot to the other. The wind kept blowing hair into my face, and after several swipes at it, I finally held my hand there, clasping it to my head.

'You know, I keep meaning to call to see you. But what with one thing and another…I was away, and then with the children…I just don't seem to get a moment.'

She smiled at me apologetically and I made some noise about how it was as much my fault as hers, and we both agreed that we'd make more of an effort in the future.

'Tell you what,' she said suddenly, her face lighting up as if just struck by a new idea. 'Why don't you come to ours on Sunday for lunch?'

'Oh, well, I—'

'Do! I'll invite Stella and Guy along as well. Stella and Guy Naseby. Have you met them?'

'No, I don't think so…'

'Then you simply must come. You'll love them. Is three o'clock okay?'

She fixed me with the fullness of her gaze, and I was too stunned to think of an excuse.

'Em, yes. Thank you, Sorcha. But please don't go to any trouble on my account.'

'No trouble,' she sang out happily. 'In fact, it's a disgrace that I haven't asked you until now. And no need to bring anything, just yourself.'

She gave my arm a quick squeeze, favoured me with the dazzling warmth of her smile, and chirped 'See you then' before hurrying past me into the bank that I had just left.

For a moment, I stood there in a sort of daze, staring about me, gasping in the air, wondering what on earth I had just agreed to.

*

There's a wall in the middle of the town between the credit union and the neat row of box-like houses that edge away down to the church, and when I was growing up here, it used to be covered in graffiti. 'Free Bobby Sands.' 'IRA – the undefeated army.' 'Eat shit and die.' 'LB is gay.' 'TH and KS forever.' 'Advertising is corporate heroin.' 'JP is a dickhead.' 'I love you Una P, my heart is yours forever.' All these statements of love and hate and spurious gossip sprang up when no one was looking, clandestine scrawls in the night.

But after Sorcha left me standing there in the middle of the street, I stared across at that wall and saw that a mural had been painted over it, a cartoonish depiction of a castle with a moat, four fat white swans with regal necks suspended in the water, and a host of laughing children in medieval costume dancing by a tree. The effect was garish, and slightly ridiculous sandwiched as it was between the austere elegance of the credit union building and the neat houses with their window boxes of geraniums. The title of the mural was painted in a looping black script above the moat: 'The Children of Lir'. But crossing the road, I saw that the mural had been defaced, for after the title, the words 'are cunts' had been scrawled in black spidery letters, a succinct appendage. I could almost hear the snigger unleashed from whatever smart aleck was brazen enough to make this mark.

I turned from the wall, past the credit union, and as

I walked I remembered the time my own name had appeared on that wall, red lettering slashed across it. 'Lara Symons is a slut', the statement had screamed in its angry blood-red ink. It was there when I walked to school that morning, the word 'slut' flung at me from across the street, hitting me like a brick. Anger, red and pulsing, gripped me, chased by shame, that horrible paralysing shame. What person bore me such malice that they would do such a thing? Tears had sprung in my eyes and a hard pain in my belly while I rifled through the names and faces of the people who I thought could hate me enough to inscribe my whole name, not just my initials. And as I turned away from it, slinking past the houses and the church, rounding the corner onto the school road, I began to wonder about the truth of that statement. I thought of all those evenings after school, up behind the old barracks, shoved up against the crumbling wall with the ivy creeping over it, my schoolbag discarded in the nettles by my ankles and some boy pressed up against me, fumbling with my clothes, feeling the press of his face against mine, his hot breath, sometimes the crust of acne or the prickles of a fledgling moustache grazing my skin, hands pulling at my skirt, but always that hot pumping sensation as I felt swirled away in a haze of desire, letting it take me, losing myself in it.

Could it have been one of those boys, I wondered? Which one had slunk away dissatisfied, spurned in some way, his sticky kisses and groping hands mocked or rejected? Or perhaps it was not a boy, but a girl, seething with jealousy. Perhaps I had gone with the object of some other girl's desire, and this was her way of unleashing her wrath, this terrible, screaming vitriol let loose on the wall for the whole town to see. That day in school was hellish, the whispered asides in the corridors, the nudging and pointing and sniggering, my eyes casting around for the guilty party, looking for red ink like blood on their hands.

But on the way home that afternoon, as I approached that wall and its screaming slander, a new resolve took hold of me. *Fuck them*, I thought to myself. *Fuck them all*. I threw my head back, tossing my hair, my chin jutting forward defiantly. I stuck out my chest and sashayed past, my hips swaying wildly from side to side with all the sex I could summon up. If that's what they think, let them have it, I decided as I strutted past. And the next day, as I walked past that lettering, I did the same, infusing my body with a sexiness that was brazen and vaguely threatening, a pout on my face and fire in my eyes. I swung my satchel over my shoulder and thrust my chest forward, feeling the power of that walk, that bold strut. I kept it up until that angry lettering was painted out, and by then the walk had become so fully ingrained that I couldn't let it drop, but continued to sashay with that proud swagger, that conceited gait.

I had long since abandoned that walk, that confident strut I avoided eye contact with other people, whereas before I used to seek them out with my eyes, challenging them silently. And something of the shame of that morning came back to me, chasing up from the depths of my past. I thought of Christy, the light of hope in his eyes as he had said those words to me – 'I love you' – and I, all the while, thinking *this has gone too far, this has to end*. I should have said those words out loud. I should have turned then, and walked away. But instead I had launched myself at him, my lips silencing him, and before I knew it, we were making love, and what kind of message was that to send him?

Lara Symons is a slut. The words had been painted out long ago, and yet a trace of them remained with me. Walking past the wall, I was sixteen all over again, that word screaming at me, as I slunk away pulsing with shame and hurried home.

17

Christy intended to make himself scarce for the duration of the preparations for two reasons. The first was that he wasn't particularly effective when it came to these catering events – it was just about all he could manage to put together dinner for the four of them when called upon to do so. It seemed to him that he chopped too slowly, lingered too long at the sink, stirred inadequately and lacked the aesthetic sensibility to set the table appropriately for these kinds of gatherings, perceiving Sorcha's exasperated silences to be a reproach for his shortcomings in the kitchen area. The second reason was that he wasn't entirely sure how he felt about this lunch. When Sorcha had announced it to him, he had felt aghast at the thought of sitting down to lunch with his wife and lover and a host of spectators. He remembered standing at the sink drinking deep from a glass of water and how he had slammed the glass down on the counter, the water spilling a little, and turned to her suddenly with eyes flared open, a dark look coming down over his face, and said: 'What?' There had been heat in his voice, although it was almost a whisper, but the punch of disapproval in it was unmistakeable, and despite himself, he had allowed the air to become threaded with the soft hum of an un-spoken threat.

'It's just lunch,' she had said, and he heard the involuntary tremor in her voice. 'She's our neighbour. I felt it was about time we invited her around.'

'And Stella and Guy bloody Naseby?'

'It's our turn,' she had insisted, stronger this time.

He had stared at her for the longest time and felt himself grappling for something to say, reaching around for some argument or excuse which, in the end, evaded him so all he said was 'Fine' in that short, low voice that really meant it was not fine. Not fine at all.

But as the hour drew closer and the tempo of preparations grew more frantic, he suspected that his and Sorcha's feelings towards this lunch had become transposed. He could tell by the clip of her heels over the tiled floor, the brisk quality to her voice and the slight quaver of panic in her hurried gestures that his wife was in danger of losing control. All was not going to plan in the cooking department. Sorcha was making an elaborate Eastern dish, which Christy thought was a mistake, but he knew better than to advise her other-wise. Part of him admired her ambition in tackling such a risky and exotic concoction. At the centre of her preparations was a simple roast chicken. That at least should be easy enough. He watched her taking the chicken out of the plastic bag, dropping it onto the counter with a dull thud, and regarding it with distaste. She didn't like handling dead things. When she was pregnant with Avril, she had found herself to be excessively squeamish, and he had been called upon to prepare the meats for their meals. The smell of it made her nauseous, she had told him. The coolness and damp touch of it made her innards bubble. This afternoon, he watched her breathing through her mouth as she picked up the small black knife and, grabbing a hold of one leg, began slicing away at the excess fat, the gristle.

'Do you want me to do that?' he offered, moved by a sudden need to please her.

'No, that's all right. I've got it under control.'

Her voice was breathy with the vigour of her enthusiasm, but he thought he detected something harder underneath, the steeliness of her resolve amid the rising panic.

He stood for a moment longer, watching her rubbing the chicken with garlic and sage and dribbling olive oil and a squeeze of lemon juice over it before she shoved the two squeezed halves of lemon, a peeled onion and some cloves of garlic into the inelegant open orifice. Irritated perhaps by his lingering presence, she said briskly, 'Don't you have something to do?'

'Of course,' he said cheerfully. 'You're absolutely right. I may as well correct some essays until they get here.'

She glanced across at him then, and he thought he caught the faintest glimmer of suspicion in her eye. His good humour was a surprise, as much to him as it was to her. He contemplated the meaning of it as he went into his study and sat at his desk, drawing down the first of the fifth-year copybooks and opening it in front of him. He wished that it stemmed from some noble obligations towards family and home, an old loyalty to his wife. It was possible that it was just the thought of seeing Lara again, allowing her into his inner sanctum, his home. But he knew that what it really meant was a nearing finality. All of this would soon be over. Lately he had been assailed by a sense of impending closure. Soon he would have to tell Sorcha and have it all out in the open. This couldn't go on much longer. And while the thought of that conversation brought a sudden burst of acid in his stomach, with it came the sense that what would follow was a sense of completion, of calming, of destiny fulfilled.

His red pen passed over the pages, making ticks, correcting spellings, underlining phrases and finally fixing a grade and a brief explanatory note before he flipped the copybook closed and dutifully pulled down the next. He viewed the name scrawled in spidery handwriting on the front cover and inwardly groaned. Carl Ring. *Is it even worth reading?* he thought to himself, examining the graffiti on the cover, the bold, aggressive strokes of the pen. Carl and his one-page essays – unimaginative, lazy and riddled with a sneering arrogance. He had come to dread marking these, routinely doling out Ds and Es, the same sad pleading notes at the end, urging the boy to apply himself, not to waste the opportunities he was being given. The usual words of restraint like 'disappointing' and 'unacceptable', when he really wanted to write 'abysmal', 'pitiful', 'soul-destroying'.

Opening the page to the latest essay, entitled 'Clouds', Christy found himself startled. Four pages written in Carl's spidery handwriting, but it was evident that the boy had made a serious attempt. For just a second, the thought wandered across his mind that he had the wrong copybook, or else that this was a clear act of plagiarism, but turning to the first page, Christy found his eyes drawn over the words, a curious sense of amazement opening up within him as he read Carl's account of the sun setting over the ocean, the gulls circling and wheeling away, the empty sky, light fading on the water and the shadows of clouds moving over the hills. The sparse beauty of the language sent a thrill of surprise through him as he read how the protagonist (presumably Carl himself) sat on a grass verge, hidden among the leafy foliage of an attendant tree, watching the movements of the dark clouds, quietly appreciating his solitude as the sky filled with darkness, turning purple, then black.

The mood of the piece changed when suddenly a car appeared, its headlamps swinging and briefly illuminating the branches of leaves all around Carl, before swinging away again. And then the engine cut out. After a brief pause, a second car appeared. The boy waited. He heard a car door open and slam shut again, the click of heels across pavement, and then another door opening and closing. Still he waited. Christy felt his heart thrumming, a low-pitched beat, something cold stirring in the pit of his stomach. And still the boy waited. The sky was fully dark now, the hour late, he must be getting back. But somehow he felt afraid. The presence of the cars unsettled him, so he crept along the outside of the car park, keeping low, hiding behind the foliage. And as he passed the second car, he peeped above the bushes and to his amazement he saw a woman sitting in the front seat with her back to the wheel. She appeared to be moving slowly. She wore something green, one side of her dress pushed down from her shoulder, dark hair falling down her back. He couldn't see her face, but he saw hands on her back – large hands gripping her and roaming over her, grabbing her hair, running over her shoulder, disappearing underneath her dress. The boy didn't see the man's face. But he saw the car. The same car that was always parked in the same spot in his school's car park. And alongside it, the empty car was red and rusty, an old model. He had seen that car before too.

Christy felt the bile rise suddenly in his stomach and tried to swallow it down. A dread was opening up inside him like a yawning hole. It felt cold and it hollowed out his insides. From the kitchen, he heard noises, Sorcha's voice ringing out in welcome. But inside his head, his own voice echoed down the corridors of his mind. *Oh no,* it whispered, like a whining wind.

Entering the kitchen, Christy found his wife embracing each of the Nasebys in turn as they stood by the back door through which they had entered.

'Stella! Guy! You're early,' Sorcha remarked. 'Hello, Elijah.'

There was a reproach in that statement that only someone who knew Sorcha as well as he did could detect.

Having offloaded some kind of dish with linen gauze covering it, Stella saw him now and came forward.

'Hello, hello!' she said, holding her arms out to him. She was wearing some sort of crimson smock with a tight-fitting bodice and a plethora of tiny sequins sewn into it, so that she appeared to shimmer as she approached him, reaching around his neck with her short arms and kissing him on the cheek.

'There now,' she said, drawing back, her little eyes fluttering over him. 'Isn't this lovely?'

'Stella, you look charming,' he said, his voice quavering with residual nerves after the shock of the essay. Sweat was leaking from his glands, and he felt a dull thud in the pit of his stomach.

Indeed, Stella did have a certain charm, and there was something different about her eye make-up that made her seem pretty, although her alarming breasts had been hitched up to fit into the bodice and appeared to reach her throat. It was hard not to stare at her cleavage but he did his best to avoid it.

'Christy.'

'Guy. Oh, now that wasn't necessary,' he admonished, taking the bottles of wine proffered by the man whose hair looked newly washed and slicked back off his head. There was something jaunty about his clothes, a black leather waistcoat over his blue denim shirt. He looked like a country and western singer, Christy surmised, and peered down at his feet, half-expecting to see spurs and pointy toes.

'You look tired,' Stella said, not unkindly, reaching forward to pat him on the cheek. She was a very tactile person, Stella. 'And a little flushed. Working hard on the book?'

'Yes, yes. Working away.' He tried not to look at Sorcha.

'And how's it coming along?'

'Okay. Okay.'

'Oh, Christy. Such a shame about that poetry competition.'

'Uh-huh,' he said, looking for a trace of satisfaction or sarcasm or something beneath her face. But he found Stella hard to read – the deadpan thing stumped him.

'We couldn't get over it when we read the shortlist in *The Times* yesterday, could we, honey?' she asked Guy, who stood behind her, hands behind his back, his head bowed to hear her, but his eyes looking up at Christy, so that his expression, the tilt of his head, seemed somehow humorous, as if he were trying to share a joke with Christy behind Stella's back.

'Well, never mind,' he said. He was tempted to tell her that he hadn't entered the competition, but didn't like to think of her reaction – upset, scolding, aghast. 'It wasn't meant to be.'

'They're fools,' she declared to the kitchen. 'Absolute bloody idiots.'

She shook her head sadly, and for a long minute nobody said anything. Then Guy, ever the diplomat, sniffed at the air and turned to Sorcha.

'What is that? It smells absolutely divine.'

'Oh yes,' Stella crowed, quickly forgetting her glowering sense of injustice. 'It smells kind of spicy.'

'Now, don't get too excited.' Sorcha moved quickly to manage their expectations. 'It's something new I'm trying out, which I know they say is a bad idea when you have guests coming, but—'

'Oh, what the heck,' said Stella.

'Live dangerously,' said Guy.

'Seriously, though, I've no idea what it's going to taste like. I just banged all the ingredients in together. A bit of a mish-mash.'

Christy watched his wife's face go pink at the edges, seeing her valiant attempts at masking her apprehension with this gutsy show of gaiety, of nonchalance. She had been working on this meal all morning, and part of last night too – he had come into the kitchen before bed and found her in the midst of a storm of chopping, ingredients marinating in bowls on the counter.

'Why don't we all go through and have a drink,' he suggested, looking to rescue her, but needful of a drink himself to calm his nerves.

'Good idea,' Sorcha said, brushing a damp strand of hair from her eyes and casting a weary eye around at the scattered evidence of her culinary efforts.

In the sitting room, he fixed them all gin and tonics, and while Stella brought hers and Sorcha's back into the kitchen, Guy and Christy remained behind. Neither one of them sat, both preferring to stand about in a proprietary manner. Guy offered a few words to Avril, who was curled up on the corner of the couch, flicking through a magazine and sulking. She hadn't been consulted about this lunch, and a row had broken out earlier that day when Sorcha had sprung it on her, insisting that she attend. Now she was retreating into the extreme hostility of her personality, and after a few moments of gentle ribbing from Guy, she got up and left the room, barely civilly. Guy didn't seem to notice, and if he did, it didn't appear to trouble him. He moved to the window, sipping at his drink, and looked out at the vast stretch of the bay. From the kitchen, the women's voices rang out, and through the door that Avril had left open, he heard noises from down the hall – the boys playing the PlayStation in Jim's bedroom. Guy didn't seem perturbed by that either, despite the strict rules of Elijah's wholesome upbringing.

'So tell me, Christy,' he started, turning with a slow smile and a raised eyebrow, 'did you really enter your poetry for the competition?'

He thought about it for a moment, considered lying, then decided against it.

'No.'

Guy shook his head, chuckling.

'I thought not.'

He didn't elaborate, just took another sip of his drink, and Christy wondered what he meant by that.

'So, I believe there's another guest arriving?'

'Yes. Lara. Sorcha's cousin, remember?'

'Ah yes,' he said with what seemed to Christy to be

an elaborate recognition. 'I'm looking forward to meeting her.'

All too often, Christy found that he didn't know how to take Guy – his smile that displayed too many teeth, his quiet, assured manner and the ambiguity over his meaning. Somehow, what he said seemed to be loaded with innuendo, but delivered with such a deadpan expression that it was difficult to tell whether he intended it or not. Christy watched him, feeling queasy as he thought back to that night a few months ago, standing on the veranda with Guy, inhaling the evening air heavy with lilac. Guy's words came back to him: *Something sexy about a sorrowing young woman...the challenge of comforting her...the possibilities that lend themselves to that situation.* A shiver inadvertently raced down his spine.

'Another one?' he offered, indicating to Guy's almost empty glass, which he handed over enthusiastically.

'Why not?'

They were both drinking quickly. As he poured the gin and watched the tonic fizzing up in the bottle, he heard Guy say something.

'What's that?'

'I said – the lady of the hour approaches.'

The tone of his voice, high and light and so forced, made Christy feel, when he looked down at the figure striding across the beach – a flimsy skirt billowing about her legs, hair tossed in the breeze – as though something had slipped down inside him, cold and smooth as a pebble.

She wore a long skirt in a daze of aquatic colours, so bright it made the navy of her sweater seem sober in comparison. For a moment, he felt that heady sensation of joy tinged with pain that observing her caused him, as she lifted her skirt at the rocks, stepping up onto the softer sand. The tide was coming in fast, and a swathe of seawater advanced suddenly towards her, threatening her dry feet, and turning to it, she seemed momentarily startled. Something about her slight loss of balance at the wave told him that she had perhaps been drinking already. Even from this distance, he could perceive she was unsteady.

'She *is* a looker,' Guy said next to him, sounding almost aggrieved, as if Christy had told him otherwise and he now saw that he had been deceived.

There was nothing to say to that, so he said nothing, watching her negotiating the steps with her head bowed, studying her feet, passing by the window without looking up. If she'd seen him, she didn't let on. In the kitchen, he heard the voices raised in greeting, felt a sudden lurch within him, and paused, steadying himself for what came next.

Both men stood there, listening to the hellos in the kitchen, before the door opened and Sorcha entered, looking flushed from her cooking exertions. Behind her, he could see the tall willowy form swathed in those glorious blues and greens, and the disparity between the two of them, his wife and his lover, occurred to him in that moment. Lara's body as she entered the room appeared long and svelte, making Sorcha appear short,

almost dumpy in comparison. And dowdy – he looked
and saw the black trousers and beige sweater she was
wearing under a navy pinstriped apron smeared with
something green like avocado. He surprised himself
with a short pang of sympathy for his wife, how unfair
it was on her, and how that injustice would worsen
shortly when he told her, finally, that he was leaving her.

'Now you two, another guest,' Sorcha announced,
ushering Lara past her so that she was standing right
next to Christy, her arm not an inch from his elbow.
'Lara, this is Guy Naseby, Stella's husband and a dear
friend.'

Guy stepped forward on cue and reached for Lara's
hand.

'Guy, this is Lara, my…oh!' she started, then laughed
as Guy bent forward and planted a kiss on Lara's hand
in an overblown gesture of chivalry. 'Well! As I was
saying, Lara and I are cousins. You remember Lillian,
don't you, Guy? Lara is Lillian's daughter.'

'Of course. She was a charming woman, your
mother,' he said, giving her the once-over and not bothering to hide it. Christy felt a small kick of annoyance.

'Lara,' he said, touching her elbow. 'You'll have a
drink?'

'Oh, I brought this,' she replied, suddenly remembering, and raised a bottle of wine in one hand.

'Now, you shouldn't have done that, Lara,' Sorcha
admonished good humouredly. 'Should she, Christy? To
bring yourself is enough.'

Christy began to feel battered by his wife's boisterous

high spirits, and as he retrieved the wine from Lara's hand, he tried to catch her eye, wanting to transmit a shared sympathy, a meaningful look. 'What torture this is', he wanted the look to say. But taking the bottle from her, she avoided his gaze, staring resolutely ahead, and despite himself, he felt the slight of her coldness.

Stella's voice called out in the kitchen – a cooking crisis had occurred, and Sorcha slipped away, making her apologies.

'So,' Christy heard Guy say, steering Lara away to the window, 'I hear you're quite the wanderer. South America, was it?'

'Yes.'

'Which parts?'

'All over, really.'

Guy launched into a detailed account of a holiday in Ecuador with his first wife, and as he spoke, Christy observed Lara while he fixed her drink. There was something different about her today, something dazed, slightly sedated. He wondered if it was nerves on her part, but suspected that there may be a pharmacological reason. He noted the dull unfocused look in her eyes as he handed her the glass, fizz spitting over ice. Her reaction to Guy's story, his unabashed charm offensive, was distinctly muted, which led him to believe she was already stoned. Outwardly, she appeared calm, cool. But surely inside she must feel awkward, uncomfortable, aware of her words and movements, a heightened sense of everything around her. Since her arrival, his fingers had been shaky, his palms sweaty. How he wished he could take something to blunt his own edges, to calm the tremblings and secretions of his body.

Guy persisted with his boastful account of Ecuador.

'And you've never been to the Galapagos yourself?' he asked incredulously. God, the man was insufferable.

'No. I never made it there,' Lara said.

Guy nodded to himself, chasing the prideful look from his face with a quick smile. And Christy, suddenly bold, feeling reckless, said, 'We were going to go though, weren't we?' and felt a flash of satisfaction at the question in Guy's face.

'Em… yes, we were,' she agreed, and he heard the waver of doubt in her voice.

'Years ago, Lara and I planned a trip together,' he explained to a watchful Guy, whose eyes darted from one to the other as they stood side by side. 'We were going to travel the world, once I had finished my degree and school was over for Lara.'

'And what happened?' Guy asked, looking for a story.

'I went alone.'

Her words seemed to cut through the air, like a warning, pulling him back, and she flashed him a glance that seemed to suggest that despite whatever she had smoked or drank, she wasn't oblivious to where he was going with this. Watching Lara now, that fixed faraway stare, the slight sway of her body, he realised too the low hum of fear running alongside the warning. He was unpredictable today, dangerous. He feared what he might be tempted to reveal.

But at that moment the door opened and Stella swept in clutching a stack of plates, her face red, her forehead shining.

'Dinner is served,' her voice sang out as she moved to the table.

The lunch was a disaster, pure and unmitigated. Sorcha stared at the charcoal ruins of the skewered kebabs lined up in rows, her nostrils assaulted by the pungent odours of burnt cardamom and that sickly clove smell of cumin. What had she been thinking? Remembering those hours spent chopping and grating, skinning and deseeding, pounding and stirring, and all there was to show for it was this yellow pulpy mess?

'Not to worry,' Stella had breezed. 'You've got peas in the freezer, and sweet corn. That'll do just as nicely.'

Stella, well meaning as she was, had done little to improve Sorcha's mood. Somehow her capable presence in the kitchen seemed to make Sorcha more nervous, thoughts turning over in her head of Stella's perfect sauces, her bottled chutneys, that bloody goat tethered in the backyard producing milk. It was all too much. And here she was in this steam-filled kitchen, the smell of scorched butter and charring in the air. She hated this kitchen, this outdated ode to the 1970s with its orange Formica-clad cabinets, the elaborate gilt handles, the roughened beige tiles. How was she supposed to produce a triumph of culinary skills in this jumbled mess, this ageing relic?

'Ready?' Stella asked, her head and upper torso peeping around the door.

'Coming now,' she called out, lifting her voice.

Arranging the chicken on the serving plate, she breathed in the warm salty scent of it, thankful she'd had the foresight – or perhaps it was the lingering knowledge of her own potential failure – to pop this bird in the oven as a standby. But as the scent wafted upwards, invading her nostrils, it took on a new odour – the whiff of failure. There was an ache in the back of her legs. She felt tired and suspected she was getting her period. That this lunch had been her idea was little comfort at this stage. Pausing at the door, armed with a roast chicken, she closed her eyes momentarily, offering up a brief prayer for strength before rearranging her features into that hostess smile and pushing through the doors, crying out, 'Now, everyone! Food at last!'

As Christy set to work carving the chicken, the rest of them, at Sorcha's encouragement, began helping themselves.

'Rice? We're having *rice*?' Avril asked, her pretty face snarled around a frown.

'Wonderful spread, Sorcha.'

'Thank you, Guy,' she beamed at him.

'Who eats rice with roast chicken?'

'Well aren't you in a beautiful mood,' she told her daughter airily, the smile for Guy dying on her face.

'Plenty of people would give their eye teeth for what

you have before you,' Stella said not unpleasantly, and was rewarded with a glare. 'You must have witnessed terrible poverty in South America, Lara.'

Sorcha looked up, surprised by this remark, unsure as to whether she should be offended by it. Was this a meal palatable only as an alternative to starvation? But Stella's eyes were fixed intently on Lara, hungry for details of street urchins and child prostitution, lurid accounts to feed her fetid imagination. Sorcha had seen her friend's bookshelves, knew all the details of her private fascinations with how the Third World lived.

'Yes, I suppose there was a lot,' Lara answered thoughtfully. 'But you kind of get used to it.'

'I'm not sure I could. I'm not sure I'd want to become that complacent.'

'Well now, I don't think you'd call that complacency,' Guy said reasonably, standing up for Lara.

'What would you call it then?'

'I don't know. Acceptance. Normality. A way of life.'

'You would accept poverty as a way of life, would you?'

'You're playing with my words, Stella.'

'I'm just saying.'

Lara's eyes were darting from one to the other, looking bewildered.

'They were rich in spirit,' she offered weakly, and Stella fixed her with a pitying look that seemed to say that's all very well but what did they eat?

Earlier, when Sorcha had left Lara alone with the two

men, Stella had given her a funny little look when she returned to the kitchen.

'So,' Stella had said, 'that's the famous Lara.'

There was something underpinning the air in which she said it – disapproval. People rarely referred to non-famous people as being famous unless it was to cast some sort of aspersion over them. Sorcha hadn't been altogether sure how to answer, and had assumed a noncommittal position by laughing generously and saying, 'That's her.'

'She's awfully pretty.'

'Do you think?'

'If a bit stoned.'

'Really?'

'Oh come on, Sorcha. Surely you saw it in her eyes? They were so glazed. That slow handshake? Definitely. That one is fond of blowing jays for sure.'

Sorcha had felt a current of shock rippling through her, comprised of a number of things. The most notable was the fact that Lara might be indulging in some kind of drug habit, which now that she thought about it wasn't entirely unfeasible, and would certainly explain a good deal of her recent behaviour. But she was also taken aback at Stella, that she should recognise these traits so easily, that she should be familiar with the lingo. There was a sneer in her voice that brought back to Sorcha those names she had tried out on her – Iris, Mavis, Enid – and felt the small, hard scab of that wound pinching at her.

Looking across at Lara now, she tried to detect some

signs that she was high. She was eating slowly, giving her food long looks before guiding it into her mouth. When she looked up at whoever had addressed her, her eyelids seemed heavy. In fact, her whole head appeared heavy, weighted with wine. Guy had taken the seat next to hers and had managed to snake a proprietary arm around the back of her chair, but casually, as if he were just resting it there.

A lull seemed to fall over the table, and Sorcha looked around at the faces, the thoughtful chewing. Tension lingered in the air following the exchange between the Nasebys and she wondered if it had any-thing to do with the rather close attention Guy was paying to his new companion.

'So, how are the renovations going, Lara?' she asked brightly, feeling someone should make an effort at lifting the mood, and noting Christy locked deep in concentration with the breast of chicken on his plate. 'Lara has been working on her house for the past couple of months,' she explained to the others.

'It's, um, well, it's better than it was. Though I haven't done a whole lot to it.'

'I've always loved that house,' Guy declaimed. 'Haven't I, Stella?'

'Have you?'

'When we first moved here I said to Stella, what the heck is a house like that doing here? A clapboard house with a porch and a screen door? That house has no earthly business on the south coast of Ireland! Didn't I say that, Stella?'

'I can't recall.'

'And who, might I ask, had the brilliant idea of building such a gem?'

'It was a cousin's house. Well, a grand-aunt, I suppose you'd say,' Sorcha explained. 'She had been living in America for some years before she was forced to come home. A marriage had been arranged for her, isn't that right, Lara?' She paused, waiting for Lara to elaborate, but her eyes were flickering past over to the heads of the two boys, Jim and Elijah, who were engaged in a process of bartering their food. 'She didn't want to come home, refused to agree to the marriage. But some pressure was brought to bear, as happened in those days, and eventually she agreed, but on one condition. If she had to go through with the marriage, then she wasn't going to live in any twee thatched cottage, any labourer's hut. She wanted a proper clapboard house with a porch and a run of steps leading down to the beach. That was the deal.'

'Amazing,' Guy breathed.

'What's so amazing about an arranged marriage?' Stella asked, and Sorcha began to wonder exactly how much she'd had to drink.

'Did they have children?' Guy asked, ignoring his wife.

'No.'

'Hardly surprising,' Stella murmured to herself.

'It must have been dreadful.' They all looked up and stared at Christy, partly because he hadn't spoken a word all afternoon, and partly because of the pained sincerity in his voice.

'Indeed,' Guy nodded his head thoughtfully.

'Being forced into a marriage like that,' Christy continued, going at his chicken with a knife and fork. 'Against your will.' His movements became savage. 'Locked into a loveless marriage.'

He paused then, as if conscious of having said too much, and Sorcha felt a sharp shock of pain as if she'd suddenly been doused in cold water.

At that, Lara began to explain to the rest gathered there how eerie and depressing she had found the house on her return from South America, how anxious she had been to throw out all the furniture, to start from scratch. Sorcha felt a flicker of gratitude at Lara's intervention on her behalf. What had Christy meant by that? She sought him out with her eyes, and as he looked up briefly she scoured his face for meaning. There was nothing but an empty gaze.

'Dessert,' she said weakly, getting to her feet.

Dessert was more successful than the rest – pavlova with winter fruits and whipped cream. In the kitchen, she glared at Christy as he brought through the plates, setting them on the counter by the sink.

'What was all that about?' she asked quietly under her breath.

'What?'

'About the house? About arranged marriages?'

'It was nothing,' he replied irritably. 'I was just making a point.'

'Are you all right?' she asked then, stopping what she was doing to turn and look at him – the tension in his shoulders, something dark at the back of his eyes.

They stood there, staring at each other like that for a couple of seconds, before he answered, 'Yes. I'm fine.'

Picking up the bowls and spoons, he turned and left the kitchen, and she followed shortly with the pavlova. On re-entering the dining room, she felt the tension still lingering. Guy was emptying another bottle of wine into Lara's glass, and Stella was slumped in her chair, glaring across at him. As Sorcha took her seat, she caught Avril's eyes and saw them flare briefly before flicking across at Guy and Lara. Sorcha paused, wondering what it was her daughter was wordlessly telling her, and then, as she turned and looked, she saw what Avril was alluding to. Guy's hand had disappeared from the table, but the angle of his arm seemed to suggest it was resting on Lara's thigh. For a moment, she felt a wave of panic. Looking around the table now, it was clear that most of the others had noticed it too. Christy was staring down at his placemat with a face black with rage, entombed in what seemed to be a furious silence. Stella was narrowing her eyes into little slits, and in that moment, Sorcha saw how dangerous she was, building up to something.

'So, Lara,' Stella began, 'I believe you're working in Crazy Prices.'

'That's right,' Lara answered, clearing her throat quickly, leaning forward, and Sorcha spied the quick movement of her hand under the table, flicking away the unwanted guest.

'And how are you finding it?'

'Fine. It's grand, actually.'

'Very different to markets in South America, I'm sure.'

Sorcha wondered where she was going with this. As Lara launched into a tentative description of markets in Peru, Stella sat there nodding her head, a small smile creeping over her face, and Sorcha wondered, now that she had succeeded in eliciting this description from Lara, how Stella would send it crashing apart with the easiest of kicks.

'And tell me,' Stella said slowly, remaining perfectly still, 'is it true what they say, that most children who are snatched are snatched in markets?'

In the stunned silence, no one spoke, no one moved, not even the two boys who up until this point had been shuffling in their seats, whispering asides to each other. But now, they all sat there, eyes fixed on Lara, waiting for her to say something. Sorcha feared that her response when it came would be shocking.

'You bitch.'

She blinked and stared across the table. Christy was looking at Stella, his eyes dark and threatening, honing in on the smirk that was dying on her face.

'Christian,' said Lara, in a tone of gentle warning.

'You absolute bitch,' he said to Stella again, who was staring resolutely at her placemat, her mouth a grim line in her face, locked in the understanding that she had gone too far.

'Please,' said Lara, getting to her feet, 'I should go.'

'No,' said Guy, his hand grabbing her wrist, restraining her. 'Please stay. She didn't mean that, did you Stella?'

'No,' she said sullenly, before making a brief attempt to look Lara in the eye. 'I'm very sorry. I don't know what came over me. I think perhaps I've had too much to drink.'

'Please sit down, Lara,' Sorcha pleaded in a conciliatory, appeasing tone. 'At least have some dessert.'

Lara looked down at the creamy fruity pile in her bowl, then looked at Sorcha again, and tears were standing in her eyes.

'I'm sorry,' she croaked, a tear leaking out and spilling over her cheek. 'I can't.'

Stumbling away from the table, freeing her arm from Guy's grasp, she seemed unsteady on her feet, visibly distressed.

Sorcha pushed herself away from the table, and Christy did too. Stella was leaning forward with her head in her hands and Guy sat back addressing his wife with a thunderous glare. In that moment, it seemed to Sorcha that this lunch couldn't have gone any worse.

At the door, she caught up with Lara, who was fleeing quickly.

'Lara,' she said and watched her cousin spinning around, giving her a tear-stained, sorry look. 'Please stay. Stella shouldn't have said that.'

'No. I'm sorry,' Lara said. 'You've gone to such trouble and I feel like I've wrecked everything.'

'Nonsense.'

'I shouldn't have come.'

'You're upset, that's all. You've been through a lot.'

'This was a mistake. This has all been such a mistake.'

She seemed so distraught, so dramatic in her vehemence, that for a moment they stood there together at the door and something seemed to change about Lara's face – it seemed…pained. It seemed guilty.

'You're so kind, Sorcha. Such a kind person. And I'm just such a—'

'Lara, don't distress yourself.'

'I'm so sorry.'

Sorcha felt something passing between them, something meaningful that she didn't fully understand.

Christy was standing beside them now.

'I'll walk you home,' he told her.

'Oh no…'

'I insist,' he said, already getting into his jacket, and just then, Sorcha saw a flicker of consternation in Lara's eye, a look of lingering regret, and something about it raised questions in her, before Christy opened the back door and led her out into the night.

The party broke up, a tearful, remorseful Stella ushered away by Guy and Elijah. Soon enough, Avril disappeared too, so it was left to Sorcha and Jim to clear away the dishes. Christy hadn't returned, and as she stood at the kitchen sink, her gaze fell out the window to the long stretch of sand. The beach was deserted, and in the shadowy darkness, she saw lights on in the house, the flickering shadows of two dark silhouettes. How much you can see from here, Sorcha thought, standing in the darkness of her own kitchen, and she remembered all those nights she had listened to Christy pacing about down here. Was he looking then too?

'Christian', she had called him.

The light went off in the house and Sorcha's eyes traced away, down to the silvery stretch of sand and his slow trudge home. She thought again of the look on Lara's face, how weighty her apology had seemed, and she remembered Neil's words – how his speculation had created a doubt inside her, and at that moment, Sorcha felt something rising up from her stomach, cold and sharp and acidic. It tasted like vomit, like bile, in the back of her throat. It tasted like the beginning of something, the dawn of realisation, the coming of knowledge – knowledge of his betrayal – and promised to bloom into something large and cavernous and frightening that she wasn't sure she had the strength for. Silently, she slipped away from the window and retired upstairs to bed.

18

We walked in silence along the crest of the beach, and in the silence I could hear the movement of fabric, the lash of my skirt against my legs. I felt kind of up and down, like I'd been underwater for a long time and had suddenly bobbed to the surface, out of breath and gratefully gulping air. The wine I had drunk, the gin and tonics, the grass I had smoked that morning, all of it swished around inside me, making me feel nauseous and unclean. But everything seemed clear and distinct under the light of the moon, and I could feel his body close to me.

'Are you okay, Lara?' he asked, and for a moment I didn't know how to answer. I wasn't okay, and yet I was afraid of what comfort he would try to provide if I admitted to that. I could feel the slow end of things coming between us, but knew it would come as a shock nonetheless.

'I'm okay.'

'You seemed a bit freaked back there.'

'Yes. I know. I'm sorry.'

'You don't need to apologise.'

'Don't I?'

'No. Stella had no right to say what she did, to upset

you like that,' he said, his voice all tight and wound up, so that I glanced across at him suddenly, saw the pinched hurt that was there, the fury, and saw, too, his pity for me. 'I can't tell you how much I wanted to lean across and smack her in the mouth.'

He looked at me then, but there was no violence in his expression, and suddenly, the way he was looking at me was too soft, too tender, and I had to look away again.

'It's been a weird kind of day,' I said at last.

'That's true.'

I thought then for a moment about telling him, then decided not to. All the way up the beach, I tossed it over and over in my mind. The silence between us was loaded with unspoken things, and I felt the weight of them crowding in on me. I thought again of the meal, of the bent heads of those two boys and how I could hardly take my eyes off them. And all the while I looked at them, especially Elijah with his dark hair, his mischievous eyes, I kept thinking of my son and what he would look like now, whether his hair had grown or had it been cut, and if so, by whom? How much taller was he? Did he still laugh as often? Were his milk teeth coming loose and falling out? I tried to imagine him with a gap in his smile, the frills of new teeth breaking through pink gums. Part of me knew that it was a mistake to cave into these fantasies, and yet it was difficult not to. It was a disposition. Another part of me felt that imagining what he looked like now was an act of faith in his continued existence. Besides, it was hard not to, given the day that was in it.

As we approached the run of steps to my house, I turned to him, seeking out his eyes in that dark face.

'It's his birthday today, you see.'

'Whose birthday?'

'Nacio's.'

He didn't say anything, at a loss for words, and I could see the shock in his eyes, the sudden tenderness, and I had to look away or it would make me cry again. His face had twisted into an expression of pain, a pain that was not his but mine.

'Lara,' he whispered.

'He's six today,' I said, gaining control over my voice. 'Somewhere, he is six. He probably doesn't even know it.' I tried to smile but my face just twisted and melted, my chin trembling dangerously.

'I think you're very brave,' he said solemnly, and I shook my head, tears close now.

'No I'm not. I'm not brave at all.' I thought of that night after Alejo left when it was all too much and I couldn't go on any longer. I remembered the feel of all those pills in my mouth, the chalkiness of them, that bitter taste, crunching between my teeth, sticking to my tongue and palate. I remembered, too, the hot, angry tears I cried, staring at all those pills spat out into the toilet, and thinking to myself: *What a coward I am.* I thought of my promise to myself on returning home, that I would clean up my life, that I would get myself together. And instead, here I was standing in the dark half-drunk, half-stoned, with a married man I had been fucking for a month now. I wasn't brave in any way at all.

'Why didn't you tell me?' he asked gently.

'I don't know.'

But that was a lie, because I did know. I didn't tell him for the same reason I had avoided his gaze all through lunch, for the same reason I had dipped into my pharmacological rescue kit that morning. Because I didn't want to admit it to myself. Didn't want to remember. And admitting it to him made it all the more real, and it was going to be hard enough getting through that lunch without the weight of that between us.

'You're shivering,' he noticed and clasped my upper arms. 'Let's get you inside.'

I allowed him to steer me up the steps, all the time turning the words over in my head, casting about for a phrase to use, something gentle, something firm. Part of me knew that it was a mistake to let him come up, to let him into my house, but at the same time, there was something so sad about him that I couldn't tell him out there in the cold night air with the waves licking blue against the sand.

Once inside, he set about turning on the lights, and I stood there watching him fixing up a fire in the grate and I thought to myself what a serious man he was, what a caring person, and I had to admit that for a moment I almost changed my mind. But then I remembered my mother's face, this look she'd sometimes give me when I'd come home late, my shirt untucked, face flushed and hair mussed. I'd catch her looking at me, her eyes small and bright, this expression like she wasn't sure what I had been up to and was wavering over whether or not to say something to me. But always behind that look was the sad trace of disappointment, and sometimes it made me strive to be good, to be a better daughter. Other times it made me cross and defiant. But tonight, as Christy straightened up, examining the fire taking light, I felt my mother's watchful gaze again, and felt so small and filthy and ashamed that I knew I couldn't carry on like this.

'I can't do this any more,' I said, and watched him turning to me, his eyes searching my face.

'What?'

'This thing between us. It's too much,' I said, shaking my head, avoiding his face, that look of surprised anguish spreading across it. 'It has to end. Now, before it goes any further.'

'You don't mean that.'

'Yes, I do.'

'Lara,' he said then, his feet coming unstuck from the place they had been rooted to. He approached me now, his face all sincere. 'You're upset.'

'Yes, I'm upset, but I still mean it.'

'Hush now,' he told me, his hands around my arms again, trying to draw me to him, pulling me towards his chest. Part of me wanted to go there so badly, but the other part – the stronger part – resisted, pulling away from him, detaching myself from his grip.

'Christian. It's over.'

He shook his head solemnly. 'No.'

I was getting that floating feeling again, my heart beating somewhere in the air in front of me, and I had to sit down. Backing away from him, I found a seat. He was still looking at me, his face a mixture of defiance and hurt, like a schoolboy, and I could tell that he was unsure of what exactly to say. Mostly, I just wanted him to leave, but felt I owed him something – an explanation, I suppose – so instead, I just sat there and lit up a cigarette.

'Today, sitting there, in your house,' I began, keeping my voice steady, 'I felt like a criminal. Like a fraud.'

'Lara.'

'Your lovely home, that lunch Sorcha had made, all the trouble she had gone too…I just felt dirty. Too dirty to sit there, sullying the atmosphere.'

'Don't say that.'

There was a quiet but determined edge to his voice that made me nervous.

'Don't you see?' I asked, looking up at him, his dark eyes, the square set of his jaw. 'This never should have happened between us. What we've done is so wrong. So terribly, horribly wrong.'

'It's not like that,' he said again, steel in his words.

'Christian, it is. Sorcha is your wife. And my cousin. All this time we've been carrying on behind her back – it makes me feel so disgusted with myself.'

He gave his head a fatigued shake and came and drew a chair up next to mine. Up close, I could see the vein pulsing in his temples, his jaw working determinedly. I could tell by his face that he wasn't about to accept this lying down. His eyes confirmed this when he turned to me, lit up with zeal, crazily hopeful.

'This is difficult,' he began, 'of course it is. We knew it would be from the start. It's understandable for you to be frightened now. I am too. To take the next step is going to be scary for both of us – for everyone concerned. But I believe that it will be worth it.'

'Christian—'

'Wait. Just hear me out. I know today was hard. Christ, it was tough for me too. I mean, do you think I want to hurt Sorcha? Or my kids? Do you think I would willingly put them through this?'

He was such a serious man, and I could tell by the intensity of his gaze that he was hurting over his family.

'But the point is,' he said and reached for my hand, 'that this is not something that is within my control. This is bigger than me. Bigger than both of us.'

His voice had dropped away to a whisper, but his grip on my hand was firm.

'I have loved you all my life. From the first moment I laid eyes on you.'

'Don't do this,' I pleaded, but he continued on.

'From the first time I met you, there, outside on that beach,' he said, pointing towards the window, and I could see the distant roll of the waves. 'It's always been you. All those summers I came here from Dublin – what did you think, that it was to see my grandparents? It was to see you, Lara. You were all I ever thought of. Even in university, when my friends were all spending their summers in America or London or Paris or Germany, I kept coming back here. Did you never wonder why that was? Did it never strike you as odd that I would choose to work the summer behind a bar in this town when I could be working in a bar in Boston or New York?' He paused, searching my face for a response, but I was lost for words. 'All those years I couldn't have you. All those years of waiting, of longing. Even when I was in college and with other girls, I still thought of you. And when I came back here that summer after first year, and you began talking of going abroad, of seeing the world, and gradually that developed into a plan between us – how hopeful I was! How happy it made me to think that finally, after those long years of waiting, of having to make do with your friendship, that finally I was going to be alone with you – that you would be mine.'

'That was a long time ago,' I said slowly, carefully. 'A lot has happened since then.'

'Yes,' he acknowledged, a hint of regret in his voice, a low note of sadness creeping in. 'All these years since that day on the beach – the last time we saw each other – I've been thinking to myself *what if*, torturing myself with alternate histories had I not been so foolish, so hasty. So bloody quick-tempered. But don't you see, Lara? You coming back here, it was meant to be. I knew it that first day I picked you up in my car. I could feel the connection between us, the electricity that charged the air. And I know you felt it too. I know you did.'

'No, Christian.'

'Look at me,' he demanded, and wearily I brought my gaze up to meet his. 'Of course you're having doubts – that's only natural. And if there were any way of doing this to avoid hurting Sorcha and the kids, then I would go with that. But there isn't. And I know that when I tell her about us, it's going to be dreadful. Unbearable.' He shuddered then, as if living the moment of revelation in his head. 'But once it's out in the open, we can all deal with it, and then start to move on.'

'How can you just sit there and speak about this as if—'

'They'll get over it in time,' he said softly but firmly. 'It will be hard at first. Devastating, maybe. But they will come to terms with it.'

He reached out and cupped my chin in his hand, gazing serenely at me, while alarm jumped up in my throat at the seriousness of what he was suggesting.

'You're not going to tell them?'

'Of course,' he said. 'They have to find out at some stage.'

'But why?'

'So that we can be together.'

I shook my head out of his grasp, sat up straight and studied his cool, handsome face, marred by the insanity of what he was suggesting, and I tried to fix on the enormity of what he was proposing. He gave me a long stare, his dark eyes drawing attention to themselves. And I knew in that moment that there was no going back – for him or for me. I knew, too, that I would have to leave this place. How could I not? There was no way I could stay living down the beach from him, living in that close proximity, not after all that we had done.

'We can't be together,' I said gently. 'Not any more.'

'Wait, Lara. Just listen. It will be tough at first, but once we get through it, we can be together.'

'What? You'd just pack your bags, stroll down the beach and move in here, is that it?' I asked, a stern note entering my tone, but I was starting to become alarmed by what he was saying.

'I've been thinking about it,' he began, dismissive of my sarcasm. 'We could leave. You could sell this place and I have money put by anyway that I was going to use to travel.'

'Are you out of your mind?'

'It will be like we always planned, you and me, all those years ago. We can go anywhere we like.'

'And what about Sorcha? What about Avril and Jim?'

'They'll have the house. We can work something out,' he said quickly, with a degree of irritation.

'Have you any idea what you are suggesting?' I asked, somewhat incredulous. 'You're talking about leaving your wife and children.'

'I know that, Lara. Don't think I haven't thought this through. Christ, I've thought of nothing else for weeks now.'

'But they're your family. Your life.'

'You're my life.'

'No,' I said firmly. 'No, I'm not. And you're a fool if you think you could just walk away from them. A fool to imagine that I would ever want you to. Just stop for a moment and think what it would be like. Not seeing your children again. Not being there to see them growing up. The pain of being separated from them. The guilt of it. Just think about it for one minute. See how unbearable that would be.'

He blinked and looked away. After a moment he took a deep breath, swallowed, and then he looked at me, his gaze steady, and when he spoke, his voice sounded husky and uncomfortable.

'If there has to be a choice…I just couldn't bear the thought of losing you again.'

I closed my eyes to him for just a second, and thought of that morning in San Pedro when I felt the ache of separation, the weight of Alejo sitting on the edge of the bed, the soft pain in his eyes, his voice weary: 'No more, Lara. No more.' What I felt then was a pain so deep and unyielding that I knew it was the beginning of terrible sorrow. But this thing with Christy was different. Despite the concoction of drink and substances I had consumed, there was a clarity to how I felt about him now, what I knew must happen. When I opened my eyes again, he was looking at me with a watery gaze, and when he spoke, his voice was utterly sincere.

'I can't live without you. I won't.'

'Don't say that.'

'But it's true,' he insisted, his voice rising a fraction.

I thought about that for a second or two, then thought about his wife, how guilty I had felt when I'd seen the sympathy in her eyes, how small and filthy it made me feel to have her bestow the warmth of her kindness on me – I, who had been fornicating with her husband for weeks. What kind of person was I anyway? And all at once, the enormity of what we had been doing – the wrongness – seemed to overwhelm me, and I thought I might not be able to breathe. I stood up suddenly, moved away from him, over to the fire, and stared into it.

'I think you should go now.'

'Not until we've sorted this out.'

'There's nothing to sort out,' I said strongly, wheeling around, impatient with him now.

'I love you.'

'No,' I insisted, shaking my head.

'You can't deny you feel the same way too.'

'That's enough, Christian,' I said, my voice rising. 'I don't want to hear any more.'

'Just look at me and tell me that this isn't love.'

Everything seemed to still in that moment, and I felt a kind of heaviness gathering in the air between us. His eyes were fixed on me intently and I saw the determination in them, the conviction that he felt.

'This isn't love,' I said coolly, without emotion.

For a moment the air shrank around those words, and something seemed to move in his face. His eyes became bright with tears, and the colour seemed to drain from his cheeks so that I could almost see the latticework of veins under his skin.

'You don't mean that,' he said hoarsely.

'This isn't love,' I said again, louder this time.

He looked at me with his eyes narrowed a little, like he didn't quite know how to take what I'd just said. I thought about saying something more, but then decided to just let it sit there between us, sinking in. After a minute he got up and I thought he might leave, but instead he walked over to the fireplace and I began to dread him pacing around in front of me, working this thing out.

'It's getting late,' I said. 'Sorcha will be wondering—'

'Let her wonder,' he snapped, and I saw the first trace of annoyance in him.

He stopped pacing, a hand to his head, before shaking it suddenly and turning to me, apologetic now.

'Sorry. It's just that…everything is so confusing. I need to get my head clear.' He paused then, and I felt my heart become possessed by a heaviness. 'Lara, when you left, all those years ago, it felt like something in me broke. It was like a piece of me just broke away after you'd gone. And now…don't you see? Something amazing has happened here.'

His eyes seemed to flare open, the amber flames dancing there, forcing a new optimism, giving it one last desperate shot.

'We've been given a second chance. How many people get that? Don't you see how lucky we are? You coming back here, at this time, it was meant to be.'

'Don't do this, Christian.'

'All those plans we had,' he persevered, 'we can still achieve them. Just think, Lara – everything we once spoke of together, we can still do it. We can go wherever we want – Asia, Africa. Pick a place. Go on – anywhere you like – just pick it.' And I remembered that day I saw him coming out of the betting shop, and I saw now the gambler in him. 'We could go back to South America,' he continued. 'I could help you look for Nacio.'

I looked at him then, something in me recoiling in horror, and shook my head firmly.

'No.'

'Lara, sweetheart,' he said, grasping hold of my arms, and I felt the strength in his hands, felt pinned by them. 'Just think about it. That's all I'm asking you to do. You don't have to decide now. It's a lot to take in, I know. And we've both had a lot to drink. But tomorrow, when you're sober, when your head is clear, think carefully about it. Trust me. It was meant to be.'

'Why aren't you listening to me?'

'Shhh.'

'No!' My voice grew loud and shrill with a new urgency. 'This has to stop. You have to listen to me!'

I looked into his stricken face, the enthusiasm dying in his eyes.

'This isn't love,' I said clearly, emphatically. 'This is loneliness. This is a crazy fling. This is trying to revive something that belongs in the past. This is trying to fill a void with something not real, not genuine.'

'That's not true.'

'It is true,' I replied to his baffled face. 'I've been in love before. I know what it feels like. And this – all these weeks, this secrecy, this deception, fucking in your car – don't you see? It's all a fake. It is not love.'

'You don't mean that.' His voice was hard and he fixed me with a hollow stare.

In that moment, I became conscious of my breathing, watching a tear creeping out of the corner of his eye. Something moved in me when I saw that tear, his eyes rimmed with fatigue, and I felt struck with an enormous sadness. But more than anything, I felt a sharp disappointment in myself. I had come home to try and rebuild myself, make new my life, and all I had succeeded in doing was ruining his. His expression was unclear as we stood there regarding each other, blurry and indeterminate.

'Christian,' I said, softer this time. 'It's over. You have to let it go.'

He seemed to tense then, withdrawing his body from the space next to me, and I felt moved to appease his pain.

'This is my fault. I should never have let things get so out of hand. I shouldn't have let things get started in the first place.'

And then he did something that clutched at my heart. Squeezing his eyes shut, he pushed the balls of his hands against them, holding them there, not moving, and when he withdrew them, the light picked up the rounded shine of his tears and I saw that his hands were shaking.

'I can't do this,' he said with a vigorous shake of his head. 'Please don't. Don't leave me.'

His voice wobbled as he said this, and I was torn between remorse and a certain embarrassment for this bewildered pleading, this sorrowing. I thought of that morning in San Pedro, when I had stepped outside onto

the dusty street, listening to the sounds of dogs barking, the chiming of bells in the distance, and breathing
in I had smelled the smoke and the dust and the engine
fumes gathering. There was heat on my face as I stood
there and thought: I am alone now. And walking
through the town, trying to come to terms with it in my
mind, the knowledge kept drilling through my calm
thoughts. I knew. Right away I knew that this was the
beginning of sorrow. My whole body had wanted to lie
down and let it all pass over me. And yet I forced my feet
to keep moving, to keep walking, thinking as I walked:
this would be the worst I'd ever know. That nothing
would ever hurt this much again.

A shadow of that pain was passing over me now, and
the thought that I was inflicting a reflection of it onto
him filled me with remorse. But I thought again of
Sorcha, the warmth in her tone, the genuine sympathy,
and the guilt rose up so strongly inside me that I knew
I had to be harsh.

'It's over,' I said again, working hard to keep the
wavering doubt from my voice. Then walking to the
door, I opened it. 'Now I think you should leave.'

After a moment, he got up and slowly followed me,
both of us avoiding each other's eyes. He paused briefly
in the doorway as if considering saying something
more, then thinking better of it.

But as he stepped out onto the veranda and into the
night, he turned back to look at me, his mouth twisted
and sarcastic, his eyes reproachful.

'You've broken my fucking heart,' he said.

He held me there for a moment with his eyes before stepping away from the door. I stood there watching him descending the steps, down onto the beach, his hands jammed into his pockets, my own heart hammering in my chest, as he walked slowly and sadly away from me.

19

Days passed and he felt them growing shorter. He went about his business as usual, functioning in a mechanical way – getting up in the morning, going to school, getting through the classes as best he could, busying himself in the evening in his study, locking himself away. He tried to work on his book, but found he had lost faith in it.

The nights lengthened and he slept poorly, having nightmares he couldn't remember when he woke up. Instead he was left with the strange feeling of having been visited by something sinister. It left a shadow over him when he woke, a mark that stayed with him as he passed through the days. Waking in the night, he no longer rose from the bed and padded downstairs to the dry cavern of the kitchen. He didn't want to linger by the kitchen window, to gaze out at the black spread of land, to wait quietly as his eyes grew accustomed to the dark, blindly picking out the dark shell of her house, hopeful for a flickering light, some kind of message, some kind of signal. Instead he forced himself to lie there, his wife's gentle breathing rising and filling the room.

He rose early, hours before he needed to, and sat in

his study with a mug of cooling tea, listening to the house waking up, rousing itself around him. At breakfast, he sat quietly eating his toast, unwilling to become involved in the early morning bickering between Avril and Jim, refusing to be drawn in. Unobserved, he watched Sorcha as she moved about the kitchen preparing lunches for the children, refilling the teapot and the toaster, attending to the surly demands of her family. She seemed outwardly unperturbed by his brooding. A couple of nights ago, burying his pain, he had almost, but not quite, made love to his wife. Afterwards, she had kept her hand on his collapsed penis, stroking it softly, and he had felt tears of shame leaping in his throat. 'It doesn't matter,' she had whispered, and he had wanted to cry out in shame. Afterwards, he had held her in the darkness, willing himself to feel something, desperate for some kind of connection. Instead, he had felt a seam of panic opening inside him – panic over the knowledge that this was to be his lot, his whole life spanning out in front of him. This was what he had bargained for.

In the bathroom he brushed his teeth savagely, attacking his gums painfully as if trying to scour away the words she had said, *it's-over-it's-over-it's-over* running endlessly through his head. Greeting his own reflection in the mirror, he saw the haggard look about his features, the dark shadows lurking in the corners of his face, skin sagging around his jaw, daubs of purple like bruising beneath his eyes. *I am a broken man*, he announced to his reflection before tapping his razor sharply against the enamel of the sink, wrenching his concentration away from this indulgent self-pity.

He kissed his wife goodbye and felt the bitterness in his heart as he left the house behind him. In the car he drew a deep breath in preparation for the hours that lay ahead, another day he must get through. Tiredness stretched through his limbs, across his back, communicating itself down the length of his spine.

He didn't know how he got through the morning. He got the boys to read aloud or to study quietly, unable to engage with them in discussions. There was a band of pain clinging to his forehead and temples. He sat back in his chair and rested his head against the blackboard, his attention drifting in and out, incidents and events from the last few weeks tumbling back over him in waves – the image of her walking alone at the side of the road that day, lost and forlorn; her sadness that day of the regatta when she told him about Nacio; the soft caress of her voice when she said his name; the heat that rose up to greet his fingertips every time he touched her. All of these things surrounded him, these and a hundred other things, some real, some figments of his imagination. In his mind, their affair had raced on ahead through the days and nights, becoming something firm, something lasting. It had charged on ahead, tackling those difficult decisions that would have to be made, the twisting apart of the knot of his marriage, wrenching himself away from his life, his family, his work.

In those hours of daydreaming, he had faced up to

the guilt, the horrible gut-wrenching knowledge of the crime he was committing by breaking the bond with his wife, leaving his children, turning his back on his family, his home. What kind of a man could do such a thing? That is the question that would be asked of him. But by then he would be gone. They would be gone. And no one would ever hear his explanation of how he couldn't go on any longer, how he couldn't live a lie any more. He had done it for fifteen years, and to carry on like this would kill him. They would put it down to an early mid-life crisis. There would be some who would point out that they had never liked him, never trusted him. Those with longer memories would hark back to the rushed marriage, the premature birth of his daughter, and comment to each other that it was always doomed to fail. With that kind of a start, it was inevitable that things would fall apart.

Some would blame Lara, the types that always put the blame on the woman – seducing a married man – not realising that he had given himself willingly, that he had ached for her in ways they couldn't imagine. All of these things had echoed down the long corridors of his mind. But now they were drowned out by a newer, bleaker thought – she didn't want him.

'It's over,' she had said, her voice low and firm.

Shockwaves passed through him at the memory, and something deep within him moved – a new knowledge, absolute and unsinkable, that they must be together. They were meant to be together. He had known it from the very beginning, all those years ago on that sunny afternoon, the power that seemed to move between them. He had been a fool to ignore it, to do nothing about it. And now, to undermine what they had in any way was a sin, a crime against nature. He looked into the future without her and saw the endless stacking up of days and nights and years stretching out ahead of him, the endless spiral of time. It could not be. He must find some way to persuade her, some way to exert his will.

At lunch hour, he left the school grounds and hurried to the telephone box on the corner outside the church.

'It's me,' he said urgently, hearing that whispered panic in his own voice, trying to calm it down, to pull it back. There was silence on the line, and when she responded, it was in a quiet voice. He heard the heaviness, the weariness in it.

'There's no point to this.'

'Wait. Just hear me out. Those things I said the other night – I should have thought them out first. I know I seemed a bit intense—'

'Christian.'

'No, wait. I'm sorry I blurted everything out like that. If I frightened you, I truly am sorry. I want you to know that.'

He heard a long sigh at the other end of the line. He pictured her leaning against the bureau, the receiver tucked under her chin, those grey eyes casting out over the bay through the window. As if trying to catch a glimpse of the same sky, he turned and faced west, saw the expanse of pewter, clouds scudding across it, rain on the horizon.

'Okay,' she said at last. 'Is that all?'

'No. No, that's not all. I…I wanted to…'

'Christian.'

'I love you.'

There was a pause.

'No.'

'I do. I love you. I can't pretend that I don't – I won't pretend it.'

'Stop it.'

'Why? Why should I? Are you so afraid of the truth, Lara? Are you scared of being honest?'

'Don't you dare try and take the moral high ground with me.'

'All your life you've been running away. Running from here, from your mother. Skipping from place to place, never settling, never giving anything a chance. Well, I'm not going to let you run away from me – from us.'

'Don't lecture me like I'm one of your kids.'

'I know you love me too,' he said, and he heard the wheedling tone in his voice and hated himself for it, and said again, stronger and more resolute, 'I know you do.'

A silence developed. She was quiet for the longest time. He felt blood pounding in his temples and he leaned his head against the glass, felt the coolness of it against his fevered skin. He was standing on the brink of a precipice. What she might say, the words she might utter, could send him sailing over the edge, falling down and down into oblivion.

'No,' she said at last, and he felt something kick inside his chest. 'I don't love you.'

'You…'

'I have never loved you. It was just sex.'

The word cut him like a blade slicing his flesh. Her voice when it reached him sounded cool and metallic, tainted with a new bitterness. There were no tears in her voice now – her emotions were steady.

'Lara.'

'It's over, Christian. Don't call me again.'

And with that, she put down the phone.

He heard the dismissive click of the receiver before the long, slow beeps. It was a few moments before he could return it to the cradle. Outside, cars moved in the street, traffic roared and kids in their uniforms sauntered back towards school. They travelled in packs, laughing and shouting, thrusting their fists into bags of crisps. All of these sounds filtered through into the box, penetrating his consciousness, but inside he was filling up with white noise – and the start of something else. All he wanted was to sit down and cry.

In the afternoon, the pain in his head worsened. It was twinned with an ache in his chest – the ache of a new knowledge that this was it, this was to be his lot. This life he was living was to be his happiness, nothing more. He was bound to go back to the life he had been living before she returned. Days and years stretched out ahead of him and he felt a great sorrow opening up within him.

Through the haze of tiredness and grief that lay like a fog over his brain, he became aware of a raised hand, and a low snigger rippling through the class.

'Yes, what is it?' he asked and Robert O'Shea put his hand down, earnestly leaning forward on his desk.

'Sir, you haven't asked any of us to read out our essays.'

He groaned inwardly. It was customary for him to ask one of the boys to read his essay aloud on a Friday afternoon. But at that moment, he wasn't sure if he could withstand the stilted, awkward prose and the painful probing and needling required to get the boys to have any meaningful discussion of the piece beyond 'it's boring' or 'it's crap' or some other mindless banality.

'Okay,' he conceded. 'Robert, seeing as you asked, why don't you read out yours.'

'If you don't mind sir, Carl would like to read his out.'

He felt a sudden invasive alarm and his response was immediate, fuelled by his panic.

'No.' A sharp syllable, fired from his mouth like a bullet.

'Why not?'

'Don't question me, O'Shea, just read your essay.'

'But I only got a C minus and you gave Carl a B.'

Christy felt his panic rising with O'Shea's desperate wheedling tone. And even though Christy knew he was being unfair, knew that what he was doing was wrong, preventing the boy from reading out his essay, the first essay he had put some effort into, indeed the first time he had shown any enthusiasm whatsoever towards his studies, and here was his own teacher suppressing it – still, he couldn't bring himself to allow all of that to come tumbling out. He refused to look at Carl. He could feel the heat of his piercing gaze, knew already the smirk that had come to rest on that acne-riddled face. After an angst-ridden few days spent agonising over the essay, the implicit threat it contained, what to do about it and how to diffuse the situation, he had come to the decision that he would say nothing. Instead, he had awarded the boy a B – a higher grade than the treacherous little essay deserved – and hoped that it would silence him. And now, today of all days, when he felt forlorn and vulnerable and raw with pain, his plan was unravelling before his eyes.

'For the last time, O'Shea,' he snarled, his anger rising, 'read out your bloody essay or shut up!'

Something was said then – a word – he couldn't be sure of it, or who said it. The whisper of it lingered in the air around them.

'Who said that?' he demanded, and was greeted by silence.

Fascist. That was the word. He was sure of it now.

'Who fucking said that?' he screamed.

Yet still there was silence. He looked down at Carl, knowing that he was the culprit.

'Was it you?'

'I don't know. Maybe. Tell me what it was, and I'll tell you if I said it.'

A ripple of laughter scaled across the room. His head was thumping, bile in the pit of his stomach. He felt how dangerous this boy was to him and suddenly experienced a surge of hatred so powerful it made him rock back on his feet.

'Get out,' he said in a low voice, barely controlled.

Carl just sat there, staring back at him, testing him, taunting him with the coolness of his gaze and suddenly waves of anger surged upwards in a jet of rage.

'Get the fuck out of here!' he screamed.

Slowly, Carl got to his feet, shuffled his books together and, tucking them under his arm, turned to face his teacher.

'By the way, Mr Archibald,' he began tentatively. 'How's your girlfriend?'

They stood perfectly still for a moment, teacher and pupil, looking straight into each other's eyes. Christy felt a tremble of murderous rage. The ground seemed to be tipping away from him, his legs suddenly weak. And just then, something snapped within him. He could almost hear the sound of it breaking inside his head – the snap of his momentary departure from reason. And there, in front of the whole class, he drew back his fist before sending it crashing into the centre of Carl Ring's face.

20

We came here when I ten years old, all the way from Basingstoke, England. There was the long drive across England and Wales, and then the boat from Hollyhead, the three of us up on deck where it was cold and the wind hurt my ears. Someone was being sick over the rail. But my mother wanted to catch the first glimpse of Ireland, our new country. She was wearing her belted raincoat that day, and a scarf over her hair to stop it getting messed up in the wind. Her eyes were hidden behind big square sunglasses, but I remember the brightness of her smile – that splash of red lipstick. 'A touch of glamour,' she used to say before drawing the colour over her wide, smooth mouth.

I remember, too, the pitch of excitement that hung in her voice as she described the house to us. 'It's beautiful,' she said as the three of us sat huddled together on a wooden bench, the spray from the sea filling the wind with salt. 'It has high ceilings and wooden floors, loads of space and light. And there are antiques, and an open fire and a beach on the doorstep. An incredible gift,' she said again, and I remember how she had looked from me to my father with that bright smile, her face all tight and stretched with hope. 'It's the best thing,' she had said out loud to nobody in particular. 'The best thing for everyone.'

By the time Dublin Bay came into view along the horizon, she was almost giddy with excitement. I watched as my father tried to lift his spirits to meet hers, but the brightness of her enthusiasm had grown shrill, her smile stretched thinly across her face, lipstick on her teeth, and watching the grim set of his features, I began to wonder whether the glowing descriptions and listing of advantages was more for his benefit than for mine. I looked out at the sea, grey and unforgiving, and held myself tightly.

As we leaned against the rail while the ferry drew into Dún Laoghaire harbour, I saw my mother wrapping her arms around his waist, pressing her body into his back, and I could barely hear the words she whispered down the coil of his ear – 'Everything will be different now.' I knew that was why we had come here – because of that flimsy hope she was clinging to. But there were pretty women in the south of Ireland too, and it wasn't long before it became apparent that nothing much had changed at all.

People don't change, after all. I learned that lesson early in life. And on this late October afternoon, with the wind outside filling up with autumnal leaves, I made the depressing realisation that I was no different, that nothing about my recent behaviour was new or unexpected. It was an old pattern, a familiar weakness, this need to seek solace in the arms of someone else and all the destruction and chaos that came with it. I looked about me at the clean bright walls of my mother's house, the varnished floorboards – remnants of the great effort I had made to start afresh – and wondered again, what had it all been for? A chill from my past had come over me; the sordid trappings of another mis-guided, ill-conceived relationship and all the difficulties of disentangling myself from it. I thought back to the men I had become involved with before Alejo and felt a grave disappointment in myself that I had allowed it to happen all over again.

In one corner of the room, my bags lay packed and ready. As yet, I had made no arrangements, no flight bookings, but the desire to go had sprung up so suddenly, blooming within me from the moment I first opened the envelope and read what lay within, the latest of his cryptic messages, and yet this one was different. It had arrived in an envelope, the postmark was Parati, Brazil, and it contained a birthday card. And this time, he had written in it.

It was lying there now, resting on top of my luggage, along with the other cards and a framed photograph of Nacio I'd found in my mother's bedroom. I had looked over those cards again and again – all day, I couldn't get away from them. The vividness of their colours, the love they still stirred up inside. But the card that had arrived this morning was different. The whole house seemed to shrink around it, that one small card, the enormity of what it contained. Blues and greens, a cartoon mouse, a badge pinned to the top right hand corner – '6,' it said, in bright sunny yellow.

All day that number had weighed like a stone inside me. It was a week late, but true nonetheless. Six. He had remembered. But far more than that, there was the possibility that he believed again. I felt flooded with this new hope, so sudden and unexpected. All the possibilities that I had begun to close my mind to, that I had started to shut myself off from, were suddenly alive again, the door flung wide open. Questions jumped inside me, multiplying, spawning new questions, bouncing underneath the surface of my skin. It seemed certain to me that this card was a gesture of his renewed faith in our child's existence and I thought again of those small words printed inside – so small and so few, yet clamouring and swollen with meaning. After all this time, all this waiting. I turned them over again in my head. 'I miss him. I miss you.' And staring at that card, my bags packed, the house holding its breath, I knew I had to get out.

The sky was filled with ribbons of light as I stepped out onto the veranda. It was a relief to escape the confinement of the quiet house. All day, the air had been thick with his scent – that little-boy scent, like warm milk and sleep and a far-off whiff of urea – so that each time I entered a room, I could smell him, like he had just left as I entered. I had to get out of that house full of ghosts, out to where my mind could breathe. Although the beach was empty, I was wary of walking it, scared in case I met Christy, and I thought again of the conversation we'd had on the phone that afternoon, the desperate notes at the edges of his voice, and I thought again of his wife and kids, and made a kind of vow to myself to try and sort out my own life without fucking anyone else's up. I decided to steer clear of the beach with its low tide and its own whispery ghosts, and instead I headed for Cooscrom for an evening swim.

The road narrowed, its banks alight with mont-bresia, the sheep staring lazily as I passed, and as I walked, I tried to feel some kind of goodbye. I was leaving, and I knew that I would not be coming back. I thought again of the cautiously optimistic e-mail I had received from the private detective in Brazil, and felt impatient to be back there. Reaching the turn, there was a gentle hum from the ocean, and in the distance I could make out the archipelago of islands shaped by the sea's relentlessness. The water was reflecting the evening sunlight, and for some reason I thought of my father, of the evening strolls we had taken long ago, before his abrupt departure, and the stillness that would sometimes come over him in those moments – how rare those moments of calm were, instances of serenity amid a turbulent, complex personality. People thought he was charming. 'Your father is a hoot,' they used to say to me. 'A gas man.' He liked to introduce my mother to people as his 'current wife' and smile beatifically when greeted by their laughter. My mother would stand there smiling throughout, silently bearing it – she, too, wore masks in public. But later, when I had grown up and knew something more of the world, I thought of my mother and how those words must have stung. The cruelty of them, the veiled threat, conducted so publicly, drawing snorts and snickers. She must have felt they were laughing at her, always the butt of his jokes.

As I walked, I remembered my father in one of his calmer moments, when his only audience was his thirteen-year-old daughter, walking down to Cooscrom in the fading light of the day. Reaching the wall, we had looked out onto the rocks, the pebbled cove, and on one occasion there lay the dead body of a seal stretched out on the stones, a bullet wound in its belly. We stood over it together and he shook his head sadly, his comment about the local fishermen and their callousness lost in the breeze. But then he said something that I caught, words that I held onto. 'The sea always gives up what it takes away, Lara. It might hold it hostage for a while, but eventually, it will surrender what it has stolen.' This wasn't long after the baby had been washed up onto the beach, and we both felt the resonance of his words as we looked down on the inert body of the seal, the ocean whispering in the distance.

For a long time, I had forgotten those words. But almost twenty years later, standing in a police station in Brazil, my little boy's sandal in my hand and that pain convulsing in my chest, those words came back to me, echoing up from the tunnel of the past. They seemed to act as a poultice against the wound that had opened up inside me. That if my son had drowned, then there would be a body. And as days and weeks and months went by, my father's words seemed to nourish the hope within me. That if Nacio had drowned then the sea would wash him up on the shore. And as the sea refused to yield up a body, I knew he couldn't be dead. I refused to believe it. Now, standing here alone, peering over the wall, I remembered those words again, and they seemed to shore up the hope that lay within me. Those words nestled alongside the lines Alejo had written – *I miss him. I miss you* – and in that moment I didn't know whether they made me happy or angry with myself for coming so close to losing faith.

The water in the cove was calm, a gentle tide pulling back and releasing, spilling salty bubbles over the cold grey sand. I was alone. Some part of me craved the ocean – an old longing. The sand felt cold and hard, and after stripping down to my swimsuit, I picked my way down the stony descent.

Once – a long time ago now, when Alejo and I had been together a year, maybe longer – I stepped into the sea at Parracas and swam out beyond the pier, out into the Pacific Ocean. Past the floating buoys, out to where the cliffs ran jagged into the swell, to Dead Man's Point. It was our first time there together – summer – and I remember the brown bodies, oiled and iridescent, stretched over the rocks, the bright colours reflecting off buckets and towels and bikinis. There were roars from the boys who were hurling themselves off the jumping ledge, the spluttering impact of their bodies penetrating the ocean. Gulls screamed overhead, and far away there was the drone of the fishing boats, green and blue and white in the sun. Suddenly I became overwhelmed by the energy, the sheer force of life emanating from that corner of the world. I turned to Alejo, lying on his towel, a hand raised to shield his eyes from the sun.

'I'm going to do it,' I said.

'What?'

'The swim. Out there.'

He followed my outstretched arm with his eyes.

'No,' he said, shaking his head. 'It's too dangerous.'

'I can do it.'

'You're crazy. A crazy lady.'

He smiled and ran his hand across my tanned belly, fingering the elastic of my bikini, teasing.

'You watch,' I said. 'I'll show you.'

And he did watch. He watched me stroke through the water, strong and purposeful. When I reached the buoys threaded through with blue rope stretched across the bay, I looked back and saw him standing at the edge of the water, hands on his hips, shaking his head.

Dipping under the rope, I reached out and swam, past the pier, out, out to where the water dragged and pulled, feeling its strength, its tenacity, its power. I swam until I became afraid, until I felt the water tugging at my limbs like slippery hands rising up from the deep to clutch at my ankles. Such foolishness, risking everything on a whim. What was I trying to prove?

When I got back to shore, stepping out of the water, dripping and exhausted, he came forward and folded me in a towel, still shaking his head, and smiling at me, that broad grin, those white teeth, exasperated and proud.

'You are truly crazy,' he said, rubbing my quaking limbs. 'You could have been killed.'

'I know. It was stupid.'

'Promise you won't do that again. Ever.'

'I promise.'

It was autumn now, and far from that sunny corner of the world. There were no swimmers this evening as I waded alone into the empty water. The shock was palpable, blue-green cold that climbed from my feet, its icy fingers clawing at my limbs, its nails forking my flesh, making me gasp with pain. I forced myself to go deeper, the tide rising, sucking up through my swimsuit, drenching the fabric as it crept over my flesh.

Standing with arms outstretched, the water had reached my breast, my heartbeat and breathing quickening with the heightened sensation. The cliffs were black and threatening in the distance. I held my breath, poised for the certain pain that would follow. Then, closing my eyes, I allowed myself to be drawn into the water – arms, shoulders, neck and chin. My feet lifted off the gritty seabed, and I was suddenly adrift, consumed with pain, my movements frantic and clumsy as I struggled to swim, desperate to escape the cold by plunging deeper into it.

As I swam, I thought of that stretch of beach outside Ubatuibe where they found his sandal, that long arc of sand nestled into the forest, palm trees and conifers and deep green jungle creepers. I remembered the waves, their height and glorious power, the roar of them as they rose above the water, toppling over each other, exploding onto the beach. Out here in the water, amid the ferocious chill that sucks at the limbs and clenches around the heart, I tried to feel whether this might have been the end for him. I tried to sense the distress of his jaded body, how it might have battled against it. But I couldn't feel it. I couldn't believe it. And still I went deeper. Further out into the bay, I stroked the resistant water with weakened arms, chin held tensely over the water, eyes fixed firmly on the pier. Tired muscles sent out indignant protests at the sudden effort required of them. They tensed and strained, making themselves leaden, pulling on each tendon and nerve.

And then I stopped. I was alone, stranded, out of my depth, treading icy water in the empty bay. I turned my head to look all around. The rocks, gilded in the last rays of the setting sun, looked so benign, an innocent mask over their deadly edges. High up behind the pier, cattle were grazing on the hill, the sun behind them casting their big sleepy silhouettes against the shade of Killealan Mountain. The silence was broken by the cries of the chough bird, casting out its lonely goodbyes across the bay.

It was then that I saw him. The grey pier, with its blue netting and mossy steps leading down to the boats, was all but deserted. Except for the boy. He stood there, small limbs emerging from black shorts and orange T-shirt, his dark hair lifted by the breeze. I couldn't read his expression. My hand came out of the water. It was white and bloodless. All my extremities were numb with the cold. But my little boy didn't wave back, just stood there, watching me. And as the sea swept around my body, I felt each cell and pocket, every pore and crevice, being gathered in. My body was being reclaimed by the sea, like a raisin plumping out in water, and I knew it couldn't be true. I knew it was not him.

Something bubbled up inside my head, endorphins stirring themselves and a cry rose up from my lungs, the lump bursting in my throat. I turned away from him, my body enveloped in brine – soothing, forgiving. And as I offered my flesh to the waves, I waited for it all to pass, waited for his image to fade, for it to be washed away by the water. I felt the pain of the sores on my heart, like open wounds licked with brine, and I knew what it meant, seeing him again like that. He was calling me back. And what I wanted more than anything was to be there, in the place where I had lost him, to start again with a firm resolve, and this time I would find him. The strength to start that search all over again seemed to invigorate my tired limbs. The goodbye I had been seeking was echoing all around me, the sea whispering an apology.

Evening was closing in over Cooscrom as the sun crept further west. Killealan Mountain cast its cold shadow over the sea. Dressed and still shivery, I walked away without looking back. I knew why I had come back here to this place of my childhood. The need to escape South America for just a little while – its colours and smells, its heat and noise – all of this had served as a reminder too painful to endure. And so I had returned here, to a place he had never been. But that evening, as I walked, I could feel the green waves behind me rising proudly before crashing against the cliffs, their energy pulsing through the cove, their buoyancy, their tenacity, their terrible life-affirming beauty. And something inside me stirred, something old and engrained – an instinct, a hunger to find him, and I steadied myself for the journey that would follow, poised to begin again.

21

Sorcha began with the mushrooms, spilling them out onto a tea towel and brushing the dirt off them before reaching for the knife and chopping board. As she sliced and shredded, she said their names in her head – girolles, chanterelles, blewits, porcini. It calmed her to recite them over and over like that. Pausing to glance at the recipe again, spaghetti with wild mushrooms, she took a sip of wine, Chianti – it seemed only fitting – then ran her hands swiftly down the front of her apron. Outside, the sky was filling up with wind. Grey clouds scudded above the sea.

The oil in the frying pan began to sizzle, and she dropped the first handfuls of mushrooms in, then checked on the veal under the grill. She added the remainder of the mushrooms, then garlic and chilli and a pinch of salt, and began cooking the pasta. There was something restful about her preparations, the love that went into them. His favourite meal. As she took the pan off the flame and squeezed in the lemon juice, she thought of their honeymoon in Italy all those years ago, and a meal they had shared one night in the Tuscan hills – succulent veal, an exquisite mushroom sauce, a roll of steaming pasta served on a white plate. Afterwards, they had walked hand in hand back down along a stony road, both of them feeling a little drunk and lecherous, the avenue flanked by tall dark trees and bats flapping above them. Some nights are magical, rare in their potency, their bewitching power, and that night was a diamond in her memory. She thought about it as she took her glass of wine and wandered into the dining room, and knew she was hoping that the meal being prepared might stir up the memory of that night for both of them, breathing life back into it.

She had opened a second bottle of wine and left it to breathe. It sat on the dining room table amid the New-bridge cutlery and John Rocha glasses. The candles were lit, the napkins folded, and Sorcha caught sight of her reflection in the mirror − rouged cheeks, lipstick, diamonds sparkling from her earlobes. Returning to the kitchen to make the final preparations, she heard his key in the lock, the familiar sound of the door opening and closing behind him, and felt a skip in her heartbeat − anticipation at the prospects for the evening ahead, what she hoped they might achieve, what might be rekindled.

'Hello you,' she said breezily, watching him surveying the kitchen, the scent of food greeting him, this offering she had made.

'Sorcha.'

'You're home late,' she remarked in a voice possessed of determined good humour.

'Sorry.'

'No need to be sorry,' she laughed. 'Just glad you're here.'

She flashed him a swift smile before turning back to the stove and felt the force of her own optimism.

'Are the kids home?' he asked.

'No. Actually, they're not going to be home tonight. Avril is staying over at Annette's and Jim is going to Elijah's for the night.' With the food prepared, she turned to face him now, her back against the counter, and looked up at him with hope in her heart. 'I'm cooking veal and mushrooms. Your favourite. I thought, seeing as it's just the two of us, we could make a night of it.'

His eyes were on the food behind her, and something about the slump of his shoulders spoke to her of a weariness that seemed to threaten her enthusiasm, shrinking away from the reach of it.

'Look,' she said brightly, pointing at the open door, and watched as he looked past into the dining room – the table set for two, candles, the good silver, wine waiting to be poured. 'Just the two of us,' she said again, breathily. 'Just like the old days.'

She was standing behind him and was aware of the proximity of her body to his. From his silence she could tell that he knew what this dinner meant. As if to reinforce it, she reached out, placing her hand in the small of his back, and gently began to massage his spine. He used to find it soothing, during the first years of their marriage. But time had changed all that and she found that he was tensing to her touch, twisting away from her, and turning, she caught sight of his eyes, the fear that was in them. They seemed unfocused and she could smell alcohol on his breath. She stood perfectly still for a moment, looking straight into his eyes.

'What's the matter?' she asked quietly, her eyes darting all over his face.

'I…I…'

But as he struggled for the words, the phone erupted in the hall, and she turned from him warily, going to answer it, when he caught her arm, pulling her back.

'Don't answer it.'

'Christy? It could be one of the kids.'

'It's not. I'm telling you.'

'What's gotten into you?'

He kept his eyes on her, and she felt her throat grow dry and stiff. Watching him, he seemed to struggle for the words to say. When at last his voice came hoarsely it was in a whisper she hardly recognised.

'Something happened today at school. Something serious.'

The phone stopped ringing. Sorcha stood very still.

'I've done something,' he began, faltering as her eyes filled with a new fear. 'A boy at school – one of my pupils – he…I hit him.'

'You *what*?'

'I hit him. Punched him.'

'Oh my God.'

'I don't know how it happened. He just provoked me and I—'

'Was he hurt?'

'I don't…he was bleeding…'

'Jesus Christ. Oh, Jesus Christ.'

She pulled her arm away from him and leaned back against the counter, suddenly weak as the full implications began revealing themselves to her – that her husband would probably lose his job, his pension, their financial security suddenly gone. Her mind filled up with nightmarish images of court cases, civil injury suits, unemployment.

'I don't understand. How did this happen? Whatever possessed you to do such a thing?'

His hands covered his face – a nest of fingers – and from behind it, she heard a low moan and a thin, small voice breaking through. It distressed her to see him like this, and she was moved to come towards him, reaching out and taking his hands in hers, moving them gently away from his face.

'What happened, love?'

'Sorcha…Christ, I just lashed out at him. It all happened so suddenly. The things he was saying…'

'What was he saying?'

'He knew. His essay – I wouldn't let him read it out. I couldn't let him tell everyone…'

'Tell them what?'

He was looking all about him, refusing to return her gaze, and she smelled his breath and wondered again how much he had had to drink. There was an incoherence about him, a wildness, that was disconcerting, and the panic was starting to buzz in her brain.

'He had seen me with her…oh God, I can't look at you when I say this.'

He dropped her hands and turned away from her then, and Sorcha, leaning against the counter, heart pounding in her chest, saw the defeat in his shoulders, the tension running the length of his spine. Breathing in the nourishing scent of her cooking, in that instant, all of her earlier hopefulness, her optimism, her tentative affection evaporated, blown away in the brisk wind of his account. The scent invoked memory, a night of love in the Tuscan hills, and the memory seemed particularly cruel at this point in time. One word was resounding in her head – *her*. It drilled right through to the core of her being, and she knew, even then she knew who he meant. It was as if she had known all along. She asked the question anyway.

'Who?' she said slowly, knowing the answer but needing to hear him say it, admit to it. 'Who did he see you with?'

His hand went to his face; it was as though he couldn't bring himself to look at her.

'It's Lara, isn't it?' she said quietly. 'Isn't it?'

There was a sickness in her stomach now as she watched him turning to her, reaching inside himself for words to grasp and simplify and soften everything he had done, to try and explain it all away. She stood there, riding the roll and swell of her nausea, and when he finally brought himself to look at her and she saw the treachery in his drawn face, she clapped her hand to her mouth, sudden tears in her throat. For a moment, neither one of them moved.

'How could you do this?' she demanded in a voice fractured with hurt.

'Sorcha.'

Without warning, she began to cry. Her whole body shuddered noiselessly as she wept, and all at once she felt stunned and useless in the face of this great sadness rinsing through her. He was looking at her with an air of expectant sorrow and she found herself repeating quietly, 'How could you do this?', her voice a whisper, almost as if she were saying it to herself.

Stepping away from him, back to the sink, she struggled to compose herself. He was staring at her, ready to talk, to explain, now that she knew his secret, and it seemed important to her that she was calm, in control of herself, for what would come next.

'How long has it been going on for?' she asked, keeping her voice low and steady.

'A couple of months.'

Silent calculations in her head.

'Not long after she came back here, so.'

'I suppose not,' he replied, sounding a little hollow.

'And is it serious?'

He didn't answer immediately, just bit his upper lip, a furrow of tenderness appearing in his brow, and she saw immediately that it was as serious as it could be, and a new anger bubbled up inside.

'Sorcha. I didn't mean for any of this to happen.'

Without really meaning to, she gave a derisory snort and moved to the stove, seizing the pan, her lovingly prepared meal, and crossing the room to the dustbin, she flung the contents into it, slamming the empty pan into the sink. He stood by silently, witnessing her vibrant aggression as she returned for the veal steaks that she had so carefully pounded and seasoned and grilled, lobbing them into the bin on top of the pasta, waves of discontent billowing out from her like breath in cold air.

'That's what people always say, Christy – that they didn't mean for things to happen.'

'I know. But it's true.'

'Rubbish. You must have had a choice. There must have been some point when you could have stopped yourself, when you could have held back, reasoned with yourself, realised the damage and pain and hurt…'

She broke off, her voice cracking with a sudden emotion and she lowered her head, thinking of the room next door – the candles, the wine, the pristine white napkins.

'I suppose that's true,' he conceded. 'There probably was a point. But I was overwhelmed.'

She rolled her eyes and turned away, not wanting to receive his pleading looks, unprepared for any emotional account.

'I knew it,' she told him. 'All the time I knew it – the way you acted around her, how secretive you had become. She's hardly back a wet week and already you're…' She let the sentence hang there, shaking her head sorrowfully. 'God, I'm such a fool! I should have guessed before she even arrived back here. But me, like an idiot, thought that maybe the last sixteen years might mean something to you. That maybe I might mean something to you.'

'Sorcha—'

'Oh, spare me,' she said, anger and disgust knotting in her voice.

She pushed past him into the dining room, and felt him following her, standing by as she briskly gathered up the cutlery, tossing it noisily into the drawers.

'Stop this,' he said gently. 'Let's sit down and talk about this properly.'

But she ignored him, concentrating on putting away the glasses, corking the wine, extinguishing the candles with her finger and thumb, all the while trying hard to hold it together. She wondered if that would be possible once he had told her the details, and yet the need to know was building inside her.

'All right then, let's talk about it. First of all, tell me where?' she asked coldly, and from his quizzical expression, she could tell he couldn't fathom what she was asking him.

'Where did this boy see you two?' she clarified, hearing her own voice, not recognising it.

He sighed. 'Does it matter?'

'Just tell me where,' she snapped.

'Down at the Reen Roe Hotel,' he said meekly. 'In my car.'

A laugh rose up in her then, a gasping wheeze of disbelief, before she recovered, drawing herself up and shaking her head.

'I should have guessed,' she remarked and her voice sounded peculiar to her, high-pitched, shrill, with a deliberate cruel sweetness. She couldn't help it.

'What's that supposed to mean?' he asked coolly.

'I mean the apple doesn't fall far from the tree, does it?'

'What?'

'Oh come on, Christy – Lara's father? Hello? Don't you remember all those rumours about him? What I'm saying is that it wouldn't be the first time that Datsun has been parked up at the Reen Roe.'

He was looking at her now with a hollow stare, but the anger was bubbling up inside her.

'But that you would take her there, given that place's reputation. Jesus, Christy, I thought you had more imagination than that.'

'Well, I'm sorry to disappoint you.'

She felt the argument changing, a new cruel and vicious tone entering the space between them.

'Come on then,' she said, facing him, challenging him now. 'Where else did you do it?'

'For Chrissakes…'

'No, really. I want to know. Tell me. Where else did you two go to carry out your sordid little affair? How about here? Hmm? Did you ever do it here? Did you fuck her in our bed?'

'Jesus, Sorcha!' His fury rose involuntarily. 'Don't use that word. Don't describe it like that. Don't pervert it like that.' She saw that he was offended, her use of the word 'fuck' making him cringe. An inconsolable thought – it wasn't just sex.

'Well, where then?' she demanded, biting down on her scorn, her tears. 'What about her place? I'll bet you had her there. I'll bet you had her in every room in the house.'

'Stop this, Sorcha.'

'Was it good?'

'I'm not answering that.'

'Why not? I think I have a right to know. After all, I *trusted* you.' For a moment that hung there between them, the word *trust* bouncing off all the hard surfaces in the room. And when she spoke again it was in a different tone. 'I hope it was good, Christy. I hope it was amazing. That you would risk everything for bad sex with some drugged-up grieving little cow would make me sick!'

This anger that came from deep within her, emerging with spite and venom from her mouth, was new and shocking to both of them. She looked at him now, her cheeks glowing with glorious rage, the furious workings of the release of her anger. He was looking at her as a stranger might look at her, but his eyes were guarded and she couldn't guess at his thoughts. He seemed so distant from her. And yet her life had been knitted up with his. But looking at him now, it was as though she had given everything of herself to him and he had taken it, while giving little in return. Her whole life seemed to be stored up in him. His body seemed bloated with all he had consumed. Realising this now, there was a sudden bitter taste in her mouth. Sharp feelings had risen to the surface and she felt them swelling inside him too – all this acrimony, all this hatred. Then the argument split open.

'It was good,' he began in a low, quiet voice that seethed with vengeance. 'It was fucking amazing. The best sex I ever had. And God knows I waited a long time for it.'

'Well, it's hardly surprising. After all the men she's laid back for, she was bound to learn a few tricks.'

'You don't know the half of it, Sorcha. She is amazing. An animal. A breath of relief after the coldness – God, the sheer fucking boredom – of your bed. We fucked each other with abandon.'

He seemed to tremble with murderous pleasure, and she in turn regarded him with a hatred she hadn't felt before – it was pure and unadulterated.

'And what about me?' she snarled at him. 'Putting up with you and your moods, your distance? You say I'm cold to you in bed, but God almighty Christy, you've been cold throughout your entire life. You've never fully engaged with us, never properly embraced your family. Always withdrawing into your own little world. The hours you spend locked away in that study wasting your time working on your precious book, telling me that it's almost there and then inventing agents who are interested in it when really, you've done nothing at all!'

Instantly she regretted this, but it was too late. His eyes narrowed and he looked at her suspiciously.

'You've been going through my study?'

'How is it *your* study? It was my father's study and then you—'

'You talk to me of trust while going through my stuff behind my back?'

'I was worried,' she began, anxiously backtracking, prompted by the sudden turn in the argument. 'All the time you were spending, locked away in that room, the children growing up around you and you hardly even noticing. Christ, just think about what this will do to them.'

'Don't take that line with me, Sorcha. Don't try and make out that I don't love my children.'

'Then why would you do this to them?'

'I've done everything for my children.'

'You don't think an affair would hurt them?'

'I've sacrificed everything for them. Without question, without ever saying a word. I've given up everything I ever wanted to be here for them.'

She stared at him for a moment, absorbing the struggle in his features, trying to control his emotions, trying to say everything there was to say without having to utter the words.

'Say it,' she said to him now, taunting. 'I want to hear you say it.'

He thought about it for a moment before his voice – cold, controlled – broke like ice on the surface of water.

'All right.'

On this night of all nights, when there was nothing left to lose, they were past caring, both of them reckless.

'I think you got pregnant on purpose – with Avril. I think you did it to keep me here.'

The words once uttered seemed to flap about in the space between them like a bird trapped in a room, caught and desperate to get out. She nodded slowly, almost triumphantly. He had at last said what she had known of him all along, and in that moment she felt enormously and finally sick of herself, sick of him, sick of what they made up together. She sat down slowly, and after a minute, he joined her at the kitchen table. They sat together under the low-hanging kitchen lamp, exhausted, their two faces looming in a pool of light.

'Do you love her?' she asked finally, a quaver of fear trembling in her voice.

He nodded his head slowly. He couldn't bring himself to look at her. Controlling her emotions, she asked him, 'Do you love me?'

The question sat between them now. She felt the weight of it. Both of them knew that to answer no would be dangerous. It could cancel any chance of redemption. The events of the day, his career in ruins, the revelation of his infidelity, the meal that she had so carefully prepared – her offering of love – a meal that would never be eaten, all of it seemed to fill the air around them now. She held herself carefully, her heart labouring in her chest, and as he looked up at her, she could tell by his eyes what the answer would be.

'No,' he said softly. 'Not any more.'

The words seemed to expand in the air between them, a living thing, as though a new force had entered the room. Something seemed to move behind her face, a crack of pain, of remorse. The chair beneath her seemed to fall away and she felt like she was spinning down, endlessly falling. She didn't tell him she loved him. She didn't say anything at all. Instead she got to her feet slowly, as if her flesh had become heavier with the weight of his betrayal, with the heaviness of this new sorrow. She drew away from the pool of light and moved to the window. And in that moment, she felt her marriage coming apart – that one word he had uttered, that cold and final 'no' slashing it open right down the middle. There was nothing left inside her. She felt drained of everything. Behind the window, the sky had grown dark, rain falling now. She stood there for a moment, waiting. But with nothing left to say, he went away.

22

The rain was falling softly now, clouds spilling out above the sea, as I sat on the veranda with my back to my house, watching the fading of the day. I was thinking of all those places I had visited trying to find my boy, the crazy pattern to it, first trawling the streets around Ubatuibe, then going further afield to São Paolo, that sprawling city, trying desperately to find him, a needle in a haystack. Then, acting on small clues gleaned from our search, we moved on to Argentina, hunting around the border by the Iguaçu Falls, then back to Brazil where we concentrated our search around Bonito before heading back to São Paolo again and then on to Rio. Round and round we went. We had visited these places before at a leisurely pace, soaking up the atmosphere, whereas this time our journey was frantic.

As I sat on the wooden bench and watched the ribbons of light in the sky turning orange, then purple, then deepening to black, I thought of the comfort I had taken in the strangest of places. Sitting in a bus shelter in São Paulo, exhausted and deflated after showing Nacio's picture to countless strangers, a small, squat woman had come over to me and given me a cup of coffee and a sandwich. I didn't know the woman, I hadn't asked for the food. She simply gave it to me, squeezed my shoulder and moved away again. I remembered, too, the official in the Irish Embassy in Rio, who had clasped my hands in his as we stood there in the cloistered silence. He e-mailed me still, every week, simply to show that he had not forgotten. And Alejo – even when he had lost faith, even when we had grown so far apart – still he was a comfort, for in him, I saw my son.

The air was growing cold around me and the rain became heavier, and soon I went back inside. I picked up the card again, felt my fingers tracing over the writing, the way he wrote my name, a flourish in the loops and tails of the letters, and looking at the postmark, my mind cast back again to that time we were in Parati together, that old slave town on the southeast coast of Brazil, where I first discovered I was pregnant. I knew it already, but it wasn't until Parati that I could get to a chemist and buy a test and wait for that inevitable blue line and the slow bubbling of uncertainty that it provoked. But by then, it was just a confirmation, a cementing of the facts. For all the way from Bonito, along that bumpy, dusty road, being thrown about in the back of the van for nearly a week, my body was in turmoil. Limbs that felt heavy, like they were filling up with water. Sudden hungers. My stomach in revolt. I kept all these biological clues hidden from the others, smuggled under the veil of travel sickness, the bumpy road a blessing. But in Parati, I couldn't escape from the truth. A baby. It seemed as

weirdly removed from me as an elephant or an alien. I
remember stepping along the narrow cobbled streets in
a daze, my eyes passing over the colonial buildings, the
whitewashed walls, the brightly painted window frames
and shutters and eaves, my mind swelling with the new
knowledge that I carried inside. I imagined the zygote,
that tiny clutch of cells, spinning around and bouncing
off the walls of my womb. Even then, my body was
drumming home its new state, the sudden nausea at the
smell of fish washing over me at the harbour.

I wondered how I was going to tell him. Fear gripped
me at the thought of it. There was no place for a baby
in our rootless existence. A child would be an
impossible burden to carry from place to place, moving
with the weather, with the tourists, with the mood.
Children needed stability, foundations, a home. That
would mean giving up the road, settling down. I
thought of Alejo, the way I could tell when he was tiring
of a place, how his eyes became hungry, busily moving
as if searching something out. How his conversation
withdrew, his words growing clipped and scarce. In
those times he seemed to hum with impatience, nervous
tics becoming apparent – a jiggling knee, fingers
drumming on a table – and I would watch his eyes
casting about and wait for him to say the word, and we
were off again.

I knew all of this. I held all of this inside me, a knowledge just as real and immediate as the knowledge of
this baby. I couldn't ask it of him. I didn't know how to.
As I pondered the words that I could possibly summon

to break it to him gently, the toe of my flip-flop became caught between the cobbles and I fell against the kerb, landing heavily on my hands and knees, shockwaves dancing up through my body, a white noise filling my head. Two women came to help me up and I remember the strange looks they gave me as I got to my feet and moved away from them. I must have been as pale as milk. Blood was thundering in my ears and I was struck by a sudden vulnerability, a new fear. That to hurt myself now meant hurting the bunch of cells dividing and multiplying inside me, something so tiny and vulnerable. I felt overwhelmed, suddenly frightened as the enormity of the situation bore down on top of me.

That afternoon, sitting together at the harbour, I sipped guiltily from my beer, toes dipping into the water. There was music coming from a boat – a low crooning, the pluck of guitar strings, Jack Johnson on the stereo. I could feel the warmth from Alejo, the glow he carried with him when a place was new to him and unexplored. It lit him up like a firefly. He seemed to buzz with excitement, with contentment. I almost hated myself for doing it, for breaking the spell, for tossing those words out into the space between us, unable to look at him, squinting out across the ocean. He didn't speak for some seconds after that, nor did I. Not a word. The air around us grew tight and I thought I wouldn't be able to breathe it in. The silence seemed to stretch between us and I felt his eyes upon me. Turning to look at him I saw his face, the tilt of his smile, his eyes bright. And I saw the sudden joy there. I was stunned by it. He didn't say a word, just leaned in to kiss me, his mouth tentative against my own. I felt suddenly lifted by this great new thing between us, this live, pulsing joy, buoyed up by it, the fear inside me caving and falling in on itself, crowded away by this warmth spreading through me.

All of it returned to me now in a flood of feeling. The bright colours of that place, the warmth of the sun and the warmth inside me, so clear and immediate that for a moment I forgot the rain falling steadily outside the window, the dark, threatening sky pushing up against the house. I forgot the sorrow that had slipped into my bones, and just how fucked up my life had become. For a blissful moment, I was free of all that. Then a floorboard creaked behind me, and I turned my head and saw his dark form filling the doorway, his hair and clothes wet and plastered to him. My heart stirred inside me as I looked up into his eyes. In the shadows, they were red-rimmed with fatigue, small and bloodshot, and I saw his face drawn and ravaged with grief.

'Lara,' he said hoarsely and something sank in me, an old tiredness, as I slowly got to my feet.

We stood there, the two of us, regarding each other warily. Darkness had sprung up around me while I'd been sitting there, with only a reading lamp for light, and as I moved towards the old Bakelite light switch on the wall, he spoke.

'Leave it,' he said. 'My head is splitting. I couldn't bear the light.'

I was standing close enough to be able to smell alcohol on his breath, close enough to hear the snagging sound of his breathing. I could tell he'd been crying.

'What do you want?' I asked, feeling a small ripple of nerves in my stomach. I wasn't sure yet how I felt about him happening in on me like this, his face shadowy and stretched, the taut pull of his emotions close to the surface.

'Everything's finished,' he said into the darkness. 'All of it. Everything's over.'

He said this in a reasoned, measured tone, but there was something beneath his voice, something brittle and dangerous and barely controlled. I took a moment to observe him and saw something wild about him. It hovered behind his eyes, which appeared bright and unblinking in the dimness of the room. I didn't want to sit down, didn't want to move, afraid that any movement in any direction would be taken as an indication that I wanted him there.

'Sorcha knows,' he said.

'What?'

'I told her. She knows about you and me. There's nothing left for me there. She won't try and stop us.'

'Christian,' I began carefully, feeling something plunging down into my stomach. 'You should go home.'

'Didn't you hear what I said?'

'Go home to Sorcha. Try and reconcile with her.'

'What for?'

'Because she loves you.'

He shook his head and smiled benevolently, the way you might smile at a child, the light from the reading lamp picking out the angles of bones in his face, and I felt fear move within me, scared now at his behaviour, unsettled by the dark disquiet in his eyes.

'She doesn't love me. She just thinks she does because we've been together all these years.'

'But—'

'It was never love between Sorcha and I. Not really. She knows that now. An accident of fate, that's all it was. I did my duty. I stood by her all these years. But my heart has always belonged to you. It was just a matter of time before you would come to reclaim it.'

His face seemed so open, his spare countenance hiding nothing – all the hurt and hope and love and desperation huddled around his handsome features. My first instinct was to look away. He continued to stare at me, waiting for my reaction, and I was forced to look back at him.

'This is crazy,' I told him.

'I know,' he laughed, but there was a dangerous edge to his laughter. 'It's crazy and stupid. Pure madness. But amazing too. You and me – we were always meant to happen. It just seems crazy because it's taken so long. The circumstances—'

'Stop this,' I said, bitten by a growing alarm.

'I can't.'

His words reached me, plaintive and true, and

suddenly I was so tired of this, tired of finding myself caught in another awkward, deceitful situation, and it left me with a longing for something pure and true, a love that I hadn't let go of despite the distance between us.

'I want you to leave.'

'And go where?' His face seemed to fall a notch before he shook his head and ploughed onwards. 'Don't you see? My place is here with you. We belong together, you and me. There's no point in fighting it.'

'It's over, Christian.'

'No.'

'It is,' I insisted, but he shook his head so vehemently that I feared what he might say.

'It isn't over. It can't be. You can't tell me that this has all been for nothing.' His voice grew shrill and I could feel the heat in it. 'I've given up everything to be with you – my wife, my kids, my home, my job…'

'What are you talking about?'

'All of it's gone.'

'You lost your job?'

'But that's not important. None of that matters. What matters is that I have nothing to stay for any more. I'm free.'

His voice seemed to tremble with this announcement. I saw the emotion moving through him and he seemed so tired and crumpled and desperate in that moment that I was torn between my alarm at his delusion and a great pity for him.

Behind him, out the window, I saw the dark boil of

the sea in the distance, a crackle of lightning through black clouds on the horizon. A silence opened up between us, trembling with unspoken things, and I could feel him waiting, poised for me to submit to him, and I could sense in that moment how convinced he was that this would happen, and the fear inside me turned over. He seemed dangerous to me in that moment – a man with nothing left to lose.

'I know that you love me,' he said into the stillness between us, and I closed my eyes and shook my head.

'No. I don't.'

The smile on his face – that slight, self-congratulatory twist of his mouth – seemed to slip suddenly before recovering and he nodded his head slowly.

'Yes, you do.'

I turned away from him then, exasperated, and reached for my cigarettes on the coffee table. His eyes followed me, and as I lit up I noticed my hands were shaking. Looking back at him then, blowing smoke out into the darkness, I saw his eyes remained fixed on the coffee table, the cards that were gathered there, the picture of Nacio, and from there, his eyes moved to my bags, packed and sitting on the floor beside the table.

'You're leaving?' he asked quietly.

'Yes.'

'You're going back?'

I nodded my head and looked away, taking short, quick drags on my cigarette.

'Were you even going to tell me?'

I shrugged, wary of what lay beneath the controlled

tone of his voice. His form seemed dark and threatening in its proximity to me.

'Don't you think I deserve even that much?'

'Please. Let's not do this.'

His eyes rested on me, and something seemed to change about them then, overtaken by a new hope. He took my free hand in his own and I felt the tremble of his emotions.

'Let's leave together, the two of us. Let's give it one last shot. Away from this place. We deserve that much. We deserve to be happy.'

Something twisted inside me as he said this, his pain, his desire so raw and vulnerable that I hated myself all over again for doing this.

'This can't happen,' I told him softly. 'It was a fantasy. A pipe dream. Nothing more. You and I – even when we were young, travelling around the world? That dream belongs in the past. Let's both walk away from here now, before one of us says something we'll both regret.'

'It's too late for that.' His voice trembled as he said it. 'I can't walk away. I've waited too long. My whole life, all I wanted was you. Please, Lara.'

Sliding my hand out from his grasp, I told him softly, 'No.'

'But—'

'No, Christian,' I said, firm this time.

He stood and stared at me. 'So that's it, is it? I just walk down the beach back to Sorcha with my tail between my legs and we just pretend that this never happened?'

'I'm so sorry.'

But he shook his head at this.

'No, Lara – sorry is not going to cut it this time. Sorry just won't do. I've given up everything to be with you, my wife, my children, my job, and all you can say is sorry?'

His voice wavered unsteadily, breaking like a teenage boy's, and I wondered again what he meant about his job.

'You haven't lost them. Sorcha – your kids – they still need you.'

'No, they don't. They barely tolerate me. Avril thinks I'm an embarrassment. Jim hardly notices I'm there. And as for Sorcha, she's just terrified of being alone.'

He sank down into the sofa, suddenly exhausted.

'Plenty of children get by with just one parent,' he said quietly, in a new coolly detached voice.

'You don't mean that.'

'Don't I?' he turned and fixed me with a piercing gaze. 'I look at my children sometimes and wonder what exactly they've gained by my being there. Sorcha accused me tonight of being absent for the last fifteen years. In a way, I think she's right. It feels like a part of me has been missing all this time. I felt incomplete. And then when you came back, when we were finally together – God, how long I had to wait! – I felt whole again. I ask you, is that not love?'

I took a seat next to him, keeping distance between us, and felt his eyes flickering upwards to the ceiling.

'I'm so tired, I can hardly think straight,' he said.

I didn't know what to say, and so I said nothing, waiting, praying for him to leave, for all this to be over. I looked down at my luggage, and suddenly couldn't wait to be away from this place.

In the silence, he leaned forward and picked the cards up off the table. He flicked through them, examining them one by one. I watched him opening the birthday card, fought the urge to snatch it from his hands, while his eyes passed over the words written there.

'You're going back to him, aren't you?' he asked in a quiet, tight kind of voice.

I didn't answer, fearing how he might react.

He studied me for a moment, a new hardness coming over him.

'You're still in love with him, aren't you?'

Slowly, I turned and looked him in the eye, and I guess he saw everything there was to see there, and something mocking entered the look he gave me.

'And suddenly it's all back on again, is it? The big search? Your big love story? All of it revived with a few lines on a fucking birthday card? Jesus, this guy must be something. A couple of lines and he manages to bring a child back to life?'

His words sent a shiver down me as I slowly straightened up.

'What?'

Everything seemed to still in that moment, and he looked at me sideways, his eyes small and mean, and I realised that he was about to shatter the last ounce of trust I had in him.

'Nacio is dead. Or at least as good as. You're never going to see him again. Snatched kids? They're normally dead within the first forty-eight hours. And if they're not, you still never see them again. You know it. I know it. And you can be damn sure that Alejo knows it. And if you can't see *this*' – he released the card, flicking it onto the table in front of him – 'for what it is, a cynical ploy to get you back, then you're even more stupid than I thought.'

Blood was thundering in my ears and for a moment I was paralysed, convulsed with fury. All this time, all his sympathy, none of it had meant anything. The comfort he had provided, all those words he had poured out about not giving up hope, about believing that Nacio was still alive – all the time it had been lies. In that moment, I was overwhelmed by the degree of his faithlessness, his falseness, dumbfounded by his dishonesty.

'You really think that?' I gasped.

His eyes were wary now, shutting down defensively.

'So do you, Lara. Why else did you come back here?'

'What does that mean?'

'If you really believed he was alive, you'd have stayed in South America. You would never have come back here and set up a life for yourself. By coming home, you as good as admitted he was dead.'

'Get out,' I whispered under my breath.

'All this sorrow you're clinging to, all this grief – you have to let it go. How else are you going to move on?'

'Get out!'

My heart was thumping crazily in my chest, my fear clambering up my throat, and all the while I felt my convictions dissolving around me, that wall I had built of them suddenly crumbling with his declared loss of faith. Our voices seemed to bounce off the walls, and as I felt tears crawling down my cheeks, he stared at me and I saw the change coming over him. His anger seemed to contract. It was as if he had been absent from his body, and now, re-entering it, he was shocked by what he had done.

'Lara. Jesus, I'm sorry. I went too far.'

He came and sat next to me. I felt the weight of his body, the heat from his breath, and became afraid.

'Lara, sweetheart,' he said, a gentle coaxing, but there were nerves quavering in his voice that unsettled me.

'Please just go,' I whispered, the tears coming fast now.

'Shhh, baby.' Through the blur of my tears, I watched his hands reaching for me, and felt myself tense to it. 'I can't leave you like this. Not like this.'

With his finger he rubbed a tear from my cheek.

'Please, Lara. I shouldn't have said that. I didn't mean it. You know I didn't.'

His hands were about my face now and I tried to shake them away but felt the firmness of his grip.

'Please,' I whispered, his face coming towards me.

'We can't leave it like this.' His voice was a throaty whisper only inches from my face.

I felt for his wrists, trying to release myself from his grip, but my hands were trembling and the dark felt

oppressive around me and something like a scream rose
up inside me but got trapped in my throat, clogged up
in the tears and fear gathering there as he leaned in and
kissed me.

'I didn't mean it,' he whispered, kissing me again,
and I could hear the fear in the ragged edges of his
breathing, could see him searching his thoughts for the
right words to appease me, to undo the damage he'd
done. 'Sweet Lara. Of course he's still alive. Of course
he is. Shhh now, don't cry.'

He kissed me longer this time and I felt his teeth
coming at me behind his lips, forcing down on me,
silencing me, while a great panic bloomed inside me,
petrifying my body. A terrible emptiness like a great
wind was blowing inside me. And as I felt his body
leaning down on mine, it seemed to me that all the
memories I had of him – taking my hand on the
veranda, holding me in the silence of my bedroom,
and lately, the passion that leapt between us, the
comfort that I drew from him – all of it seemed
crushed underneath the weight of his kiss, his mouth
covering mine, forcing an entry with his tongue, so
savage I couldn't breathe. The panic lifted inside me
and found voice. My mouth broke free of his and I
began to scream, and the screaming grew in pure
voice. He reacted to it, his hand reaching up to cover
my mouth, an urgency in his voice as he told me to
stop that, to be quiet. As we struggled against one
another, killing every tender feeling that had ever
passed between us, I felt so dirty and sordid that I

wanted to retch, to rid myself of everything dark and fetid that I held inside. I knew I would remember this feeling, this weary regret like my skin was too small and tight and grubby for me to live in.

And just as this feeling rose sharply inside me and I thought I couldn't stand it any more, I heard a voice, one that was not my own but that came from somewhere beyond me. Looking up, I saw a figure, and it took a second to identify Avril through the blur of my tears.

'What the fuck?' she asked, her voice a breathy wail of disbelief and horror.

For a moment, I was too stunned to say anything. I only saw the confusion in her eyes, and the slow realisation of what she was witnessing. Christy drew back from me, his eyes wide with alarm, his hair sticking out at crazy angles to his head.

'It's not what you think,' he told her, his voice shallow with fear.

Looking up, I saw her expression change to one of pain and disappointment. She shook her head, then looked down at me briefly and I saw everything in that look: hurt, disgust and betrayal. But I had no words for her. They were all lost deep inside me. As I lay there struggling for them, she turned abruptly, and after a brief and stunned silence, he followed after her, leaving me alone in the darkness.

23

The room suddenly felt too small. In that moment, with his heart throbbing behind his ribs, his head filling up with heat, Christy had no idea what he should do. He just stood there, listening to that beating organ filling up his chest, the crash and hurl of the sea outside, until he became aware of another sound – Lara crying softly on the couch below him. He looked down and saw she had curled herself into the foetal position, protecting herself, and he realised with a sudden crushing shame that she was protecting herself from him. Part of him wanted to kneel down next to her and apologise profusely, but he knew that they were beyond that now. The door was banging in the wind, left ajar by Avril as she fled, and he thought again of her face, the light and the shadows in it, her eyes round with horror, and in that look he had seen her innocence splinter and come apart. The crying died away and he looked down at Lara, cradling her head in her hands.

'Just go,' she said to him, rocking gently. 'Just go.'

Stepping out onto the veranda, he felt the wind whip his hair back, and from this height, he could see the dark outline of Avril's figure against the silvery sand. He called out to her, but her name was lost in the wind. Hurrying down the steps, slick with rain, he almost lost his footing and reached out a hand to steady himself. There was a need to steady his thoughts too, his own heartbeat, the tremors of panic running up and down his spine. But instead he started to run, chasing after her, needing to catch up with her before she reached home. With no idea of what to say, what kind of explanation he could offer her, he charged down the beach after his daughter, the sand wet and heavy beneath him, clogging his movements, an ache communicating itself all the way down the backs of his legs. She had a good head start on him, so that by the time he reached the path to his house, his lungs heaving, his chest fracturing with the effort, she had already disappeared from view.

Stumbling up the path, his breath wheezing and rattling in his chest, he saw the light from the kitchen window. Something made him stop where he was. Peering in, hidden from those inside, he watched them carefully. Mother and daughter, together under the harsh fluorescent light, holding onto each other, rocking back and forth. Although they were the same height, he could see that Sorcha was clasping her daughter's head to her chest, her two hands lost in Avril's dark hair, while she whispered a litany of comforts into her ear. He couldn't see Avril's face, but he saw Sorcha's, all pinched with worry and confusion, and he saw the gentle shuddering of Avril's body, saw her hands disappearing around her mother's back. Standing there, soaked to the bone, he felt his heart burst in his chest as he watched his wife draw back her daughter's head to examine her, and he saw the crumpled, tear-streaked face and felt a sorrow and regret rise up within him so suddenly that he thought he might choke on it. His eyes ached with the light from the window and he wanted to draw away, but was riveted. His chest felt collapsed with fatigue, his neck and shoulders stiff, and he was so thirsty his mouth felt like a dry, dusty cavern. Yet still he kept his eyes on them, watching their faces as words were spoken that he couldn't hear, but he knew all the same what they were. He badly wanted to go in there to the warmth and safety of that kitchen, but he knew that to do so meant breaking the spell of their tableau and incurring the combined force of their anger and hurt and acknowledgement of the very depth of his betrayal. He knew that he could not go back there now.

He stood there holding his breath, the rain pelting down around him, for three, maybe four full minutes. He tried to calm himself, searching his thoughts for what to do next, but found only a blanket of heat unfurling behind his face. In that moment, he felt lost, abandoned, an aching regret taking hold of him. He was hot-faced and mute with shame. Taking a step backwards, he turned from the window and stumbled away into the night.

*

With nowhere to go, he walked aimlessly, unaware of the rain that was easing off now, or the sand wet beneath his feet. Thoughts rushed through his head, a stream of images. He remembered another night like this one, only many years ago, when he stumbled out, his heart scalded after happening upon Lara yet again with another boy. Burning with the knowledge that she didn't want him in that way, he crawled away from that painful love and into the shelter of something comforting and real. That night he had found Sorcha and taken her into his arms, feeling the warmth of her, the gentleness of her nature, and pressed her to him like a poultice to a wound. And even though he had turned to her on that first night with a vengeful heart, his anger had been blown away by the warmth of her comforting hands, her familiarity. This memory rubbed up against others and he thought back to a more innocent time, walking along the beach with his family when the children were small, picking out the gulls and the oystercatchers and the snipes. He remembered them standing there, that little group huddled by the lapping shore, pointing out the kitti-wakes. 'But they're seagulls, Daddy,' Avril had corrected him, and he explained to her the identifying call of the bird, how they repeated their own name, and standing there together in their boots and anoraks, all four of them had cried out, 'Kit-wak! Kit-wak!', their voices lifted on the wind.

As he walked, he began to cry. Tears spilled down his cheeks and he didn't wipe them away, allowing them to thread down over his face, disappearing down his neck.

He thought of his son, who could walk before he was a year old, that pale, anxious face, more Sorcha's than his, and how the rarity of his smile these days seemed to clutch at Christy's heart. And he thought of his children splashing in the waves when they were younger – their small bodies, open faces, how beautiful they were to him, the joy of folding them wet and shivery in beach towels, the sight of his wife manoeuvring their busy limbs into their clothes. And with that thought, he was filled with an old love for Sorcha, a love of sixteen years, a love that he had confused with nostalgia. He had deceived himself with his own complacency, his own impatience and longing and unwillingness to settle. And remembering what he had said to Sorcha that night, the treachery of his words, he felt something break within him.

Reaching the spit of rocks, he climbed up, his head banded with heaviness and alcohol, waves breaking in the distance, blue under the light of the moon. The word that Sorcha had used all those weeks ago about Lara came back to him now. *Broken.* 'I am a broken man,' he said aloud, offering the words to the night, but they sounded different when spoken, whimsical and foolish, and he was at once struck by his own vanity and pride, the weakness that lay within him. The realisation of this brought a new and unexpected resolve. It wasn't too late for him. He could still go back there, enter that kitchen, brave the words spoken in anger and pain, offer up his heartfelt apologies, make promises he would endeavour to keep. He thought, in that moment, that whatever else happened in his life, he must win his family back. The resolve that formed within him had tentacles that strayed into the other pockets of his life – he would ditch his dismal excuse for a novel; he would go crawling back to Arthur full of remorse and apology; he would even swallow his pride and express contrition to Carl Ring. And Lara? He would stay away from her – that was his conclusion, distrustful of what he might blurt out if he tried for an apology.

In the moonlight, the rocks were black like tar. Avril and Jim had played on these rocks through the years. They rose up out of the sand, great humps, garlanded in moving sea, and he used to tell the children they were like whales in their colour and power and dignity. When Jim had fallen here once, opening a gash in his shin that required stitches, they had joked afterwards that the injury was a whaling wound.

Clambering now, far out along the spit, the beach falling away behind him and the water lapping around him, his thoughts fell back to his own childhood – arriving on the beach that day, his slow progress picking through the longshore drift, sand between his toes, his hair and shoulders warm in the sun, shells in his pockets, grit under the soles of his feet, and looking up he saw her, unaware of him still, her long arms plunged into water, droplets on her skin catching in the light. His heart turned over in his chest at all that had passed since then. And in that moment, with the sky black above him, despite his resolve to make new his life, he still wanted to hear her voice, one last time, to stretch out next to her and rest his cheek on her bare breast and smell the salt on her skin, heat on her breath, and listen to the beating of her messed up, melancholy heart. He wanted to feel her all around him, and under him and through him, like liquid, like brine. But what he felt instead was the ground slipping away from under his feet, and then the sharp crack as it met the back of his head and something seemed to break behind his ear. And then he was lying there on the rocks, the water cold and lapping at his feet, and as he lay there he thought to himself how ironic it was that he should pick up his own whaling wound, and then he felt the sea whispery about him and something trickled out of his ear, and the sky was all around him and filled with stars, and then he felt nothing at all.

24

At first there was bustle of the bleakest kind. I watched from my window as they came and swarmed over the beach and surrounding coastline – officials in uniform, and people from the town. They sprawled over the rocks where he had last been seen, and beyond over the crest of the headland to The Point. There hadn't been that much activity since the time the baby was found twenty years before, when the beach was cordoned off and all those Gardaí from Tralee and forensic experts from Dublin and a whole battery of journalists flocked to the place. And while officially it was a missing person's case, I knew that what they were scouring for was a body. The sea hissed and bubbled in among the rock pools, washing the evidence away, and while the searchers walked head down, eyes alert, I watched from my veranda, aware of the pull of the ocean, and I knew that they were silently waiting for it to surrender that which it had claimed. And while the beach became pocked with their footprints, the smooth sand broken up and scattered by their persistent combing, I was all the time aware of Sorcha and her children in the house at the end of the bay, the anxiety and fear crouching in around that desolate place as they waited for news of the inevitable. I couldn't bring myself to visit them, although I had seen the cars pulled into their driveway, knew of the constant stream of well-wishers bringing food and comfort. I would not be welcome there. Sometime during those first few days, I looked down from my vantage point up above the beach and remembered another bleak search along a different beach at the other side of the ocean. And I thought, too, of the small sandal hidden away in the depths of my packed suitcase – a relic of another loss. As night fell again and the beach became deserted, all that remained was the sea brushing up against the long expanse of shingle and sand.

On the third day, there was a knock at the door and I opened it to find two gardaí standing on the veranda with grave expressions, and I knew it could mean only one thing. Although I had been expecting it, as inevitable now as the tides, I still felt the lurch in my stomach, my chest filling with spangles, and I clapped my hand to my mouth instinctively. They introduced themselves solemnly and confirmed my identity before asking could they step inside, and I knew what that meant, so that when the younger one shut the door behind him and they both sat opposite me on the couch, my heart was already filling with dread.

'He's been found, hasn't he?' I asked, nerves quavering in my voice.

They looked at each other then before looking back at me, and the older one nodded his head.

'Yes, Ms Symons,' he said gravely, 'We believe so.' He had dark brown eyes and an accent that wasn't from this place, and for a moment he seemed a little surprised that I had guessed at their reason for being here.

'Oh my God,' I whispered, my eyes stinging with bitter tears, blinking them away, trying to remain calm, trying to hold it together. 'Where was he...his body...where was it found?'

They paused then, the older one opening his mouth to answer, when I saw him stop, consternation crossing his brow.

'No,' he said then. 'There wasn't a body. You seem to have misunderstood me—'

'No body?'

'Ms Symons, he was found alive.'

I shook my head, unable to take this in.

'But I thought he went in the water?'

'Ms Symons.'

'They said there was blood on the rocks. But now you say he's alive? I don't understand. Christian's alive?'

And then I saw the mouth of the younger one dropping open, and something seemed to change in the room, a sudden jarring, and I became frightened by it.

'We don't want you to be alarmed,' the older one said.

I sat perfectly still – it seemed important at that time that I remain unmoving, clear of all thoughts, and something bubbled up from far down inside me, something quiet and reverent and deep within. A prayer. All of my being seemed to crouch in around it. In that instant, I forgot all the other prayers I had offered up, those Faustian pacts made deep in the night. The prayer that rose up within me now seemed to overpower them all, pure and true as it was. There were sounds surrounding me – the screech of gulls outside, the drone of the sea, the creaking of my old house – but I heard only my own breath and this prayer within me: *please let it be him, let my son be alive.* I stared into the careful expression of that sergeant, a dam waiting to burst behind my eyes, and willed him to say the words I so desperately wanted to hear.

'Nothing has been confirmed,' he began cautiously, 'but we have received preliminary reports that a boy who fits your son's description has been found. They have him in a hospital in São Paolo. His father has been contacted and is on his way, and he will able to identify him. I must caution you, Ms Symons, that until that happens, there is still the possibility that it is not your son. But they seem hopeful that it's a positive match.'

Those words spun around me. They formed a cloud in the air, and then the air filled with sound and I felt the vibration of it in my head and chest. I couldn't breathe, couldn't see. His name curling inside me, ancient tears flooding my whole being, and all the while, my voice offering up his name. I filled the room with it.

It was three days before Christian was discovered, his clothing tangled up in wire enmeshing the rocks of the groyne, his body joining with that groyne to form a defence against erosion. When the news reached me, I felt a sort of relief followed by sadness, and I thought of his family, the sorrow they must be feeling, and I felt a fresh wave of shame at what I had done.

The funeral followed swiftly and was well attended. Sitting at the back of the church, I listened to the priest in his eulogy speaking of a good teacher, a kind neighbour, a loving husband and father. He used words and phrases like 'tragedy' and 'taken too soon', and I bowed my head along with everyone else as the coffin passed, the boys from the school flanking the road in a guard of honour. Standing in the churchyard watching that coffin being carried away, I heard the talk around me beginning to trickle about what might have possessed him to take to the rocks so late at night, slick and treacherous as they were after the rain. It seemed that everyone had heard of the incident in the school that day and then someone mentioned seeing him emerging from the off-licence on the afternoon of the accident, an agitated look on his face, and soon theories were being put forward and conclusions arrived at. There were some who dared to suggest that perhaps, in some small way, it was a mercy on his wife and children that things turned out this way. After all, you can't prosecute a dead man, and no doubt there would be an insurance policy, and at this I turned and walked away, unable to listen to any more conjecture.

A few days later, the paper ran an obituary that mirrored some of the language used by the priest. A couple of his poems were also printed, and people read them and shook their heads, and murmured again of the tragedy. A substitute teacher was found to fill in the classes until the end of the year, and things began to return to a type of normality. Winter drifted in, and sand was lifted and carried across the beach in gusts of wind, so that soon the marks of that frenzied search were nowhere in evidence. By the time I left, the days had grown chilly, a cold front drawing in from over the Atlantic.

25

'Have you been to Rio before?' asks the man sitting next to me.

'Yes,' I tell him. 'I was there just six months ago.' He cocks an eyebrow before telling me that this will be his first time there. He's an older man, in his fifties I guess, whose facial hair has started to grow a little wild. He tells me that he's going to Rio to deliver a lecture series on European jurisprudence. I'm not sure what that means, but don't let on, and as it happens he goes on to explain that he intends to deal mainly with trial by ordeal. 'Trial by fire, the use of torture,' he lists briskly, casting out those image-evoking phrases in a businesslike fashion.

His explanation is interrupted by the safety instructions, and then the low rumble of engines as we accelerate up the runway and lift into the air. I have a window seat, and turn to look at the frosted fields around Heathrow, the neat layout of housing estates, a river snaking across the land. My companion resumes his conversation.

'I was in South America last year,' he tells me. 'Argentina. Buenos Aires – again with work.'

I tell him I've been there, and we talk for a while about tango in San Telmo, the graveyard at Recoletta, the colourful buildings of La Boca. His office, he says, was close to the Plaza de Mayo, and I ask him did he ever witness the weekly demonstration there of the Madres de Plaza de Mayo.

'Yes,' he says. 'Yes, I did. Although to be honest, I couldn't help but think the whole thing was largely futile.'

'Why is that?'

'Well, it all depends on what they're trying to achieve,' he explains. 'I mean, here you have these mothers, congregating on a weekly basis, demanding to know the whereabouts of family members that went missing back in the seventies. What is it they call them?'

'*Desaparecidos*,' I tell him.

'What I'm saying is, if what they're trying to do is draw attention to the injustices of a military regime that's been defunct for over twenty years now, then fair enough. It's certainly enough to grab the attention of passing tourists. But if they're expecting these protests to deliver up their loved ones who have long since disappeared, well,' he pauses, shooting me a glance that seemed to me to be partly apologetic, partly condescending, 'I think they're fooling themselves, denying the plain truth that these *desaparecidos* are most certainly deceased, and it is unlikely that we will ever know what really happened to them during that dark time.'

I think about this for a minute, feeling the stirrings of an old argument inside.

'Perhaps they're still holding out hope of finding them. Even if it is a fool's hope.'

He smiles at me then, pleasant but unyielding.

'You may call it hope, my dear. I call it denial.'

I think about saying something more to that. I think about asking him if he has any children. But then the in-flight entertainment starts and he leans forward, reaching for his earphones, and the moment seems to pass. Or perhaps I just don't feel the need for that particular crusade any more.

Those officers had returned a few days later, this time with a photograph they'd printed from a computer. I was still wearing black, not long home from the funeral mass, and I sat there with trembling hands as I looked into that blurry image and saw his face – recognisable, yet unfamiliar, and still a shock to me now when I take it out to look at it. At the time I had sat there, nodding furiously, my hand over my mouth, the ventricles of my heart filling up with emotion. But in the days and nights that have followed, worries have crept in any time I have unfolded that picture and examined his face. There is a toughness about it. He is unsmiling. Older, a vague expression on his face that seems slightly threatening, and when I consider this, my mind starts to wander down corridors filled with theories of where he has been, what he has seen, what he has been forced to do. There is a hardness in his eyes that I don't remember. It calls to mind a loss of innocence. I think of pictures I have seen of child fighters – young boys in Burma with cigarettes dangling from their mouths and AK-47s resting in their laps and a dull sneer seeping out over their small faces. But then I remind myself that he's alive. That is a miracle in itself. I try to calm my impatience, telling myself that there's time enough to fill in all the gaps, time to discover all that happened to him. Time, too, to learn how to be a mother all over again to this tough little boy, this vulnerable creature, my own living, breathing paradox of a son. I ache to see him, to hold him in my arms again, to feel my face buried in his hair, the smell of him filling my senses. It's a twelve-hour flight to São Paolo and from there a forty-minute drive to the hospital. There will be a car to meet me at the airport. I glance down at my watch and calculate the hours left before I see him. His father is with him, and soon I will be too.

Outside the clouds roll past the window before the plane breaks free and we are soaring above them in a blaze of blue sky. My companion has fallen asleep, the earphones still in his ears. Looking out the window, I see pillows of pristine cumulus, pushing up so brightly that I have to close my eyes to them. In the lidded darkness, I think of the time that has passed, of the place that I have left behind. The letters I sent will have arrived by now – one, a letter of resignation out of courtesy only; and another containing no words of explanation or apology, merely the keys and the deeds to my house – a poor consolation, but it was all I could offer. And as we wheel away across the sky, I think of Sorcha opening that letter, and remember with shame how I had wronged her. My thoughts turn to Avril and Jim and the loss they must bear, and I wonder yet again what might have happened had Avril not fought with her friend and come to my house that night seeking comfort. I think, too, of Alejo and the stilted, awkward conversations we've had over the phone in recent days and hope that things may be different when we're face to face. I remember my mother and picture her standing on the veranda looking out to sea, a mug of warm tea held to her chest. I think of my son, recovering from his unfathomable ordeal, and the distance that has grown between us, a distance that I pray will be bridgeable. And then I remember Christian, that dark need in his eyes, the desperation inside him on that last fateful night; that he should die, while my son is saved. And I reflect again on the great mystery of it, the chance that separates the living from the dead.

But then I open my eyes and everywhere is blue and white and bright. The engines hum and a man's voice is speaking over an intercom, information about altitude and flight times filtering past me. I gaze out the window, my thoughts drifting away again, and lifting my head up slightly, I offer my face to the warmth of the sun.

Acknowledgements

I owe a debt of gratitude to a number of people who, in one way or another, helped bring this book into being. Thanks to: Sheila Pratschke and the Tyrone Gutherie Centre at Annaghmakerrig for a residency where I worked on some of this book; Ann Sugrue for a unique and special residency at her home in Kerry; Ciara Considine and the team of wonderful women at Hodder Headline Ireland for their valued support and hard work; my agent Faith O'Grady, for her steady guidance and commitment; Emily, Dom, Becca, and Helen for their good company on my South American odyssey; Thomas – title master extraordinaire – for explaining longshore drift to me; Conor for providing me with the final incentive. Veuve!

Lastly, deepest thanks and much love to my family and friends for their patience, enthusiasm, and indefatigable support.

Permission Acknowledgements

The five lines from 'The Stolen Child' by W. B. Yeats are reproduced with kind permission of A. P. Watt Ltd on behalf of Michael B. Yeats.

Despite our best efforts, the publisher and author were unable to contact all copyright holders prior to the publication of *Longshore Drift*. The publisher will make the usual arrangements with any copyright holders who make contact after publication.